The Unseen Path

A NOVEL

J.D. DE PAVILLY

Matador
9 Priory Business Park,
Wistow Road, Kibworth Beauchamp,
Leicestershire. LE8 0RX
Tel: 0116 279 2299
Email: books@troubador.co.uk
Web: www.troubador.co.uk/matador
Twitter: @matadorbooks

ISBN 978 1789017 748

British Library Cataloguing in Publication Data.
A catalogue record for this book is available from the British Library.

Printed and bound by CPI Group (UK) Ltd, Croydon, CR0 4YY
Typeset in 12pt Bembo by Troubador Publishing Ltd, Leicester, UK

Matador is an imprint of Troubador Publishing Ltd

Contents

....

For the Armenians, in the centenary of their genocide, the Greeks, the Syrian Orthodox, the Yezidis, Nestorians, Assyrians, Mandaeans, Zoroastrians and others too many to mention. May all things be restored one day. They will. And to my wife, Samantha, who restored me and still does, every day.

For those who encouraged me to publish despite the discouragements. To my friends Susanna Smith, for proofing, cover design and the use of her photography, to Stuart Beaker, for starting me down the publication route, and to Brian Firth for the first editing. And to Going Postal (www.going-postal.com) for allowing me a voice in a time of increasing obstacles in the path of new authors, especially those of a book like this.

Explanatory Note

··

The section headings used in this novel relate to the ancient Celtic church's Easter dating system, which was used in much of Britain before the progressive adoption of the Roman Latin church's method of dating Easter, following the old Anglo-Celtic kingdom of Northumbria's recognition of papal authority at the Synod of Whitby in 664 AD. The differences between the two traditions as to the calculation of the falling of Easter in any one year led to occasional disagreements as to on which Sunday Easter day should fall.

For reasons that will become apparent, this story employs the Celtic Easter cycle, whereas some of the characters within it are following the modern western usage of Easter dating. This may cause some confusion in the mind of the reader, for which the author does not apologise on the assumption that any reader that enjoys this novel is both sufficiently intelligent and curious to cope with this and other antiquarian references. They are important components of the book's central premise.

To Calliope,
Please understand that while forms change,
intent does not

Falling, falling, deeply falling,
Down towards the rosy glow,
Passion claws and fires rage,
Strength fails and grip erodes,
The tide pulls, the current gains,
Fight against where they'll go.
Attraction overpowering, mortal weak,
Gravity catches and desires bite,
So love twists and hopes elude,
And then down fall to the trap below,
But faith endures and will must fight
Against the honey scent of glorious night.
We live by day and dream long of light
That love persists and true hearts know.

It begins

....

The man about to die pulled the green framed glass door shut and glanced furtively up and down the street before locking the door and placing the key in his jacket pocket.

His would-be assassin stretched his right index finger to relieve tension and took a slow deep breath to reduce his heart rate before cradling the rifle stock firmly against his shoulder. Using the open rear window of the van, his mobile hide for this hunt, to frame his target, he carefully sighted on his intended victim through the sniper scope attached to his weapon. The light remained weak in the overcast early morning conditions and he flicked on the scope's target illuminator. It was taking too long for the target to turn around to face the street so that he could get a final identification, but long enough for the tension to build again though, for his heart rate to rise and his palms to feel clammy, long enough for the doubts to begin anew. He knew that killing his first human quarry, even a man such as this, put him on the far side of something, but the far side of what: a moral or spiritual chasm with only Hell for an escape? Whatever it was, he only knew there could be no way back once the trigger had been squeezed.

Chief Inspector Andrew Bowson stretched out to shake his slumbering colleague into consciousness. Their third long night of surveillance on the bounce was coming to an end and the muggy atmosphere of the van was proving particularly soporific on this early spring morning. As the dawn established itself he put down the night vision viewer and picked up the binoculars, allowing him to get a good look at the man they had been observing, firstly from a distance and now more closely, for the last six days. Five-nine, wiry build, curly black hair and beard, non-descript clothing – all perfectly normal in this immigrant populated part of Birmingham – but there was something about the way he carried himself though, an arrogant assurance that ensured he stood out to the trained eye. It was definitely him, another ideological psycho, a walking bomb, primed to explode at any random moment.

These people took up all his time now, most of that of his colleagues in the other Counter-Terror teams too. How many had he investigated, watched, then raided over the last few years? Far too many to recall, that was for certain. When Andy first considered joining the police family he was told that this should be where to specialise: exciting, vital, high profile, all the requirements for the ambitious young man on the rise. All true, but what he hadn't really appreciated was the addictive intensity, the inability to ever turn off the adrenal tap, the career narcotic that demanded increasingly more of him as he rose through the ranks. His family life was suffering too, his work consumed him, and they were paying a heavy price; he'd need to make it up to them and soon.

"What's up?" Detective Sergeant George Edward said stretching into life, his reddish-blond hair now complemented by thick stubble.

"He's just coming out of the house, let the relief team know he's on the move and he's all theirs now; we can stand down."

The sniper watched the target glance surreptitiously right and left up both sides of the street. A sign of training, a marker of suspicion, further, but not final, confirmation of his identity. Now he was looking down the street leading directly away from him in front, lined on both sides with cars and vans, the red brick terraced housing gently cascading down the hill and rising again up the other side of the low valley, intersected regularly by other roads, until it ended at another residential street, perhaps two thirds of a mile away.

"Target confirmed."

The rifleman grunted assent to the confirmation of his spotter beside him, exhaled gently as the target pulled a car key from his trouser pocket, and squeezed his index finger, doubts stifled by the habits of long training and the impersonality of it all, and then saw his target, one Mohammed Amallifely, hurled back into the green door, his chest a fragmented red mass slumped against a now shattered front portal. Already the shooter's rifle chamber was recharged, he was barely aware of the action, the aiming point varying just a fraction, steadying, exhaling, trigger finger pulling for the second time.

"My…"

Andy Bowson never got the chance to finish his profanity as a sound like the air being torn asunder by a street level ballistic missile engulfed his vehicle and resounded down the street. The suspect was thrown backwards like a rag doll into and partly through the now broken front door, glass, wood and blood clouding the air like sea spume. As the body settled against the door's remains, the banshee-like scream came again, only this time his shaking binoculars saw the victim's head struck by the invisible force, flying backwards in a red mist.

"Get the support team and an ambulance here soonest, and let local liaison know as well," Bowson ordered Edward as he reached for the van's sliding door.

He retained enough self-awareness to know that he was in shock, but adrenalin and training took over as he stepped down into the street and broke into a run to where what could only be a broken corpse lay partly hidden by the doorway. Thoughts that they were in a hostile neighbourhood with a gunman in the immediate vicinity never even reached his consciousness. Reckless he told himself later. By the time he reached the shattered front door he could hear the siren of the unmarked support car as it turned into the street, and Edward just behind him with his handgun out as the car pulled up to a stop.

Bowson rose from the body and looked down the adjoining streets, breathing furiously from his exertions, the body... Well, he had seen nothing quite like it. Dimly viewed shapes were peering through windows and doors were opening. The support team of two were by him now, and the wail of sirens could be heard in the near distance.

"You two, keep the scene secure while the Sergeant and I check the house."

"Success" whispered the spotter, in a language which only a tiny handful in the country could have understood, as he moved to the front of the van and turned the key in the ignition while the sniper packed away their equipment in the back.

"That second was a beaut, 1,000 yard head shot. Shame it wasn't really needed."

Slipping backing into English tinged with the remains of an Australian accent, its inherent warmth contrasting with the clipped delivery of the cold-blooded statement.

The shooter spoke for the first time since he'd pulled the trigger, "Didn't come all this way not to make sure."

The equipment all now secure in building tools cases, the marksman remained in the back with his thoughts. So, what they had taught him was right, the training kicked in and mastered the fear, albeit the doubt was racing back now. He could feel his raised pulse, which he knew would be followed by an overpowering exhaustion, and a certain elevation of spirit, the endorphin effect, they called it. The target deserved it and much more, but his conscience was conflicted, hopefully his maker would understand. But of one thing he was certain, not just his, life but his world, would change dramatically now. A lot more would inevitably follow.

Blood on his hands, blood on his soul. So, he had done it after all; he, Sam Penwarden, the names he normally used these days, really had graduated now. He sat in the back of the second change vehicle as they drove towards the meeting point with the lifting team, as they were jokingly nicknamed. The van they had used had been left flaming in an abandoned warehouse, although the plastic liner in which they had wrapped the interior had been removed for burning at the farm. Good luck to any forensics experts trying to use it to find them. The second vehicle, belonging to a family on holiday, had been returned to its owners' home without anyone being the wiser.

People said he had had a hard, young life, but nothing in it had fully prepared him for what he had just done or what he would do in the future. A life involving drugs, petty crime, being shuttled in and out of care, rough sleeping, all the usual markers of a life with an absence of real direction, meaning or luck. Then quite unexpectedly he had been found, offered meaning, value, companionship, true wonders which smashed the carapace that had accreted to him and given him a path to a new home, a new country, a new family and even a new name. All things which created debts he could never hope to repay, but must try or lose his new self-respect. In finding his soul, he must risk its loss, its final pollution once again. Ironic, he knew, but once that first shot had been taken, the path he had willingly trod had become as one of those moving travellators one saw at airports. There was no turning back, just an onwards rush impelled by forces far greater than himself. But it had been his decision.

Sam looked at the back of his spotter and boss on this mission, Alan the Aussie, who was driving. Here he was on the other side of the world from his homeland; something had reached out and drawn him here to this place, this purpose, just as it had drawn him from the hard streets and harder lessons of his native south Bristol and then the alien London. He envied his colleague's apparent lack of introspection, his antipodean cool, but suspected that the older man was, in reality, just more self-possessed than anything else. Well, when he returned home his confession was going to be a long one.

They were pulling up now. The other team couldn't be far away unless something had gone wrong. They drove into the waiting barn, closed the door and unloaded their equipment before approaching the farmhouse to be met by one of the base team holding open the front door and looking at them quizzically. Alan's broad, relieved grin answered his unspoken question.

Mohammed Badr's morning run proceeded as usual as he headed out of the city up into the hills on the edge of town; this was going to be a long one, twenty miles at least, as he built up his training schedule. He would visit the gym later for martial arts class, and then maybe some resistance training. The sirens were particularly busy today, the kaffirs' stooges inflicting harassment on some poor victims. No matter, his record was clean, and he had been careful, and was headed away from the gathering commotion which seemed to be concentrated some way away. He had time to clear his head and focus on their mission.

He was in the small country lanes now, climbing a narrow hilly section passing just the odd farm driveway or cottage. There was rarely any traffic to contend with at this time of the morning up here, but he could hear an engine in the distance and moved closer to the wall in anticipation.

A Land Rover came around the bend towards him, picking up speed as it descended the hill, it was getting hellishly close to him, leaving him with nowhere to go…

"Nicely done Art."

The speaker was trussing the recumbent body expertly, ankles, knees, elbows and wrists, while his partner gagged the mouth and checked that no evidence was left on the ground by the collision site. They lifted the unconscious man into the back of the van, which as a commercial model lacked windows, administered a sedative and drove away. It was all over in less than two minutes.

The speaker looked at the back of his companion, Art, from his vantage point in the rear of the vehicle. Art seemed a real deep dyed West Country yokel; a laconic giant of a man in his mid-twenties, strong and dextrous from a life spent sailing small craft in all seasons, but surprisingly funny when in the mood. He wasn't in the mood now, even for a few words.

"Okay Art, you know where we have to be and when to meet the others, let's be on time without rushing."

Even as he spoke the words Georgios Tredare knew them to be superfluous; it must be his half-Hellenic nature, this need to talk in the silence. He was an older man, in his mid-forties, but fit and slim with thinning grey-black hair. The excitement of the taking made him itchy and again he checked his handgun and its attached silencer just for something to do. Not that their prisoner would give them any trouble for quite some time: the bruises and swelling were starting to show, and trickles of blood were apparent, but nothing significant, and it appeared there were no breaks or major dislocations, but a thorough check up would be needed when they met the others. He understood the victim was Turkish which made it all the better.

'Henry', well, that's what everyone called him these days, was burning up his reserves of patience, sitting here in his anonymous office in central London. The first anticipated call, the unofficial one, a text message on an unmonitored one time pay-as-you go phone, was, strictly speaking, superfluous. The official call, which should follow the first within a couple of hours, would be the one that gave him the entrée he needed. But it was the first, the waiting for it, which was consuming him; the heralding of the opening shots of a new war, well at least another side joining a war which was already raging, even if most of the powers-that-be adamantly denied it. It had been over a decade in secret, silent preparation, every step fraught with self-doubt and fear of discovery, drawing on resources and people from the most unlooked-for corners of the world. Failure now, at the outset, could prove fatal to the task he had set himself all those years ago in the aftermath of baleful times. Times that haunted him almost every…

Rescued from his unwilling reverie by a buzz on the unofficial handset, yes; the text he had been waiting for. Short, to-the-point and containing some of the most reassuring words he had ever received. Good boys. She'd be pleased if she had had any inkling of what was planned, but of course she couldn't have. Strictly need to know. She was sufficiently professional to understand that, but a small part of him, that inner boy that can be harder to eradicate than a vampire, longed to tell her, to impress her. Pull yourself together you fool, you can't ever go there, it would jeopardise everything; besides, he thought, you're marked by a prior claim... You're slipping, not back there either, concentrate.

How long for the second call? No matter, he had it planned. First a call to Gerald, Director-General of MI5, the Security Service, to explain his intervention and a request that they, his little band of brothers and sisters, work alongside their more visible and far larger sister agency. Most previous DG's of MI5 would have told him to clear off, only not so politely, but Gerald was different, if not a friend, then "simpatico" as the Italians termed it. He understood the need for them, what they had to do, where they had to go, the places his people couldn't, and then fade out when required, and he didn't ask superfluous questions. Thank God for Gerald.

That second call, the official one, informing him of the killing of a suspected terrorist in Birmingham in front of an anti-terrorist police surveillance team, led by... who... Chief Inspector Andy Bowson. Must read his file while travelling to Birmingham.

The call to Gerald, straight through,

"Gerald, Henry here, you've heard about the shooting of Amallifely in Birmingham?"

"Just. I wasn't aware you had an interest in this operation?"

"You know we're always interested, sounds like a sniper. I assume it's not anybody on our side?"

"If it's not you or any of your confederates... No, I'd have known."

"Would you?"

"Don't scare me. But yes, I'm certain."

"I'd like to look into it, on your organisation's behalf as well, report everything of course. If it's internal, something new, well, you know that's what we're here for..."

"I see," Gerald's voice faded to silence, ten seconds, then, "alright, Henry. You'd better get moving, they're planning to meet later today when the dust's settled a little. We'll tell them you're one of ours and we'll stand our people down."

"Thanks Gerald, I appreciate it. I'll call you afterwards with a full report."

"Are we quits now?"

"Of course."

Sally Bowson felt a tear slide down her cheek as she locked the door behind her, looked around the back garden of her home once more and walked to the car in which Josiah, her three-year old son sat, already secure in his child seat.

"Where're we going again Mummy?" he asked as she drove out of the drive of the home she shared with her husband into a residential street in west London.

"Granny and Grandpa's in Devon like I told you."

"Is Daddy coming?"

"Not this time sweetie, he's got to work. We won't see him for a while."

"Catching bad men again?"

"Yes Josey; now here's your lollipop."

She felt guilty about distracting him with sweets, but it was going to be a long journey and he was a bright boy who had an unerring knack of launching into a series of questions with a remorseless childhood logic which she currently felt too fragile to withstand. She had sworn to herself at his birth that she would never lie to any of her children, an oath she had barely managed to sustain so far.

As the car drove onto the M4 a little later her mobile phone buzzed to indicate the arrival of a text message, almost certainly from her husband. She hadn't replied to the last few he had sent over the past twenty-four hours, a coward's way out she knew, but she needed space and time to sort herself out. Her mind wandered, driving on autopilot;

the city was too big, too alien, and too impersonal for her to get her mind and feelings straight. Now she knew how much she missed the wide-open country and small communities of her native north Devon. Like so many of her peers she had left for college and the bright lights of the city as soon as she could, then fallen for an attractive young class mate who ended up becoming a rising star in the police of all things.

Married for seven years, they had imperceptibly grown apart since Josey's birth as Andy had hardened in response to the unspoken things he faced in his job, especially since his transfer to the Counter Terrorist Command of the Met. Not that she thought he could see it for himself, but the cold of their growing lack of mutual understanding had chilled them both. In reaction, her love for her child had rekindled her childhood Anglicanism, just as she increasingly realised that there were unlikely to be any further children. And so, she had left, for how long exactly she didn't know, but she had to get away. At least Josey sleeps in the car, she thought.

So, she drove steadily westwards on the M4, stopping occasionally to give Josey a break while still aiming to arrive at her parents' house by early evening. She had called them to say she was on route; they hadn't expressed any surprise at the unannounced news that she was coming down, but she knew the questions would come after she had arrived.

'Damn the woman, why did she have to go so distant to him now?' Andy Bowson thought to himself as he sat waiting outside the meeting room in West Midlands Constabulary headquarters later that day. 'She didn't play this hard to get when we were going out, if only she hadn't rediscovered God.' As soon as he thought it, he chided himself, but he had sent eight text messages over the last few days and had only a single monosyllabic response to the first.

He was broken from his reverie by the meeting room door opening. George Edward rose beside him and ran his fingers through his ill-kempt hair. Both men looked a mess after twenty-four hours without a break, but Bowson knew that this was the least of their problems right now. The Chief Constable's assistant beckoned towards them somewhat sympathetically, "You can both go in now gentlemen."

Bowson led the way in and Edward followed closing the door softy behind them.

"Please take a seat, gentlemen. Would you like tea or coffee? You've had quite a night and day of it I understand."

It was the first time that Bowson had met the local Chief Constable and the man surprised him by showing some welcome old world courtesy, something he was not used to from his own superior, Chief Superintendent Martin Dager, who sat next to the Chief Constable. The Chief Constable continued, "May I introduce you to our local elected Police and Crime Commissioner, my Deputy Chief Constable and a colleague from the security services who says we can call him Henry."

Politicians and spooks already here for what was surely only an operational policing matter, albeit one with particularly sensitive connections. Oh well, it was above his pay grade.

After the assistant had provided refreshments and left the room the Chief Constable, who clearly wanted to dominate a meeting on his own turf, invited Andy to recount the events of the last twenty-four hours.

"… so the media seem to be concluding it was a drug related killing, a gang turf war, at least so far." Bowson concluded a few minutes later.

"So, who was it?" broke in the Commissioner.

"A little bit early to speculate don't you think Alina?" interjected the Chief soothingly to the plump, PCC with the dyed red hair.

There was a tension there that even the worn Bowson could sense, but fortunately, before the PCC could respond, the spook intruded. "More to the point, whoever it was used something special. You think the shot was taken from well over half a mile away and was from a large calibre rifle, probably 0.50 inch, so much so it blew his head off and took the front door with it? Nothing like that's been used here since the 1970's when the IRA got a few US military sniper rifles and caused consternation among the security services. Fortunately, they didn't have anyone good enough to use them to their full potential and they were recovered fairly quickly. Whoever was behind this is serious."

Bowson was impressed, perhaps the guy was ex-military, he had the look. He had certainly got to a conclusion that Bowson was only just reaching. This meeting was a minefield, potentially a career limiting one, lots of agendas and prejudices. He spoke slowly, almost as if reading from a written report, treading gingerly.

"Well clearly the heroin and other narcotics we found in the property indicate there is a serious drugs connection and the young girl we found there suggests it was another case of grooming and exploitation by a local ethnic criminal gang. However, the nature of the killing almost confirms our, and your, interest in the victim."

He inclined his head to the MI5? man who still hadn't fully introduced himself.

"Ballistics will take a few hours to confirm the details, but we don't expect it to help much, they were far too professional. All we have is one report from a witness over half a mile away of an unknown grey van driving away, quite unhurriedly, just after the second shot. No cartridge cases, no strange lodgers, nothing. House to house enquiries are continuing, but the locals aren't particularly volunteering anything and quite a lot purport not to understand English, so we're having to use interpreters which slows us down. Nevertheless, I suspect you're right – the weapon was clearly large calibre, the shooter highly expert and unlikely to be working alone – but it's just speculation at present."

The spook ignored the other would-be questioners. Was he the one with real authority here?

"I assume you are calling in any nearby close circuit camera tapes for examination? Yes? Not that they will tell us much. Unless we are miraculously lucky, perhaps the best we can hope for is to find the getaway vehicle burnt out somewhere. I'd be surprised if the bullet fragments tell you anything, it's just too professional."

The PCC would not be denied any longer. "This is intolerable, this... gentleman," Bowson noted that her tone suggested otherwise, "Informs us that a highly expert hit-man has murdered a local resident in a heavily populated street of my city in broad daylight. A resident that the Counter-Terrorism Command have been watching for a week without anyone informing me, and a colleague from the security services says we shouldn't expect to find out who committed this heinous act. Why are they involved in this anyway?"

The Chief Constable sighed and tried to take back control of what was turning into a 'scene'. "Let's not forget Alina that the victim was clearly involved in drugs racketeering and apparently child exploitation, he had an illegal firearm in the house, and he is suspected of involvement in other very serious activities, hence these gentlemen's presence in our city. Besides these are highly sensitive operational matters and it is only my regard for you Alina" he paused briefly and smiled winningly at her "and the political sensitivity of these events that led me to invite you to this briefing. Has anyone else anything to add?"

Only Bowson's boss, Martin Dager, ignored the Chief Constable's attempt to defuse the brewing row by curtailing the meeting. "I'd like to thank Officers Bowson and Edward for this clear briefing and their work to date on this investigation, but due to their direct public involvement other colleagues will follow up on the ground in support of the local constabulary. Given the press' speculation that this is just an unpleasant criminal matter, the Counter-Terrorism Command's involvement will ostensibly fade into the background. My colleagues will return to London for further debriefing and to consider our next steps with higher authority."

Bowson saw both the Chief Constable and PCC bridle at his boss' citing of superior authorities in London as he followed him out of the room. He glanced at George; his face betrayed dismay at their apparent dismissal from the case, an emotion Bowson felt only too acutely himself. It looked like Dager was distancing himself from the failure of the operation. Just typical of the man, thought Andy.

He stepped into the gents to wash the perspiration off his face and hands, and on emerging was surprised to be faced with the loitering spook. No one was sufficiently close to hear his hushed tones, "Well done, especially after what you went through only a few hours before. Get home, get some rest. Don't worry about the internal politics, leave that to others. You won't be off the case."

He turned and took a step as if he were finished, then, inclining his head back to Bowson, he smiled and whispered so quietly that Bowson almost missed the words, "Of course they've all been terrified for years of a serious nativist backlash, not the ranters on the streets and web, but something more… considered, it bears consideration. See you around."

And with those words, 'Henry' turned and sauntered off, leaving Bowson to pause and then make his way to join his superior and assistant at the front of the building. What was the meaning of the spook's words, a nativist reaction? Why mutter it to me rather than say it in the meeting? What's going on here? Who was he anyway? Then, unbidden another thought came as if intuition and instinct rebelled against years of inculcated practice, perhaps best not to say anything to Dager or George yet. Why not? Because he had been invited to share a confidence? Why had 'Henry' spoken to him like that? He wasn't sure, but he told himself, go carefully.

Andy's focus snapped back into life to see Dager looking at him unsympathetically, which wasn't unusual.

"Got all your belongings? Good. Stow them in the back of my car: you can both come back to base with me and go through things again. Hopefully we may get some preliminary forensics on the bullets by the time we are back."

Bowson's spirits sank a little lower: no space to myself, even for a few hours.

Alina Mackintosh left the office early that night. That patronising Chief Constable, he clearly thought he knew how to manage her… and that creep from MI5 or where ever, with his tame coppers. When the Islamic hotheads started up, with their "community leaders" not far behind, she would be the one in the firing line, and she faced re-election only next year. She picked up her personal mobile and dialled the council leader, to whom she had once been deputy. A voice answered. "Paul, there's more to this killing than meets the eye. You need to know, I can't tell you everything and they're not letting me know the half of it, but it's for the good of the party… and the city. Can I come over?"

The evening was advancing towards night as the car carrying Chief Superintendent Dager and his subordinates passed the M25 ring-road and entered outer London. Dager and Bowson were just winding up a full review of the case so far, getting every item straight in their minds in preparation for a full debriefing to higher authority the following morning, exactly how much higher was not yet clear.

Used as he was to working on highly politicised and sensitive matters, this felt slightly different to Bowson and it appeared to have unnerved his boss as well. He had been shocked, if not entirely surprised, by the presence of a senior Security Service official at the meeting with the Chief Constable, their normal MI5 liaisons not even making it into the room. Henry, the spook had called himself, and he hadn't disclosed his rank or department, which implied that he was sufficiently senior or 'discreet' not to need to, odd and worrying in equal measure.

It would have to happen now when they seemed to be making real progress on the investigation. GCHQ had informed them about web chatter which had led them to what seemed to be at first a lone wolf. Careful observation had identified Mohammed Amallifely and now they were in the process of trying to identify his associates, of whom there were potentially dozens. It was like looking for needle in a haystack, but Amallifely was interesting because he was clearly experienced if not totally a professional. Unexplained absences, no clear means of support, apparent involvement in criminal activity, sedulous attendance at a local mosque with a radical reputation, were all usually good indicators, but not proof. He was clearly plugged into some sort of network, but probably not central, and could have acted as a gateway to others for the investigators.

Now their best lead was gone, publicly assassinated while under police surveillance; Andy and his team were going to be a laughing stock. The local Chief Constable seemed tractable, but that PCC! And the security services would demand more powers over the CT Command on this sort of investigation. Inter-service politics were bad enough without spooks and politicos pursuing their own agendas.

As for Dager, well, Bowson's relationship with him was professional at best and now the man was fuming. This couldn't have happened at a worse time with his annual evaluation coming up in the next week. Andy was ambitious, looking for his next promotion; it was hard enough in today's service being white, middle class, hetero and male, the last sort of officer the HR types and his superiors wanted to promote. It wasn't as if he hadn't paid the price in full already, potentially broken marriage, a distant child, few real friends and a life consumed by his profession... Bowson knew there were plenty of others in similar positions, scrabbling for every ounce of professional fulfilment, maybe even a vicarious validation of their choices... Damn it. He knew it wasn't fair to blame Dager either, who after all was not that dissimilar to himself, save for a fading Derbyshire accent, but he was inevitably going to catch some of his boss' frustration. If only they had got some sort of lead on the assassin...

Bowson felt like the world was bearing down on his shoulders. Even Dager, worn by his own concerns, noticed. "What's up Andy? You look like this case is the least of your problems?"

"Been trying to get hold of the wife without any joy sir."

He couldn't, didn't, want to elaborate and Dager, his attempt at fellow feeling exhausted, lapsed into introspection which invited no further comment for the rest of the journey.

There was a call on one of his secure pay-as-you-go phones. "Abdul, it's Suleiman here. Amallifely's been martyred, shot outside his house this morning. The police are all over it and have been searching the house and asking lots of questions of everyone."

"Then why are you calling me on this number, it may have been compromised? Meet me in forty minutes at point B."

The younger man was panicking he realised, his inexperience showing through. Better contact his leader, Badr, to confer. They might have to accelerate or abort their mission, but it wasn't his decision. One more call with this phone then dump it. No answer. Thirty, sixty, ninety minutes later, still no answer. Concerns began to rise. Alternative numbers not answering either. Better go around – a risk he knew – give it twenty-four hours then. Low key for the rest of the day other than meet Abdul and the others; they can ask questions of local sympathisers to try to fill in the gaps.

He turned on the local news. There had been a drugs related murder according to police, in Amallifely's street. He was really worried now; it was too much of a coincidence. Something had gone seriously wrong and his leader had disappeared. Yes, too much of a coincidence, Badr had all the contacts outside their cell; if he were taken they could all be rolled up. Amallifely, Badr's deputy, would have known what to do. They were taught to be flexible, self-sufficient and unpredictable. They might not have very long so they had to move fast. Allah would steer them and provide. Devotion, dedication could overcome all, even in this hostile infidel land. As next in authority now, unless Badr re-emerged, it was his call. Strike now before it was too late, even if not fully prepared? The panic, the fear began to recede as he came to his decision. It would be tomorrow evening at the softer alternate target then; now to tell the rest of the team.

Sally Bowson turned the key in the ignition again, and again, nothing, dead, no electrics at all. The last vestiges of daylight were fading into the west over Cornwall, blending with the early moonlight to barely illuminate the moorland stretching away all around her. The car would pack up here, on one of the loneliest roads on Exmoor, a road she had taken hundreds of times to her parents' cottage just beyond the western fringe of the moor. The clear early spring night was already bitterly cold and clear, and the heater had gone with the electrics. "Are we at Grandma's yet?"

"Nearly sweetie."

"Why have we stopped"?

"Just resting the car."

She picked up her phone. Her Dad could come and get them: it could only be nine or ten miles. Please Lord, let there be some signal. The phone seemed to be off. It wouldn't turn on. Had the battery died? She had no spare with her. No, Lord, no, not now. She wasn't normally one to panic, but she had Josey in the car and it looked like a freezing night. The stars were coming out now, the sky was clear and yes, the temperature was going to crash. That settled it. There were farms, even up here less than every mile or so: it could be hours before a passing vehicle came by. She leaned back in the car and released her son from the seat straps. "Put your coat and jumper on sweetie, we've got to go for a little walk."

She reached over and pulled out the torch she normally kept in the glove compartment. No light, damn, the batteries must have run out. She got out, let out Josey and they headed west along the road. She touched his head. Ouch, the crackle of static made her jump, the air seemed to be crawling with a pent up electric charge, weird. She went on a few further paces and looked up. The Northern Lights! It was a long time since she had seen them this far south, let alone such a magnificent display – greens, blues, purples – almost as if they were all around her now. The charge in the atmosphere was getting worse. Something wasn't right. Better not hang about. She swept a faintly protesting son into her arms and set off, jog-walking, eyes down, looking for that first farm gateway. Words from her college years broke into her distracted mind, 'In the middle of the journey of our life, I found myself in a dark wood, for the straight path was lost.' Dante's Inferno wasn't it?

She was fearing a physical loss of direction now, not just an emotional one. A mist seemed to be rising, diminishing the brightness of the lights in the sky; visibility was very faint, but there it was, a gateway, or at least an earth track with an open rusted metal gate slumped to one side. Second thoughts rose, but a sixth sense or mother's intuition impelled her not to retreat. She hurried down the falling rutted track, the heather closing in on both sides so that finally only the wheel tracks remained. There was no sign of light or habitation. On the point of abandoning this track as a false start and heading back, she heard, or thought she heard, something like animal footsteps rustling the heather away to the right. "Hello, hello?"

No answer, Exmoor ponies, or sheep? The rustling footsteps picked up speed seemingly coming towards her and there seemed to be more now, both to the right and behind. She felt fear, the real primal kind; this was no longer the moorland she knew so well and had loved so much, but an unfamiliar hinterland of unseen menace. She stumbled down the track, the heather snapping at her jean wrapped legs and ankle boots, her dark brown, almost black, neck length hair sweeping across her eyes as she clutched an alarmed Josey to her breast, his dark brown eyes staring up at her, her mood silencing the normally interminable stream of questions and observations.

Whatever they were, they seemed closer now in the strangely coloured darkness, on all sides but not in front. She was running now, praying not to lose her footing. Out of the night came a guttural whispering, a subdued cacophony of communication between unseen terrors.

"Dear God," she heard herself gasp as she glimpsed a dim yellow-orange luminescence ahead, almost similar to the patina of light given out by the oil lamps her parents used to keep for the frequent power cuts of her childhood. There was another, and another... and then, a faint metallic squeak, and another, again from ahead.

The sounds behind were very close, almost imminent, possessing a feral intensity. She was exhausted from stumbling along with a mute Josey in her arms, bathed in a cold sweat, her heart pounding, pushing up towards her throat. The mist and twisting, writhing sky lights were all around as she finally lost her footing on the broken track and fell headlong into the heather with a cry of despair, cut short as her head slammed into a protruding lump of granite. For a split second, part of her retained just enough consciousness to later recollect a shape running up to her, a swinging light in one hand and something dark in the other, with other lights swaying up behind…

In silence, the Abbot left the chancel along with the Brothers, a silence they would all observe until the following day, with the single exception of himself. He turned and followed the cobbled path up to the stone built fort of ancient design which doubled as the Duke's small palace. The Chamberlain met him at the main door as he did every night at this same time, something that they had been doing for many years now after a string of others before them. It was held to be a vital tenet of Duchy tradition, the importance of which the old man himself had stressed to him after his election. So, here he was again, following the Chamberlain slowly up the candle lit stone steps, pausing at the ornate oak door along the landing and following him through into the chamber.

A wood-burner was chugging away in a corner of the room, holding the evening chill at bay for the sleeping occupant in the silk covered bed. He always marvelled at those silks, a gift from the east of exquisite construction, the byzantine designs and colouring reminding him of the icons held within the Abbey. There he lay sleeping on the bed as he always was when they came to bless his recumbent form and to pray for God's protection of the ageing man beneath the covers. White haired, he looked like as a man in his sixties might look after a life of hard service. His face was always expressionless, as if he never dreamed or as if his soul were somewhere completely "other."

He gave the blessing and made the short plea for divine protection as normal, and then it was over for another twenty-four hours. He had never lingered in this room, had never seen it in the natural light. For him the silk window hangings were always drawn across the barred glass, the hanging oil lamps lit, keeping the darkness at bay, the wall tapestries and floor rugs of uncertain detail in the dim light. He followed the Chamberlain out; looking back into the room and on to the form of the figure about whom so much was said.

The waiting night servant locked the door behind them and sat on the chair beside the door as he always did. The guard on the top of the stairs nodded wordlessly to them as they descended. Another would be up there as well in the room opposite all night. No one would take any chances, not even somewhere as safe and secure as here. The Chamberlain thanked him, as he always did, and went back to his own quarters in the fort. The night porter locked the main door behind him as he blessed the man as he always requested, and headed back to his cell. His mind, reassured by the continuity of the ritual, the timelessness it seemed to possess, began to think of the dawn and the coming of Easter and of those in harm's way on the outside.

It was almost eleven as Andy Bowson made it to his hotel room for the night, just as his personal mobile phone rang: it was Sally's mother, "Andy? Justine, it's Sally, we were expecting her here hours ago with Josey, but she's not arrived, her mobile's going straight to answer phone and she isn't at home as far as we can tell. She phoned this morning to say she was coming down today and never turned up. Her supper's ruined. Have you heard from her?"

"Don't worry Justine, I'm sure she's fine" he found himself replying almost automatically. "If we don't hear from her by morning I'll get my colleagues on to it."

He knew things hadn't been right between them, but she had never taken off to her parents before without discussing it with him first. And she hadn't contacted him for over thirty-six hours now; better not wait until the morning. He picked up the phone again to speak to the local duty officer at Devon & Cornwall Constabulary. After all, they were all members of the police family.

Thursday

....

Alan Dare watched Mohammed Badr wake slowly from his drugged stupor; the man must be dying of thirst, he thought. They were in a large barn, bare and devoid of content other than some animal stalls, all occupied except for the one in which Badr was bound and chained. A door was ajar, letting in some of the limp early morning light, joining that which filtered through the dirty high-level windows.

Alan knew the floor was freezing, softened only by animal litter, but could read the prisoner's face sufficiently to see that the man's feelings were colder than his body as he realised that he was surrounded by three men, all masked and in grey overalls. One, Art, would seem a virtual giant, another, Georgy, almost Arabic in appearance from the look of the uncovered patch around his eyes, but clearly no brother from their expression, and Alan himself, blondish haired.

"Good, you've re-joined us. You must have been tired; you were out for almost twenty-four hours. Let me tell you how it's going to be. You will tell us all we want to know, every last detail without hesitation, just the truth. If you don't, you will not survive the consequences. Clear?"

Art removed the gag in Badr's mouth.

"I've rights…"

The kick slammed him into the left-hand stall. Art picked him up and lifted him over the stall and held him seemingly without effort. Badr could see the pigs, unclean pigs, in the stalls beyond. Alan sighed.

"Wrong answer, I see you've noticed our evidence disposal team. Good. Here's proof of our intent."

Badr tried to scream as the fingers of his left hand were laid flat on top of the stall partition while Alan pulled out a small cleaver. Art pushed the gag into Badr's gaping mouth, the man was shaking and trying to flail himself free until the moment white hot pain coursed through him and his appalled eyes saw Alan drop his digit into the neighbouring stall where it was welcomed with happy squeals; with that Badr slumped back into unconsciousness.

Alan stepped back. "Lord help us, I'm not sure I can take too much more of this."

"He's done worse to others, innocent women and children. There should be no pity, nor guilt."

Alan looked at his companion with mixed emotion. Georgios Tredare was carrying something personal, an ancestral loathing of the Muslim Turk passed on from his Greek mother, despite his birth and upbringing in Britannia. How different from his own privileged Australian childhood, a culture without ancient hatreds. He had left aged eighteen for a year's tour of the old world, arrived in England and never gone back. And now, some nineteen years later, life had transpired to make him a killer, a torturer, in a bleak old barn on a remote god-forsaken farm, with his wife and children blithely unaware of what he was now doing. Jesus forgive me, he thought. He couldn't though let his companions see his lack of strength of will or courage lest they doubt him; he was already confirmed in his belief that moral courage is more precious, more easily eroded, than the physical: he felt his draining away with every second in this place of horrors. Focus, remember why, pull yourself together; the prisoner was already showing signs of stirring. He nodded to Art, the giant.

"Wake him." A pail of icy cold water slammed the prisoner back into consciousness.

"Now Mr Badr, time is short and so is our patience and, if you continue to defy us, so will be your anatomy."

When he came to Badr found himself trussed to a plain wooden chair, with one arm tied behind his back to the chair and the other, his left swathed in a rough cloth and tied across his chest. His mouth was free of the gag again, but he felt the presence of one man, surely the giant, behind him with a hand clasping the nape of his neck. Another, the Aussie seemingly, sat on an identical chair two yards in front of him. To his left there was a table with several metallic implements which he struggled to make out in the dim light, fainter now that the barn door was closed. The third man stood just to one side and behind his companion, directing a video camera on a tripod.

Must be some kaffir black operations team Badr thought, but even they had limits, especially as he must still be in the UK. His spirits rose, only to be dashed as the pain from his hand finally intruded into his mind. How had they traced him, who was the betrayer?

"What you have done to me? Who are you? What d'you want? Why am I here"?

"We ask the questions."

The presumed Australian nodded to the one behind him. The agony in his neck was stunning in its speed and severity, he felt sick, faint, on the verge of collapse. The pressure was released, but he knew that it was only a second away. He was frozen, hungry, thirsty, racked with pain, and almost totally disorientated.

"We understand that this situation is familiar to you from your past in Iraq and elsewhere, only this time from the other side of the camera. Firstly, you will make a full confession of your activities in spreading terror to the innocent. If you do not, or attempt to mislead us in anyway, then each time you lie another part of you will go the way of the first, until there is nothing left to follow, am I clear?"

"I'll never betray my holy trust to you damned crusaders. All you do is offer me welcome martyr…"

Before he could protest further the pain in his neck returned, followed by the gag. The cameraman switched off the video recorder, removed the prisoner's right running shoe and sock and pressed the foot flat to the floor. Alan came forward holding the cleaver, just as the combined pressure on his neck and his struggle to breathe through the gag sucked him into brief unconsciousness, only to re-emerge once more into pain-wracked awareness.

Two hours later, after several more sessions, Mohammed Badr's will to resist collapsed. Nothing in his training and experience had prepared him for this. Western agencies weren't supposed to behave like this; they had rules, limits and weaknesses to be exploited by the certain and death seeking.

After three further hours he was done. He was allowed a little water, but remained tied and gagged. The Australian, the apparent leader, disappeared taking the camera and notes he had transcribed as they went and made for the farmhouse, saying to the others, "I'll send a couple of guys over to replace you. We need to start following up what he's given us. Hose him down, put him in the bunker, give him a little water but keep him wet, hungry and cold."

Semi-conscious, Badr felt himself pulled across the barn floor into an occupied stall where the straw and litter covering had been scraped aside and a concrete hatch pulled out. Hunger, cold and loss of blood meant that he was only dimly aware of being lowered, none too gently, into a black void. The hatch above him was replaced and he could hear faint scraping as the litter and straw covering was re-laid. He lay shivering in absolute darkness as the swine shuffled about just seven feet above him. The darkness about him though was as nothing compared to the blackness within as total despair and the realisation of failure gripped him: if he could have ended it all by mere thought he would have. A last flicker of resistance ebbed away as he felt his way around his new refuge to realise there was nothing but bare concrete surrounding him and the hatch appeared to be immovable from below. Despair surged through him once more and this time there wasn't even a spasm of resistance as he felt his chance of entering the place for martyrs fading away. He had failed. They had broken and brutalised him, treated him as he had done others. He saw for the first time the realisation of his actions, the consequences: it was as if this dark room was brightly lit and mirror-walled, there was nowhere to hide from himself, his abjection was total.

The sound of nearby soft, almost furtive, movement prompted Sally Bowson into wakefulness. Lord, her head hurt. Reflexively she tried to open her eyes, her right one she was barely able to open at all such was the pain and swelling, but the grey-blue left one's emergence caught the attention of the source of the nearby movement in the room. In the half-light of the curtained room the shadowy figure settled down on the end of the bed by her feet. Sally realised that she was in a bed under layers of sheets, blankets and a quilt. The room appeared to be quite small, with whitewashed rough plaster walls, a simple dark wood door, and similar cupboard and chest of drawers. Her vision was still unclear, vague and surely not to be explained just by the lack of any form of internal light.

"Welcome back. How d'you feel? That's quite a knock on the head you've had. By the way, my name's Martha, Martha Penwarden."

The voice was rich in a thick, slightly stilted West Country way, almost as if English were not her first language. She was tanned and weather-beaten in complexion, with lightish eyes, and dark, slightly greying hair tied back. Late forties perhaps? She was wearing a plain grey woollen top.

Something was nagging at the back of Sally's mind. "Where am I, what's happened to me?"

"You're safe in my home, the boys found you out on the moor; you must have had a nasty fall so they brought you here. Would you like some light?"

The speaker got up from her place on the bed and went to the window, pulling back the plain blue curtains and letting in the rapidly brightening Spring morning light.

"Would you like some tea, water, something else? Tea? Ah, good, I'll go and get some. My husband would like to have a word with you."

As she went to the door and on to what was clearly a landing beyond Sally took in more details of her host and her surroundings. A simple rustically furnished bedroom, thick cotton sheets, plain blue quilt above, her hostess of medium height, slim, whose grey top was revealed to be a knee length jersey dress; a simple unassuming elegance combined with practical comfort and lots of pockets. The room was cool with no source of heating other than that ebbing in from the landing. She tried to sit up, but the pain in her head was reignited by the attempted movement and she retreated under the covers once more, a slumbering lethargy overcoming her despite the feeling of that nagging unarticulated question vying for her mind's attention.

The woman who called herself Martha was speaking to someone downstairs in an unknown language, to which there came a similarly incomprehensible reply, and then the sound of footsteps climbing the stairs. Martha turned to face her, "Sorry, force of habit. My husband, Iltud, will try to answer any questions you have."

"Iltud, what kind of name was that, was she in Wales"?

A dark haired tall man of middle age let Martha, his apparent wife, pass on the landing and came into the room. Worn tweed trousers, grey shirt, green pull-over, he was dressed like a well-to-do but working farmer. He too was weather-beaten, obviously a man who spent most of his life outside.

"How're you feeling? Your son is fine, and he's sleeping. We didn't want him to wake you. Martha trained as a nurse and while she's cleaned and bandaged your head wound; she thinks you have concussion. We've sent for the doctor again just in case."

"Where am I, what happened? I must see Josey."

She asked the questions by instinct, but partly to mask the guilt about forgetting her son in her confusion.

"Of course you must, but it is best he sleeps. Have something to eat and drink and get looked at by the doctor while he rests."

There was assertiveness in this man's manner, a gentle authority. Before she could argue he went on, "You travelled further than you realise last night, a woman walking alone across the moor at night with a young child, you must have known better? What were you thinking?"

Words poured out of her in a torrent. "My car broke down, no phone signal. I grew up by the moor. What were those things chasing us? Where am I? I need to call my mum and dad, and my husband to let them know…" The panic of last night started creeping back as questions flooded her mind, "I want my son, you've no right…"

She hadn't been aware of more footsteps climbing the stairs carrying another chair. Similarly dressed to Iltud except for green military style trousers and boots; a taller and younger man ducked through the low doorway, placed his chair by the window, sat down and looked at her from keen grey eyes.

Iltud cleared his throat. "This is Mark the Seigneur for this parish, of which I am Steward. After what you went through last night I don't want to give you another shock, but we have to, our laws…"

He paused uncertainly, looking back at his younger companion, who nodded. "I'm sorry, I wish you had more time to recover, but… You're in what we call "The Pocket" and you won't find it on any map. I don't know how you found your way here, but it's not unknown for strangers to stumble upon us, runaways, the lost, those guided by greater forces if you like. However, once here you will have to make a new life with us and there are no means for you to communicate with the outside world, or to leave. You're not our prisoner, but one 'of the land', as are we all."

Her jaw dropped. She could barely register what he was saying, he was making no sense, and it must be the concussion…

The man known as Mark had been watching her intently, clearly impatient at Iltud's diffidence. He broke in. "You're not going mad, and neither are we, as you will see when well enough. Last night did your vehicle lose its electrics, also your other devices? Did you see what you thought were the Northern Lights? Did you feel a crackling in the air, static electricity like you've never felt before? I can see from your face that you did. That's just what happens when someone crosses the barrier. Everything Iltud here has told you is true, and plenty more besides, like no electronic devices work here. Don't ask me why, I'm not a scientist. There are no cars, nor lights other than oil lamps and candles, no telephones or radios, or and such like, not even thunder or lightning. No one on the outside knows we're here and that's the way we like it to keep it, and why, once you find us, you've really joined us whether you wish it or not."

She goggled at him, as he continued. "Did you see what you thought was hunting you? We call them the Guardians, but it was just as well we had business in the area and found you."

"This is some sort of joke…" but her response was interrupted by Martha pushing aside her husband and entering the room carrying a tray holding tea and some sort of sandwich, followed by an older grey-haired woman carrying an old-fashioned doctor's visiting bag.

"There's a time and a place for everything Seigneur and you Iltud should know better. It's too soon; she needs rest, time to recover and to see her son, not you overwhelming her. Explanations and questions can come later; she'll come to understand."

"You know the laws with new incomers Martha," replied the Seigneur who was clearly the senior figure despite being the youngest by some way. "They were near her, too near. You know what that means, the barrier was weaker. It's growing again. More like her must be expected."

Sally could see that the Steward's wife was clearly not one to be overawed in her own home. "She's a guest in my home and Doctor Gillian here needs to examine her. Come back and bother her this evening if you must."

Her husband clearly didn't know where to look and the younger man smiled bashfully at the chiding. Suddenly Sally sensed the tension in the room had gone and a warm humour surfaced among her hosts, relaxing her as the two men nodded at her and ducked out of the room speaking in their strange language or dialect. There was closeness between them all, a trust that only comes from long familiarity and shared endeavours.

Doctor Gillian, another simply dressed but spry looking older woman smiled at her and sat by the bed while Martha hovered at its end. "Let's all have some tea and you can eat your sandwich while I check you over."

Fifteen minutes passed as the doctor cleaned and re-bandaged Sally's gashed head and, other than heavy concussion, the doctor pronounced everything else to be minor, recommending a week's recuperation in the cottage; Sally noticing Martha's apparent pleasure at this, seemingly having a young child to grandmother was her main motivation in her now childless home.

The Doctor sat back in her chair, studying her closely. "It's almost too much to take in isn't it? Those born here in the Pocket can't really understand the impact it makes on us outsiders for the first time."

"What do you mean?"

"I'm a stray like you who came here by accident, at least that's what I thought then. I've been here nearly twenty years. Trained as a Doctor in Edinburgh – I'm from Islay originally by the way – have you been there?"

"I'm sorry, no."

"Shame, I would have liked someone to tell me what it's like now. Anyway, I worked in Bristol, Frenchay. My husband left me, no children, my life just slowly dissolved I suppose – any of this ring a bell? I quit my job, gave up my flat and came west one night not knowing where I was going, I think the western moors reminded me of my childhood. Hiked across the moor and found myself here…"

"But those things, what Iltud's friend called… What were they again?"

"I must have been lucky; I came straight through unmolested, thank God."

What are they Doctor?"

"I'm not sure I can answer that. You'd better ask Iltud or someone in authority. Just be glad that you made it through intact, not all do. I won't describe some of the things that have been brought to my door… Anyway, here I still am. I'm not sure anyone looked for me very hard, just another lost soul who disappeared with no obvious evidence of foul play. I was as out of sympathy with the world as it was with me. It must have taken me three months to accept my new life here though, it wasn't easy. They were looking for a Doctor for this part of the March and the upper villages, and I found a new life, even a new husband. Hopefully you can too, more easily than me."

"But, my husband…"

"Oh, I'm sorry. Forget that last part then. Sometimes my tongue runs away with me. At least you've got your young son with you. He's fine by the way. I examined him last night when you were brought in and gave him a mild sedative to get him to sleep. I hope that's alright?"

She smiled anxiously at Sally through her blushing cheeks, picked up her things and made her goodbyes, promising to look in again the following day. How many times has she given that speech, thought Sally? It's well practised, a sort of ongoing conversation with an old part-abandoned self, almost as if she is still trying to come to terms with the disjoint in her life?

Martha came back after letting the Doctor out. The day outside was maturing now and a beautiful bright spring sunlight played out across the room, enlivening those within. "Do you want to get up and see your son? He's asleep in the next room. You'll need a bath – it's downstairs in all these cottages I'm afraid – and the boys found your vehicle last night and brought your bags back. Then I suggest some more rest."

Suddenly the unrequested kindness in the older woman's voice unlocked a pressure reservoir of suppressed emotion within the younger woman. Perhaps it was the loneliness of her recent months punctured by a stranger's concern, perhaps it was the bewildering situation, the confrontation with her and her son's mortality, but she reached out and hugged her hostess to her, crying like a baby, "Thank you, thank you, thank you…"

Andy Bowson and George Edward were in their offices by seven the morning following their return to London. Overnight updates from the teams in Birmingham had to be gone through and preliminary ballistics reports were expected mid-morning. On top of that, potentially relevant snippets of data, received from various agencies required review before a twelve noon inter-agency sub-committee meeting which had been set up on their journey down the previous evening. Dager was also in the office early and he called Bowson into his office.

"This thing seems to be snow-balling Bowson. I understand we will be meeting senior representatives from GCHQ and MI5, probably our mystery friend from last night, our own Commissioner, Command head, and potentially the Home Secretary with associated hangers on. Something's touched a nerve and we aren't getting any time or space to do the job properly. Just get ready for it; you know what's at stake."

Bowson had never seen his superior like this before, he reflected unsympathetically. The pressure's getting to him, the prospect of thwarted ambition and not being able to glide away from a debacle unscathed. Why hadn't Sally called, what was going on with her? Surely she hadn't walked out on him now? Had she left a letter at the home he hadn't visited for so many days? Why now with so much else on? A chill settled on him, tipping his shaky equanimity into another train of thought. Was it something to do with this case, had she been targeted in some way because of his job? He needed to get home right now, but was trapped here. Should he call the local station to send someone round to have a look at his house? No, that would look panicky. Just as he had decided to pick up the phone to his local station his mobile rang. It was a Devon & Cornwall police sergeant.

"Chief Inspector Bowson, you reported your wife missing late last night? I'm sorry, but your wife's car has been found abandoned on a road on the south-west fringe of Exmoor with an empty child seat. It was unlocked and if there was any luggage it's been removed. There's no sign of her or the child. We closed the road for forensic tests and are making enquiries with the locals: there are only a few farms up there, but we are stopping any traffic to see if anyone passed that way yesterday and saw anything. We've ordered a helicopter search of the surrounding moorland which will start shortly, but you know what it's like up there. I believe her parents live locally; will you be able to come down?"

Shock, stunning shock, a momentary stopped heartbeat for Andy Bowson. It can't be, it's not possible… His brain clouded and then his heart-rate rose as his body tried to compensate for the additional load of stress that had landed on him. A busy, all-consuming professional world briefly lost its grip on him as he tried to take it in, only to reassert its iron control at the prompting of his telephone correspondent, "Chief Inspector Bowson, are you still there?"

"Sorry? Any… Any clues, evidence of foul play, where she might have…"

"I'm sorry, nothing obvious… perhaps forensics will help?"

A long, slow exhale, don't go to pieces man, you're a professional.

"I'm not sure I can make it today, I've got something on here. I'll need to get permission, I'll have to get back to you…" Almost as an after-thought, "Do her parents know?"

"Not from us. Do you have their details? Do you want us to call them?"

The implication in the man's voice was clear, 'You're taking it too well. What the hell's wrong with you? You should call them…'

"Okay, I'll speak to her parents and make enquiries from this end. And I'll try to come down asap."

"Understood."

"Can you keep me informed of any developments? Thanks."

He placed the phone down, got up and walked to his boss' office.

Halfway over he checked himself and headed for the coffee machine, brushing aside questions from a couple of his team on the way. What was he doing? Admitting to Dager of all people that his personal life was in melt-down, that he couldn't cope with the pressure, that he'd have to abandon the biggest challenge of his career to race down to the West Country after his errant wife? You've got to be professional, report it to your superiors and leave it to the local force to find her. That's what they would expect of a dedicated career officer. The hard, professional veneer was reasserting itself, pressing down the fears for his son, and, yes, for his wife whom deep-down he still loved. 'Don't you?' he asked himself, 'I must do, haven't really thought about it like that, for how long now? A wobble, get it over with before you lose it, face it down.'

He breathed deeply and walked into Dager's office, closing the door behind him.

"Can I have a word boss?"

Dager gestured silently to him.

"My wife and child have disappeared on the way to her parents in North Devon. The car's been found unlocked and abandoned, but intact, on the moor… Any luggage she was taking has also gone and I've heard nothing from her for two days. The local force is out searching and they consider her a missing person, but there's no trace. It seems from my conversation with her parents that it must have happened some time yesterday evening."

Dager looked at him, apparently stunned. "What d'you want to do? What do you want me to do? I, we, need you, here. And you know the protocols…""

"I need to go home to see if there is anything there that might give us a clue, but that can wait until after the meeting later. Can you chivvy the local force to step up the urgency? What if it's linked to my job?"

"Okay, but if any evidence at all emerges that it's linked to your job, you'll have to stand down from this investigation. You know the issues, especially if it's blackmail." He sighed, "Almost certainly it's got an innocent explanation, but I will make a few calls; I'm sure it will be resolved happily."

He took that as his dismissal. On the way back to his desk he thought that Dager had almost been genuinely human for once. Yes, the pressure was definitely getting to him too.

Later that morning on their way to the midday meeting Dager related his calls to both local chief constables, given that the car had been found close to the force boundaries. "They both understood the import of this… development… and promised to do all they could. I also took a call from my boss reiterating the need for you to be here. Apparently, someone in MI5 requested it. Care to explain?"

"News to me Sir."

The mysterious 'Henry', what was the man up to? It had to be him. Who else could it be? Would he be here? Bowson looked about him. The meeting room in the Home Office was of the highest security status and most secure in the building, it was also full to capacity. Civil servants, special advisers, police high rankers of various descriptions, a Lieutenant Colonel, various representatives from all the major security services and penultimately the Home Secretary herself were present. The last entrant was his friend from yesterday, 'Henry', assuming that's his real name, joining immediately behind the minister. You're just a fly here, a humble junior liable to be stepped on by the big beasts as they dance their steps of power and evasion.

The Home Secretary cut through the usual pleasantries and protocols. Bowson reflected that career women of such advancement often felt empowered to ignore the unspoken rules that gave succour to the 'little people'. Perhaps breaking the glass ceiling meant dispensing with courtesy, the shards of broken glass slashing away the soft tissue of human empathy. God, he must be losing it. He awoke from his reverie as Dager asked him to describe what he had witnessed and to summarise the progress of the investigation, or lack of it, so far. His boss was back to his old tricks, almost by reflex.

A few minutes later he was winding up his summary. He glanced across to his new spooky friend of yesterday who nodded almost imperceptibly and allowed a faint smile to grace his lips.

"… So, on the ground enquiries have yielded nothing of substance so far. The getaway van, or its remains at least, were found five miles away, thoroughly burnt out and apparently cleaned beforehand. Forensics are pessimistic I'm afraid. Preliminary ballistics test confirm the weapon was a high powered rifle, 0.5 inch calibre, probably fired from over a kilometre away. We're speculating that the weapon was a US military type Barrett sniper rifle. It seems to be custom made ammunition, not commercially manufactured, but all this needs checking. Enquiries have been made with the FBI, but it could be another twenty-four hours or more before we can confirm this prognosis with any confidence. No one has claimed responsibility, which at least allows the press to continue to pronounce it as simply a gang killing. At this point our best hope of progress is to further our investigation of the murdered man and his associates. His killing, particularly its manner, I think confirms that our suspicion of his involvement in terrorism is correct, and as such we should prioritise our resources in this direction."

Several other agency representatives spoke up, unwilling to be seen as having nothing to contribute, although none added anything of note to Bowson's summary. The mumbles and side conversations then started as the meeting suddenly ran out of substance.

"This is entirely unsatisfactory gentlemen," broke in the Home Secretary, "Professional snipers shooting presumed terrorists on our city streets in broad daylight with the police looking on. Untraceable weapons, no real evidence; if the press get on to this there's no knowing where it will go. Who is the most likely culprit, a splinter faction within the organisation? We all know these people turn on each other with as much viciousness as they do on their innocent victims"

So that was the cover story they were going to use if it should get out, thought Bowson. That's their main worry, looking impotent. The man Bowson was starting to think of as his spooky friend was whispering in the ear of an older man at the table, someone he later realised was the Director of MI5, who spoke when the Home Secretary finished.

"If I may Minister? In truth this is not the style of a factional dispute, they usually settle their differences with bombs or close quarter killings, not this way. Of course, they are unpredictable and do adopt new ways of operating, but I don't think we can assume, at this point, that a factional struggle is the most likely explanation."

"What is then?" interrupted what seemed to be a ministerial official.

The first speaker responded with a degree of lordly distaste. "I'm not sure that speculating will help anyone conclude this matter, but we should not rule out a foreign secret service's involvement or even a new domestic group with ex-military involvement, much less likely I know. However, it still surprises me that, with the now long and unfortunate series of Islamic inspired terrorism we have experienced, some sort of reaction has not happened before; however there is no evidence to support either theory at this point, other than the manner of the assassination. A foreign security service may be our best bet at the moment, perhaps the Israelis? Perhaps the Foreign Secretary could help?"

The question was put with childish innocence, but even the tired Bowson could see the sharp point of the verbal stiletto it contained. The Foreign Secretary was tipped as one of the Home Secretary's principal rivals in any future succession race. The blankness of her face said it all.

"I want daily updates gentlemen; meanwhile I will constitute a steering group to oversee this investigation and to prepare for different scenarios. My assistants will be in touch."

With that she and her entourage got up and left the room, leaving the remainder to wander out in small fissiparous group-lets exchanging muttered sentences, before breaking and then reforming with others, like mutating cancer cells. Dager began talking to a senior Met officer on his right, so Bowson got up and left the room without anyone even looking at him. He was small fry who wouldn't even have been invited if it wasn't for his accidental witnessing of the events. He turned the corner to the lift, went down to the foyer and was not entirely surprised to see a now familiar figure loitering by the revolving door. "Got a minute for a coffee Chief Inspector?"

'Henry' was smiling. They headed out and walked deep into the side streets for seven or eight minutes, without speaking, before entering an anodyne and unmarked domestic side door. The room was windowless, painted white and plainly furnished other than for several wooden chairs and a table with coffee and tea already set out. Bowson looked about surreptitiously.

"You may not believe me," smiled his host, "but even we have to have places which are unmonitored, it's one of the privileges of being in one of the more obscure and autonomous branches of the service. Tea or coffee?"

He looked at his interlocutor. Mid to late forties, fit but no longer the athlete he must have been once. Light brown hair steeling into grey. Yes, definitely ex-military, probably special forces. He carried himself with understated confidence. Still he hadn't introduced himself or even said which part of the labyrinthine state he worked for. Certainly not to be trusted, at least not yet.

"You can call me Henry, most other people do. By the way, I'm sorry to hear about your wife and son. Anything I can do to help?"

The suddenness of the remark was like a physical blow. Careful now, cool. You can't really trust anyone in this world. "How d'you know? Who told you, Dager? What d'you know?"

"Not your esteemed superior I can assure you. Quis custodiet ipsos custodes? Were you a classicist? No? I believe your wife was once though? Who watches the watchmen? That's part of my remit, among other things. Our colleagues at Cheltenham are so helpful after all."

"You're tapping my phone calls?"

"Among other things."

Affability was flicked off like a switch as 'Henry' pulled his chair up so that his head was only eighteen inches from Bowson's. His voice dropped away almost to a murmur. "Listen Chief Inspector, I think you are very probably a good man, at least for now, who has fallen into something none of us really understands, least of all you. But whatever it is, it's leading to something bigger…"

The older man's attention faded into introspection; Bowson sensed a withdrawal on the part of his host, a glimpse of a deeper weariness gaining a momentary advantage.

"Everyone in the meeting was so thrown by the mystery sniper and his motives that we hardly considered the target. But they frighten me, something tells me they're bigger this time, more far-reaching and that we haven't begun to scratch the surface. I was amazed no one suggested the possibility that it was a blind, a diversion to distract us. Perhaps his own people sacrificed a pawn. Perhaps they thought him a security risk…"

Bowson just stared at the man. He must have a mind like a cork-screw. His eyes are on me now, no, they're looking through, somewhere else, like I'm a ghost. This isn't helping, get his attention.

"Perhaps not, but if we work back from the victim… What d'you know about Sally?"

"We know her phone was on and winked off the network on that road on Exmoor at 7:12pm, 1,200 yards from where the car was found and that it's still off air. Details will be forwarded to the local force after we have finished here. There are no mysterious messages or unknown calls logged. Nothing more, alright?"

Bowson was reeling. His wife had been under observation, or were they just going back through the records now? But there was no point in arguing, this man might be able to help. "Back to my main point, I asked you here to give you that information as a mark of good faith. It's up to you, I don't expect you to trust me, but perhaps we can help each other."

Here it was, almost disappointing in its nakedness. "I want you to continue to do your job, but to share with me the things you won't be ready to report formally; your suspicions, your hunches, the unsubstantiated connections your mind will turn over in your dreams. I don't want confidences, I can get those already. I don't want you to withhold anything from your chain of command, just report to them as you would anyway. Tell me who you trust, who you don't. What d'you think of your boss?"

Andy thought for a second or two before replying "A professional and highly capable officer, ambitious, but a decent man. He could go far."

"Spare me the anodyne guff. You're a fool if you can't see that he was a decent man, but frustrated ambition is undermining his integrity. Not in the usual way. He knows the odds of advancement are unfairly stacked against him unless he compromises, perhaps sells out. Time isn't on his side, as it still is for you."

"Sell out to whom? What're you talking about?"

"You'll see when it happens, it's not far now I fear, too late to be recovered. Watch how close he gets to HR."

"He's got his annual evaluation on Monday; I think he's worried all of this will prejudice him."

"I know. Look, it's your call. Most people don't understand the real nature of the modern state. They think it large and complex, human with flaws and wrinkles, but essentially moving in broadly straight lines and therefore somewhat clumsy but generally comprehensible. But they're wrong; those things are superficial. Society no longer shapes the state, not since the long march through the institutions took off in the forties. It's the other way around now, but there's a sort of dysfunctional feedback loop. A more complex society – I think 'diverse' is the preferred term – presents less resistance to the objective, but the state has to become more complex to manage the process, more cost, more intrusion, more bureaucracy, more people like me, I suppose you could say. Understand?"

He was smiling to himself now, he's fading out again, but let him talk, that's why we're here.

"Well not like me, nor like you really. But it's got so... too... complex and the monster's getting beyond the control of its inventors. Some of them seem quite happy about that, but most are in denial. It's not just here by the way, it's across all the major democracies as they believe themselves to be, and many others as well, but we are amongst the worst."

He paused and then continued, even more quietly. "Keeping up? It's become a roomful of spider webs twisted up like a bag of rubber bands, impossible to separate and falling to bits at any attempt. Heard of Gordian's Knot? And the spiders are still in their webs clashing with one another, not sure where one's domain finishes and another's starts, and increasingly too preoccupied to find the flies."

He chuckled at his own analogy; a bit odd, but certainly not mad, thought the increasingly bewildered Bowson.

Henry was looking at him, "We've got to help each other find the flies, repair the damage to the webs where possible and, who knows, even separate a few out?"

Bowson sat back. What was the guy talking about? He was clearly highly connected and nobody's fool, maybe he was much more. He was trying hard to give him the impression he wanted to help him. A bit too hard? But getting this man's support could only help with the recovery of his family and he wasn't being asked to break professional commitments, but it was a major step in that direction and was unlikely to be the last. He had certainly summed up Dager pretty well and would definitely be a help with his own career.

"Is it down to you I'm still on this case?"

"Not directly, but I did have a word in a helpful ear or two."

"Can you tell me how the assassin, if that's what he was, knew who, what and where the victim was? Did they know we were watching him? If they did, there must have been a security breach on our side."

"No, I can't, and that's because I don't know. A leak is entirely possible, and it's being investigated thoroughly. Neither you nor your immediate colleagues are under any suspicion at this point though."

Until this moment of temptation, with someone who could be a devil or an angel, he had never broken protocol. His service record was as clean as they came.

Angel or devil? That was the question. What to do, the safe road that could well lead nowhere, or the other one, the high stakes one? What's more important to you, your career and all that goes with it or your family? Or is there a middle way? Can't see it. And what if you turn him down? So, go along with him, at least for a bit.

"Okay, I'll do my best, but I won't break the rules for you."

"I know, that's why I asked you. Here's a secure pay-as-you-go phone, the number's under Henry. I'll give you a new one each time we meet or by other means if we can't. Give me a call whenever. I'll get hold of you if I make any progress on your family. I'll show you out."

The door closed softly behind him. The new phone was stashed away. He set out back to the office to get Dager's permission to go home and then down to his parents-in-law and meet the locals on the case. He would come back tomorrow afternoon and get back to work. The last few days had left his head spinning. He needed to focus on something concrete again.

'Henry' left the building and went to an office, his sanctum, in another street. So, his judgement had been right. It had been a risk taking him to one of their buildings, no matter how clean and peripheral, but anywhere public was just too exposed. He had bitten. Hardly surprising. He hadn't died inside yet unlike so many others and was probably more desperate now than he even realised. Whether he would if he progressed in his career was a moot point, many did and few didn't compromise those ideals with which they had joined. Henry had started out with them, the desire to serve in the hardest circumstances, to protect.

Bosnia had come as a huge shock, but little compared to what came after, Iraq, Afghan and other things which threw them into the blender along with most other aspects of his, well, the totality of him really. What was that line? Something like 'everywhere cruel sorrow, everywhere fear and all the images of death.' Virgil, wasn't it? Yet still he thought himself lucky to come out so changed, so clear, so intact, but scarred in some ways he didn't want to recall. Bosnia had confused him, the aftermath scoured him clean of any illusions and the other conflicts, cleaning up others' filth, the friends lost, the lies they were forced to swallow, well, those that came after had shown him what had to be, what was being surrendered… And so, he had begun.

He tried to keep the memories compartmentalised, filed away to be brought out when he needed. To be distilled as motivation when the loneliness and magnitude of his adopted task threatened to morph into despair, but always they attempted to snap their bonds, straining and struggling with his subconscious, threatening to break forth through his dreams, her most of all. It had been so hard, much harder than he would have ever thought possible when he started out: he had come to a full sympathy with Sisyphus, trying to move an immense stone in the dark. Perhaps today represented half an inch of movement and promised more.

The call connected and was picked up. "Hello, oh it's you. I was expecting you a while ago. Yes, I was there. They're pretty bereft really.

Whoever was responsible is unknown to them all, no leads other than to go through his associates step by step. They think it's probably foreign, possibly Israelis, less possibly something domestic. They've no idea how he was identified. A leak inside probably, but no one's found any trace and they're looking hard. That was unwise of the Chief Constable. Luckily, she's on the side of the angels, even if she doesn't know it. We can't afford this to leak out, got to keep a lid on things. Steady as she goes has brought us a long way. We can get it cleaned up later if required, but only when it's died a death, but probably don't need to, these things have a habit of fading away, just being forgotten. But we have to find out who was responsible, they could be a problem. Okay."

The line went dead. Better tell some of the others.

She had come downstairs wearing Martha's dressing gown when Josey woke in the afternoon. He was full of it, Martha had a young puppy, some sort of collie, and that was sufficient distraction for now. Sally could see Martha had a way with young children. They sat by the sitting room wood-burner drinking tea while Josey ran inside and out with the puppy who was clearly delighted to have a new young play-mate.

It was astounding, a hidden enclave in rural England, big enough to have its own steam railway line, a small harbour, a population running into the many thousands with a language descended from sub-Roman Brythonic, loosely related to Welsh and Cornish. Hidden for over 1,500 years, protected by a barrier that allowed no one to leave other than a chosen few, keeping out almost everybody without their being aware of it, just a few finding the gateways which closed and opened to those from the outside quite unpredictably. Governed by a High Steward on behalf of a reclusive Duke, with a Council of largely hereditary Seigneurs and elected parish based Stewards. No internal combustion, electricity or electronics of any kind, so still running on horse and steam power, illicitly importing certain benefits of the twenty first century such as medicines and insulation, but otherwise self-sufficient in its network of one principal and several subsidiary valleys, surrounding moorland, forest and hills, about the size of one of the smaller English counties. She had to pinch herself. There was so much to see and learn, her intellectual curiosity, which had lasted beyond her university days studying Classics and Italian, but had been ground down by the realities of working for the Foreign Office and then motherhood, was sparked into renewed vigour. How? Why? What were the drawbacks; it can't be a utopia, which after all means 'no place'?

Josey fell over the dog and started crying. "That's enough questions for now," smiled Martha, "I need to prepare some dinner as Iltud will be back by six I should think. Perhaps he will be able to help you find some more answers, but don't worry, there's no rush and you need to recuperate."

Sally went to the front window after stilling her son and looked out. It was on the lower slope of a long valley looking south-west. In the far distance she could just make out the sea beyond a bay holding what seemed to be one large and several small mist-shrouded islands, the cold clear air aiding visibility. The sun was heading west glinting on the waves, such was the clarity of view on this fine day. The village, really a hamlet, was all around them, pretty stone and cob built white washed cottages, chimneyed, tiled roofs, gardens front and back which were clearly used for fruit and vegetables, often fringed by adjoining farm buildings, with the dirt and stone road between them descending the valley in a thick fringe of wild flowers.

It was idyllic, and then the memories of the previous day came rushing back, the fear so over-powering, her abandonment of her husband without having the courage to explain to him. Her shame, her deep shame. She heard the church clock strike six, out of sight to the right. She would go there first thing tomorrow and offer her penitence and thanks, but she needed more answers, perhaps Iltud would be receptive.

She heard the kitchen door close behind her and a man's voice speaking quietly in the unfamiliar language, punctuated repeatedly by Martha's softer tones. "When's dinner Mummy? When will we see Grandma and Grandpa?" Josey's time clock had clearly gone off despite the puppy's distractions.

"Not long now sweetie. Why don't you go and wash your hands, you can't eat with doggy hands."

I've just told him another lie, another promise to myself broken, another selfish failing.

Evidently satisfied by this little bit of their own domestic routine, he toddled off to the water closet. At least they had some, albeit primitive, plumbing, and hot water for baths. Cleanliness seemed to be highly valued; thank heavens it wasn't medieval in that respect at least.

The kitchen door opened, it was Martha's husband. He smiled, somewhat stiffly she thought: he clearly wasn't a natural extrovert and seemed to find the presence of complete strangers in his home something of a challenge, but he seemed to be trying to put her at ease.

"Martha says dinner won't be long. You do eat fish? It's Lent and we are quite traditional about it. Fortunately, the waters off the coast are rich here and it compensates for the 'hungry time' as we used to call it. A diet of salted meat and cheese would be so boring otherwise, and we try to minimise what we bring in from Logres."

"Where's Logres? And what do you mean by the 'hungry time'?"

"Sorry, England, the rest of the mainland really. The 'hungry time' is the old expression for the time at the end of the winter and before the new season's crops and animals are ready for harvesting, when we have to live off preserved foods from the previous year, salted meats, cheeses, winter vegetables, fish when the boats can put out. We don't go hungry, probably never did given our local climate and the sea, but it was never easy and pretty monotonous."

"How're you feeling, the boy? Martha says you are making a good recovery, but never stop asking questions, but can I ask some? Where's your husband? Why do you think you ended up with us? Tell me about your life? You may as well rehearse it because you will have to tell your story many times now that you're here."

To her own surprise, she just dived in, wasn't even derailed by her returning son who was beckoned into the kitchen by Martha and clearly distracted with slices of buttered bread. Her family and upbringing which, by how the crow flies, could only be a handful of miles away, but now seemed almost in another world, her parents, her education, her job, her husband and child, his profession. She hesitated, not knowing how to go on into deeply personal matters which, now that she had to explain them, seemed so small, so petty and so selfish. How to explain why she had left home? Had she really left him?

"Go on Sally." He smiled at her. "There must be more, otherwise you couldn't have found us, wouldn't have made it through the barrier."

She looked at him. His blue eyes, wrinkled brown skin at the corners. He might have the manner of a naturally shy, old fashioned rustic but she could see the keenness of perception there, perhaps a wisdom. How to open her heart to a stranger, even one who had rescued her and taken her into his own home and treated her only with kindness? Her loneliness had made it impossible to speak to anyone about these things, even her parents or so-called friends, let alone Andy.

"If you tell him the rest we might be able to help you know." Martha had re-entered the room, bearing what looked like a bottle of cider and three glasses. She filled them, offering one each to her husband and guest, "To your safe arrival, your health and happiness and for the gift of childish laughter in my home again."

She went back into the kitchen, shooing Sally's son with her. Sally took a deep breath: there was more tenderness in this house of strangers than she had experienced for a long time; it was a matter of faith, of trust and she, almost heedless, chose to trust. Out it spilled, disjointed, discursive. Her husband's growing pre-occupation with his career, his hardening in response to the things he had to cope with, her increasing loneliness and isolation in a huge city which became ever more alien, her retreat to her childhood faith and the wedge it drove between her husband and herself, the pouring of her energies and emotion into her son, her growing sense of being adrift, what she had thought she was doing when she had left home only the previous day. She stopped, surprised at her almost complete unburdening, ashamed of how trivial it must sound to a stranger. And he had just sat there, quiet, attentive, just soaking it up, not questioning, not commenting, just looking at her gravely as if trying to convey sympathy through his stillness.

"Do you still love him?"

"He's my husband and I don't want a divorce, there's Josey to think of…"

The question had been gently put, but puncturing in its directness.

"That's a legal and spiritual state. Do you want to be with him again?"

"I don't know, I suppose…"

"Well there's no rush, I'm blessed never to have experienced what you have, but it might matter a lot… to the shape of your future. You say he's in the Counter-Terrorism Command, a senior officer? And you were in the Foreign Office and speak fluent Italian and know Latin? Yes? You also know some other languages, not so well, but French and Spanish? Greek?"

"GCSE Ancient, a bit at University, but not since and that was a long while ago now."

"Mmm, could be helpful."

Martha called them through. He relaxed. "Very few come here entirely by chance and even fewer bring children. We are truly fortunate today. It's your turn to ask the questions over dinner, after you."

The two vans came off the M42 and pulled up the slip road signed for the NEC; despite the loss of the missing Badr and their martyred brother their alternate target was almost as glorious as their primary one. A convention for the senior officers of the world's largest spirits multinational, nearly 500 in all, was taking place at one of the hotels on the site. Even better, their wives and husbands, politicians including a Cabinet Minister, an Opposition would-be minister, bankers, diplomats and major customers would be there for the dinner and entertainment, after a hard day's planning how to corrupt the youth of the world. Well over a thousand people in all. Abdul Patel and his seven fellow martyrs were going to put Mumbai in the shade. One of them was already working in the kitchen. Security would be tight but discreet, and certainly not prepared for what was coming.

Abdul smiled to himself as they paused outside the car park. A couple of guards on the barrier, one police and the barrier operator, a couple more police patrolling outside the dining room and ballroom where the main event was in full swing, others inside by the lobbies, just as they expected. The explosives were to be primed for contact detonation when the two suicide drivers hit the main entrance and the dining room side fire exit, the brother on the inside would blow the back lobby, and then he and the other brothers, having dismounted as the vans came through the barrier, would get into the remains of the hotel and cause mayhem with their AK47s and knapsacks stuffed full of ammunition and grenades. They were not coming out, but would take hundreds more infidels with them.

Their vans came on again, slowing just before the last but one roundabout before the car park entrance. Suddenly, without warning, the windscreen shattered with a scream as he and the driver beside him were riddled with bullets. Can see nothing, feel little, can't move, ambush... Just fire behind, those in the compartment and van behind, dozens of rounds impacting, the shooters must be in the car-park on the other side of the entrance road... Then nothing at all, at least nothing earthly.

Both vehicles had skidded to a stop, one on the pavement and the other on the mini-roundabout in front, rendered in seconds into inert colanderised metal cans. The staccato shrieks made by the bullets lasted all of six seconds. Alan Dare's magazine was empty, his arms still shaking from the strain of controlling the automatic rifle's attempts to pull away from his target. He dropped it like a hot brick, motioned to the others who did likewise and turned for the bikes parked up behind them. Later they would learn that six would-be mass murderers had died and one would be confined to a wheel chair for the rest of his life.

Meanwhile, Abdul's comrade on the inside, hearing the shooting, ran to the rear lobby and set off his pack-bomb, blowing out both sets of lobby doors and bringing down the ceiling.

The guards on the gate had dropped to the ground as ricochets screamed about them and the bomb went off behind them. Deafened by the explosion, ably supplemented by a cacophonic orchestra of car alarms set off by the ricochets and flying debris, no one heard two motor-bikes picking up speed as they headed for the bridge over the motorway.

Alan was breathless as he sat on the pillion seat. It was too unplanned, too last minute, too many police nearby, too risky, but what else could they do? They had had to move fast. Badr had at least been telling the truth about the fall-back target and how to trace his team. Over a thousand lives had been at stake. Tipping off the authorities had been an option, but one equally difficult for them and from what they had learnt the authorities weren't spotless or reliable; they certainly weren't friends. Besides him, their mentor here on the outside, had said an intervention by unknown parties such as them would have other unspoken benefits. So, their hand had been forced.

The guns were clean, virginal, he was sure of that and could be safely left. The overalls they were wearing would be burnt with everything else later. The bikes would be dragged into the 4x4's trailer and covered at the first meeting point five miles away, only five minutes. If they got away safe from there they should be okay. Dispose of the 4x4 and bikes in the Cotswolds, the site was already prepared, and back home to go to ground for an extended period. He looked at his watch; they were nearly there, just three or four minutes to safety. No police cordon could be set up that quickly. That bomb at the hotel had been a real boon to their get-away, a complete diversion, and then he realised the price paid by the innocents affected. Saying a silent prayer for their souls, whoever they were, he consoled himself with the thought they had saved many hundreds of others by this evening's work; hopefully that would mitigate the price he would pay later.

He was well west on the A303 now, nibbling at the fringes of the West Country on route to his parents-in-law. They were expecting him: it hadn't been an easy conversation. Understandably they felt he should have dropped everything after her car had been found, must be wondering if he weren't quite human anymore. Was he, or was he just losing perspective or being truly 'professional'? His work phone rang, it was Dager himself.

"Have you been listening to the radio?" Before he could answer Dager continued, "There's been a major terrorist incident by the NEC at the main hotel. Some sort of company conference, a government minister and all sorts of bigwigs there as well. Reports say a bomb went off inside, seemingly suicide, some sort of fire fight by the car park outside; two commercial vehicles that seem to be full of explosives shot up in the street, along with at least half a dozen gunmen, maybe more. AK47s and spent rounds lying around like confetti. Those on the ground are awaiting the arrival of bomb disposal before they enter them. The local force thinks a major catastrophe's been averted. The target was almost certainly the hotel rather than the music concert at the NEC, but that's got to be confirmed. Look, I know you've got personal business, but I need you back here by mid-afternoon tomorrow after you've met the case officer for your wife. I can't give you any more, okay?"

Dager rang off. The near panic in his voice was clear, even via a speaker phone travelling at eighty miles per hour through the dark countryside. Bowson could sense the fear for his prospects in his staccato delivery, not his usual suave self. The speedometer had climbed to ninety-four, better slow down, being pulled over now is the last thing you need. Was this just coincidence, or had the event on a backstreet of Birmingham triggered this event? A reasonable conjecture, but he mustn't jump to conclusions. Two terrorist related attacks within a dozen miles of each other in less than seventy-two hours. No, they had to be linked. Who was doing it?

What had Henry whispered to him in that first conversation in the police HQ, the fear of a "nativist" reaction or, according to the senior spook in the meeting at the Home Office, foreign security services pursuing some private vendetta on the streets of England? Too easy to blame the Israelis, they were everyone's favourite speculative scapegoat. But the reported manner of this one was entirely different from the one he had witnessed. Well he had eighteen hours to get back: the others could cover the ground by until then. The lights would be on late in parts of London tonight and the airwaves busy. Andy had something more important on his mind, a higher priority and again he found his mind clear, refreshingly so, as he switched on the radio.

Georgios Tredare drove the Land Rover containing his three colleagues south then west by the A and B roads, avoiding the cameras of the motorways as far as possible. They were dozens of miles past the police cordon before it became tight. They were entirely untraceable, forensics would struggle to find much on what they had left behind, the bikes and get-away 4x4 were burned and buried at the bottom of a pit, dug deep under a huge barn and then refilled. The other team would follow up, but let it all cool down, the authorities would be distracted by other things soon enough.

Alan had let Georgy deal with the prisoner personally. Sam knew Georgy's opinion of Alan: he thought their leader was clever, meticulous, decisive, but lacking the embitterment to have a real killer instinct, let alone to do whatever needed to be done. And Georgy had enough bitterness for all of them; his immigrant mother's stories of her homeland and her family's history saw to that. As for Art, well, he was harder to read, quieter, ruthless enough to do the job required, but lacking a personal motivation or grievance. As for me, the baby of the team?

Lots of reasons…

There would be no evidence. The bunker had been burned clean along with his clothes and the other items, then doused in caustic and swilled out, as had the stall where the prisoner had been "interviewed." The pigs were happy, and their faeces would be cleaned out and put with the mountains of other animal waste, the bones ground into powder and scattered on the roadside behind them along with the ashes from the flames. Even now the other stalls were being carefully hosed out and cleaned up. They had a saying, 'diligence and preparation are the handmaidens of freedom.' Corny, but utterly true. Nothing remained other than their memories. Another four hours and he would be at the last staging point before home.

Sam was stretched out on the back seat, jostling with Art for the most space, pretending to be relaxed enough to sleep. Seventy-two hours ago it had all been talk, hypothetical preparation. Now it was all too real. Gunning down the occupants of the second van had been child's play compared with the killing of Amallifely. How many were in there? Several for sure and the press would report the answer later. How many had he hit? He would almost certainly never know. They were just abstract invisible targets in the commission of evil. Amallifely had been an individual, someone he had stalked, whose face he had studied through the rifle scope as if close to, someone he had turned by a twitch of his finger into a lifeless shattered corpse.

Yes, the second had been easy in comparison, but their blood was still on his hands; he was well across the divide now and headed deeper. Too late to turn back, to recant, too many others were counting on him, most of all his team-mates. They all said he was probably the best marksman they had. His instructor, that leathery old Texan Green Beret bastard Hendricks had sought, in the time remaining to him, to pass on all the craft he had learnt in half a dozen best forgotten conflicts in this poisoned world, but the cancer had denied him the chance to hear how his star pupil had put his learning into action for the first time. He suspected what Hendricks would have said though, 'Only 1k range, straight, unsuspecting target, little wind, not bad, but you've still got a long way to go.' Yes, he wouldn't have been happy, satisfied perhaps. God forgive him.

Her gentle interrogation of her hosts was really a two-way process she realised, only cut off by the arrival of Doctor Gillian as promised, and the need to put her son to bed. The Doctor pronounced herself satisfied after changing her dressings and hurried home. Coming back downstairs after making sure Josey was comfortable, she found her hosts with Mark the Seigneur, or whatever he was called, in the living room with two other youngish, fit looking men. Mark looked up at her as she descended, but caught sight of a reassuring nod from Iltud, which she noticed too. She was okay then, if not to be trusted just yet it seemed, at least she wasn't a problem.

"You and your son are comfortable? Feeling better? Good."

It was odd how this man, who clearly held some high level of authority and the respect of the others in the room, came across so stilted in his questions to her. Perhaps she worried him more than she did the others. She caught sight of some vicious looking military style firearms propped up against the corner of the room along with three unlit oil lamps and, now she noticed it, she could see they were all wearing military style clothing and boots. Fear surged back, a rude shock after such a homely afternoon and evening.

Martha's husband noticed the reaction. "There's nothing to fear Sally. Mark and some of the boys are going to spend the night on the moors by the barrier…"

"My apologies, I didn't mean to frighten you. Your arrival, while cause for joy," he nodded at Martha, "coupled with what we saw and sensed last night when we found you, means that the barrier is weaker than normal. Things can press in further than usual and it's my job to prevent that in this area. It also means it's more likely that other wanderers such as you cross through and like you they may need our help…"

"This barrier you say I crossed? How does it work? Why did it let us through, but you say it keeps everyone out and all but a few in? It doesn't make any sense. Surely if it let us through, it would work the other way too?"

Iltud and Mark looked at one another as if to defer to the other to answer. She noticed that Mark wilted first.

"So asks every arrival. They all get the same answer: we don't know, or if any here do, I, the rest of us, have not been told. Some of us can, if specially selected and subject to an annual ceremony, come and go. Outsiders can enter if touching one of us as they cross, but it doesn't work the other way around…"

"Why not?"

"Told you, we don't know…"

"Or you don't want to say so I don't try to leave…"

Mark's face was flushed now, his authority challenged in his little domain. "You can try, find out the hard way. That's if the Guardians don't find you…"

"Mark," Martha face registered shock and dismay, "how can you say such a thing, it's a fair question." She smiled reassuringly at Sally. "It's true Sally. Ask Gillian if you won't believe us natives. We've no idea, nor why some outsiders make it through unaccompanied, but it seems to happen more when the barrier is weaker, as Mark said…"

"Are you trying to tell me it's some sort of magic? I'm not stupid…"

Iltud sighed. "We're not Sally… It just goes back to the first days of the Pocket. The monks say it's divine will, that we're a sanctuary and those who find us need what we can offer, that's all. Something in you needed us, somewhere safe, the barrier responded, that's all. But it's one way I'm afraid."

Frustration. Credulous fools, or liars, or both. Be fair, they may believe it, yet not understand, it's some quirk of nature, like something out of a sci-fi film. "But why now, why is it so weak now?"

Mark had used the respite to master his temper. "It's difficult to explain to an outsider, but the barrier weakens when the Pocket expands and takes a while to build up its strength again so most of the Seigneurs will be out tonight along the barrier. It also seems your disappearance has caused an unusual stir on the outside; there's been lots of activity there since they found your vehicle. Unfortunately, we didn't have chance to move it as we had our business to complete and you to bring home safe. It means that we will have to delay further business with Logres, by land at least, for some time. I'll report back later to you Iltud and head back to the Council in the morning. When will she be well enough to attend?"

Sally realised he didn't mean to be rude, talking about her like this. He wore his duties heavily, a bit like her husband she thought, and was preoccupied with events he must feel to be threatening. Perhaps not long in his position, he didn't want to be thought less than completely dedicated or competent.

"A day or two, but it depends on the Doctor, sooner than we thought last night anyway."

He nodded at her and his hosts, picked up his effects and left with his two mute acolytes, closing the door behind them.

"We go to bed early here," said Martha, "my husband was up most of last night, so I hope you don't mind?"

That was as clear a dismissal to bed as she had had since her childhood, she reflected as she got under the covers and extinguished the bedside lamp. So much to take in, too much to comprehend in a short time, and then the weariness closed in around her...

Two hours later, her mind sparked into life. The police and others had found the car and would be looking for her. Her husband must be with them, surely? Could she get to them, did she want to see him, how would she explain? The ambiguity of her response shocked her.

What was it her hosts had said at dinner, outsiders who come through the barrier can't leave, it's a one-way trip, down to some freak of nature? Most outsiders just see and step through it straight to the opposite side of the Pocket as if they have just gone an extra sixteenth of an inch without even noticing the slightest sensation of displacement. But from this side of the Pocket it was an impermeable and invisible barrier above and below ground as well on it. The same was apparently true out at sea.

She knew from the TV that astrophysicists were speculating about the existence of bubble universes, ekpyrotic universes, whatever they were, thousands of other dimensions, all attempts to explain away the singular creation of the Big Bang without a deity. Well, perhaps there's one here right under their very noses on Earth. What did that mean for her faith? Was Andy's disillusionment with it right after all?

They had argued bitterly over it at times, neither making any headway against the other, just deepening the divide between them further every time. And now they weren't even trying to win the other round any more, not from toleration or a desire not to hurt the other, just from weariness with it all.

Only those who had been 'touched', whatever that meant, could leave and few incomers were that privileged. Many, most, never wanted to go back anyway, even for a short visit and of those who did, they had to prove their complete loyalty or have something uniquely required. A few incomers, a tiny handful over the centuries, had never settled and tried to escape, almost always unsuccessfully. Some who had received the 'touch', both native and incomer, had tried to leave; some had been caught and confined, one or two had made it out and been judged lunatics or worse by the outside world when they tried to tell their stories. Life in an asylum or punishment as a witch was hardly an incentive to escape, and no one had tried for well over a hundred years.

Why had they been so interested in her background, her career before Josey, even more than her husband's job? Most acquaintances were much more interested in him than her; it was almost flattering in a way.

Chief Superintendent Dager had been back in the office for the last ninety minutes, having been called by the duty team. Late and overnight duties had diminished as he had climbed the ranks, but in some ways he found it oddly comforting, not exactly a spider at the centre of the web, but certainly much closer to it than the periphery, or so he thought at the time.

If the atmosphere in the command room was not chaotic or panicky, there was a thread of tumult and uncertainty twisting its way among those coming in from their homes and private lives, among them a couple of Home Office civil servants, at least one of whom was an aide to the Secretary herself. His boss, the Command head, Assistant

Commissioner Ted Armstrong, was in situ, trying to make sense of events on the ground at the NEC, and the morass of patchy intelligence reports relating to the previous killing. Dager checked himself: why had he called it a killing rather than murder? Was it because buried deep down he had a sense of pre-emptive justice rightly done? He stifled the thought.

All the subsequent reports received from those on the ground were confirming what he had told Bowson on the phone and little details kept being received to colour his bare sketch of the events of a few hours earlier. Four abandoned assault rifles, over eighty rounds fired, almost all hitting the vans. Four dead men in the two front cabs, two dead in the back of one, one critically wounded in the back of the other, all with multiple gunshot wounds. It was a miracle that neither vehicle's fuel tank had ignited nor the estimated two tonnes of commercial explosive been detonated. Dear God, if the target was the hotel they would have reduced it to rubble.

The buzz in the offices was distracting as he studied the fragments of information like a papyrologist trying to make sense of the latest discoveries from Oxhyrnchus, not knowing whether the key fragment to make sense of the others was lying before him or still lost in the Egyptian desert. A couple of witnesses had seen two motorbikes travelling on to the motorway bridge at the nearby junction, carrying four people they thought. No other details. The relevant camera footage was being accessed and analysed already, but this was the heart of the UK road network, if that was them they could be hundreds of miles away by now. They just needed a break.

It was a feeling reciprocated by the Assistant Commissioner, joining with much darker ones after having put down the phone call from an incandescent Home Secretary. That bloody woman. Off duty officers were being recalled, resources diverted from other investigations, other agencies asked to do likewise. Why? Here he ascribed an accurate, if uncharitable, answer. The call had been received just after the late evening news''What the papers Say' slot had flashed up the tabloids' late edition headlines. 'SAS Foil Britain's Mumbai in Massive Shoot Out', 'Islamic Loony Gang Banged Out on Motorway' (he struggled not to laugh at that one), 'Massacre by the Motorway'. Totally irresponsible and largely inaccurate of course, but they were happier printing the rumour than incomplete facts in these situations. But worst of all were the broadsheet headings, 'Shoot to Kill on Britain's Streets?' or 'War on the Streets – Has the Government Lost Control?' His political superiors were going berserk, demanding to know if the MOD had a rogue death squad roaming around the Midlands or, if not, why were the police not telling them that it was they who had foiled the attack?

Ted Armstrong permitted himself another rueful smile. He wasn't too far from retirement which gave him a certain objectivity and immunity to external pressure. He liked to think of himself as old school, not an ardent careerist, and was increasingly uncomfortable at the way things were going, the unfair pressures put on younger, still ambitious subordinates.

The Prime Minister had called another COBRA committee meeting for nine tomorrow morning, which meant that the Home Secretary would want to see them at seven, just to look in control, wasting more hours of precious time in talking rather than investigating and analysing. He must be getting old and cynical. They called COBRA meetings for the slightest thing these days; it was all an illusion of control. As the state got ever bigger and more bloated it became ever more impotent, unresponsive and more desperate to pretend it was otherwise. They had hacked the police and armed forces into near impotence to fund their interest groups, and never stopped to consider why their other demented policies' consequences were now leaving them like a giant dinosaur's brain, unable to cope with the rapidly changing environment around them. You could sometimes almost smell the gangrenous flesh of some of its decaying extremities. Well, back to the task in hand, just try to finish with a good record and integrity intact.

'Henry' switched off his phones and the television news. Too much chaff to discern meaning and pattern at the moment, let others establish the facts. He needed to remain bright and alert to make the connections, come up with explanations, and play the game. His time in the military had taught him the importance of rest in times of crisis. He eased back in the bed in the single bedroom of his small flat in an okay part of London, his lack of wealth meant he couldn't afford anything in the best areas, those which had been colonised by the trashy foreign super-rich or Croesus like financiers. He found he had less and less need for money: life on his own had its compensations.

The train of thought carried him back through the years. He knew where it was taking him, he didn't want to go, but was powerless in the face of the longing that was its engine. His first Bosnian tour as a subaltern in a rifle regiment, based near Banja Luka in the last months of the raging conflict; the Serbs were on the slide now. His patrol, his little command, two Warrior APCs and an armoured car detached from a cavalry regiment. Both regiments had gone the way of all things flesh since; curse them, cutting him off from something that might have been a family. Twenty men and him, rumbling up to the outskirts of a small village, dust kicking up all around from the tracks, the armoured car in the rear. Traversing their turrets left and right, watching for snipers, peering through their apertures for hints of roadside bombs. A shot up ahead. A small group of armed men in combat gear, looking at a body in the dust at their feet, pointing at something in the ditch by the road. They pulled to a stop twenty yards behind them.

He dismounted, taking three of his boys and his interpreter through the rear door. His sergeant, still one of his best friends to this day, was in the turret ready to bring down covering fire, the other vehicles, as they had practised, covering left, right and behind. He walked up, Bosnian military uniforms he noticed: his interpreter became agitated, "Chechens" he whispered, "a couple of Bosnians as well."

He stiffened; he knew the Chechens' reputation, the worst of the worst for unpredictable brutality. Show no fear was his first though.

He could see his sergeant wasn't happy about it at all; he had seen it all before, this was his third tour in this hellhole already. The body was that of a young boy: fourteen, maybe fifteen, lying in the dust with his own blood congealing beneath him. One of the guilty men reached down and pulled something gold from the corpse's neck, wrenched it free and showed it in triumph to his colleagues, but they were more interested in the cowering figure at the bottom of the ditch. Filthy, plastered with mud and dust, terror seemed to radiate from her, unnerving him. She must be older than the dead boy on the road top, sister, wife, girlfriend it was difficult to tell. A couple of small back-packs were lying beside her, half protruding from the brackish ditch water. The gunmen were ignoring him quite pointedly.

No, no, please don't take me there. Not tonight. He knew what they were planning; you could read it in their body language. He nodded to his Sergeant and five more of his men from the Warrior dismounted and strolled up towards them, their safeties were off, he knew. Keep your own hands away from your weapon, cool it down.

He had now got their attention. There were seven of them. He pointed to the crouching girl and beckoned to her. They didn't like it he could see, their voices started to rise, his interpreter began to translate, but he cut him off. "I'm not interested in what they've got to say, tell them that's the way it's going to be. We have the numbers."

Something in the flat way he spoke seemed to have more effect than the words repeated by the translator. Grumbling and scowling they made to move off. By instinct alone, despite himself, he reached forward and put a hand on the gold chain that the looter had pulled from the corpse moments before. The man made to pull it away, another moved his gun, and then caught site of the weapons trained on them, causing him to release it into his grasp. It was an orthodox crucifix and chain. They tramped off up the road muttering, covered by his men.

He was moving purely instinctively now, some deep human impulse brushing aside his professional training and the will emanating from his men not to do anything silly. He stepped down into the ditch and reached out towards her. She was utterly terrified, filthy in smock and torn jeans, quaking, looking at him through lank muddied hair plastered across her face. Seventeen, five or six years younger than me perhaps? She shrank back. He smiled gently. Her eyes slid over him, alighting on the Union flag on his uniform. He reached towards her. She let him, didn't resist when he lifted her into his arms. She was trembling now, wetting him with the new tears that were starting to pour. She was as light as a feather, malnourished for sure. He tried to pass her up to one of his boys on the road top three feet above, but she clung all the tighter. In the end, it took three of his comrades to lift and pull both of them out together.

He had nodded to Jonesy, the Sergeant. "Let's get back and get her to the field hospital, recover that poor sod, and their bags."

Top man Jonesy, it all just happened; they turned around and headed back to base. He was inside the transport now; she was clinging like a limpet, not answering the gentle questions of his interpreter. Shivering, sobbing quietly, plainly fearful of being in the belly of this beast of war, holding on to him as if her was her one chance of re-emerging into God's light. Jonesy sat beside them.

"Bad business Sir, Orthodox, almost certainly Serb refugees, the poor devils." He was looking at the crucifix twisted around his boss' hand. She caught sight of it and touched it, the tears rolling again. He pushed it into her hand where her fingers enclosed it like a Venus flytrap.

The ride back in the vehicle was tomb-like, only punctuated by staccato radio conversations and the mechanical noises all around them. The boys kept glancing at him, weighing him up, their natural black humour stilled, almost as if they were at the graveside of the young lad in the body-bag secured on the outside. Jonesy told him years later that some of them, those on their first tours here, thought him mad, others reckless. One had even leered a joke and been struck down by a comrade. Hard bitten, foul-mouthed, cynical, they were all of that, but he was learning they were so much more. What was it George MacDonald Fraser had said in his memoirs about the Burma campaign with the Cumbrian regiment which he had read so avidly over the years? Ah, there it was, 'Whenever I think back on those few minutes when the whizz-bangs caught us, and see those unfaltering green lines swinging steadily on, one word comes into my Scottish head: Englishmen.' He was still a romantic at heart he knew, but it was true also of many of his boys, especially the veterans whose tenderness was nearer the surface through exposure to, well, Hell.

He had had to carry her, still clinging to him, to the old warehouse that counted as a small field hospital, one of the guys bringing the recovered packs along behind with the interpreter. They had a devil of a job persuading her to release her grip, she screamed and wept, distraught beyond reach. They sent for the local Orthodox priest to see if any of the locals knew her. The presence of the nurses seemed to slowly still her, helped by that of the priest, and she finally relented when he promised to return at the end of his watch. He left her cradling the crucifix as if vampires were all around her.

He debriefed and went to see Jonesy. "You did the right thing Sir, if I may say so."

No, stop there, no further please. Please have pity. He had returned at dusk. He was intercepted by the Sister just outside the women's ward. They had cleaned her up, re-clothed and fed her. She seemed to speak very rudimentary English. She was called Jovana, he had later learnt it meant 'God is gracious'. The irony had struck him hard; He certainly hadn't seemed to be in her case: she had been brutally raped some time ago and badly beaten. The boy was her younger brother, sole survivors of a family of Krajinan villagers 'ethnically cleansed' from their ancestral home by the invading Croat army. They had been fleeing to some distant relatives they thought were in Banja Luka when they fell in with her brother's now murderers. Their bags contained all they had in the world, little enough and the crucifix that had belonged to her mother was probably the most valuable thing she now possessed. All this the priest had discerned before going to find her relatives.

"The doctor said she may never have children now, but will need a proper scan and tests in a modern hospital to tell."

Why had the Sister said that, was she looking at him oddly? He went through and sat beside the girl, not sure what to do or say. He knew no Serb at all other than please and thank you really. She looked up at him, as if unworthy, afraid. He smiled, "Jovana?"

Her face was impassive, no trace of the unbounded emotion she had displayed earlier today. She was quite pretty, dark shoulder-length hair, grey eyes, very slight of build. It came as a surprise. She seemed to be weighing him up. It was unnerving; she must still be in deep shock. She pushed out her right hand into his and placed something warm and hard within his palm. He looked down; it was the crucifix and chain. Her cracked lips moved, "Life… gift? Thank you for…"

He had looked up at her and been sucked over the precipice by the vortex of her utter vulnerability. Yes, that had been it, not desire, not admiration; they had come later, just that vulnerability against which he had no defence. The desire to protect was his crowning weakness, the spur to his flank. No more please? I need rest. But he knew there would be no respite, he had been here hundreds of times. The chained crucifix round his neck was cutting into his chest, just as his memories of her sliced into his mind.

He had gone to see her every day, twice a day when possible, a practice he continued after she went to her relatives' home. They were dutiful towards her no more; she was a burden and an embarrassment. And then, suddenly it seemed, his tour had ended and back home he went. His relationship back home fizzled out within days, his thoughts elsewhere. A fortnight later he took leave and flew back to the Balkans breaking the rules and working on autopilot, using his contacts still in situ, carrying a small box. He returned, to the consternation of friends, family and colleagues a husband, then spent the next six months bringing her home.

Nine months of true joy followed, perhaps the only real happiness he had ever known. The doctors confirmed there would be no children and then found something else; the real nightmare began, the relentless, pitiless spread through her body, possibly, they thought, triggered by the trauma. Temporary victories raised hopes, only to be crushed by subsequent tests. And then she was gone, to him another casualty of evil. She never cried, never complained about anything after he brought her back, as if put beyond mental anguish by her earlier experiences and the intensity of her bond with him. That was the only consolation he could take. He had been lost, bereft, drifting, investing his entire persona into his military and subsequent careers, until events had catalysed something in him that had been lying dormant since her passing. Is that it? Is it over for tonight? Have mercy. And then the sounds of the River Lethe washed over him for a few short hours. One day, one day, it would be the waters of the Jordan instead, perhaps then he would be with her again.

Friday

....

He had left his parents-in-law by eight o'clock the following morning, heading to the local station to meet the officers leading the search for his wife; it had been a sombre evening, but not what he had expected, he had done them a disservice. They were frantic about their daughter and grandson, but had tried to shield him from their feelings, clearly concerned for him too. They didn't probe about why he hadn't come down straightaway, assuming it must have something to do with last night's dramatic news. They didn't know why she had phoned to tell them she was on her way down so unexpectedly, perhaps he had wanted her away from the big city with all that was going on? He hadn't wanted to disabuse them of this comfort.

They displayed an old-fashioned English sang-froid, motivated by a selfless concern for others, it was quite admirable really. Yes, in his selfishness he had misjudged them. Now to apply a boot to the arses of the local boys and then back to face what seemed to be mounting hysteria in the higher echelons in London. Oh yes, he had spoken to a couple of colleagues who had been summoned back. What a mess, although old Ted Armstrong seemed to be winning new admirers.

Sally was up late the following morning, awakened only by her son entering and climbing on her bed; her headache had diminished, and she realised how clean and fresh the air felt. Sea air. It always made city dwellers like she and Josey sleep deeper and longer for days before they acclimatised. She opened the window and looked down the valley. It was still clear, but she could see a hint of cloud on the western horizon, perhaps auguring a change coming.

She washed in the bowl on the chest of drawers, almost icy cold, dressed and came down feeling less stiff, a little fresher. Martha heard her descending and came out to call them through for late breakfast. "Iltud's walking down to the station with the Seigneur, the others have gone home. They found nothing, just a few more yards of new moorland. I've invited my grandson, who's about Josey's age, round to play to give you a break. Is that alright with you? Why don't you have a bath and then come with me for a walk while my daughter-in-law keeps an eye on them? See some more of it for yourself; the fresh air may do you good."

Her hostess really was one of the nicest people she had ever met, a natural at putting her at ease and stilling her worries. She nodded assent and tried to lose herself in small talk about everyday things.

'Old Ted' Armstrong hadn't been able to avoid attending COBRA, sucked into the black hole of blathering, as he termed it. He was getting too old for this; he was employed to use his judgement and make decisions based on a lifetime's experience, not exhaust himself, out all night at the scene and then back here, sat at a desk for hours taking calls from all and sundry wanting to be 'in the loop'. Oh Lord, the PM was channelling Churchill again; why do all modern politicians imitate the great man in anything resembling a crisis? Most weren't fit to lick his boots. A giggle broke in, but he stifled it, the barely subdued hysteria in the room was infectious. Concentrate man, your mind's wandering. The Home Sec's lizard-like eyes were on him now, get ready for it.

"And perhaps the estimable head of the Counter-Terrorism Command would like to recount any unreported details of last night's events and the course of the investigation so far?"

Well he was ready for them. "Thank you, Prime Minister. You are all now familiar with the outline of last night's events. A major atrocity was averted, by forces unknown to us, saving perhaps over one thousand lives, including a Cabinet Minister. Seven suspected terrorists were killed, one by his own hand as he detonated a bomb in the hotel lobby. The others, preparing to suicide bomb the hotel with over two thousand pounds of explosives and then launch a Bombay-style gun assault on any survivors and unfortunates in the vicinity, were shot to death before they could unleash their carnage. The sole surviving suspect is critically injured and in a coma, but should live. We are running traces on the suspects' identities; four have been confirmed as British citizens so far. All bar one have no known terrorist links, the other only marginally so. The others remain unidentified and may well be foreign nationals; we are in contact with several governments, but it may take some time. The estimated number of innocent victims is six dead, fourteen injured and three missing, but the rubble means more bodies may be found."

"We believe that there were at least four suspects. Two motorcycles were seen leaving the area very shortly afterwards, carrying four riders. We believe they entered the country roads south of the motorway, thus minimising camera coverage and have effectively disappeared for now. We recovered four AK47s of Chinese pattern from the scene, no serial numbers, but our experts think they may well be North Korean in origin, same for the ammunition. Hollow tipped and full metal rounds were used. The fact that they just abandoned them suggests they are confident we won't be able to trace them via the weaponry. I trust their confidence is misplaced, but time will tell."

"Whoever did this was highly expert. The thing that is most impressive is the quality of their intelligence. They seemed to know when and where the suspected terrorists would be launching their atrocity and killed them red-handed so to speak. Quite a neat job if I may say."

He paused for effect. No one was stirring. Time to step out on to the stage.

"We now suspect that this event is connected to the killing of one Mohammed Amallifely in Birmingham less than seventy-two hours ago. He was a suspected Jihadi and was under observation. He was killed by a highly expert sniper on a city street at very long range with a high-grade military rifle, but no weapon or other evidence has been recovered. So far the press haven't made the connection, but that may well not be the case for much longer. All resources available are being deployed on this investigation, but whoever has done this is highly expert and has remarkable intelligence and resources."

Now to tie their tails together and watch them scrap so that his officers could focus on the job with as little meddling as possible. "As to who might be behind it, all we have is speculation, informed by one or two important observations. Firstly, they are highly resourced, professional and well informed. The latter suggests a splinter faction, as possibly does the manner of the second incident, but this theory does not fit well with either the professionalism or resourcing required. Furthermore, they have thus far exclusively targeted would-be terrorists, no one else, which makes it a less probable explanation. So, although a possibility, it's not the most likely."

No one had interrupted him; they were rapt, out of their depth here. "Secondly, a foreign security or intelligence agency, the first incident might suggest this, but not the second – too high profile and risky. I can't believe even the Israelis, Russians or an Arab government would indulge in such dramatics on our shores unless they had lost control of one of their security services. Perhaps the Foreign Office could venture their opinion?"

He carried on before the purpling Foreign Secretary could collect himself and make a denial to hide his ignorance. He was enjoying himself now; he struggled to suppress his Lincolnshire tones, so long moderated in the cause of his career, but having a tendency to regain their grip in times of excitement.

"Thirdly, our own security or armed services have been running an operation of which we have not been made aware, or some of their agents have taken it into their own hands and slipped the leash. The nature of the targeting might be said to support this speculation."

The heads of MI5, MI6 and the Chief of the General Staff looked up sharply. What game was being played here?

"Fourthly, some ex-military personnel, perhaps one of the various contractors used by various arms of Her Majesty's Government for its more deniable activities in the defence of the realm, have started their own private war for their own reasons. Again, this is supported by the targeting, Frankenstein's monster, breaking out of the castle so to speak."

'Henry', standing as an apparent junior here, suppressed a smirk. The old boy was inspired; if this was his final bow it deserved an Oscar and a knighthood. His audience was on tenterhooks, wondering where the weathervane was going to point next; some were looking at one another with barely concealed distrust, suspicion even. It was like a field of dry stubble waiting for the inevitable lightning strike and the inferno to begin. Point the finger at the MOD in some way; everyone blamed them for everything, failing the Israelis or Russians? They had scapegoat written all over them, especially with the oaf currently sitting in the seat of Minister of Defence.

He drew breath. The atmosphere in the room was thick, sullen almost, like a storm waiting to break. Good. "Finally, I hope, a new, possibly native force, completely unknown to us. Hardly credible I think as we've heard nothing of it at all, no rumours, no signs, unless the Security Service has not been fully forthcoming, which I am not at all unduly reluctant to discount entirely."

People sat stock still trying to unpick the increasingly tortured syntax employed by the old man, muddied by his now revivified provincial accent. Had he just insinuated that agencies here weren't being entirely open with what they knew or were running their own paramilitary operations on the mainland with no political oversight?

The PM, whatever his faults, was one of the brighter ones in the room. The last thing he wanted was a major row between Cabinet colleagues who were fractious at the best of times, let alone to stir up the endemic distrust that existed between the various agencies represented here. But it was also a chance to take down the Home and Foreign Secretaries a peg or two, and to relieve the stress by kicking the Secretary for Defence.

"Thank you for that masterly summary Ted. We can leave it in your hands, for now." The threat was made, what had the old boy been thinking? "Speculation is an enemy here, but Foreign Secretary I would like your categorical assurances that we have no evidence that a foreign security service is conducting paramilitary operations on our shores? Home Secretary, this is on your watch, I'm sure you appreciate that." Her rectus smile made his heart sing. "Minister of Defence, it strikes me your team have a lot of questions to ask. That's all everybody, thank you."

'Henry' slipped out of the room first. Too bad the old boy was heading for retirement; he would have been worth cultivating. He had taught him a thing or two about holding court in such company. Well, well, well, whoever would have thought that an old plod could out-dance them all?

He picked up the phone and pressed the numbers. Two rings and it was answered, the recipient had clearly been awaiting his call. She was very keen to play, she knew all the right words, seemed a true believer, at the least she really wanted to be on the inside of whatever it was. Her vanity made her malleable. "I'm not sure quite what I witnessed. Your man came through it all unscathed. Quite a master, shame he's not ours." She liked the "ours." She almost purred with shared complicity. "But how much longer has he to go? Hmmm. Who's favourite to succeed him? Ah. Anyone for us? Disappointing. Dager, I've heard of him. Surely too much of an outside bet, too junior, besides, he's not on side? Not yet? I understand, but soon you say? You've got the buttons to press? I hope so; it would be quite a step forward. You could deliver it you think, I wasn't sure you had that much sway? Let me know how you get on won't you? Good morning to you."

Very eager to please, to ingratiate, to advance, confident that she could deliver. It would be another step forward and a feather in his cap if it came off. Oh well, back to those who thought themselves his masters. He smiled mirthlessly at himself in the mirror as he adjusted his tie.

The walk was just what she needed, invigorating in the Spring sunshine among the reams of wild flowers lining the track sides and field fringes, helping to clear her head. The climate was more like that of southern Cornwall here, a microclimate established by the alignment of the surrounding hills, moor and tree topped in places. Running, broken only in a few places by side valleys, down to the shore line, if anything gaining height as they did so until they cut out into the sea, curving around the enclosed bay like a mother's arms sheltering her baby, almost entrapping the mist obscured islands in the bay, leaving only a few narrow channels out to the ocean beyond. "What are those islands?" she had asked Martha.

"The big one's Apple Island, where the Duke lives, the Abbey is there too. The little ones we call the Hermitages, after the monks who sought solitude on them. One or two still do."

She was introduced to locals they passed, all seemed friendly if reserved; eventually they came to a large stone and tiled building, like a great barn. "This is the warehouse and beside it is the station for the railway with the general store attached. There are several trains per day normally, not Sundays though. Look, you can see where they are extending the track."

Five or six hundred yards further up the valley side a gang of men were laying metal rails on newly levelled ground which appeared to be cut from the hillside. "I think they will be ready to blast another section next week. We all have to go inside when they do."

The track looked narrow she thought, like one of those in North Wales. Josey would be in heaven, puppies and steam trains, what three-year old boy could want for more? They headed back to the house, passing the church entrance on their circuit. A few stone graves projected from the grass and Spring flowers surrounding it. It wasn't a church really, more a small chapel built out of stone and tile, with small plain glass windows, no tower or spire, just a bell towerlet at one end.

"Can I go inside? I've got some things to think about and it might help."

"Of course, it's never locked in the day." The older woman smiled, encouraging her, "I'll see you back at the house, the boys will be getting hungry."

She hesitated in the porch, steeling herself for what might follow. She pushed the heavy door open, and stepped in, closing it so softly behind her. She looked around, plain whitewashed stone walls, exposed roof timbers, only one small stained-glass window above the altar, the rest clear, and a couple of stone plaques mounted on the walls of the nave. It was clearly not old, just built to look old.

She heard movement behind her. She froze for a second and then turned around. There was a priest, a large youngish reddish haired man coming out of a side door, no; he was wearing light monk-like robes. "I'm sorry, I didn't know…"

He smiled. "Sally, isn't it? I heard you might come in today." How did he know? "I'm the priest for this parish, and yes I'm in Holy Orders and a monk. Is that a problem?"

"I'm sorry, I didn't recognise your, ummm, tonsure?"

"Clever of you to spot it." He bent forward; he had plenty of hair other than a gash shaped shaven patch running from ear to ear. You won't have seen one of those before?"

"No."

"That's because the Synod of Whitby, as it's called in Logres and the outside world, never happened here. We're the last refuge of the native Celtic Church. The church of Columba, David, Aedan, Patrick, Pelagius and Joseph of Arimathea you might say. When's Easter?"

"Umm, nearly three weeks away?"

He chuckled. "Not here, we still use the old method of calculation;

it's a week sooner this year, although even we moved from the Julian to Gregorian calendars ninety years ago. Can I get you some coffee?" He winked at her. "I keep some special coffee in the vestry for visitors who want to talk…"

The last free member of the late Mohammed Badr's cell was watching the TV news for the umpteenth time in disbelief. Shaitan himself must be upon them, fighting for the kaffir surely? What to do with the video swansongs they had all recorded before starting off on their fateful journey? Post them up on the web, don't hide them away. They had still died martyrs, however unsuccessful: they deserved their memorials.

What was he to do then, all alone? Lay low and wait to be contacted, praying that friends found him before the authorities, who seemed to be in a killing mood, or undertake a lone glorious action on his own initiative? For all his fervour in company he was not a naturally brave man and was better with keyboards than weapons, which is why he had been given the job he had. So, lay low and wait, for now, for twenty-four hours. Perhaps the missing Badr would turn up, perhaps he had been called away by other contacts, other operations, perhaps it wasn't as bad as he feared and the rumours were false, put about by the infidels to confuse the righteous.

Helena put down the tablet and logged out of the web browser. The journalists and commentators were in a rising frenzy of reportage, with speculation building on rumour in a kind of media arms race. Now the foreign media had dived in, with even less restraint and no worries at all about any consequence. Some were even speculating that the killing, in a Birmingham backstreet, of a Turkish immigrant could be related, as he seemed to be known to at least one of the identified jihadists. One admittedly notorious web-blogger had even picked up a local rumour that another associate of theirs had just disappeared, but no one reputable would want to be seen dead associating themselves with the opinions of such an 'out-there' commentator so it remained a dead strand for now.

She hadn't known what they were up to, wouldn't ask, but it had been an unexpectedly good return on investment. She mulled it over, as good as that which her best private equity deal had produced, a truly embarrassing IRR in a few months? Luck and timing obscenely magnifying the results of the good judgement that had made her reputation and her fortune, made her courted and influential in the shadowy private finance world. When the media and politicians went on about bankers, they hadn't a clue what they were talking about: the real power lay within unremarkable town-houses and behind office doors bearing anodyne brass name-plates in select streets around the West End, so understated that one would think them the offices of small provincial firms of solicitors or chartered surveyors. The City was for drones.

Well, whoever they were, they had done her proud. Perhaps when this was all over, when her drive to win had finished burning itself out, she might be allowed to meet them, share a couple of bottles of her favourite Musigny with them over dinner in some forgotten rural pub. The juxtaposition tickled her.

The money was nothing after the first few mill. She was free of that endless desire for more, unlike so many of her colleagues and competitors. She didn't really earn it, she made it; it was real people who earned it for her doing thankless jobs, people she would never meet. So why had she never lost perspective, why had the rewards she gained, which so obsessed and twisted other people around her, only clarified her thinking? She had been empty, a futile vessel of outwardly immense success, and then she had met him in a lift in the West End. He had smiled at her. She had been alone at the time, contemplating giving it up, but for what? He was reasonable looking, older, gracious, understated, very good manners, elegant almost, assured but not arrogant. And light years away from her world.

She had asked him for a coffee there and then. He was surprised, disconcerted almost. That had amused her, but she had wanted him all the more for that, wanted to sleep with him to make him hers and had tried for some time without too obviously throwing herself. She now realised she never got close. She wasn't unattractive, and he didn't seem to give a damn about money or status. He was very hetero, but closed off; she only found out why much later after she had swallowed her pride and settled for friendship, something she now valued more highly than his, well, passion.

She had tried to check him out, as she did if she were seriously interested in someone: credit checks, that sort of thing, until the firm she used got cold feet and resigned the case. He had little money, a military pension and one from the civil service, decent schooling but no college, and wore well cut gents' clothes purchased from a nice, but staid, gent's outfitters. His flat was ok, but not registered to him, no close family any more, non-descript car, seemed to give quite a lot of his income to charity, nothing about his job other than that he was a government employee, all very dull and not really her. But, bit by bit, as she got to know him and a very little about his world, he had started to fill the void she had feared to recognise in herself. Three, four, five years, several lovers and one husband had come and gone, but no one had come close to matching his meaning to her as their friendship morphed into something close to the deeper love of companionship she now realised was what she had craved most of all. Cynics said it couldn't happen between man and woman, there were movies made about that storyline after all. Well he, in so many ways for her, showed her how.

Then one day, just one unremarkable day, he had met her at her penthouse flat in Chelsea. She had seen the burden was crushing him, whatever it was; he was tired, at a loss, she had never seen him like this before, it was shocking. His vulnerability had reawakened the old feelings, part of her had wanted to seduce him, comfort him, make him hers; fill some of the void within her, perhaps even all of it. But, being always more of her mind than her body, she had feared that to attempt it could only ruin what she had from him, so she had locked those feelings away deep down once more. She offered him anything he needed, a home with her, money, contacts, secrets. She had shocked herself with the fervour of her generosity, her desire to repay something of what he had given her.

He had looked at her for a long time in silence, in that quiet penetrating way of his. She had felt naked before him, totally exposed. He had warned her of something of the consequences, had made her swear to never disclose anything. He was almost touchingly naive in some ways; oaths meant little in her world, water-tight contracts were obstacles sharp minds could circumvent, the American way of doing business was now utterly dominant. Still, she would have promised him anything at that point and she would keep it, of that she was sure.

So, he had told her, just a little of it, to whet her appetite. But then she had doubted, briefly, his sanity, when he told her more. But it was still him, still that quiet, determined romantic hidden under layers of obfuscation and detachment, working towards the goal he had set himself to assuage the emptiness. And then he had introduced her to somebody else, living proof he wasn't a fantasist. That had been enough. Getting the resources in the right places was child's play to her, she had access to far more than he thought he needed. Tracing it would require the attention of experts on several continents, and because it was lots of small, everyday amounts it wouldn't even be flagged up unless someone really knew what they were looking for.

Now, four years later, she only really continued in her job to help him and his 'friends'. Her part to play, to work on something far greater than herself, something to make amends to the real people even if they would never know, perhaps to close that remaining hollow, even find redemption maybe?

If it was what she thought it was, she whispered a prayer to the deity she couldn't believe in to get them home safe. Perhaps he would call round this weekend, she found herself missing his company.

The PM took the call; the Chief Executive of the company targeted last night was one of the few who could always get through to him. It was one of Britain's best industrial success stories, worth hundreds of millions in exports each year, hundreds of millions in taxes, thousands of high value jobs. The man had survived unscathed, but lost some valued management as well as their spouses. He would be emotional, demanding, understandably so and would need careful handling. The PM spoke first, balancing the unctuousness with the directness he was advised sounded so good.

"Peter? How are you? I can't express my sorrow for your loss. Are you all getting everything you need? May I say I regard the attack on you and your colleagues as an assault on the entire UK?"

His PR adviser listening in on another phone gave him a thumbs-up, the right tone was vital.

"Thank you, Prime Minister, but that's not why I'm on the phone to you."

His gruff, Yorkshire voice accentuated by stress; he was not prepared to be charmed by anybody at present. He was clearly on the edge, emotional like the PM had never heard him before.

"I and my colleagues want to thank those members of the security forces for saving us last night, in person."

Damnation, he had bought the rumours about the SAS; this was going to be tricky.

"We, and those of the business community who have called us from around the world, have agreed to pledge a total of £50 million. Twenty for armed forces and police charities, twenty to establish a trust fund for the dependents of those killed and wounded last night, and ten to those whose skill killed the terrorists and saved all our lives. I and my Board want to hand the cheque to them in person in the next few days at Hereford, and I expect to see medals for them as well as HM Government's contribution. We will also offer a reward of a further £20 million for information received which enables the conviction of any other terrorists or their supporters involved in this… this… We are issuing a press release to that effect shortly. I trust you will support this initiative. Thank you for your time and solicitation."

The line went dead, he had put the phone down on him, the PM; he was clearly addled with emotion at his near escape. Only later did the PM learn that the man's new wife had been heading to the rear lobby when the bomb when off, leaving her dazed, but otherwise uninjured. Had she walked just a little quicker, hadn't had to press through the crush of guests, he would have been a widower for the second time.

His PR chief stood up and drew a finger across his throat; the others in the room looked at their feet. The PM was not a foul-mouthed man, but for once gave vent to an extraordinary sequence of expletives to the effect that they were royally screwed by someone who was obviously out-of-his-mind, no matter how distinguished. His PR man stepped into the breach, somewhat bravely, the other occupants of the room later reflected.

"We've no choice, we've got to issue a statement to head this off to the effect that we don't know who topped those murderous lunatics, but it wasn't us; otherwise we'll be a right royal laughing stock around the world."

"Can't we slap a D Notice on his press release?" joked someone to ease the tension, and promptly wished he were invisible such was the boss' withering look.

"Do it, write it now, I'll sign it. Get it out in the next five minutes." His Cabinet colleagues would go bananas, let alone the security services and police, but there was nothing else for it. They were stuck and they were losing containment.

Brother Peran, as he introduced himself, was unlike any pre-conception of a monk she had ever held. He had sat her down on a leather chair in his vestry while he boiled a kettle on the top of the woodburner and made a flask of filter coffee. "Two of the greatest things the outside has given us," he had smiled, "coffee and the modern wood-burning stove, from them comes warmth of body and warmth of companionship."

She looked around her at the little room crammed with a small oak desk, two upright leather strapped chairs, a rug partly covering the stone floor, and oil lamps hanging from hooks. What caught her attention most of all were the shelves full of books, some modern looking, others clearly very old. They were piled up across the desk, spilling on to the floor. He passed her the coffee and milk, noticing her searching eyes, trying to read titles. "Oops, sorry, what a mess!" he stepped back and picked up the pile of books lying on the floor, simply to create another stack on his desk.

"Father Abbot would make me do a week's penance if he could see them like this. He thinks me too fond of the world of learning and libraries. That's why he sent me here, told me I had to do a real job serving people before I could return and really understand the wisdom in books. Ten years at least he said, well six to go, but he's at heart a kind man and lets me borrow some from the library every month. Besides, I have more freedom here in some ways, so it's not as bad as I thought back then. So, what can I do for you today?"

He sat down, the end of his robe slipping aside to show a pair of black jean clad legs underneath. He readjusted his robe and smiled bashfully, "Just because we are given up to His Service does not mean we should torture ourselves with the cold…"

"Father, I think I need to confess, things of which…"

"I wasn't aware you were a Roman?"

"No, I'm not, just a sort of Anglican, that's all."

"There's no 'that's all' about it. It has always struck me that the Anglican tradition has been a sensible compromise in the outside world, the golden mean the Hellenes called it. All these divisions are the scandal of Christendom, arguments over power and position, minor points of theological speculation, matters adiaphorous to the Lord. He must weep more tears over them than anything. Each tradition should be free to commune with all others as long as they believe in the resurrection and its meaning."

She had clearly got him on to a subject of some passion. "What does adiaphorous mean Father?"

"Sorry, it means 'matters indifferent', minor matters which followers of the Way shouldn't quarrel about; mysteries of the divine you might say. I understood you knew some Greek?"

News travelled fast here she realised, they didn't seem to need social media. "Very little really, I'm sorry to disappoint you."

She needed to see if she could talk to him, if he could really understand. How could a sworn celibate understand the challenges of marriage in the modern outside world? Keep him talking while she weighed him up; see if he could be trusted.

"Can you tell me more about this place? How it happened, why you have cut yourselves off?" She could see he was becoming uncomfortable, "Your faith, what it's about here, what's special about it, why you hold onto it?"

She sensed he was relaxing again as if he perceived she was letting him stand on home ground once more. She felt again the evasions of some of the answers to the questions she had asked others, as if there were an invisible barrier within the Pocket itself, separating her from others settled here, they can't still trust her. She was being unrealistic; she'd only been here a couple of days, but had been starting to trust them, well at least Martha, Iltud and the doctor. She was still disappointed though, surprised how she had started to fit it and wanted to be liked here without realising it.

"I can't, won't try to answer some of your questions. Those you will have to ask of much more learned and senior authorities than me. But I can explain something of our history, our folk lore, if you like and our traditions. Some you already know I believe."

"Please Father?"

"Tradition says that the Celtic Church was founded by the refugee Joseph of Arimathea, at what is now Glastonbury, less than ten years after our Lord's Ascension. He and his followers found a welcome among the Celtic tribes of Britain, it is said, at least some of whom were already effectively monotheists, as were some Druids, the Culdees. They were suspicious of the growing attention of the Roman Empire and welcomed anyone they thought its enemies. A few years later Rome invaded and fought brutal campaigns against us which took decades, hundreds of thousands died or were enslaved. The Britons fought back, Roman historians said they were the hardest nation to conquer they had yet come across, and indeed a sort of truce was arranged in the end. Never fully conquered, they retained much self-government in treaty with the Emperors while notionally being part of the empire."

He nodded at the books his eyes were sliding back to longingly.

"Or so tradition says. Strangely, some of your latest historians are now saying much the same thing as our tradition: my brother gets books for me when he goes into the outside world on business. I can let you see one if you like? Anyway, what Rome's armies couldn't achieve, its peace and wealth did. Some of the Britons abandoned their ways for those of Rome and servitude in the pursuit of luxury, but not all. Those north of the wall remained free, as did those of the west, particularly the Dumnoniae of Devon and Cornwall, and we here. Meanwhile Joseph's foundation spread slowly among the freer tribes in the south and west, despite Roman persecution in the areas they controlled, so much so that one hundred and eighty years after the incarnation of our Lord, Lucius, the prince of the Atrebates, became a Christian along with his people, the first nation in the world to do so. Rome remained dominant, but could not contain the spread of the faith so that even junior western Emperors such as Constantius wouldn't implement in Britain the persecutions ordered by senior Emperors like Diocletian the Terrible. And then Constantius' son Constantine the Great converted and went on to reunite the whole empire. So, the British were never subject to the Roman Church and had ultimately saved the empire from paganism. We therefore respect the Roman church, but pre-date it and hold fast to our God-given tradition. Do you understand? I'm not boring you I hope?"

"Well then, the empire passed in the west, falling to the tribes from the east and north. Here our tribes fought one another, led by leaders greedy for power and then the barbarians came: Irish, Picts, Saxons and others from across the sea. Saxon speakers were already here; some had lived in the east of Logres since before Roman times and others had settled as Roman mercenaries. They made a grab for power and the British, weakened as they were by their faithless civil wars, tried to fight back under leaders like Ambrosius Aurelianus, with some success. You probably know the story. After decades of peace, the plague came from the east and the princes started to fight again, and then the Saxons and their allies overran the lowlands of Logres, marrying the women and enslaving the men, but God preserved us."

"Dumnonia fought on virtually alone and in vain, but in the wreckage the Lord took pity on a remnant of his faithful and protected this little land. The Pocket we call it; it sits in a hidden fold in the firmament, still part of the world, created so that the first people to embrace his salvation would not be entirely annihilated by the pagan invaders. Some say prophecy from that time says we are a fortress for the faithful for the end times, a gateway for the forces of the Lord to break into the world to cast down the Anti-Christ. Who knows? Trust not prophesies not contained in the scriptures we say. Anyway, since then he has maintained us and we have kept our faith. How could it be otherwise? Gildas himself wrote his final books here, but never mentioned this place for the obvious reason. He's buried in the Abbey grounds; you should be able to see his grave one day if you wish."

He sat back, looking at the impact of his lecture on her. He had clearly enjoyed giving it. She had heard the stories, the legends and the folk tales of course. What Briton hadn't? But not all of it, and this affable, scholarly man in this unreal place clearly believed the thread of it even if he ascribed some of the earlier parts to 'tradition.' He looked up as if he had realised he had forgotten something.

"Please don't think me rude with my talk of murderous pagan Saxons, that's long in the past, such hatred long since forgiven. The Saxons became our brothers in Christ, followers largely of our tradition, intermarried with us so closely over the years that we became one people. They have their language, we have ours, but here we speak both and welcome both if they find us."

"Eventually they, like the Celtic peoples of these Islands succumbed to the lure of Rome, but here we have remained untouched. In time most of them, Celt and Saxon, repented and found their freedom again and are not so different from us in some ways, certainly some of the

Anglicans, but again we welcome all traditions here so long as they respect ours."

She decided to move him on before she had to sit through a detailed rendition of the theological events of the last millennium.

"What about today, more recently?" She gestured. "Wood-burners, coffee, steam trains, medicines, books," she shuddered, "weapons of war? You seem to be well connected with the outside today. Why? Isn't it risky coming and going across the barrier?"

He looked uncomfortable again, and paused before responding. She could see that now he was picking his words carefully, not in full heart-felt flow like before, as if fearful he would reveal more than he felt empowered to.

"Well the centuries passed and things went on as they were. A few strays found us every decade or so, and we sat here, perhaps complacent in our security and certainty of divine favour, interacting little with the outside. What you call the Reformation came along and then the civil wars across Logres, bringing new refugees with new learning, stimulating us to take more of an interest in the outside again in case the prophecies were coming true. It went quiet again, but outside the world speeded up. Then came the terrible wars, firstly against the French Emperor and then two more, far worse, against the forces of darkness from the east. Each time we wondered if we had reached the end times, but each time they passed. Yet still it speeded up, new ideas, new machines, and outside the faith declined and the people were enslaved to the new gods they erected, and one day, just after the last cataclysm, the Ducal Council decided to prepare, fearing that creation could not survive another."

He was in full flow again, almost poetic in his delivery, the words in his thickly accented second language becoming stranger sounding, stretching out towards song, hardly breathing. "They started, ever so slowly, so carefully, establishing a presence again in Logres, to observe, to search, bringing back what was useful. And then, unexpectedly, they found us, from the Ocean, the men from the Middle Sea. They had thought themselves alone, isolated for centuries, granted a final refuge by an ultimately merciful Lord after centuries of punishment for their arrogance and folly. But the second cataclysm, that of a century ago, had affected even them: the heaps of the dead by their barrier, the stench and weeping of the afflicted, piercing their hearts in their sanctuary. So, they had started to search, to learn, to make ready. But they had one advantage over us; they knew of one place in the outside where they would be welcomed, helped and not betrayed; the Mountain they call it. They started to travel further afield, building their strength within and without, and finally, after decades, they found us. How I don't know, but they did. Praise to the Highest! We were not alone anymore!"

She focused on him. He was almost in a trance, eyes closed, mind elsewhere, joy suffusing his features, verging on ecstasy. She couldn't tell him he had ceased making any sense; she just had to let his story run its course.

"But they were still proud, haughty and untrusting. Only slowly and reluctantly, they started to share with us some of what they knew. They say that even today they have not disclosed half their wisdom to us. But trust grew slowly, we were patient, we had been waiting over one and a half millennia and, finally, they allowed some of us to go back with them, to establish trade and exchange."

"Then fourteen years ago, twice the holy number, that of the Father Himself, he came to us. He was no stray, no fleeing refugee, he was brought here, not by chance, but by a broken and contrite spirit they say. I met him once you know, down by the Abbey, just before he went back. Some say he came to answer the old prophecies, someone from the deep past sent back, but he seemed just a man to me. What he and the Council, and then the Duke and the old man themselves, discussed is not known. But he was touched and after only a short time sent back, something unheard of before. And then others of us followed him, crossing to and fro, bringing back new things, exporting our wares in exchange. And all the while, since the final cataclysm, the land itself began to expand. We didn't notice at first you know, but more like you started to find us, a dozen or more each year, and more were found and brought back by us from the outside. Our people began to grow strongly again, no longer a small, fearful diminished rump of what had been lost so long before, but planting new villages, settling the outer valleys. Building wonders of science such as the railway."

"And then you come, with a young child, so rare, so precious to us all, a mark of His continued favour. Now Easter approaches, His Blessings on us and you! and you sit there before me, in my little sanctuary, so wondering, so fearing, so doubting, so regretting, not sure whether to mourn or sing, to trust or distrust."

Suddenly, he seemed to run out of steam, the engine of his poetry exhausted. He leaned forward, elbows on knees, looking at her directly for the first time since she had sat down.

"What do you really need of me?"

She was dumb-founded, this bewildering, unpredictable, eccentric, kind man. If forty-eight, seventy-two hours before someone like him had recounted even half of what he had just said to her she would have been calling the mental health authorities and edging away. She couldn't believe the half of it, but he clearly did, and then again he was a scholar of some description. She had lost track, she needed time to process it. What had she wanted to ask of him? Ah yes, but could she? Start gently and see.

"Father, I'm not sure why I and my son made it through the barrier. But I know that things in my life weren't right and I was adrift in the world. My husband and I…" She couldn't say it.

"You still use the present tense of him; you still wear his ring, yes? Have either of you been unfaithful?"

"Why no, not me and I don't think so for Andy, I would have known."

He smiled. "I have not been outside, my place and purpose is here within. But I have had this conversation, this confession you call it, with others who have come here for the first time. It is not for me to judge; there has been no adultery you say, of the heart or body?" She shook her head. "From what I know, the life currents of the outside have become too strong for many to withstand, they are swept this way and that, slowly going under in their despair and faithlessness. It strikes me that you were swept here into a safe harbour, guided by your faith perhaps, so while you may have much to confess and repent of, it is not this. It is the Lord's will, Blessings upon Him! I will not question His Judgement. May He, in His holy wisdom, direct the currents carrying your husband here to your side in His own time."

He reached out and grasped her hands in his with surprising strength and said a brief prayer.

She walked through the open door and into the light outside as if it were a new day and made her way back to the house, where her son and his new friend were busily demolishing lunch.

'Henry' switched off the news feed on his laptop. That press release put out by the PM's office! Whatever had possessed them? He must try to find out. It was crudely transparent, wildly unnecessary, surely? It reeked of fear, of powerlessness. He knew it was all rotten of course, he saw the signs most days, but even he hadn't realised it was quite this far advanced; well they said the fish rots from the head. The self-delusion, the faux cleverness of 'youthful energy' substituting for the wisdom of experience, the shallow pursuit of position and the means to self-gratify, 'self-actualisation' Mintzberg had termed it, as if it were admirable rather than self-indulgence on an epic scale. And now, when the little boy threatened to show that the emperor had no clothes, they panicked, lied to themselves and then went on self-deceiving as to the rot around them. It would be funny, in fact, it was funny, if the consequences weren't so serious.

She would be pleased, he knew. Perhaps they could spare him for a couple of hours this evening. He could buy her supper. She wasn't with anyone at the moment as far as he could tell. She would like that.

Andy Bowson got back to the office just in time to avoid a tirade from his boss. What a waste of time! Not from the perspective of seeing her parents, he owed them that, but the locals seemed to have made no headway at all. The car forensics turned up nothing, from the foot prints she seemed to have walked a few hundred yards west along the road, with a small child, stopped, and then simply vanished into thin air. No witnesses, local farmers had seen or heard nothing, no evidence of anything from the helicopter's thermal imaging camera. One of the local bobbies, not realising who he was, had told him with an unearthly lack of tact how several people every year, more than they liked to admit and certainly more than the papers ever realised, disappeared without trace on the moor. It was all he could do not to deck him there and then.

The senior officer on the case was solicitude itself, but little more. They had thrown plenty of resources at it and even the locals were combing the ground for someone they regarded as a local girl. But that was all. He knew the form, the longer it went on, the less the chance of success, a prospect he couldn't bear to recognise. Resources were now being deployed from Bristol and as far away as Hampshire, she was after all one of their own, but they didn't seem to be optimistic. Well he could do no more on the spot. In a black bitter humour on the return drive he wondered if his new self-appointed friend 'Henry' could see if the Yanks had a satellite trained on Exmoor at the time. Speaking of Yanks, they seemed to be taking a long time on those enquiries about the weapon that killed Amallifely; mind you, the US was so awash with firearms of all descriptions it could be a task beyond even the FBI.

Shortly after he got back to his desk and started to go through the reports he realised he had done the FBI a disservice. Their ballistics experts had identified the weapon as almost certainly some sort of Barrett 0.5 inch sniper rifle with an effective range of about two miles. The problem was the bullets were home-made, by experts with machine tools it seemed, but not being commercial or military they were effectively untraceable. Their view was that this was to be expected, professional marksmen often made their own rounds. Furthermore, there were thousands of possible weapons circulating in the US, let alone those sold abroad. Many would have simply dropped out of sight and could be anywhere if someone knew how to move them overseas. Worse still, eighteen months previously a batch of thirty-two military variants, with sound moderators and the latest thermal sights, on route to a US infantry regiment based in Alaska, had simply vanished along with unspecified other equipment. Logistics error they had assumed, they should turn up eventually, but now the bells were ringing. My God, if someone with evil intent had got hold of them they would be in a position to start their own guerrilla war.

He had had a brief interview with Dager, who had asked in a perfunctory manner about his errand to the west, almost as if on autopilot. He looked dreadful; the political storm was raging just above his head, his chief had angered some of the other agencies who were now not proving unhelpful, his annual evaluation was fast approaching and he was having to work not just day and night but through yet another weekend. All of this because some nutcases were fighting their own private war on the streets of Britain's second city.

They were getting nowhere fast; the bikes had disappeared, the AKs and rounds were useless as trace aids, the camera footage told them nothing they didn't know anyway, no useful witnesses had come forward, and the dead they had managed to identify, while of interest, were not revealing anything very useful. The only flimsy lead they had was that some of the terrorists seemed to have been connected with a shadowy male resident of Birmingham, a certain Badr, who had apparently disappeared without trace. Great! "Much more progress like this and they would all be catching speeding motorists somewhere on the A1" he exclaimed, sarcastically. Bowson couldn't wait to get out of there.

Getting back to his desk, he smiled ruefully at George next to him, who raised a query with the arching of an eyebrow. Bowson gave a little shake of the head and turned back to his papers. 'Poor sod,' thought his assistant.

A couple of hours later he had reached the end of what little his colleagues had managed to establish. There were surprisingly few loose ends to follow up, other than the identified and still unknown terrorists, while the injured survivor was still several days away from being able to 'help them with their enquiries', according to the doctors. Tracing and checking out all their associates, family and other contacts would take weeks, even with the level of resources now deployed. The local force had literally just come up with an address for the 'Badr' who was supposed to have dropped out of sight. They didn't seem to put weight on it, preferring to focus first on investigating the families of those killed and wounded, working on the principle that this type of terrorism was like a virus, spreading most readily between those closest to one another.

He needed an excuse to get away from the office. Dager was raging at some poor young subordinate in his glass cubicle, for something minor probably. Bowson got up and headed over and stood outside the closed door. Dager saw him, drew breath and motioned him to enter. The poor lass within looked at him like a drowning sailor would look a lifeboat and fled. "Well, what do you want? Got something?"

"I'd like to head back to Birmingham boss; the locals are stretched pretty thin and not following up this lead about the possibly missing associate. Just instinct I suppose, but I would like to take a look at it for myself if it's ok with you?"

The man was really irritated he could see.

"It's almost certainly a wild goose chase, but if you must. I can't spare anyone from here, just take Edward and see what the locals can give you. I want you back here first thing tomorrow. Understand?"

"Right boss." He left before the man could change his mind, motioning to Edward to grab his things and follow him out, muttering "Friday night in Birmingham, lucky me."

They had had a call from base to turn around and go back; too much activity around the final staging point. The base team had had time to finish sifting through their late unlamented prisoner's long, rambling confession: there was at least one more, their IT man, may be others.

They had a name and an address. They were already watching him from a distance, but needed support, more resource. Alan could tell his boys weren't happy; the foxes needed to burrow down deep in their earths when the hunt was roaming about, not go looking for more prey.

"Just this one more, then home, I promise," he had told them. Pushing their luck. They had reluctantly assented, all but Georgy: his eyes were shining.

Helena sometimes wondered whether he had a bug in her mind. He had texted her, inviting her out for dinner. She couldn't really be herself with him in public, let alone ask the question. You could buy in great food for home-delivery in London these days, so she had insisted he come around to hers. Of course he would. She knew what he liked. She went to see her PA to set it up.

It was a little branded coffee house near the British Museum. Bustling with mainly foreign tourists jabbering away, killing time before and after their visit to the great treasure house, flirting with one another, completely disinterested in the more soberly dressed occupants of the quiet table in the dimly lit back. Museum curators or perhaps academics they would have thought, if anyone had even noticed them. A dowdy woman in her early fifties and a blandly dressed bespectacled balding man, a little older, were whispering away quietly, as if testing out a new illicit affair.

"I assumed they were much more competent than that. We were assured they knew what they were doing. No, it's certainly not the authorities, not unless someone in the sec… has declared UDI. Quite spectacular I understand. Pity it was on the way in, not the way out, that would have been much better, for us anyway. Two birds with one stone. My so-called 'masters' are in a spin and that's a concern. They can behave unpredictably at such times."

"They will use it to vote themselves new powers, spend more money surely? That helps us indirectly I would have thought?"

"All in good time, it seems it's now a four-hand game, our 'masters' thought it was two, themselves and our useful 'friends', but now they see it's three. We know it's four, not three as we had counted previously. That's both troubling and threatening, especially as they are a blank, whoever they are."

"But our hand in the game is still unseen?" She was tiring of his analogy as it became ever more forced, but he seemed to like such word-play. He thought himself very clever; that was clear.

"Yes, but our 'friends' know we are there in the background and they are not predictable, nor even as capable as we had thought. They think themselves to have the winning hand as long as they don't call the game too soon. They over-estimate themselves with their unearned wealth and seventh century attitudes. They will be, are already being, left behind by history, dragged back by their ridiculous certainties, but they're a useful catalyst, a distraction. We must be doubly cautious. Now, tell me about your superior's scandalous divorce. I hear it's quite salacious. It might even be useful."

Sally Bowson couldn't settle that afternoon. Over a late lunch she had pressed both Martha and her husband about the priest-monk's fables. They had smiled patiently, confirming them, insisting that those in Holy Orders would not lie, perhaps not tell everything, but certainly not break one of the Ten Commandments themselves, least of all Brother Peran. They seemed quite fond of him, if amused by some of his eccentricities, but were unwilling to elaborate further, pleading they could add little to his scholarship. She doubted that, but it was unfair to press too hard.

Iltud had then gone back to work on his small-holding, but it was increasingly clear that Martha had been relieved of whatever nursing duties she had to keep an eye, no, that was too suspicious, unfair on such kind people, to look after the new immigrants. Her son just loved it here she could see, so easily absorbed by new friends, puppies, farm animals, roads, streams and fields. He could wander freely and safely about with the other children he was getting to know, coming back scratched, wet, muddy and beaming with excitement about his latest little discoveries. All so different from London.

It took her back to her own childhood two and a half decades ago, one with an unusual freedom even then, now almost completely obsolete in the modern world outside. Outside, she caught herself, almost starting to think like a native. I want my life back, not as before, but to see my family, my parents, my husband again. How was he? Was he missing her? Was he bereft at their loss to him, or just their son's? She knew he had been even more closed, more preoccupied than normal recently; perhaps something big had been building? She hadn't stopped to think, consumed in her own unhappiness; she had missed the signs, not asked to share his cares. Her spirits, lifted by the absolution that Brother Peran had seemed to confer, sank again. Blinded by his loquacity, she had not done this morning what she had set out to do. She would return to the little church, get down on her knees and ask for guidance, for answers, to be able to forgive herself.

Firstly though, she had to help Martha at home, to repay a little, start to feel useful. The afternoon wore on, filled by the endless little household chores of all homes. She began to see the drawbacks of a life without electricity: no vacuum cleaners, no washing machines and no hot water at the flick of a switch. If she had harboured any illusions about this being an antiquated Disneyland, an earthly paradise of peace and contentment, those few hours started to shred them. And then she thought of the men's weapons, cold killing implements – she had never liked Andy keeping his handgun in the house – needed to maintain this place against something Mark had said was trying to press in. Everyone here seemed to feel safe enough, but it wasn't Eden that was certain. She would ask the priest about them, what they were called, the Guardians, when she returned to the church later, perhaps before dinner. She had meant to this morning, but like so many of the questions she wanted answered, they had been lost in the flood of his poetry. Perhaps, he was even brighter than he looked? She would not be so easily distracted the next time.

She went with Martha down to the little general store by the warehouse, accompanied by her son and Martha's grandson, both of whom she had promised to treat if they were good. She felt that, as a guest eating and sleeping at their expense, she should contribute to the cost of the household, buy some things for her hosts. Martha had smiled and shaken her head, explaining that not only was there no electronic money here, invisible money she called it, that even her paper notes and coins would not be accepted. Indeed, with no calculators or computers, they had never decimalised, had never seen the need to use tens rather than dozens; a reluctance reinforced by their remembrance that decimalisation was the invention of the French Emperor Napoleon, the author of the first cataclysm as they called it. So, they were still using pounds, shillings and pence.

Martha had shown her some of the coins; let her examine them in her hands. Some were old, a hundred or more years, worn by repeated handling. Many of these were from outside, from Britain, she realised with a shock; there was even a golden guinea from the reign of George IV. Martha was proud of that, it seemed more an heirloom to her than a sum to be spent. Other coins looked locally produced, but modelled to resemble the ones from outside, although not-so-fine as if made with less sophisticated machinery.

With a start, she realised there was no paper money, the higher value amounts were all denominated in gold and silver, the smaller in bronze. Farthings, ha'pennies, pennies, three penny bits, silver sixpences and shillings, half crowns and crowns, ten-shilling coins and pound coins, and that one golden guinea. Martha explained how they still used sovereigns for the largest value transactions, largely for the business of the authorities. She looked at the silver coins again, most were local, portraying Britannia with the spear and shield. The classics student in her recalled Britannia was, in origin, the Greek goddess Athena on the on of Alexander's Successor Lysimachos. On the obverse the head of a late middle-aged man, the Duke, Martha explained, and a small Celtic cross with no lettering. The designs of the local coins seemed to vary little between types or level of wear or age. Simpler in some ways, more complex in others, she realised.

They walked past the warehouse on the way to the little station halt and store. A train was pulled up; steam hissing quietly from funnel as if at rest but not sleeping. Other than a small coal wagon, there seemed to be a passenger coach, one open goods wagon and two enclosed, whose side doors were open. Her son broke free of her hand in his frenzy and sped towards it onto the open platform. She raced after, scooping him up in her arms just as he about to try to climb in one of the good wagons' open doors. A man came to the doorway carrying a large cardboard box, he must be in his sixties she thought, but he handled it as if containing little weight. He grinned at her; he had been a little boy once.

She carried the squirming Josey back towards Martha at the edge of the platform. As she retreated two younger men came out of the warehouse's open double doors, one empty handed, the other pulling a small hand-cart. They smiled at her, they were clearly relieving the train of its cargo. Her eyes glided past them into the semi-darkness of the open warehouse behind; it was almost full, mainly cardboard boxes similar to the one the older man on the train was passing down to his empty-handed colleague on the platform. Besides them she could see some heavy looking wooden packing cases stacked low on one another, and various other boxes and metal drums of different sizes that were harder to make out in the shadows.

The older man had got down and approached them, embracing Martha as he did so. He smiled again at Sally.

"This is my brother, Docco, who works as the guard on this service."

He rolled his eyes. "Sometimes I wish there were not such a fashion for naming us after our native saints. Welcome, isn't she grand?" He pointed to the little engine and, looking at the wriggling Josey who was still fighting to break free, smiled "Would the young boys like to come up into the cab and see her in all her glory?"

"Good idea Docco, for once." Martha was laughing now. "You can avoid the hard work and play trains with your two little friends, while we go to the shop in peace."

Sally's son gave her the most beseeching look she could remember and, promising to be good, toddled off squealing with his two new friends. "Come on," said Martha, "let's use the peace to get what we need."

She tried hard not to be disappointed by the village shop. She had imagined it to be like an Aladdin's cave, one of those old shops you saw in children's films, stuffed full of oak and glass cabinets running floor to ceiling and wooden counters, all piled high with jars, packets and boxes of all descriptions containing many coloured wonders from around the world. Passing hessian sacks of coal and other similar goods on the way in, she saw it was tiny, containing mainly basic commodities in sacks, jars and boxes holding items such as flour, salt, a little sugar, potatoes, dried pulses, preserved meats and fish, a few bottles of cider, beer and lemonade, boots, tools, soaps, belts etc. She looked beyond the little shopkeeper who was busy serving Martha. There on a couple of back-shelves were more highly coloured items, goods brought in from the outside as she was increasingly thinking it, clearly expensive relative to those produced locally. Her spirits rose a little with the familiarity contained there, some tooth-paste (what about dentists, do they have them here, she shuddered), brushes, cleaning materials, razor blades, cartridges for guns, tinned foods, rice, some spice jars it seemed, matches, a few other items, but Aladdin's cave it wasn't.

She followed Martha out and round the back onto the platform where the train was now building steam and Martha's brother was holding his two charges by the hand. He was smiling as broadly as they were, "I'm sorry, but I couldn't keep them off the coal bunker."

They were filthy with soot and coal dust, but clearly heedless. Before she could admonish her son, Martha lent forward and gave them both a decorated ginger bread man she had bought in the store, scolding her brother, "Honestly Docco, I swear you are more a child than either of them."

They waited, watching the train puff out of the station the way it had come in and disappear into the distance down the line before they commenced the walk back to the house with the children. The warehouse was now locked up again and the men had seemingly vanished. She tried to probe Martha on what they kept inside, but her hostess became cagey once more, trying to change the subject. This time she would not relent, repeating her enquiries. Sally was starting to worry now.

As they entered the front gate, ushering the children through, Martha conceded defeat. "I shouldn't discuss that, you try with Iltud tonight. All I will say is we can't pay for the things we need to bring in from Logres just by exporting our preserved meats and fish, and lobsters and crabs."

Sally gave up. She would clearly get no further until this evening. She helped put everything away, cleaned up the boys and then, excusing herself, headed back up to the church. Brother Peran wasn't there, or at least didn't answer her knocks on the locked vestry door, so she went up to the altar, knelt down and tried to pray, to confess her failings and her fears, but she seemed to get nowhere. Her mind was full of unanswered questions; this place wasn't clearly all that it seemed. She felt as if she were in some mystery series on TV, a character trying to survive the twists and turns of the plot, near helpless in the hands of others no matter how kind they seemed. She needed answers to be able to think straight, to make decisions on behalf of her and her son. If only Andy were here, they could decide together, take strength from one another. Should we try to escape and, if so, how? Were they lying to her about the need to be 'touched', whatever that was? She shuddered at the thought of trying to go back the way she came; she felt trapped by the uncertainty, only answers could allow her to work it out.

She left the church and headed down the path through the little churchyard; as she closed the gate she glimpsed something towards the back wall of low dry-stone; a grave stone, not a Celtic cross like the others, more like an eastern cross, Greek or Russian? Odd. She had to get back to what she was starting to think of as home in her weaker moments: Iltud would have to help tonight or she would lose her mind.

It was no use; the waiting and the wondering were killing him. The police could be following him already, waiting to pick him up any minute. How much did they know? They didn't seem to be playing by their normal rules anymore. He knew it was a Friday, but there were dispensations for times like these. Omar Lemani, the last free survivor of Badr's group, was being eaten alive by the uncertainty. It was the isolation, sudden, dramatic and confusing that unnerved him; this was his first time and now there were no older, more experienced brothers on which to fall back.

Night was falling as he made his way to Badr's house. He had to find the cache of memory sticks holding his leader's links to the rest, the resources available, safe houses, money. There would be ciphers, encryption, but that was his baby and he knew most of them already. Ask Badr's wife, his widow probably, what she knew and then vanish. The rain was heavy now, driving people off the streets. His superior had lived in a better area than the rest, mainly semis, not fully colonised yet, nearer the outskirts, with old white residents slowly giving way to the newcomers; those left had little means of escape other than by way of the grave or nursing home, they were the left behinds. But it was still mixed and people kept off the streets, avoiding their other, alien neighbours, especially on a night like this.

The street was deserted. He walked past the house, nothing unusual, curtains closed against the falling night and to protect the modesty of the women within from the eyes of non-believers. He went around the corner and sheltered for eight or nine minutes to see if anyone was about, or following him, as he had been taught. He headed back to the house and up the step to the door. He looked around. No one. His heart was pounding: the exposed, vulnerable moment.

He knocked. Seconds passed. He tried to suppress the worry, the slight trembling spreading through his body from his accelerating heartbeat. The light in the front room went out and the curtain twitched aside, someone was looking him over as he stood under the glare of the external light above him. Footsteps from behind the door. Someone must be peering through the fish eye aperture. He looked straight back and nodded. Bolts and a chain were unfastened and then the lock turned. His hand reached into his jacket pocket to grasp the comfort of the small handgun it contained.

The door swung black slowly, a burqa clad figure peered round and gestured him in. He walked past her as she closed and locked the door; she seemed taller than how he remembered Badr's wife. His arms were grabbed from behind and a huge man in a balaclava and gloves, followed by another holding a pistol of some sort, came from the front room door and pinned him, while what was now obviously a man dressed as a woman pulled a gag across his mouth. His shock at the speed of it stunned him. Within seconds, it seemed he was bound and gagged, kneeling on the floor in a back room alongside a woman, presumably Badr's wife, and a younger girl, the concubine servant Badr had brought back from Iraq, a devil worshipper he had said, borne to serve, supposedly now much more biddable than his wife.

Who were they? They didn't speak, just quickly searched. They were in a hurry he could see, fearing every moment they stayed could result in their discovery and entrapment. They had clearly been rough with the wife, as her two swelling eyes showed, but the pile of laptops, phones, passports and memory sticks on a nearby sofa indicated that they hadn't been wasting their time. In three minutes they were satisfied or felt they had to leave. Some sort of message was received on one of their phones; the one reading it gestured frantically to the others. There were four of them at least now he could see. They turned off the light in the room and motioned to their prisoners to keep silent. One raced silently upstairs, one stayed by the door; the giant retreated to the front room while the burqa-clad one went back to the front door. He realised they were repeating what they had done to him.

The front door was knocked on and he could hear a muffled voice. The door was unlocked and opened as before. "Sorry ma'am, Police from the local station. We hear a man, registered as dwelling here, one Mohammed Badr, may have disappeared. Your husband, yes, may we come in?"

The speaker clearly didn't wait to be contradicted; he simply walked past into the hall followed by others. The door closed, "Oh sh…", moments later three men, two in plain clothes and one Asian-looking and in uniform, were led into the back room at gun point. Three of the masked men, all armed, one with a small submachine gun and two with long nosed handguns, were securing and gagging them, relieving them of radios, two pistols and their official identification: all disappeared into the holdall with the computer equipment they had already gathered. The phone buzzed again. The man read the message and gave the others the thumbs up. They must have an accomplice in the street outside, spotting for them.

Two went out of the room, leaving the large man with the machine pistol. There seemed to be a muttered, rapid conversation. Two masked men returned, one holding a discarded burqa – he looked Mediterranean or possibly middle-eastern he thought – and a plastic jerry can. He felt fear, real terror, now. He could see the other prisoners, other than the young girl who looked utterly broken, goggling as the realisation dawned. The giant and the third one dragged out the girl and the uniformed officer through to the back of the house. They came back for the plain clothes men, who tried to struggle, but were powerless, and took them away too. The olive skinned one covered the remaining pair with a gun which he could now see held a silencer. 'So, this is it what death looks like when it comes,' he thought. 'I didn't do anything! I'm just the errand boy!'

The giant had removed the can lid and was carefully pouring it around the room, trying to avoid splashing himself. The dark one, the devil he could now see, came closer and suddenly turned and without a sound shot the woman beside him through the forehead. Her body snapped back, slumping against the now bloodied wall behind her.

The devil took off his mask and looked him in the eyes, "For their untold numbers, we remember," and shot Omar Lemani through the right eye.

Art poured the rest of the can over the two recumbent corpses, and dropped it by them, as Georgy replaced his balaclava and left the room carrying the holdall. The smell of gas was becoming pervasive. They opened the back door, having locked the front. Good. Their transport was in the back alley. No one about. The four tied figures were pulled outside and the door shut. The girl was lifted by the giant and carried, lying limp as a rag doll in his arms, through the yard gate into the waiting vehicle. The boot swallowed her prone form as the lid was replaced. The remaining three, the discomforted policemen, were dragged up the garden path, rolled on to their fronts with their faces in the dirt and told in hushed, urgent tones to keep down. And with that they were gone.

The timer was set for ten minutes. For a short while people would think it a gas explosion in a poorly maintained house until they found the bound men who would almost certainly be badly stunned by the blast. With a modicum of luck they should survive it, if they kept their heads down as they had been told.

By the time the house went up, they were far away enough not even to hear it with the radio off and windows down. They had to risk the motorways this time, to put as much distance between them and the house in as short a time as possible. They were running out of disposable getaway vehicles; another twenty minutes and they would leave this one burning in a field, headed back to their away-from-home refuge. This time Alan was determined that nothing, no one, would stop him returning to his life, far away from this field of death. The mood had even seemed to prompt a subdued protest from Sam, the most laconic of them all.

"We nearly ran out of luck there Alan, those cops could have had us. We didn't have time to get ready. Sure, that monkey thought he knew what he was doing, hiding around the corner like that, giving us time to get in and wait for him, but what if those cops had arrived ten minutes earlier? How many traces did we leave behind? We need to disappear for a long time or I'm done. What's the plan for the girl?" Almost a soliloquy for him really.

"I don't know, but we couldn't leave her there like that. You know what's happened to her at their hands. Where would she go?"

Art and the one known as Sam seemed to take that at face value. Georgios Tredare had no doubts other than about his leader's ruthlessness; he had enjoyed it. Alan noticed he was smiling, that worried him most of all. To distract them he cracked a joke, "Well Georgy, that's four blokes you've entrapped with your dark, come hither eyes this evening."

She helped Martha get dinner, feeding her son and putting him to bed after a thorough clean: he was exhausted from the day's thrills. Sally knew he would be up early, but that seemed to be the way here, as with all agricultural communities. Iltud had been noticeable by his coming and going, as if trying to avoid a conversation with her, and then his wife had mentioned causally that they had invited the Doctor, Gillian, around for dinner, along with her husband Petroc. Sally pretended to be pleased at the additional company, but it seemed they were stymieing her opportunity to ask any meaningful questions. Well, she wouldn't be put off and anyway, as an incomer herself, Gillian would understand.

As Iltud went to admit their guests, Martha explained that Petroc's first wife had died of cancer; there was no treatment for it here or even diagnosis until it became obvious. She had been looked after by Gillian, who later married the widower. She had been a little shocked by this, but Martha was clear that people living here were more practical in some ways about grief and life beyond it; there were none of the illusions conferred by the miracles of modern medicine that death was somehow beatable.

She was introduced to Petroc, a small stocky farmer, slightly younger she surmised than his second wife. He was quiet in her company, as old West Country farmers tend to be; it was hard enough to get some of them ever to leave their farms other than for weddings and funerals. Gillian was smiling, re-assuring; enquiring politely after her and her son, expressing her disappointment he wasn't allowed to stay up with them. All very nice, but she seemed anxious, as if she knew she were really here to discourage their house-guest from being too inquisitive or excitable.

Fish on Fridays of course and it was Lent, Lenten grace first, then the fish, with last year's apples, cheese and home-baked bread to follow. A little cider or beer, and then they were sitting drinking tea. Small talk, local matters, the air of evasion becoming more apparent with every passing moment, she was building up inside, frustrated beyond self-control, about to explode with demands for answers…

And then. "Now then Iltud, Sally needs answers and you can't put it off any longer. It's only fair, she's my guest too and she deserves to be happy, so out with it!"

Martha was wearing a smile she could see, but there was serious intent in her eyes. The Doctor smiled nervously, her husband looked at his feet.

"But the Seigneur said…"

"Bah, he's young, inexperienced, born into authority, he's never been a stranger lost in another land. She found us, evaded them and brought a little boy. She's meant to be here with us, but how can she feel at home if we shut her out?" Martha was working up a real head of steam here; Iltud was looking like he knew worse was coming. "If you don't, I will, even if that means I get into trouble. Gillian here will help, won't you? But you can do it better and avoid the embarrassment of the Steward's wife being up before the Seigneur, so it's up to you."

He looked like a man walking out on to the icy surface of a pond. "You shouldn't have taken her to the warehouse," he heard the ice splinter beneath him, looked at his wife's expression, it was cracking fast now, and fled back to the shore. "Oh, alright, as much as I can, but there's some things…"

"I can tell you some of what I think you want to know, not everything, some I won't be party to myself. I'm just a farmer and Steward of a small parish, not in the highest councils. You were asking about the warehouse?" He cleared his throat, as if embarrassed. "I believe Brother Peran has treated you to a poetic history of our land as he does all incomers who are unwise enough to ask him." He was smiling thinly now. "So, I won't waste your time on that any further unless he missed anything? No? Well, see if anything occurs to you later."

"When we first started going back into Logres, seeing some of the wonders there which we wanted to bring back and also those we learned of from our new friends from the Middle Sea, we understood the importance of money to secure these things. We have little here of value, at least that the outside would trade for. We have barely enough gold and silver for our own needs, and no means to produce more. But we do have excellent fishing grounds, especially lobsters and crabs in the bay, finer than most available in Logres because they have never been over-harvested. So, we carefully began to export them, finding a local fisherman who became our agent on the outside; he secured a good income and as he had a relative here he thought he had lost, we knew he could be trusted. We tried to sell other produce as well, but there was little demand, so we were making some income from our fisheries, enough to start bringing in and constructing a railway, some modern inventions that could work and be maintained here, medicines…"

She couldn't hold back any longer, "What about those weapons, they aren't for hunting or pest control?"

"It depends what you are hunting, but yes we started to increase our defences, most of all in the last dozen years or so. We had some wealth now to invest in trade with our new friends, to improve our buildings, our farms, our health, but only slowly. And then he came and saw, and was trusted. What was agreed I can't say, but he left, and then we began to import through our friends from the Middle Sea more new goods, purely for trade with Logres, items highly taxed there on which we could make a good surplus. He helped us, knew the right people, so that none of it could be traced back to us, and then the wealth began to flow and we could do the things we needed more quickly, and begin our work outside."

"My God, you're smugglers! Is that what was in the warehouse, drugs? Please no… I don't believe it!"

The others just waited, stony-faced, leaving it to Iltud to find the words. He nodded miserably. "Yes, we smuggle, just like the forebears of our neighbours in the outside in former times, but not drugs, not things illegal in Logres, only those highly taxed where the government keeps most of the surplus. We do not touch drugs. Mainly cigarettes and tobacco, light and easy to transport, very profitable and easy to sell, less commonly gold and silver, antiquities and old things of value, fuel sometimes, that's all, nothing bad, I swear."

Sally looked at the others. Martha was all business, Petroc didn't seem to see what the fuss was about, Gillian was blushing. "Gillian, how could you go along with this? How could you? Is he telling the truth, no drugs?"

She nodded. "I know, it took me that way when I first found out, but that's how they found you by the barrier, they were sending out a few cartloads of cigarettes when they heard the sounds, came to look and discovered you and your child. If they hadn't been smuggling, no one would have been there in time."

Sally didn't know whether to laugh or cry, the relief of it compared to her worst fears; it was like something from Compton Mackenzie. They were smiling now, as if the worst were out and she hadn't exploded, the smiles becoming grins, she began to giggle, it was just too absurd, and she a policeman's wife. It was a wonder their laughter didn't wake her son.

They calmed down over another tea. The mood was lighter in the room now, the storm had broken. "But those things you need those terrible weapons for, what are they?"

"You know we call them the Guardians. If they have a name for themselves or if God or the Devil does, we know it not. We know little of them, where they come from, where they go, what they are. They seem to avoid large armed parties with lights, but hunt the weak and the defenceless as they press in; trying to break the barrier, but it holds them and always has. However, when the barrier is weaker, when it is pushing out, expanding, they seem to become more furious, more active. They must take several of those who would otherwise find us each year, but we do not know how many.

"Only once have we cornered one, when I was a boy. One seemed to break into the world, the outside world on the moor and spread terror, killing hundreds of sheep in its fury. Fearing what its presence could lead to, the Council decided to track it and end the threat before the outside world could. They sent our best hunters out and they searched just beyond the barrier and found where it lay up in the day when it was not out hunting. They dug a great pit and covered it with heather. The fog was thick that night and the creature fell into the pit, it was leaping up, trying to escape and it very nearly succeeded. The hunters, fearing to draw attention by firing their weapons, poured fuel into the pit and set it alight before piling the earth back on top, they then fired the surrounding moorland heather to hide their traces and returned. One of the hunters told me that it looked like a great starved black dog, with orange shining eyes and a coat of shimmering black, almost indistinct in the mist. Those hunters are all passed now; it was a long time ago. That's all I know, I swear."

A pack of feral dogs then; she had heard the stories from her early childhood, the Exmoor Beast the press had called it, speculating it was an escaped black panther. And then it disappeared and the killings stopped suddenly. "So, we are safe here, they can't get far this into the Pocket?"

He nodded his answer. He was opening up at last, if somewhat reluctantly, goaded on by his wife. "Why is everyone so ecstatic I have brought a young child, what's so special?"

Gillian laughed. "It's not what you fear, some sort of secret pagan cult lusting after the blood of young children." Sally crimsoned in embarrassment that they might think that was her suspicion, it hadn't even occurred to her. "It's just that most who come here are people like me, refugees from life, damaged, older, unable or unwilling to have children, or they do not meet the right partner." She smiled at her husband. "It must be over seven years since the last child came here; it is regarded as a blessing and augurs good fortune, a sign of better times ahead, that's all."

"And this about 'being touched' whatever that means, before someone can leave?"

"It's true," added the Doctor, "I've not been, have not asked. Why would I want to leave?" She looked at her husband. Real love there thought Sally, I'm happy for her.

"Few ask for it, many of those who do are refused. Some who do not ask are asked to receive it. It is our way; our leaders' wisdom chooses who is least likely to go astray in the outside. Martha and I haven't been asked; Petroc has, but refused."

"Why would I want to go outside when all I want is here?" Yes, real love she thought.

"Very, very few incomers ask. Most are fleeing the outside; they don't want to go back. A few are asked when they are trusted, after many years. You know about the others who ask and are refused, yes?" She nodded. "The touching requires the blessings of the Abbot and the approval of the Duke himself, it takes place in the presence of some ancient relics, and only happens on Easter Day at noon. Why this is, I again know not. That is all."

"Relics, what relics, even Catholics stopped believing in them years ago? It all sounds like mumbo-jumbo, there must be more you're not telling me."

He shrugged his shoulders in resignation and looked at his wife. "I did not say you would believe, but I've told you all I know, that I swear." He seemed to view that as the ending of his obligation to give her the answers she wanted.

"Just one more please Iltud. You say you have spoken truthfully? Then tell me about the man from outside whom you and Brother Peran have mentioned, the one who came fourteen years ago, met the Duke, was touched and left, and has since helped you with your criminal activities." She instantly regretted using that word; it was snide and unlikely to help coax him further. He winced and looked at his wife again.

"I can tell you little more. It was as you say, that's all. It is not encouraged to gossip about it, the Abbot says it's unholy."

"But Brother Peran said there was prophecy, talk he was a man sent back. That's nonsense, isn't it?"

His face was flushing with anger now, she was being unfair. "Let monks and priests have their prophecies, I have to live in the world of today, as it is, as should you. All I know is he was a man, a good one with a dying spirit they say, who came just before one Easter, met the Duke, was touched and left, that is all."

She felt spent, as if all the burning questions and fears had evaporated, leaving just a few fading embers to blow away in the breeze. The cheering thing was that they had seemed easier, more ready to share information, even if so much had ended in frustrating admissions of ignorance. Most of all, her hostess was starting to treat her as one of them, who had rights, who should be respected as an equal. She had no doubt that Iltud would not be far behind, in so many things it was becoming clear that his wife led the way.

Just before she went up to bed, Iltud caught her eye. "Because of your blizzard of questions, I forgot to give you the important news, the Council want to meet you on Monday in the harbour, St Josephs. You've no choice I'm afraid, that's the way it is. We can help you prepare over the weekend and I will take you down if you like."

Helena's door phone buzzed. She went over to the camera screen; it was him, alone, just standing there as if he had all the time in the world. She pressed the door release and watched him come into the foyer of the building. He would be knocking on her door in two minutes; she smiled. He was late, most unlike him. She realised she was excited to see him, spend time with him again, to hear his, their, news. She went to the hall mirror and looked at herself, ran her hands over her dress to dislodge any invisible creases.

She knew she was still attractive to men, still a few years to go to her forties she reflected. She couldn't bear to let herself go, get sloppy; she was too much of a control freak. She had made an effort for him, for friendship rather than desire's sake, although she knew that lurked away in some subterranean passage deep within her, waiting its chance to coming screaming out and damn the consequences. The others, they want what they see in me, power, wealth, elegance perhaps, even looks, things for them to enjoy, to possess. Unlike him, who wasn't at all interested in any of those things. His motives were entirely different, if only… Her doorbell rang. Stop, pull yourself together, you're acting like a schoolgirl on a first date.

She opened the door. There he was, standing in that way of his, smiling that slight smile, waiting silently for her permission to enter. Always the same. She motioned him in and closed the door. "No one followed me here," he said as she took his coat, not remarking on the metallic weight in one of the pockets. A habit she had picked up in recent years, an almost instinctive desire to check.

She led him through to the kitchen where they would dine. He seemed to prefer the informality of eating there, as if it were a family supper in his own home. Part of her wished it were, not only the part she had just thrust back into its locked lair.

He refused the glass of wine she offered him, apologising for having to go back to work later, then apologising again, more profusely this time, for being late and keeping her waiting. She would not drink on her own, so poured them both mineral water. He looked up at her again; his smile was back and his eyes were studying her face for any sign of thought or emotion. It really was disconcerting, almost flattering, this scrutiny.

"You saw of course. Pleased?"

"Of course, as long as they are safe."

"They are, no one has a clue. Innocents hurt, some killed, sadly, but not by ours. It's miraculous to me, they had to improvise quickly. We owe them so much."

The cynical professional side to her had to have its say. "As does the Board of the company targeted I understand, only they want to pay off their debt in specie."

"I know, they mean well; it's all they understand I suppose."

He suddenly looked tired, as if the stress he must have been shouldering, like a giant piece of blotting paper absorbing it from those around him so they could focus on the task, had suddenly sucked the strength from him. She knew from her own life that a sudden successful conclusion to something long pursued could wash away one's energy in a flood tide of relief rather than exultation. She reached out tentatively and put her arms around him, holding his still form close, her head on his shoulder. She didn't, couldn't, find the words, rarely could with him. She pulled back, "Come on, let's eat, too much longer and we will be using it as footwear."

A shell-shocked Andy Bowson and his two colleagues were recovered by the emergency services twenty-five minutes after their captors had left them. Stunned by falling debris, lightly burned by the fireball that passed over them, they were ambulanced away to the nearest major casualty department before they could collect their concussed wits and explain what had happened. A police car followed them back to the hospital, as a consequence of their bindings it was clear to those on the ground that foul play had been involved.

By then, the fire and explosion had done their work. The roof and floors had collapsed, bringing parts of the adjoining property with them. The smell of gas had been noticed by the neighbours, the report of which delayed the fire-fighters' attempts to get in at the heart of the fire due to the fear of subsequent detonations. The smell of gas had even masked the sickly-sweet stench of burning flesh as the secondary petrol-driven inferno fought furiously to consume its victims before the firemen could douse the flames.

It was concluded later that night, when Bowson and his colleagues were recovered sufficiently to sketch out what had happened, so far as they could recall, that the chances of decisively helpful evidence being recovered were very low but not hopeless, given the advances in forensic science. However, the details could take days, if not longer, to establish. The men who found the appallingly burnt bodies under the rubble, hardened as they were, were of the view that it would take far longer for them to forget what they had found.

She had thought her evening with him was coming to its conclusion by the way his words ran out until she was speaking twenty for every one of his, as if she were trying to delay his departure as long as she could. He was drifting away into thought again it seemed, tuning out almost without perceiving it. This was not the usual him, normally she had the whole of him when they were together: it had always been a comfort.

"They had to go back, to another job. They may still be there, hopefully they aren't; with any luck they'll have done it and left it well behind them. It was a fearful risk."

So that was why he was elsewhere. Had he only come around to distract himself? He had noticed, seemed to read her thoughts again. "I wanted to see you anyway, I've missed you. I fear I have asked too much, but must continue to ask more."

From anyone else, she would have written that off as BS, but not from him. "Why? What's so important?"

"Loose ends to be cut off, things to be recovered, I may need your help with that."

She didn't need to answer; he could see it in her face already. "Let me know what and when? Please? And let me know when they are safe?"

He nodded. A broadening smile creased his face for the first time since he had arrived. "Oh, by the way, I hear the Salvation Army may be thinking of asking you to become an adviser, trustee or some such. You've been a huge help to them, not just the money."

He got up to leave. As he put on his coat he did something he rarely did, he kissed her cheek in goodbye. "When I know more... perhaps dinner on me tomorrow, if you can spare...?"

And then he was gone. She closed the door behind him and leant heavily back on it as if fearing he would return and try to get in. She wouldn't want him to see her crying.

He hurried out into the night and caught a cab two streets away, alighting two corners from the office, walking the rest. She really was a remarkable woman, but not in the way she thought of herself. If things had been different, well who knows? But then again, if they had been, she might not have been interested anyway. He had thought she was past all that for some time now, but tonight he had wondered. He didn't want her wasting herself on him, but if she wouldn't or couldn't complete her life with someone else, he would have to help her fill it with other things of value.

Martin Dager was still in the office when the call came in, as if the breakthrough would come because the hidden connection would reveal itself through sheer ennui, worn down by his unyielding persistence. The office had largely cleared, just the night shift was in, along with a few stragglers determined to win their boss' good favour by their displays of stamina and dedication. He slumped forward on the news of Bowson and Edward's near escape. Fortunately, their injuries were not serious, but by now he was wondering if this case was jinxed, whether they were out of their depth.

He would have to go up to see them tomorrow morning, it would be expected. The last thing he needed, he told himself. His political overlords, especially the Home Sec, rarely understood obligations of duty and shared service. The distraction could cost him time, extract him from the games being played near the centre and lose him what little influence he might have for critical hours. He sighed. His future prospects were fading before his eyes. They would have the ideal excuse to red circle him, shunt him aside in some back-water until his pension came up. All he had worked and striven for, all the years, ending in empty failure. The bitterness, the frustration, was burning him as it coursed through his veins. He emailed his superiors, briefed the Duty Inspector and left for a short and disturbed night's sleep.

She lay awake, unable to sleep. Helena dreaded the weekend that was upon her; she no longer had an appetite for the things arranged, the people to see, work to review. Still, hadn't he asked her to dinner? She wasn't quite sure now. What she did know was that she couldn't keep going on like this, she had her pride. Anyway, what had he meant about the Salvation Army? Sure, at his prompting she had started to donate, large sums, then larger, over half a million last tax year. It went back to the checks she had once run on him; it was one of the many things that had intrigued her. He was giving over twenty per cent of his income to them, eye watering given his salary. And that wasn't the only good cause either.

At first, she had done it for him and consoled herself with the tax advantages. And then he had invited her to spend an evening with him, on the streets and at a hostel for the homeless. She had seen and heard about it of course, stepped over the bodies, hurried away when approached, but never confronted it, them, as human beings, not so different from her in most ways, utterly apart in others. She hadn't been shocked or even surprised, but perhaps for the first time she had seen clearly down from the ivory tower that had grown beneath her feet almost without her noticing, had seen how easy it was to fall between the cracks in this huge wealthy city and to be ground down with the dirt and dust. And there they were, working for peanuts between the cracks, pulling them up, setting them on their feet, not judging, not indulging them either, for a faith she didn't possess.

So, she had started helping in small ways, donating money, advising on their funds, getting drawn in, and all the while he had been there, encouraging her. Together they had found a further way to help, to change lives even more fundamentally. Now she wondered, what was he up to, trying to manage her life for her? She should resent it she knew, be outraged by his presumption, but she never could sustain anger towards him for any length of time. In truth, it was touching that with all his concerns and responsibilities he was investing that much energy in her… well-being. She stretched out and relaxed. Her sense of humour returned, she really needed to get a grip.

Saturday

....

Dager arrived at the hospital just before nine the following morning. Sleep was becoming a rare and fractured commodity for him and in the end he had given in, got up early and driven himself on the theory that the sooner he got there, the sooner he got back in the office, and the less the potential damage.

He looked terrible thought Bowson, almost as bad as me and it took an explosion to get me in this state. That unfamiliar feeling of sympathy for his boss seeped back. He might be doing it out of duty rather than genuine empathy, but at least he had made the effort, arriving early on a Saturday. "We really appreciate you coming Sir, especially with all that's going on."

Dager nodded at his two men, and then the third, the local man. He wasn't good at this sort of thing he knew. "Are you all well; that was quite a fright you gave us? At least they have put you somewhere decent: do you have everything you need?"

The three of them were in a small private ward on their own, with the curtain drawn, the door locked and an armed guard on the door, with two local armed coppers patrolling the grounds outside. No one was taking any chances. The local constable, of Indian Parsee descent, was clearly a little overawed by the company, especially when Bowson introduced him to Dager. "A good man Sir," he had said deliberately audibly so the other would hear.

"We'll be out of here tomorrow I hope and straight back to work if that's alright with you Sir? It's personal now. That's twice they've got away from me." God, he was laying it on thick, but his superior seemed to need it, and anyway, what was waiting for him at home? Edward was glaring at him; he clearly felt he had earned some R&R.

"Very commendable, you'd be welcome, but it depends on the doctors. What's the prognosis?"

"Some light burns Sir, bumps and bruises too, some concussion and temporary hearing loss from the explosion. We were lucky."

Dager grunted. "Are you up to telling me in your own words what happened, what they looked like? They got away again, they know what they are doing it seems. Not like the rag heads… Oh, sorry." Dager blushed and nodded his apologies to the constable lying in the next bed.

"No offence taken Sir," came the response, "I couldn't agree more myself; they looked like highly trained, experts to me, if that's worth anything. I've an even lower opinion of the rag heads than you."

The junior was clearly blossoming in the shared complicity of the aftermath. Of course, realised Bowson, the Parsees, the Zoroastrians, had been butchered, persecuted and driven from their homeland in Iran for the last fourteen hundred years by Islamists; there can't be any love lost there.

So, he went through the scenes, the what-ifs, the might-have-beens of the previous evening with Dager. "To be truthful Sir, I feel a bit of a fool to be taken in with a trick like that, the one with the burqa, but he did have a middle-eastern complexion about the eyes and wasn't tall. They didn't want to kill us at least; they could have done so easily. I wish we could tell you more, but they were good. Perhaps forensics might help, maybe the other prisoners? We didn't see them bring the man and woman out with us, but we had our faces in the dirt, they must have taken the girl with them."

"What seems to be a man's and a woman's bodies were removed from the remains of the house a few hours ago, not much left I'm afraid. No trace of the third… A girl you say? We think the woman is

Badr's wife, the man not sure, maybe Badr, maybe someone else. No record of a girl living there although one of the neighbours said she thought there was a foreign looking girl there who never seemed to go out of the house or speak any English. Why take her and kill the others?"

"Can't help on that Sir. I'm sorry, it's a bit of a mess."

Dager looked lost again. "Well I'd better get back, hope to see you better and back soon."

With that he was gone, handing over some grapes and chocolates clearly bought somewhere on the M40, almost as an afterthought. Bowson felt another pang of that unfamiliar sympathy for Dager; he was going to nail the bastards who had done this to him.

She was shrinking back, terrified. Not surprising thought Sam. Four masked men break into where she's living, beat up the woman she's living with, wave guns around, tie her and the other woman and man up, capture another three and tie them up too, drag her and the three newcomers into the back garden, chuck her into a car boot and drive off, leaving her in the pitch black for several hours, including another vehicle change. Then they bring her, still blind-folded, into a strange house, untie her only to chain her to a radiator in a darkened and locked upstairs room with a little food, water and bedding, and disappear. At least she didn't see the executions, we spared her that, mused Sam.

How old is she, fifteen, sixteen? Could be more, could be less; so thin and malnourished it was difficult to tell, lots of bruises though, at least those on those parts of her showing. Didn't seem to speak a language any of them knew, just whimpered quietly really. What had they done to her in that house? Poor kid, if it'd been me at that age, what would I have done? Flown at them as they untied me and tried to rip their hearts out, but I'd always had a fighting streak. He had seen others like her on the streets, in the homes of his youth, not quite as bad but bad enough. Filth, he wished he had pulled the trigger on those other two himself.

Poor kid. He was almost taking ownership of her. He had brought up more food, drink, some clothes, a bucket and loo roll, a bowl of warm water and soap, towels, even a comb. But he couldn't help wondering what would happen to her, what was to be done? She was a problem, a big one. Not even Georgy would dare suggest the most obvious course of action, at least he hoped he wouldn't, and he would have him and Alan to get past first, probably Art too. Where could they take her? Maybe he could help? He was on his way anyway; he would know what to do.

He tried to coax her, if they could find out more about her, maybe that would help their decision. He washed her face and hands with the warm water, towelling them dry; she was frozen, rigid, as if rigor-mortis had set in, in anticipation of what might come. He tried to comb her hair, but she just shivered in even more fear. He tried to smile: no response, no eye-contact. He retreated and sat on the floor by the door, smiling, willing her to eat, drink, make contact so they could help. At least he had had the sense to not to bring a gun in.

He was still sitting there thirty-five minute later when the door swung slowly open, followed by Alan and then another figure entering the room; oh, he was early. Sam hadn't heard him drive up. He stood up. Alan was hovering by the door. "There's our complication, but what else could we do? Leave her behind in the street?"

"Might have been better, certainly for you, us, maybe her too."

The speaker looked at Sam.

"Has she said anything? Any clues at all? Wonderful shot by the way, well done, Hendricks would be proud."

Sam looked back. Always the right words.

"Nothing at all, Sir. She's almost beyond fear. I think she's been beaten, maybe tortured, possibly worse. See the bruises?"

The visitor said something to her in a foreign tongue. Not a flicker. Then another language, nothing. He turned to Alan, "Can you bring my lap top up please? Also, I suggest you get the others to start packing and cleaning up. We need you safe back home."

He stood there silently, just looking at the girl, almost looking past her at something else; it was quite unnerving thought Sam. Alan came back; he had already pressed the start button. Two minutes followed while the visitor found what he wanted. He started out sounding strange words, one, pausing, another. No reaction. A few seconds later, one, another eliciting the same lack of response. He went on patiently, one after another, until a flicker, an eye movement. He sounded it again, stressing it slightly differently. She looked at him, blankly. Another word, she was looking at him directly now. He smiled at her. Another flicker, no more. It was progress. A couple more words, then three strung together. A little more reaction then passivity again. One more. He shut down the machine.

"Nothing more than trial and error, nothing clever," he smiled bashfully at their wondering faces. "Wouldn't have a clue if she started talking back. Just worked through a phrase book of middle-eastern languages. Tried Turkish, Arabic, Persian, Armenian... I think she's Kurdish, goodness knows what dialect, so many up in the mountains, but I would guess she's Yazidi, war booty of your late friend Mohammed Badr. She won't miss him. How the hell we find a way home for her I'll be damned if I know. We need time to work it out. It's probably best if you take her back with you for a while, she'll be safe enough and well looked after, while I find an answer. Perhaps our other friends can help? I'll write a note for you to pass on when you're back. Well done again; I can't tell you how impressed we are, and thanks for the sticks."

Alan went down and ushered him out shortly afterwards following a brief discussion. Sam, Samson, sat back down to watch. So far from home, poor thing. I wish I'd killed that bastard myself.

And then later, when I chose my new name, everyone thought it was because I wanted to be the strongest, but they got the wrong one. I wanted the name of the other, the most disciplined and the bravest in the hardest of places.

The air-conditioning was turned up full and a radio played local music at a volume just below loud. The weather was beginning to warm up outside, but was rarely other than hot in the day, but even so the aircon would soon make the room cold. Together the sources of noise would impair any listening devices that may have evaded the last sweep.

The three men drinking tiny cups of strong coffee were in a sour mood.

"The news from England is disappointing; it looks like that whole effort has been compromised."

The speaker was an ageing, well-built man wearing the traditional Gulf Arab robes of his class. The man at whom his statement had been directed was clad in a western style suit, but wearing an open collar shirt, running to fat, late forties, with very dark hair and thick moustache. His thick Turkish accented English of the Anatolian interior grated on the ears of his Arabian interlocutors.

"A set back, but we still have resources on the ground and others that can be directed to replace our losses quickly. As you know we always plan for losses, volunteers are not the problem. I believe we should press ahead; their will is not what it seems, whatever they say, they continue to weaken, offer compromise, concede ground…"

"So you say, but too much too quickly could spark a reaction, something which our allies, the useful fools as that damned atheist Lenin called them, and the weak of will, our wealth suckers, cannot contain. They have been surprising in their past, their history demonstrates…"

The previous speaker passed a groan of exasperation at the third speaker, a younger man in his thirties, clearly western schooled from his manner and his grasp of English.

"They are not what they were, not what their parents were and certainly not what their great grandparents, who bestrode the world, were, damn them. We have spoken of this many times; they are ashamed of who they were, have lost their faith in the things that made them great, now their force is spent. Why otherwise would their leaders scrabble for your wealth, send their royal family to beg of you, let you buy them up bit by bit, their properties, their companies, their elite schools, allow us to colonise their cities?"

"It is the slow but sure way, look how far we have come in two generations. Look how we brought your friends to power in your own country by these means, in only two generations. Even Ataturk's spirit could not withstand us." The younger man was not normally one to be argued down, but had met his match, at least for today.

"Wealth and investment can be confiscated in a moment if they awake. That way helps undermine them, I agree, but is not enough. They are already terrified of their growing immigrant populations, that fear is paralysing them. Injecting more fear into them further paralyses any response and emboldens our populations on the ground to demand more rights and special treatment, thus they concede more and more, until there is nothing left other than submission."

The eldest man made his decision. The Turk was a brute, an unrefined son of Anatolian peasants, but nevertheless he was a true believer, even if he thought his people the more cultured. Upstart Central Asian nomads they may have been, even now a quarter of them were heretics or non-believers: Alevis masquerading as heretic Shiites, when everyone knew they were really obstinate pagans, Christian Syrians who still held out after a thousand years in their mountains, devil-worshipping Yazidi too, and here they were telling us how to spread the faith. At least they had exterminated the Armenians and driven the Greeks from their ancient homelands, the rest could be mopped up later. Nevertheless, there were tens of millions of them, and they were growing quickly, they just needed direction from those who could see the longer game. Yes, the use of wealth and fear together would continue, it was working despite the recent set-backs, besides there were many thousands of would-be martyrs' dreams to be satisfied.

He turned to the Turk. "Let it be as you wish. Intensify the efforts. Have whatever you need. Keep our allies, as they think themselves to be, at a distance. When this is over we will deal with them as Khomeini did."

The Turk, as the others termed him, walked out into the street. It felt hot after the chill of the room. He had what he wanted, for now. Now to show these primitive decadents what real warriors could do.

The Home Secretary had them all in her office for nine o'clock: the Chief Constable of the West Midlands Constabulary, the Commissioner of the Met, various other senior officers including the head of the Counter-Terrorism Command, seniors from the three main security services, civil servants, political advisers, all the usual hangers-on. At least, thought Ted Armstrong, the PM's down at Chequers licking his wounds after that debacle over the press release and didn't want another superfluous COBRA meeting.

She had started with a media review, of all things. Talk about priorities he thought! The media adviser was winding up.

"… So, at least initially the media wrote it off as just another gas explosion, unfortunately someone got hold of a video clip showing the three tied up policemen being freed and taken away to an ambulance, almost certainly taken from a neighbour's camera phone. Fortunately, it's Saturday so they've been slower than otherwise in picking this up, but it'll gather strength throughout the day. I'm afraid we're losing containment; it's just a question of when they link it to the other incidents. We're getting enquiries about the identities of the three officers taken away. We aren't commenting, but it's just a matter of time before some blabbermouth in the local force spills the beans."

The Chief Constable shot him a thunderous look and started forward in his chair to protest, to defend his officers' integrity, but was cut off by the Home Secretary. She looked at the CT Command head. "So, what is your latest thinking? Is it connected to the other incidents? And what light does it shed on the interesting theories you so lucidly expounded to the PM at COBRA a little while ago?"

Those reptilian eyes, gleaming sardonically, he thought, pay-back time it seems. Oh well, she almost can't touch me now.

"Well Home Secretary, Ladies and Gentlemen, we should proceed on the basis that these events are all closely linked." No one disagreed with that, at least audibly. "Unfortunately, I.., we, don't think this fundamentally changes the balance of probabilities of the possible explanations, other than the fact that the culprits went out of their way to avoid killing three police officers, appear to have abducted a young girl of unknown identity or background, and killed a female occupant of the property and an unidentified man, possibly her husband, who may have links with the victims of the Birmingham sniping and the NEC shootings."

Somebody, one of the security service representatives, growled a protest. "They were hardly victims, they were bent on mass murder; I can't say I'm shedding any tears."

"And neither am I, nor I hope, is anyone else here today. My apologies, but they were… are, victims of a crime, unlawful killing. It appears that at least one of the gunmen was of dark skinned, middle-eastern appearance which might give additional credence to the splinter faction theory, but the other three at least appear to be Caucasian in origin. Three converts? Possible, but unlikely. Furthermore, the fact that they purposefully avoided killing four people suggests a strong desire not to kill those they regard as innocent in any way. That is highly suggestive that this is not the work of a factional group."

"Whoever it is, they are moving quickly, with considerable expertise, targeted ruthlessness and, most impressive of all, exceptional intelligence. The pathologist looking at the remains found in the house has just reported that one, apparently the female, was shot in the forehead before being set alight."

A number of the women around the room squirmed uncomfortably at this latest revelation but, he noticed, not the Minister; she remained impassive. Keep it going, keep cool. His Lincolnshire accent was almost indistinct such was his self-control. You have the beating of them today. "Consequently, this new evidence might be said to support all the other potential theories equally: the foreign services, the rogue domestic security forces, out-of-control ex-military contractors or a new group of unknown origin; although their motivation, if they indeed do exist, seem to be becoming clearer."

He looked around innocently. "Have either the Foreign Office or Minister of Defence being able to provide anything of use from their sources?" He knew very well they hadn't, at least not yet.

The Home Sec remained impassive, or was there a slight colouring in her cheeks? A low murmuring of people, deciding whether to make their invaluable contributions to the discussion, lit up around the peripheries of the room, making its way as if blown by a breeze to its centre. Just as it started flickering into life around the Home Secretary itself, she stamped on it as a fireman would a spark in a dry bush.

"Thank you," she said, "it seems that you and your colleagues are little further forward than before. Currently at least sixteen people have died violently, and more been injured as a result of this series of incidents, and now we appear to have our first confirmed abduction. It simply isn't good enough, whoever it is running rings around us and that has to stop. Let's convene again at this time on Monday morning."

As he left the room, Ted Armstrong shook his head ruefully. Don't they realise how long these things take? How much luck can have to do with it?

'Henry' hadn't needed to be in the room; at least two attendees would brief him subsequently. He had other things to do.

"Can I come over tonight; I need to ask you that favour?" Her heart skipped a beat. "I'd like to take you out for supper, but you know how hard it is to talk in public, so I was going to ask you over, reciprocate, make you supper, but I won't be back in town until sixish and won't have any time to make you anything decent. I'm sorry to let you down, I know I promised, I'll make it up to you, can you forgive me?"

No problem she had lied, come here like last night, better for talking, she insisted that no, it wasn't a problem and there was nothing to forgive. Was she so excited because he was coming over, or from wondering what he wanted to ask her, or maybe it was the news for which she was so avid? She'd hold him to that. Come over as soon you can, don't even go home, stay if you need, you know I've space. She knew she was babbling again, get a grip. Try not to sound so desperate.

He'd see, but be with her for seven he promised. Three hours to get ready, cancel commitments, now she knew. Start to cook, not cop out again by buying in, get ready and brush up. She needed the closeness, the reassurance of his presence; he was used to this type of uncertainty, people he valued in peril, she wasn't, it wasn't her world. It had been a wearing day, minutes ticking by, time dragging, waiting for news, for him, enough, wait's nearly over. She'd things to say to him. Things she should have said long ago. Things to think about.

Two hours and forty minutes later, dinner on the way, simple and easy; he would appreciate it more, her making it herself. Damn, the door phone's gone. Who can it be at this time? No, it's him and then, the warmth from within. He's come straight here; he heard it in my voice. Now there he is, like every other time, just standing there as if it's his own home and he isn't racing against the clock on a dozen matters of import. Tempting just to watch him there, make him wait a little, see how long it is before he gets impatient and buzzes again, longer and louder. He seems to be carrying something, a plastic bag, and then disappointment, no overnight bag. He was looking up at the camera now, just smiling quizzically as if aware that she was up there, watching him like a voyeur. She reached for the door release and called him in, what had she been thinking?

Two minutes, haven't had time to get ready, just to brush her shoulder length fair hair, pull it back with a clip. Just my day clothes, blue jeans and royal blue cashmere roll-neck. She relaxed again, she must have dressed for him unconsciously this morning; he had once told her that royal blue suited her, matched her eyes, it had been most unusual of him to pass such a compliment. Old, comfortable slippers, her doorbell's going, he must be there. No time to change into shoes. Warmth from within again: he wouldn't mind, maybe not even notice, but it mattered to her. She let him in, he passed the usual comment about not being followed, asked how she was, apologised for being early, but he'd decided to come direct rather than risking her wrath by being late again, handed her his coat, usual unmentioned weight in the pocket, opened the bag and handed her some flowers, just smiling at her, "Peace offering? Am I forgiven?"

Several small bunches of daffodils, looked like King Alfreds. Simple, unsophisticated, inexpensive. Look like they've come from a farm shop, she thought. At least not a supermarket or motorway services, the usual last minute desperate resort of errant husbands trying to make peace when they arrived home. Only he would dare to offer something like this. Among the few indulgences of her wealth she permitted herself to enjoy one was for fresh flowers. She had a woman from an expensive Chelsea florist who changed them in her flat every Thursday; they never lasted well inside a warm modern apartment; bouquets in her kitchen, hall, dining room, bedroom, dressing room, guest rooms when expecting visitors. It was all on account, she never dared look at the itemised bills for fear that they would reproach her for her self-indulgence. They, exquisite, extravagant, helped fill her home, make it feel somewhere to come back to when alone, make it more lived in.

And here he was, smiling now, giving her simple little yellow flowers that a young child would save up their pocket money to buy their mum on Mothers' Day, in the company of a garden of colours and scents from around the world. It was just so him, so apposite and exactly what she needed.

"Come into the kitchen, dinner's on; it's just cottage pie I'm afraid, a bit of salad, some nice ice cream to follow." Summer holidays in the Scillies with her family, the rich flavours of Jersey milk ice cream from Troy Town, the most westerly farm in Britain, another little treat. Yes, the narcissi just matched the memory. "A drink, some wine or maybe a beer? I've got you some of that Hook Norton you like, it's in the fridge and you know where the glasses are." She didn't tell him she had had to trawl three supermarkets to find it since he had called, that's why she was running so late. It took him back to the times he came and went through Brize Norton in the old days he liked to say. He smiled again. He guessed.

He went to the fridge and opened it, his back turned, guard down, vulnerable. Without stopping to think she was behind him, her arms under his, around his chest, head by his shoulder. He started slightly. "We, I, need to talk, this evening, tonight. Not now. I know there's business first, your news, higher priorities, and I don't want to burden your any further, but there's things I need to say, decisions I may be coming to, but I need you to listen before I make them. Do you mind? Please?" There, not as hard as she had feared once she got going.

He turned around in her arms and pushed her backwards ever so gently until he was standing with each hand resting on her shoulders opposite, her arms by her sides, his eyes on hers, almost transfixed she felt. That slight smile was back, unsettling and reassuring together.

"Of course, whatever you need, you know that, you've earned it…"

"I don't want to have earned it; I want to be given it, by you."

Unusual of him to make a misstep, use the wrong words. She must have rattled him; the crowbar of her need to gain purchase had opened him up a little. He looked crest-fallen, as if suddenly realising he had inadvertently wounded her. "I don't know what to say, I'm sorry. Whatever you want, as long as you want it, I promise."

Reckless, he's rattled.

She excused herself to go to the bathroom while he readied drinks. She needed to breathe deeply, regain the equanimity that had been getting harder and harder to sustain with him over recent weeks and months. She'd thought she had had it all under control, and then had realised just this morning there wasn't just one beast deep within, the familiar one that she knew how to lock away, well most of the time, but another, more subtle, more cunning and far more deadly.

When she re-entered the kitchen he passed her a half full wine glass. Moderation in all things, as ever. He had opened a beer, the burgundy and copper labelled bottle complementing the polished oak of her work-tops. He was clearly not intending to go back to work tonight and looked like he had relaxed a little following her unexpected outpouring.

She struck him once more as being really quite remarkable, just when you thought you might have seen all she had to offer, she revealed another new facet, maybe one unknown even to her, almost a lifetime's study in her own right. He asked her to turn the music on, not full, but loud enough. Bach, Brandenburg Concertos, she knew he liked them, kept them at hand. The kitchen extractor was going, whirring away. He started the microwave under the oak counter and dimmed the lights as if planning to seduce a lover. The blinds were down. "Just habit, almost nothing to worry about."

He pulled something out of the bag that had contained the flowers. A small folded freezer bag, wrapped in a rubber band containing some smaller items shielded from her sight by his hands. "They recovered these from a house in Birmingham. You've probably not picked it up on the news: they thought it a gas explosion at first, that's what the press reported, but now they know better and it will be public domain shortly, I'm sure. That's why they had to go back, take a massive risk to recover these."

He was holding a number of memory sticks. "They could be essential, we need to know what they contain but don't have the resources, skills ourselves. I'm amazed he had them in his house, it was complacent of him. You might… your line of work… decryption? But if you can help; we can't read them, there could be two, three, maybe more levels of cipher; not straight forward."

"How soon?"

"As soon as… If there's anything there its value could fade faster than those daffodils I bought you. You know how it is better than I do. But one thing, security is absolutely paramount… Don't take it on if there is the slightest risk of compromise. Please?"

He looked at her straight in the eyes, as if pleading with her to refuse it, but impelled to ask to satisfy someone else. Yes: there was a touch of emotion there, moisture behind the eyes she thought. Yes: the crack into which she had inserted her crowbar earlier was still there, had not resealed this time.

She sipped her drink and thought. Her world was full of secrets, confidences, all challenges to be mastered, learnt. Discovering others' secrets was one of the ways you stayed ahead, usually by cultivating indiscreet sources, nice dinner, few drinks, unspoken promises of favours to be repaid in future, that was the currency. But sometimes, perhaps when the quarry was openly fleeing, when the competing wolf-packs were chasing it through the woods seeking to find it first, perhaps then higher risk approaches could be justified. Certainly illegal, but hard to discover if you were careful, knew the right people and could trust them. Most of the best players did it; it was an unspoken consensus, never look a gift horse in the mouth, especially if you could steal it away at night leaving no one the wiser.

There was someone she used from time to time. Cash only, expensive, eccentric, but hadn't let her down yet. She had known him, them, for five years, they saw things like this as a technical challenge of expertise, not really interested at all in what they uncovered. It's why she liked them. And they were flexible and understood the need for immediacy.

"There's someone. They can be trusted, very good at what they do. I wouldn't use most of them for this; you know the ex GCHQ and NSA ones who realise they can make far more money outside and not have to call people sir?" He grinned; it wasn't quite like that, he knew, but he could see what she meant. "These are a bit more like the ones who stay in, almost a bit autistic, eccentric, out-of-their-depth in the real world. I believe that sort tend to be the best at this line of work? Well he's self-taught, a bit of a loner, lives in a remote cottage in the wilds of the Lincolnshire fens, so he won't be on the official register; at least he's says he isn't and he hacks in regularly to check. He's got a daughter, just lives with her I think. He wouldn't send her to school, said he distrusts official education as brainwashing. He seems to leave his tinfoil hat at home though and is not obviously nuts, just eccentric. She's a nice girl, bit different, but that's hardly surprising. Must be seventeen now. He says she's as good as he is and will be better."

"Are you sure you can trust them?"

"I'm certain I can. They bring two customised laptops, no external wifi or other connections. Just cd's and sticks. No smart phones, just simple old-fashioned pay-as-you-go phones which they constantly change. They will work here as long for as it takes, don't trust offices apparently, finish the task, give me the results on a stick with another copy, wipe and smash the hard drives, and leave everything, computers, the rest, for me to dispose of. They take nothing back, other than the payment, obviously. Very thorough and they don't ask questions: he sees it as undermining the system. If we can trust anyone, it's them."

"Sounds expensive, that sort of thoroughness, how much?"

She wasn't sure, but gave a range. He winced. "They'll be worth it; they could get more if they could be bothered to negotiate. It'll be half in cash, Sterling and Swiss Francs, and half in gold coins, Sovereigns, Britannias, Krugerrands, that sort of thing. He says he plans to buy an island somewhere in the South Pacific off the map, sail there in his own yacht and disappear; she never says what she wants, but seems to adore him. As I said, a bit eccentric but reliable, trustworthy and very good."

"When could they start, sometime next week?"

She smiled at him. "That's the best bit, if they take the job I should think they'll be here tomorrow morning knowing them, for me and for a bonus of course. And don't worry; I have that sort of funds in the safe here. You never know, he may just be right about the banking system as well."

His face was beaming at her now with the glow of admiration. She basked, it was nice to surprise him occasionally. He came up and stood before her, and gripped her elbows in his hands. "I just don't know what I would do without you."

She went to make the call; he insisted she use one of his own disposable ones, while he prepared the salad and laid the kitchen table. She seemed to prefer entertaining him in here, as if it helped her complete the making of a dwelling into her home. By the time she returned he had even got the cottage pie out of the oven and begun serving, "Sorry, I'm famished, been out all day, and besides you've done the hard work."

She smiled. The man and daughter would be here at ten thirty tomorrow, that's all, hadn't asked any other questions other than agree the fee. He seemed so at rest here. She asked him the news, how they had fared, what they had done. He owed her the truth he decided. So out it spilled, the risks, the complications of the girl and arriving policemen, she had shuddered at the passing mention of the killings, the getaway. "Are they safe now?"

"Pretty much, should be at the final staging ground tonight, then the last step when clear to go. They won't take any risks now. The policemen are ok; bit battered and deafened, but will know they were very lucky. The girl they're taking with them, we have no idea what to do with her. No, don't worry, they're not like that. It's a distraction I don't need, we'll try to find a way to get her home safely, but it won't be quick or easy."

And then they had rattled on. Wait until the end of the meal, then start, gently, but don't get distracted. He knows he's in your debt, heavily. Ice cream out softening, main course put away…

"I'm not sure she would like me any more you know."

Sudden, out-of-the-blue, where the hell did that come from? He was looking over her left shoulder, beyond the cupboards and wall six feet behind her. "If she knew, knows…"

He seemed to be waiting for her to fill the void. She'd been preparing, had thought it through, had already found the purchase point earlier, that little crack to open up, gently, tenderly, to get to what she craved inside: him. So seldom did he open up, so precious the moments. Yet suddenly, now, here, totally unexpected and unplanned, complete self-exposure and almost helpless vulnerability. Utterly disarming; the urge to mother, to defend him was over-powering her own plans, casting them aside like dross into the pit. "I never knew her, you know that. What do you want me to say?"

Had he ever spoken like this before? No, sometimes close, very occasionally, but no, not like this. No answer, just that continuous stare into the middle distance. "Why do you say that as if you have done things you should be ashamed of?" She was getting upset with him now. "Why do this to yourself? I'm sure she would understand, support you, and continue to feel the same way, as I do." There, it was almost out, in the light, but still timid. "You do what you do for others, not yourself, to protect them, that's what's important. Sometimes we all have to do hard things, so long as the intentions are good, that's all that matters." Who was she talking to, him or herself now? "You know the story of the widow's mite? That's you. That's one of the things I…"

Edging back into the dark of the cave now, terrified of the noonday sun's pitiless light.

"They, those men, they help you, risk everything. What for? Why? Because of you. They share the goals, the same motivations, sure," well as far as she knew, "they wouldn't be there unless for you. They went back twice, unprepared, volunteered because they believe in you. She'd understand, not even see a need to forgive."

His eyes slid back gently on to her. "That's what makes it harder; what if I… we, are wrong, arrogating things that aren't ours to decide?"

It was like watching a fish twisting on the end of a line being reeled out of the water, struggling to-and-fro in its efforts to escape the hook, but only impaling itself all the more deeply. The irritation was rising again; she was unused to this self-pity. "There's no easy answer, you knew it when you chose to start, but you can't give in to self-doubt now you've got them to do the things they've done for you. I thought you might be mad at first when you told me, you know? I supported you because I believed in you, for no other reason, and now I see you were, are, right, as they do. You owe it to them, us, me… I've not seen the things you have, I'm pretty sure I would never want to. She saw far more of them than me, much more, more maybe than you, but from what I know of her from you, she would still love you… even more."

He looked at her, smiled, the worries suffusing his face receding back to the very corners of his eyes, where they remained, largely sheathed, only their sharp cutting tips peeking out. "Thanks, whatever would I do without you; you're my best friend you know, I'm not sure I've ever told you? Now what do you want to talk about?"

"Later, after dinner, now, pistachio or almond?" Coward, but she needed a pause to regroup.

Andy Bowson, if he had been offered ice cream, would have cheerfully thrown it at the wall of the ward which was now feeling like a prison. The frustration and waste of it. Commencing with the day that was the downer of Dager's morale raising visit, then other visits, official and social, fellow officers, mainly locals; he had then been asked if there was anyone he needed to contact, his wife maybe or his parents. Edward had made frantic dissuasive gestures at the well-meaning nurse who put the question, but the damage was done and his ill humour magnified three-fold. His own parents were gone, his sister on the other side of the world. What about Sally's parents? They had enough to worry about, he would call them tomorrow. What about his wife, well what about her?

He asked to call the local case officer who had given him his personal number with the offer to ring him any time. See if he was serious, call him now, Saturday dinner time. Surprisingly the phone was answered and he was asked if he were alright. He explained. Long silence followed. The man was solicitude itself, relayed his best wishes and then explained progress, or lack of which was much nearer the truth, and then tried to confer a positive and hopeful spin on things, presumably for his sake. To be fair to him, he didn't try to get him off the phone, but explained how they were expanding the search radius on the moor, more locals were helping, and a couple of local amateur pilots were combing the ground to relieve the police helicopter. But he couldn't disguise the fading hopes or the fact that this type of intensive search tended to have a half-life of four or five days at most. Almost as bad, given Bowson's state of mind, the scum who had done this to him had got clean away. The duty doctor who called on his rounds later that evening with an innocent comment about being lucky to be discharged before Monday at the earliest went off duty with a much lower opinion of the manners of senior police officers.

They were ready to leave, later than planned, cleaning up behind them took longer than they had assumed. It always did and for all Alan's faults he was thorough, not in the least relaxed about that. He really wanted to make it back home, the ordinary comforts of family life perhaps acting as an antidote to the moral contaminants he feared he, they, had been exposed to over recent days. He had understood, had promised no more would be asked of them until they were ready, just their call.

The problem was the girl. Other than those few twitches of recognition when he had been here, she remained almost catatonic, having to be fed and watered by hand as if an invalid. At least she swallowed, if only by reflex. Sam almost seemed to have adopted her; he was nearer her in age than any of them, almost as if he were an older brother. Was he surprised? Not entirely, Sam was just surprising really, things from his childhood seem to rise up and sweep him in some unexpected directions. He knew a little about those things, but he suspected there was far more still lying in there: Sam wasn't the talking type, more a watcher and listener, things that made him so good at what he was being asked to do.

Vehicles were a problem now; they had used all their disposable ones and would have to use either a van or the Discovery. Couldn't risk purloining another for what should be just a routine home run. The Discovery had no boot to hold her, too risky then. It would have to be the van, but on a Saturday night, it might look unusual enough for any bored policemen to pull over to break his night shift tedium. Then what to do? Kill him, them, take him with them? More complications to be avoided like the plague. They had taken pains to avoid killing the innocent, no matter how blundering and he at least didn't want to, Sam almost certainly the same, Art, probably, Georgy, hmmm?

No, they had to go tonight. It was probably safer to stay here, even if the relief team would make it crowded, but they had to get back some time. They were owed it. Sam carried her out in the dark into the back of the van. He had removed her bonds and gag, had almost snarled at the others when they queried the unnecessary risk. He had even hidden all the instruments of death they were carrying in case they had to shoot their way out, under seats, blankets, not to keep them from prying eyes but to shield her from any more terror they might inspire. She lay there in the back, swathed in blankets, him sitting next to her like a devoted guard dog, one hand lying gently on her shoulder, not moving, just resting. Neither said a word or moved an inch until the end of the journey.

The flight into Ankara from the Gulf had at least been on time. It was nice to be back on the Anatolian plateau of his childhood, away from the effete and stifling decadence of the coast. The air was cooling fast; it would be near freezing tonight, invigorating, energising; good. Tomorrow was going to be a busy day. They had, more or less, offered him a blank cheque, something a mountain peasant's son could never spend they thought. Well they were wrong there, as bad as the westerners in some ways, their inability ever to learn, they all underestimated him, the others, those with the drive and vision. The airport taxi carried him to his home just on the outskirts of town. The first meeting would be held nearby tomorrow and there would be others in subsequent days, but the first would be the most important.

How to start, what to say. Mustn't be needy, selfish or over emotional. He's as fragile tonight as I've ever seen him, almost frightening, too heavily loaded.

They were still in the kitchen drinking coffee, she could see his eyes were fidgeting towards her wall clock, time running down, wondering how to bid her leave. Nothing for it than to lay at least her first card on the table. See how he plays it.

"I've been thinking, wondering about giving it all up."

He looked alarmed. Did he think she was planning to let him down?

"Why, has something happened I don't know about?"

"I'm not enjoying the work anymore, at least not like I did. Oh, no one's noticed or said anything; we're doing fine, really well. It's just that I would have stopped several years ago, probably, if it wasn't for you. There's still a challenge there, and it helps fill the day, but I feel incomplete, as if I should be doing something else and not wasting my life just making money I don't need or want really. I'm not having a breakdown or anything." I think. "It's quite common in my line; the intensity burns out the desire eventually, especially when money is no longer an issue."

He looked at her as if she were speaking another dialect, if not another language, not fully comprehending what she was saying, recognising the words rather than their meaning. Why should he? He had probably never done anything for money, or much for himself, certainly not for status or position, in his adult life. How could he understand what made someone great in her world and why they eventually lost it unless they first surrendered their humanity, all compassion and altruism gone, and became a machine of pursuit and acquisition? Was he thinking she didn't want to help him anymore, or worse, that she would be no longer of any use to him? The half-acknowledged fear reared over her, her fundamental insecurity with him. It was long overdue that she confronted that fear, killed the beast in its lair, regained the fortitude she had felt melting away as wax around a lit wick over past weeks. Then she might be free to choose again.

"I see. I'm sorry. It's becoming a habit with you these days, having to apologise."

She would normally expect that slight smile when he made a comment like that, but it was absent this time.

"I've been selfish, focused on things, things we have been trying to do, stave off, when I should have been concentrating on people, you especially who has given so much, too much I've feared at times, and asked for so little. I've let you down. What do you intend to do? Can I help in anyway?"

The beast shrank, shivering, back to its lair, bleeding, but not dead yet. The other was alert, preparing to rain hammer blows on the door that imprisoned it, hardly daring to breathe while it awaited the golden moment.

He looked ashamed she thought, back down where he was not so long ago. That chink was a gash now, any wider and his soul could flow out, but could she catch it or would it slip between her fingers and be gone forever? She cursed herself violently for her selfishness; what was she doing, piling more weights on him when he was already bending under the strain? That was the last thing she wanted to do; she wanted to relieve him of them, casting her own aside to do so. Play the final card or work through the hand?

"I'm not planning to do anything immediately, but there are some dates coming up which will enable me to cash in my carry… Sorry, that's slang for my rolled-up investment in the funds we manage. So, I need to decide soon and work towards, whatever I or we decide to do."

There it was, the beckoning card, lure him into the cave, not risk going out just yet.

"I'm sorry, I don't understand. I don't just know enough about your profession to advise you what to do; it would be just empty presumption. There must be plenty of others who are much better qualified, why me?"

He was sniffing at the bait by the cave mouth cautiously, backing away, returning slowly and smelling the air.

"You're still young enough to start a family, have children, build a new life, walk away from all of this… Is that what you want? I certainly couldn't blame you. I'd be happy for you. There must be a queue of men begging for you, you've got everything, they'd be damned lucky."

She snorted. "I've tried, you know that. They just want me for what I am, what they see, superficial things. They don't want me for who I am. Maybe it's my fault, I've been on my own too long, become odd, not used to compromising. Only you…"

Now we're getting to the pinch, the decision to call or fold or turn again. "You know why."

She looked at him brightly, emotions in check for once, those locks and bars were holding. She was willing him to spare her the agony of that big step into the merciless noonday light.

"I'd thought that was gone a long time ago. I thought you understood, knew… Things are comfortable now."

The intensity of his concentration, eyes sweeping through her into the distance again, they were oiling and pulling the bolts, twisting the key.

"They were, I can't express it, explain it. That's still there." She had to be honest, "But that's not what this, this is about."

He wasn't taking the bait, playing with it almost, drawing her out, just looking at her with mournful tenderness, his eyes unwavering. Fold or call. No more cards to play.

"I hadn't realised it, have probably ignored it for longer than I can remember. All this… I'm not frightened for me or the others really, but for you. If anything happened to you… I feel lonely, so alone, perhaps I'm getting old, burnt out, but I'm so alone, except when I'm with you, that's the only time it's different, like tonight."

The bolts were pulled back now, eased by the tears she felt running down her cheeks, but the lock still resisted.

"I'm sorry, I didn't realise I was making you so unhappy, hurting you, that's not what…"

She almost screamed with frustration, the beasts were hurling themselves at the barely holding doors, last card hurled face up on to the table. "Why can't you get it into your preoccupied, romantic James Bond head that I love you? I know you can't be my lover, my husband: I swear I'll never ask, but I want you with me, I want to know you will be there beside me when I need you, when I want a conversation," The sobs were coming thick and fast now, oh Lord I've completely lost it, "someone to see some mornings over breakfast… Someone to work alongside with for things that matter. I'll settle for that, and be happy. Don't you see or am I going mad?"

His stillness seemed to intensify, as if frightened that the merest movement could puncture and deflate her. The emotion had been contained, so contained; he had known she was strong, quite exceptional he always said, but he had never seen this. It had been hidden, secreted so well from him that he had almost forgotten its existence and now it had become an unseen geyser under his feet, hurling him into the air, scalding him in its heat. He frowned.

"Anything but… It's me who must be mad for not having seen. I just don't see how I, my work, my life, can be what you want; give you what you say you need. You know as little of my world as I know of yours, and I have tried my best to shield you from it as far as I can, to protect you. But I promised and I will, let's try to find a way?"

She felt exhausted, utterly drained. He got up and held her in his arms, inhaling and exhaling gently through her hair. She leant in close, pressing in, "One more thing, you promised whatever I need… One day, can you take me there, before we cross the Jordan?"

She subsided into bed. I'm getting too old for this. He had been gone a little time, pleading work tomorrow, needing a change of clothes, the usual. She could have demanded he stay, but she didn't have the energy and it would have been unfair on him. He needed time to re-orientate, consider the consequences of those rash promises. He had held her in the hall for a long time, saying nothing. Later, when he had gone, she had realised that her hair was damp.

"We need to get moving or we'll lose the dark." Art was twitchy, unlike him, the lure of home one yomp away was obviously unsettling him. The farm, their final staging ground before their run for home, was well over a four-hour trek cross-country even for fit men. The ground was hard going, deep banked little rivulets and larger streams, dry stone walls and barbed wire fences to master, steep hills, loosely grounded descents where someone could go tumbling, even without the lack of light.

Too risky to use the roads given the search for a missing local woman and child said the farmer, one of them; they all knew what that might mean. Can't stay here either, they are constantly coming to all the little farms and isolated cottages, asking for help, information. Their relief had just arrived and were packing up to go just before dawn, taking their van with them. Conversation between them was muted, anxious about the next stages of their journeys.

The girl was still dead weight. They all had backpacks to carry, their kit from the past few weeks of absence, and weapons, military rifles that at a distance would be confused for hunting rifles, poachers out for the deer, the least of the police's priorities at the moment. They might be needed though. Sam just assumed he would shoulder her. She was simply limp, mute, unresponsive, but at least calm. When the others tried to share the burden by spelling him, took his pack and weapon, then later tried to carry her, she shrank back, became agitated, until they relented. Sam just bore her along, saying nothing, breathing hard. Another cold night up here, little breeze, clearish skies, the mist was falling. Nearly home.

Sunday, a fortnight before Easter

....

She had slept late, eight thirty, unusual for her. Must be getting old. How many times have I thought that this weekend already? Up, breakfast, quick tidy up after last night, get ready for their arrival. They will have been travelling since first thing, probably earlier. Could be here any minute.

Where had they left it last night? In the cold light of a new day, last night's new certainties, answers, seemed much less clear than they had done. Had he really agreed the things she asked? Not so sure now. He had revealed real emotion, deep feeling for her, more than ever before, but she had become so unwound that she hadn't really taken it all in. Still, the tenderness, the closeness, the hair, perhaps that was all the proof she would ever want. The door buzzer rang out. To business, that must be them, into work mode now.

She let them in, a plumpish bespectacled middle-aged man, his slim teenage daughter, who would be pretty if she could be bothered, jeans, sweat shirts, country coats, almost matching pair really. She smiled fondly, better get the tea on: they won't touch coffee because that's what Yanks drink.

"Good to see you both again, thanks for coming, hope you are well? Tea's brewing. The dining room's all set up for you, here are the sticks. Just to confirm, the standard protocols apply, you take away nothing from here, read nothing, ask nothing, send out nothing, okay?

Can I have your phones now? You will as always get them back when you leave. I'll set up the guest rooms for you if you think you will need to stay. Let me know what you want to eat and drink, and I will try to provide. I'm not going out today, so let me know what you want when you need it? Hopefully, this will bring your little island a few months closer."

Whatever they may be elsewhere, they were always truly professional and domesticated here. Well-mannered even. No tinfoil hats at all. Within ten minutes they were at work, quietly, then conferring animatedly, then quiet again. She always left the dining room ajar when they were here, not that she didn't trust them...

Fifty-five minutes later, a quiet exclamation of success, surely not so quickly? She put her head round the door.

"So soon?"

He looked up at her, then at the girl, then to her screen.

"That's the first cipher broken, definitely another one beneath. Bit disappointing really, it was based on an old US mid-level cipher widely shared with NATO allies, out-of-date now. Someone has tried to customise it, decent job, but a flawed approach. Can we have some biscuits and more tea please?"

Two o'clock has passed. Sandwiches and more tea provided.

Progress much slower now, time dragging, until another, more girlish exclamation.

She went to the door, the girl's eyes fixed on the screen while his were shining with paternal pride.

"I told you she would be better than me one day! Cipher based on squares of Arabic numerals, home-made, but not bad at all. But we've found another below, whoever this is may not be the most sophisticated or expert, but they are certainly thorough."

Another two and a half hours, they will be needing to stay. I was hoping to avoid that, have something to give him, an excuse to see him again, see if it's as I hope or fear. Better go in and see if they want something else to eat. Just as she entered the room, he stood up and made a gesture of triumph, kissing his daughter on the head.

"We'll share that one, she and I, the power of two, eh?"

"All done so soon?"

He nodded, still grinning.

"Based on an old Turkish alphabetic script that's all, a few times removed; simple once you know how. We just guessed they were linked by middle-eastern languages and numerals, looks like the files are in alternate sentences of Arabic and Turkish. Wonder-girl's just making your two copies before we scrub the rest. As you are such a good customer I'll throw in a couple of middle-eastern translation discs for you gratis. Don't worry, we don't understand a word."

She smiled at them and gave them a bow.

"I wouldn't use any one else on this and you haven't let me down, as ever."

The daughter handed her two sticks and two translation discs, smiling bashfully. It wasn't her business to meddle; perhaps she would find her own way without breaking his heart. She went to the safe while they were wiping the hard drives, then taking them out and breaking them with a small hammer on the cutting board. The people down below would be complaining again. When she returned, everything was piled up on the dining table. All they had left were their wallets, car keys, clothes and the phones she returned to them. She handed them the small nylon bag containing their payment.

"There's a small personal bonus in there, recognition for such a good job. It's in Swedish Kroner; I know you don't like the Euro or Dollar."

As she let them out, acting on impulse, she gave a huge bouquet of flowers standing in the hall to the girl, who beamed something new. He just smiled indulgently. She couldn't resist the hope he would let his daughter spend some of the bonus on some nice clothes and a haircut, it was such a waste.

She couldn't stop smiling; he would have to come over to hear her news.

They were past dawn now, on the rolling down slopes into the valley, the wooded hills and moorland thinning out as they descended. They really felt as if they had been walking all night: Sam was near to exhaustion carrying the girl, lurching like something out of a low budget horror film, but she was holding him tight now as if sensing the extremity of his effort to bear her to safety.

Alan watched them from his peripheral vision, worrying that Sam would keel over and topple down into one of the rocky steep sided hill streams, but knew better than try to separate them again. Art and Georgy remained watchful, one just in front and the other behind, should be safe here, but things kept changing and they weren't going to drop their guard at the last minute. They were hungry and thirsty, but unspokenly agreed to keep going, not to stop to eat and drink, not least because Sam would not be able to get up again. On they went, downwards to the valley's head, the rising sun now above the hilltops behind them, warming their backs, encouraging them for one last effort. One last twist in the slowly widening valley, and there it was a mile and a half away, St. Leonnorus, the outermost parish and village, settled only for the past sixty years.

Just a couple of small farms nearer, lying back just off the track, almost fortified. An early farmer, bringing in his few cattle for milking, waved to them and beckoned them over to talk. Alan shook his head and pressed on to the village, they would go straight to the house of the Steward, Iltud, to make their return known, where he knew they would face a fine welcome and better breakfast. And just maybe Martha might be able to help with the girl. Sam, Samson, picked up the pace; he was almost home.

Martha had just started to prepare breakfast when the front door banged open and four filthy, hardly recognisable men stepped in carrying weapons, packs, smiles of relief and one blanket wrapped bundle in Sam's arms.

"Sam," her face beamed her delight to the boy, now man, she had come to think of as her adoptive son. He had been placed with them when he had first staggered in, years before, bewildered, lean, suspicious, almost feral, escorted by a couple of the other "outside boys" as she called them. He had stayed for months and, despite time in the harbour with the monks of the monastery just outside their little capital, then working where he was asked and now one of the "outside boys" serving in Logres, he still thought of her home as his; she still kept his room inviolate.

"Mum," her heart always rose when he called her that, his only true mum he said, "I've got someone here who needs you and your magic, just like you gave me."

She could see he was almost feverish with exhaustion, a tough, even hard, boy, beyond his final limits of endurance. He collapsed into the small leather settee near the just lit fire, still clutching his blanketed bundle with only a small, darkish skinned, almost haggard, childish face poking out, eyes flicking about randomly, trying to take in her new surroundings. Martha looked at the others, almost as far gone as the sitting Sam.

"You three, don't just stand there, take your boots off, speed up the fire, wash up, get changed, whatever. Oh, and one of you go up to the barn at the back and bring Iltud down. And don't go upstairs, we've got new guests, a woman and boy, they'll be down soon enough." By then they were almost cowering at her barked instructions, "Come and sit in the kitchen while I cook up some more breakfast and tell me the news. Sam, I will be out to see you with a cup of tea in a minute? Are you alright there a bit longer?"

His tired smile was answer enough.

Hearing the banging and voices, smelling the cooking breakfast, Sally came down leading her son. The atmosphere of the house had changed in an instant, Martha's tidy home had almost been overwhelmed by dirty, smelly, tough looking men, their weapons and kit carelessly discarded, tired voices mixing with her hosts' in the kitchen, and a young man snoring on the sofa, holding what resembled a child on his lap, rigid and clutching him tightly.

Martha came through with a cup of tea, glass of water and what appeared to be a bacon sandwich, she glanced at Sally and her son just standing there, not knowing what to do and feeling like intruders. She was in no mood for pleasantries, far too much to do, "Young lad, into the kitchen with you for breakfast, if you please."

Then back into the kitchen, "Don't you know any better than leaving those dreadful weapons lying about like children's toys when there's a little boy in the house? Come and put them away somewhere safe this instant."

Back to Sally, "Come through, there's some introductions to make." Through to the kitchen again, "Iltud, get off your backside and make some more tea." And finally, squatting before her adored Sam, "Tell me everything later, my love, all about it, your new friend, but first both of you, drink, eat."

Sally could see Martha was loving every moment.

They all did as they were told and Martha went into the kitchen while Art and Alan put their weapons and kit away before returning. Iltud, clearly seeking to avoid another chiding, had made more tea, cut more bread, and was cooking more eggs, bacon and sausages, as well as handing out more cheese and apples, while trying to have a staccato conversation with Alan and the others. Sally and Josey, briefly introduced, just ate and observed, almost in awe of the presence of these friendly but alarming strangers. Meanwhile, Martha, with Sam's help, was trying to persuade the girl with smiles and gestures to relent her grip on him, sit up on the sofa beside him, and take some water and food. The rigidity was leaving her now and the abject fear receding from her body as her uncomprehending eyes and ears sensed the warm and happy chatter throbbing around the small house, sounds she had almost forgotten existed, sounds that indicated no imminent danger and perhaps better times ahead.

Chaos reigned for an hour before Iltud took Alan to see the Seigneur to report formally, smiling at his Martha's beloved Sam on the way past. The other two strangers smiled at her, got up and went back into the living room and stretched out on the floor rug and promptly lapsed into an exhausted, relieved sleep. Sally and Josey were left alone bewildered in the kitchen. Oh well, better get on. "Come on young man, help me clean up."

Martha returned, snorting happily in mock disgust. "Those boys, lying asleep on my clean floor in their dirty things, what do they think this place is?"

She then explained to Sally who they were, that the girl was some sort of foreigner they had rescued, whom nobody could talk to and whom her hero boy had carried for over six hours at night through the hills.

"He's just like one of the knights from ancient times," she had laughed. He could clearly do no wrong for Martha, Sally could see.

Shortly afterwards Alan and Iltud came back with the monk-priest Brother Peran in tow, they had bumped into him as he was bicycling slowly up to the church for morning prayer from the little satellite monastery down the valley where he lived. Sally could see Alan was now at the limits of his capacity, talked and walked out but he was not done yet, he looked worried, almost tearful as he came up to her and asked her to sit in the kitchen with him the priest and Iltud; Martha taking Josey back into the sitting room on his nod.

"Mrs Bowson?" his soft Australian accent contrasting with his formal, almost sombre manner. "I have a confession to make to you…"

Her breathing paused; he was trembling, nerves, exhaustion?

"In the house where we rescued the girl we encountered three policemen. It was us or them; we were in the process of securing vital information from enemies of us all, when they entered the house. We had no choice, no choice at all…"

His voice trailed off.

"What are you saying? Andy? No?"

Brother Peran stepped in. "What Alan is trying to tell you, very badly I have to say, but we can forgive that given his adventures, is that they captured your husband, tied him and the others up and left them in the garden before they burned the house down. They know from the newspapers that your husband survived as they intended, is not seriously injured and is in hospital recovering, mainly from bruises and light burns, nothing worse."

"I'm so sorry…"

"Andy, I need to go to him, be with him…"

"We're sorry, we just don't know what to say, but we couldn't withhold it from you. it is your right now you're becoming one of us."

The meeting, in an obscure office in a suburb of Ankara had just finished and people were leaving, drifting out at intervals and using different exits, keeping it all very unremarkable. He was pleased, his thick moustache wrinkling, wriggling, as it responded to the broadening smile he permitted himself. From this consensus all other actions, to be communicated by further meetings over the next few days, would follow. Most of the key stakeholders were there, by far the most important of all being the Director of State Intelligence, set up and controlled by the party after their coming to power, initially to side-line the distrusted military intelligence services which had always served other agendas inimical to the party. Their remit was internal watchfulness, ideological coherence, but increasingly now the party felt much more secure, furthering their deeper external agenda, the things they never communicated beyond their most fervent and trusted followers.

Even so, some parts of the agenda were simply too sensitive to be owned directly by state employees, no matter how obscure and trusted; besides, they didn't have the resources or broader regional and international support they needed, so these parts were outsourced to an informal network run by their own carefully chosen, ostensibly stepped down, people. Those who paid for it and supplied many of the programmable volunteers, the Arabs consumed with guilt for their wealth and corruption, believed they had the final say. Well, only because we let them. For now.

The events in England had dented his, their, credibility. How many more chances would they get before their backers looked to people they considered more effective, controllable, competent? Not for the time being at least, but he needed something to show for the resources invested. Volunteers, aspirant martyrs, were already heading in, as immigrants both legal and illegal, students on visas, even a few 'business people.' Lots were already there, some had been for years, some even born there but never native. Weapons were already coming into place in abundance. Their border security was a joke. It was now about research, information, planning, it had already started some time ago, and he was good at that. Soon enough something would happen, something bigger than anyone might ever conceive possible after recent events.

Sally felt defeated, the degree of absolution bestowed by Father Peran and her hosts blown away in an instant. There was no way out, no way to join Andy, apologise, make amends, she believed that now, they hadn't been lying to her she was sure. One day, when her son learned of it, he would despise her, disown her, the worst dread of all. Father Peran looked at his hosts helplessly. Iltud left, fearing to add another injury by his inhibited clumsiness with words in his second language. Martha just looked and then nodded to the priest to pick up the thread.

"He brought you here for a reason, He brought Alan to see your husband and make sure he survived danger unharmed," speaking poetically again, "perhaps it is His Will that your husband will join you here one day, in His time. That may seem hard, cruel now, but His Mercy is endless and His ways subtle and beyond our comprehension. There are no easy answers, when all else falls short, all we have is faith."

Martha was biting her lip, that's not the way she would have done it all; she would have talked of her son, his need for her to be strong and safe here.

Her first reaction was hogwash; no loving deity would do this to me, a believer and mother of a young son? Typical of a priest, trying to lever God into everything, why bring God into the brutal deeds of man?

But then she thought of the girl in the next room. She had been taken from her home, family and culture, probably thousands of miles away from here. Her family enslaved, brutalised, exploited and possibly even killed by her captors. Isolated beyond measure she must have given up all hope, despaired utterly, but found the courage and the faith to continue. Then one fateful night, after years of endless torment, four strange men, intent only on killing, had stumbled upon her and, out of pure mercy and compassion for a stranger, knowing nothing of her or what she was, had brought her out of her prison and at great risk to themselves carried her away to another world, into a stranger's house full of kindness and hospitality. Circumstance or Providence: take your pick? Perhaps the priest was right, perhaps not, but again by comparison how much did she have to complain about? Andy had survived intact, that's what mattered: he, she, they, would find a way.

She sat up and looked at the priest. "Father, I would like to go to your service and thank God for the deliverance of my husband, son and I, and pray that He will show us the way. Would I be welcome? I won't understand much I'm afraid."

His face beamed with delight, "Of course you are welcome, all we sinners are. His Mercy sustains and restores all, no matter how cast down." He grinned again, pleased with himself she could see. "You will understand more than you think. We sing in our own tongue, psalms and hymns because we feel it a tongue more suited to lifted voices than English, but we read in English, the greatest of all for the written word, your St James' Bible, your Cranmer's Book of Common Prayer, as I told you before, we bring in for ourselves the best from Logres. Ah, if only Cranmer and Tyndale had sought refuge with us here, what other wonders could they have written in the years denied to them? And, in your honour, I will speak in English, the meaning of the first verses of St. John's Gospel and their relation to Plato's Theory of the Forms! And now I must go and prepare; Blessings on this house!"

Martha smiled at her after his departure. "I don't know what it is about that priest, he always seems to say the wrong thing and yet you always feel so much better for it."

And with that she returned to the living room to dote on her adoptive son and the girl, and to chide silently and fondly the snoring men. Sally, taking Josey, went to the church with Iltud shortly afterwards, leaving Martha on watch at home.

Alan, Art and Georgy couldn't sleep through Martha's persistent mothering and were up and washed well before lunch time. Their hostess insisted on feeding them before they left for their own homes down the valley. Sam was up, guiding his adoptive sister around the house, showing her to her room, which Josey had had to vacate; he would be sleeping with his mother from now on. They ran her a bath and closed the door on her, towels, Martha's dressing gown, Martha's daughter's best old clothes from her teenage years laid out inside.

The priest came in after the return of Iltud, Sally and her son; it appeared he often lunched here after a Sunday service. In a social setting Sally could see his scholarly exuberance was translated into a hilarious bonhomie, a natural conversationalist with a fund of often tasteless jokes. It was obvious that Sam almost worshipped him, as if he had found a new older brother of whom to be proud, alongside his new mum; it was extraordinary sometimes how complete opposites could just gel like that. Alan, Sam and Art had both asked for and taken confession in Sam's old room; Georgy just said there was no time and he would go to his home priest in St Joseph's later.

They went through to lunch, the girl not having reappeared. Sam was becoming twitchy, looking at the door as a shepherd might, who, having recovered a lost sheep, had lost sight of it again and was fearing it had strayed once more. "Mum, do you think she's alright in there, it's been nearly two hours now?"

Martha got up and glided to the bathroom door and put an ear to it. She could make out the sounds of weeping. She turned to the others, "Leave her alone, she just needs time, sometimes you terrify me so what effect you have had on her…"

She had called him straightaway, the excitement breaking into her voice as she told him the good news. He said he would pop round when convenient for her.

"Why any time, now if you want"?

He wouldn't want feeding; she had already gone too far out of her way. She ignored that, anything to prolong his presence... Lord she was slipping already, but she didn't care now that her cards had been played and he hadn't run. He had made that rash promise.

She had prepared a simple dinner, now to change, not too much though, just at home.

An hour later the door phone buzzed, she could see he was there. Just a thin brief case, nothing else, he was moving on elsewhere later, back home? Bitter disappointment, he hadn't understood then?

Her doorbell rang. Two minutes as usual. At least he didn't catch me on the hop this time. She opened the door. There he was, like normal, that slight smile, a little uncertain perhaps, not like normal then? Raincoat, well cut country jacket and slacks, just a country gent, in town for the day and can't be bothered to deviate from the norm; so him. He hands her his coat and brief case, that same unnerving weight in the pocket. He reaches down behind the door and picks up a small overnight bag, warmth inside, he had meant it then. He smiled again, broader, almost a grin really, "I keep my promises, at least try to, you know. By the way there's a small camera blind spot by the porch door, thought I should mention it."

She squealed and threw her arms around him before he could get the door shut properly. He almost went over backwards before he could recover.

"I thought I might have frightened you off, last night, I was such a wreck, not myself..."

"I promised you. I don't know why you bother with me really, you're worth so much more. I worry I'm wasting your time, misleading you..."

"Don't start that again, not unless you enjoy seeing me cry. I understand."

Warmth now, self-confidence flooding back, I couldn't have spoken like this to him only twenty-four hours ago.

"I laid up one of the guest rooms for you, just in case."

She would have got down on her knees and prayed if it had occurred to her.

He followed her into the kitchen where she put the tea on, no alcohol on Sunday evenings, a little pre-work warm-up ritual.

"I can't say how glad I am that you're here…"

You really didn't say that did you? You sound desperate, you're embarrassing yourself. Don't care, all my cards played now, and I think I won.

"I've been thinking, you, we, need an understanding to protect you. Will you hear me out? Please?"

Assent, a smiling compliance.

"The last thing, ever, I would want is to see you hurt in some way. You said you know what I can't give you and that's okay for you; right?"

Consent, slightly less happy now, but content.

"I have to come and go irregularly, no patterns, so no one remarks too loudly, can't be here more than two nights a week. No, I don't want a key, it's your home. I have to travel, disappear into the undergrowth for periods, won't always be able to tell you beforehand and certainly not why. We need to up-grade your security here, just standard form, that's not negotiable; I will put you in touch with someone who can help. And if I ever tell you to run, just go straightaway, plan where you would go, keep a bag packed, somewhere safe until I could come for you. Do you want a firearm to keep here, just in case? I can arrange it."

No, not yet anyway. Alarm now, he was suddenly all business, so unfamiliar again.

"That's the deal, take it or leave it. I know I promised, but only if you listen, can live with it, for my sake if no other."

Emotion in there again, behind the eyes, worry, for her, what he was getting her into?

"Deal."

She stuck out her right hand and grasped his. So cheap a price for what she was getting.

"Do you want them now while I finish getting dinner ready?"

She handed him the two sticks and cd's, he nodded, got out his laptop from the brief case and weighed them in his hands.

"They said it wasn't much of a challenge, something about middle-eastern languages and numerals, and an old US code shared with allies that had been modified, but not very well. Don't tell me, I don't want to know."

Later that night when she went to bed her tears were those of contentment. She had the best night's sleep in a long time, he was so near.

"I'm sorry, Jovanka, I'm sorry, please forgive, please forgive me."

Not there, that was almost the worst.

"Don't punish me; I'm not betraying you I swear, I swore, remember…"

The consultant's room, his composed face, her blank expression, the news, the prognosis, the pep talk of hope, developments, her young body's strength, so much to live for… and, later that evening, her slim lithe figure had twisted around his, gripping fiercely, trying to crawl inside him, for refuge, for rescue like before, temple to temple, ear to ear, neck to neck, flesh to flesh, heart to heart. He had sworn, she had not asked, never asked, never needed to.

"What have you done in my name?"

"I'm sorry, I'm sorry, they need me, they asked me, she needs me, she asked me. I was so blind, I promised. But I swore, I remember every day, to you. Please forgive me, wait for me, don't turn your back on me when I cross Jordan."

Monday

....

Elaine Ferris was at work in her office at just after eight on Monday morning. With all that was going on, the terrible news from Birmingham, the endless meetings, emails and conference calls in London, she felt she owed it to the man she thought of as her boss. Six years they had been together; she had stayed with him by mutual understanding as he moved from position to position, seemingly advancing up the crooked ladder of his profession. She had got used to keeping secrets, evading questions, telling half-truths, it came with the job, as did developing a second skin that she could shed as soon as she got home at night to be with her husband.

He came in late for him, just before nine; he must have been working over the weekend and late last night, she thought; hardly surprising really, given events. He looked tired but happier than she had seen him for some time.

A breakthrough?

No, can't be, the office gossip was of frustration, with no real progress at all.

So, unlikely then.

But the grapevine was saying that he was back seeing his on-again-off-again girlfriend, the city moneybags. She hoped he was, but no…

The after-work crowd, mainly the young ones, used to gossip salaciously about his apparent relationship, adding lurid speculation on top of wishful thinking as all juniors do about their older superiors, projecting their own hormonal preoccupations on to the blank canvases they assumed the old to be. Occasionally she would be persuaded to go along with them, have a glass of wine. She used to get quite irate about the things they said and plead the need to leave. They didn't mean any harm, they just didn't know him. The older colleagues rarely said anything; they knew from bitter experience how hard it was to keep love alive in this game.

Civil servant grades meant little here, it was one of the best things about this work. She had earned his, their, trust and prepared the papers, the minutes, saw his emails, had access to the internal security reviews. That was the bad thing about this place, the absolute inability to keep anything personal. They had open access to your bank accounts and financial dealings, those of your family too, reviewed your six-monthly declarations about important relationships, sometimes checked up on them too. Worst though was the feeling you never knew whether they were listening in on you, whether at home, on the phone, in the car, on-line; she had to renew the right for them to do so each year otherwise she would have to leave, and then they would probably be sufficiently suspicious to keep monitoring her anyway.

Yes, those reviews, including his own, were the worst. Some of her colleagues didn't mind it, especially the younger ones; they almost didn't seem to understand the need for a private life they had probably never known themselves, having grown up in the age of full confessionals on social media and television. His had told her more about him, in some ways, than working closely with him for six years, but in other respects it just didn't get to the essence of him at all. Yes, they contained the factual record of career, background and so on, substantial relationships, finances, all the usual, but not the essence of him.

She knew it was in there, indistinct and occluded, but it was there, if largely unknown to her. Only once had she had a good glimpse; she hadn't realised at the time, only on later reflection when her mind had calmed. She had gone into his office on a personal matter, closing the door behind her. He had smiled at her, sat her down and got her some water, saw she was wrestling with a problem. Her husband, she had croaked, the GP says he needs tests for suspected prostate trouble, his PSA test was much too high, they both knew what that meant. He needed to see a consultant but, in this overcrowded city, it could be six to eight weeks before they even put you on a waiting list and every day counted. They had little money and no private health insurance, her husband was just a parcel delivery man and she a government PA. She knew he had experience of things like this himself, what did he suggest? She had feared to reach into his past for his help, it was none of her business, but she was desperate. They were both less than ten years from retirement, their kids had left home, she was terrified of being stranded, alone.

Through her tears she had thought she saw moisture round his eyes, just for a few seconds, and then a look, a gentle smile of pure tenderness. He told her to leave it with him, not to worry, to go home straightaway, keep the phone with her. Five hours later she had taken the call. She and her husband would be picked up by chauffeured car at 9 am the following morning. Take some overnight things, just in case. They would be taken to a consultant on Harley Street and a room would be arranged at a nearby hospital if needed. No, he didn't need their money. It was all arranged, including payment.

Later, when leaving the hospital after the first course of treatment she had asked one of the administrators who had paid, if it were him. No, they had said, it was a woman he apparently knew, but she wouldn't say who. She had tried to speak to him about it afterwards, so had her husband. He just brushed it aside with a joke about owing her for being such a terrible boss all these years. They had never talked of it again. So yes, sometimes when they gossiped about him like that, she could quite easily have killed them.

She got him a cup of coffee, asked if there were anything he needed. He wasn't in the mood for small talk she could see, no enquiries about her weekend.

Hardly surprising.

She left him going through the reports and status updates, the paraphernalia of modern organisational life. She smiled to herself; this was unlike any organisation she had ever come across and not just because of its secretive nature. Once, when bewildered by its latest shift in structure and remit, his latest change of role, she had asked him about it, what it meant. She didn't even know who their head was, whether there even was one. He had tried to explain it to her: that the threats they were trying to combat were like viruses, ever changing, adapting to counter-measures, inherently flexible and self-replicating, passing themselves off as other non-threatening things to gain entry inside their prey and then eat it alive from the inside, growing at the host's expense, like parasites. It needed a different kind of organisation to deal with such things.

The old organisations, MI5 and the like were institutionalised by their history, good people for the most part. doing good work, but the politicians had wanted to meddle, calling it 'oversight', which meant more structure, bureaucracy, rigidity, the opposite of what was needed to fight the new threats. So, parts of them had burrowed much deeper, out of sight, blended with some of the others and with the fossils of the more autonomous bodies still clinging on, almost forgotten after their hey-days between the forties and eighties.

From above they just seemed to be obscure sub-departments of other organisations and agencies, theoretically at least they might still be, but in reality they were fully independent. They had no settled structures or remits, no single leader, it was more a meeting of minds of key people, resembling if anything the medieval Hanseatics, possessing no constitutions or established obligations, just shared goals and resources when needed. He had smiled at the analogy. She would look it up she said, it might help understanding.

Their funding was untraceable, no direct grants. Even the Treasury didn't have a clue, government office rents and service charges to supposedly private landlords were one of the staple incomes, but there were others. They were flexible. They chose who to suspect, what to investigate, internal and external. They believed if you had the right people, the rest looked after itself; most seemed to be ex-military, some from the other services, others were one-offs, the strays, spotted by someone and now a colleague. So, they burrowed away, inside and alongside the others. They were small, difficult to identify, harder to quantify. He had asked if she were comfortable with this. She had said she thought she understood some of it, but she trusted him with the rest. He replied that he hadn't doubted her for a minute.

Sally and her son were up early, just after dawn, to find Martha and Iltud already drinking tea at the kitchen table, their porridge slowly bubbling away on the range. They smiled at her as she came in. It was a big day.

"Don't worry dear," Martha was always faster to the start than her husband, "they will be pleased to see you. It's more about welcoming you and understanding your needs, what you can contribute, and answering any questions you might have. If I know you by now, you'll keep them busy there for quite a while. Iltud here will take you down and bring you back afterwards, he can help you prepare on the way, explain the sort of questions they will ask, who will be there, that sort of thing. I won't be able to come with you now," she spread her hands in mock despair, "now that he's come back with her. It's probably better anyway; I can look after Josey here for you if that's alright? You'll have to leave well before eight o'clock to get there for eleven, it's over an hour on the train to St. Josephs, and you've got to walk to the Town Hall.

She was starting to get the feeling that her son wouldn't mind a bit, at least during a busy day. She thanked them for their thoughtfulness and said it was fine, and, by the way, how were Sam and the girl? She had still been in the bathroom when Sally went to bed, to the consternation of a near frantic Sam, who seemed to fear that she had drowned herself. In the end Martha had got the spare key, unlocked the door from the kitchen side and had told the men to stay out while she went in alone. There she was, in about three layers of clothes and the dressing gown, spark out in a corner of the bathroom floor looking like a played-out animal. At least she had had a bath and the food and drink left in the room had gone.

Sam had insisted on picking her up, so gently that she didn't awake, and carrying her upstairs to bed. Martha, following, had had tears in her eye: She could see that all he could feel was a powerful compulsion to atone for the things he had done. He lay in the room next to hers, with his door ajar one ear, pricked like a dog, for the slightest hint of movement until even he could fight sleep no more.

"Gillian and Brother Peran are coming around at noon to see if they can help," Martha had said, "if anyone can get her talking it's the monk."

If one thing renewed the child in her, which had been on the point of extinction as a consequence of her life in London, it was that little train ride down to the bay, steam and cinders flowing past the carriage window in its wake, nine stations, eighteen rural parishes before the final terminus at St Josephs. Docco had seen her clamber aboard and stoked his brother-in-law's ire by sitting by them between halts, explaining every facet of his little command and the places they rode through.

It was just like the pictures of the old pre-war countryside she thought, something out of the Titfield Thunderbolt before the full advent of the mechanisation and medication of the countryside. Small fields, high hedges, wild flowers and a plenitude of other life; farm hands working in the fields, working horses everywhere, windmills and watermills churning away.

Hard work, totally inefficient by modern standards, but so human in scale.

All the while Iltud talked like a man possessed, cramming her with information like an anxious teacher with his star pupil before a scholarship paper, derailed occasionally by a beaming Docco trying to be helpful; almost as useful to her in her preparation as all of Iltud's extraneous facts.

Then St Josephs, a small stone and timber station with two platforms, one never used, Docco explained, it was there just in case; he didn't know what for though. The little town, which she now knew had about three thousand inhabitants, was cradled on the shore of the bay between the main valley river and one from the lowest tributary valley, and so was effectively confined to a small peninsular. It was like all other small traditional fishing towns, white washed and plain stone buildings and cottages, a minster church built in a basilica style on the highest ground in the town, a Town Hall beside it and a main street that led from the main road entrance past the two civic buildings to the quayside, lined with shops and inns. What looked like a small low-scale industrial area with a few warehouses and water-mill buildings, among others, lay between the station and the adjoining main river.

The streets here were stone-paved with small, partly enclosed watercourses running down their sides in places. All very scenic, but Iltud was in no mood to tarry, seemingly still irritated by his brother-in-law's chatter he hurried on, leaving Sally to keep up in his wake. In what seemed no time at all they were in the Town Hall waiting room as other people came and went, some looking at her curiously on their way past. The little room's walls were covered in large aged oak boards carrying the stencilled names of civic worthies dating back centuries, all very Ruritanian.

Iltud motioned Sally to her feet and they were led through double doors up to a large plaster walled room that ran along the entire front of the building, with windows facing out on to the main street below. The room contained a huge ancient looking oak table with over a half century of oak chairs around it and a small oak throne in the middle of the far side; two chairs stood on their own on the opposite side, facing the throne. Iltud gestured to her to sit in one, taking the other beside her. He leaned conspiratorially towards her, "Don't be nervous, neither the Duke nor the old man will be here; the others will arrive shortly."

They started to drift in, introducing themselves as they passed her, fourteen were Seigneurs, among them Mark. Seigneur was a largely hereditary office, with principal authority for security matters, one for each rural parish Iltud had explained. Fifteen were parish Stewards, elected annually by their parish freeholders, plus Iltud, her witness and advocate should she need it. Then came the town's Mayor, the Abbot of the Abbey church on the main island and finally the High Steward himself, appointed for a three-year term at Easter by the Duke himself from the other Councillors, effectively the prime minister of this little realm. Apparently, for the Council to be quorate, the Mayor, Abbot and High Steward all had to be present, with at least half of each of the other two categories of Councillors. They met once a week on average, usually Mondays, and had to examine all new incomers at the next meeting after their arrival.

And so here she was, so nervous she was shaking gently. Iltud started by introducing her and explaining the facts of her arrival and her background in the 'outside' and then Mark, as the receiving parish Seigneur, had to report whether or not she was a person deemed fit to be allowed to stay. They at least had the decency to converse in English before her, rather than their native tongue. What happened if she wasn't deemed a fit person wasn't explained; she was asked to confirm what the others had said and then take questions, which were largely perfunctory, the Abbot seeming to act as chairman, his gentle eyes winking at her reassuringly from time to time as if it were just a little act to be played out for form's sake.

And then suddenly, the questions became serious, focused pointedly on her languages, studies and work for the Foreign Office. Was she fluent in Italian?

"Yes."

Excellent, no one else here is anything like competent. Latin?

"Read okay, don't speak it, could brush up though."

Hmm, shame. French?

"Pretty good, little rusty, need to revise."

Good, good… Spanish?

"The same."

Very good indeed, valuable. Greek?

"Very rusty, ancient Greek, not to be relied on."

Shame, but not a disaster, we can get by. Worked for the Logres Foreign Office?

"Low level analysis mostly, trying to understand trends in the countries of the northern Mediterranean littoral, getting to know the motives of the movers and shakers, that sort of thing, certainly too junior for policy or intelligence."

No matter, no matter, still useful skills. Done any official work on the Vatican?

"No, nothing," a peculiar specialism that had passed her by. Funny question to ask? No matter. Would she be willing to revise her skills, put her expertise to the service of all if asked?

"Yes, potentially, but would depend on what I was being asked to do. I have principles and would not betray my country."

Would not be asked, almost inconceivable.

'Only', she noticed.

How did she feel about the export trade, did she understand, object?

"Couldn't believe it at first, so long as it stops at tobacco and similar, no drugs, guns or the like. Hmmm. Never drugs, no, nor selling guns illegally, nor people smuggling, very clear indeed on that.

And then they veered in another direction.

Did she think she and her son could be happy here?

"Possibly, but my husband…"

Ah yes, we understand from Brother Peran…

Him, has he been reporting on me?

He likes you, thinks you are a real asset; he's just a character witness, that's all. Anyway, your husband, a senior policeman?

"Yes, but I would never ask him to betray his duty"

Of course, quite commendable.

"Will you help me see him again, my son… There must be a way"?

In good time, it's in the Almighty's hands, we appreciate it's difficult, tragic even, but we must all be patient.

Had she had chance to think where she would like to settle yet? No? It's probably too soon, but you will need to consider your future here, we can help, provide you with a house, possibly a means of income.

Here Iltud broke in saying she was welcome to stay with them as long as she needed. Remember her child.

Ah, yes. The boy, he justifies extra help, solicitude, a great boon. A school place would be provided in the next village, a small stipend for her in the meantime, but only when she has seen the Duke, sworn an oath of loyalty. Needs to be on an Easter Day, if not in a fortnight's time, she will need to wait another year. That's the rule, no exceptions. Think on it.

"What about being 'touched' so I can come and go"?

Out-of-the-question, only if she proved herself over time, an honour that has to be earned by great trust; her skills and training make it at least a possibility in the future, but only if she showed the right attitude.

Good, good, all agreed? Yes? Welcome to the Pocket, blessings on your future lives in your new home!

And that was it, they were already leaving. Before she could gather her wits and recall the many questions she had intended to ask, it was too late. She looked at Iltud in misery, only then noticing the presence of the Abbot by her left shoulder.

"Mistress Bowson? Forgive us our impatience, but we will shortly have to talk with the outside boys who returned yesterday. Please come and visit the Abbey when you are ready, perhaps share a meal with us, learn our ways in a more conducive atmosphere. We will pray daily for your safe reunion with your husband, here of course! In the meantime, I will send you some books to study, language books, just keep them away from Brother Peran!"

Iltud seemed relieved; he was a worrier she could see, but relaxed enough to offer to show her around the town, have lunch in a small café he knew near the harbour, see the ancient Basilica, point out a few sights, pick up a few things for Martha not available in the village store. Basilica first, just next door. It was round inside, loosely hexagonal on the outside with high windows located just under the copper sheathed dome covering a raised altar under the apex. Void of seating except in the side chapels. Iltud explained that this ancient church, built at the time Christianity was legalised by Constantine the Great, was modelled on a Greco-Roman basilica in Rome, constructed for Constantine's mother Helena. She had then donated the services of one of the architects and some money to build here, had dictated the dedication to St Joseph of Arimathea in thanks for the part Britain had played in raising her son to the Imperial crown.

Like most eastern churches the windows were small and it would have been semi-dark if not for the candelabra hanging down on long chains and projecting up from the ground like hallowed stalactites and stalagmites. Romanised mosaic flooring, wall paintings and, glory-of-glories, a golden leaved and faintly coloured dome mural, a more primitive version of those she had seen in the ancient churches of northern Italy and Rome as a visiting student. Here depicting Christ, his mother, disciples, Constantine, his wife, his mother and his father Constantius just to the side of the saviour, paying dignified obeisance.

The northern side chapel was in use, a small service underway with a handful of congregants standing before the priest and sacristan. That of the south was different, of the same construction and era, but much more recently redecorated, the brightness of its gold leaf ceiling and murals of saints on the walls showing an almost medieval Greek artistry, its Orthodox inspiration shining through. She remarked on it to Iltud who just shrugged his shoulders and said that it was less than twenty years old and inspired by something someone had brought from the outside. He had then reminded her that time was pressing on, they had to get back otherwise he would get another wifely scolding, and in the meantime he had to complete his shopping list and there was still lunch to be had in the small harbour side café.

They strolled down the main street towards the little harbour on the bay, stopping at a few shops, buying some cloth for Martha, some warm country clothes that might be suitable for a small teenage girl unused to the western sea climate, trousers, woollen pullover, under-shirts, leather belt, under clothes. She had to help him out at this point as he was blushing with embarrassment, cursing Martha for the humiliation, then explaining that they would be reimbursed to a point for expenses incurred when taking in a new arrival. She could see that in the clothes and fabric shops they visited his eyes were searching for something else, without success. Then into a cobblers; he had brought the girl's shoes with him and using them as a template he bought rubber wellington boots, one of the greatest imports from the outside in his view, leather and sheepskin moccasin house-shoes and left an order for leather ankle boots. All went into the large canvas and leather holdalls they were both now carrying.

Finally, the street ran out on to the shore, ending in a small paved road along the low sea wall that encompassed the little harbour. A few gigs and smaller rowing boats were drawn up on the beach, one little fishing boat, its sail down, rode at anchor near the stone jetty projecting out and then round at an angle from the shore. A few old and several younger looking fisher-folk were out on the beach and seawall laying out nets, mending them, repairing lobster baskets. Iltud explained how most of the fishing boats would have been out since morning, taking advantage of the light winds and clement weather, and that they would return in the evening, just before night fell.

She followed him to the café on the corner of the main street and the harbour road, where a few customers were coming and going. He looked at her and pointed to a painted sign that simply said 'Thea's', but with the western alphabet crudely Hellenised as if someone were trying to paint the name in Greek for people who didn't know the script. Iltud smiled at her puzzled expression and bade her follow him inside.

It was as if someone had tried to turn a little fisher inn, with small windows, low wooden ceilings and stone floor, into a Mediterranean café with white table cloths on heavy wooden furniture. An oak back-counter and wall shelves holding glass containers of what looked like honey and seed cakes, biscuits and other unidentifiable things, bottles of spirits and wine, glasses, plates, cutlery, cups and saucers, jars of preserves, even some olives and oils, she noticed. It just didn't seem to fit at all, but nothing surprised her anymore, at least not here. The walls were covered in icons of the saints, the Holy Family and Christ Pantokrator, along with other figures she didn't recognise. Most commanding of all though was the little white haired old lady, black clad, olive skinned, smiling brightly from behind the front counter at Iltud and then turning dark, sharp eyes on her. Her thickly accented voice, shining with lively humour, ringing out across the small customer area holding a few tables and chairs, "So you finally decided to come and pay homage after all this time did you, and this is the lady I heard spoken of by my son?"

Iltud smiled. "Sally, meet Thea, Georgy's mother, notoriously the most difficult café proprietor in the Pocket, and the best." He bowed.

The little old lady, mid-seventies she looked to Sally, regarded him with fierce affection. "My rudest customer, not even to use my true name, Theophano, born of the Comneniae, descendent of the Emperors, reduced to serving ungrateful peasants in a foreign land."

Sally could see she was something of a force of nature, brown eyes sparkling at them in great humour and mock disdain.

"Theophano? Wasn't she the beautiful Byzantine princess who married the German Holy Roman Emperor Otto in the tenth century? She was one of the most remarkable women of the Middle Ages?"

Thea looked at Illtud in triumph. "Finally, he brings me someone of culture, history, appreciation. I was going to throw you out for your ingratitude and rudeness, but because of her, her learning, her beauty of mind, you may stay and eat."

She clapped her hands and shouted a string of Greek to someone in the back room, clearly a kitchen. A middle-aged woman of what must be the same line, just paler of skin, emerged looking harassed and smiled at Sally and Iltud.

"Yes, mana!"

"My daughter, also Theophano. Off you go!"

The daughter smiled at them, wearing a look of immense forbearance as if this were an everyday occurrence, and ducked into the back. Shortly after, while they were talking, she brought out little plates of dried and oiled fish, mackerel for the most part, cold boiled eggs, bread, old apples, fried potatoes, even a few olives and batons of cold carrot in salted olive oil, with a glass of white wine, Greek she said, to remind her of her native land across the Sea.

Her son, her only other child, was up at the Town Hall she explained. Normally he lived with her and his wife and sons above the café, recounting his adventures, exaggerating his heroics in the outside she said, laughing sarcastically. Sally asked her how she, a Greek, came to be here, so far from her homeland.

She looked at Iltud, "Has she been told?"

"No, she has only just been accepted. It is not our decision, perhaps after the Easter ceremony, the Duke himself or the High Steward, perhaps the Abbot..."

"Then I shall tell her, now in my home by the bay. It is my adventure, my truth as much as theirs. What are they going to do, lock me up in the castle, confine me to the nunnery? Bah, they wouldn't dare."

She calmed down and looked at Sally, Iltud seemed to think it wiser to shut up, to take the line of least resistance, at least for now.

"My child, Sally, they call you? Pretty name, but I will think of something else, another for you when you are here with me, something more reflecting your culture, breeding, perhaps Arsinoe or Anna, the princess sent to be the wife of Vladimir of Kiev, to bring culture and Orthodoxy to the barbarous Rus, just as you bring culture to this place of ignorance. Yes, Anna it shall be."

"When I say I am the descendent of emperors, I am not mad or senile like they say." She gestured round her at her unfortunate customers, who were clearly used to it and grinning as if the floor show were just starting. "I am, from Alexios Comnenos, Emperor of New Rome, Constantinople, Byzantion. I am not born of the purple, it is true, but I have his blood in my veins, blood that can never dilute down the generations."

Iltud was smiling indulgently, clearly fond of the old dynamo.

"You have heard how we found this place, guided by the monks from the Mountain when my people first ventured out to find the others they were told had also been granted refuge by the Almighty? It took them years of patience, but a divine wind brought them here into the bay, by chance they said. Bah!"

"I'm sorry, I don't understand? Why would the Greek government be looking for this place and then keep it quiet, it doesn't make sense?"

The little old woman's latent fury was roused once more, this time in earnest. "Bah, not those corrupt atheist fools. I mean the true government of the Hellenes, the real Romans, those born of the purple who reign today in their refuge in the Middle Sea, the unbroken descendants of the last Emperor of Constantinople, Constantine the thirteenth of the Palaiologoi, after the barbarous Turks overwhelmed it."

She looked at the little old lady bewildered. The latter was sipping her wine clearly delighted at the amazed expression on her face.

"You think me crazy, no? Tell her Iltud."

He nodded, "It's true, we were here, and they found us, just as the priest told you."

"I thought that was just him rambling on, he didn't say who, I thought…"

"It is true, when the Turks broke across the mountains into Anatolia, murdering, enslaving and raping after the disaster of Mantzikert, His punishment on us for our divisions and complacency, many fled to the coast from the interior. Some found a place prepared for them, as this place was, to take refuge and hide so that the true faith would not be lost entirely from our ancient homelands. There they stayed, not even venturing back when the First Crusaders helped Alexios Comnenos, my ancestor, drive back the Turks from much of Anatolia. But then more crusaders attacked the Empire a century later, exiling the Emperors, but being driven out in turn years later. By then, the damage was done, we were too weakened and the Turks, ever gaining strength, eventually conquered our whole land, enslaving us. When the final assault on Constantinople was being prepared, a monk from the Mountain went to the Emperor's palace and told him of this place, of a prophecy that the City would fall but something would be saved if he would come away with him."

"The Emperor's advisers begged him to go, to save something from the wreckage, in secret. He was a proud man who did not wish to desert his people in need, but the Patriarch and his wife persuaded him in the end, and that last night he, a few of his family and most trusted and learned advisers, artists and scholars, with a small guard, taking some of our greatest treasures of art and literature, other wealth, escaped on two small galleys to the refuge."

"But he was killed in the last stand on the walls... I know they never found his body... Oh! I see."

Thea was smiling; the embers of what must once have been her great beauty glowing once again under the soft breeze of appreciation.

"My Anna, my learned Anna, at last someone for me to talk to properly, of important things... They escaped to their refuge on the south-western coast of Anatolia, much like this, joining those already there, just a few thousands, and started to rebuild. Some of the Monks of the Mountain knew, their greatest secret among many, and they read the old books, listened to travellers' tales over the centuries, and then when the time came, after the Second Cataclysm as it is called here, when the remaining Greeks were driven from Anatolia and the Armenians were slaughtered by the million, they started to search and prepare."

"Then they came here and returned, and came again, and brought back some ambassadors from this place. One of their attendants, a young, vital, handsome mountain of a man, called David, met me, a farmer's daughter, now reduced to working the land ourselves. He was so... so alive, a great northern god. Well it caused a scandal, disgraced me, but I did not care, I came with him willingly, married him, had a family and then he passed away nineteen years ago, leaving me to struggle on, making income, tolerating ingrates like Iltud here, in a foreign land. But I am satisfied, I regret nothing."

"It's unbelievable, overturns everything... There are so many questions, almost too many. I wouldn't know where to start, to learn so much. So much was lost when Constantinople went down, how much was saved and taken to your refuge?"

"Much, some is hidden on the Mountain with the monks, but some I do not know. I am not a priest, a scholar, an official of the court. Perhaps another time… I have work to do, an absent son to make up for, and your companion there is willing me to be quiet so he can leave. He thinks I have said too much already."

Iltud blushed, "We need to get back home, your young son will be missing you and I will be in trouble. How much do we owe you Thea?"

She waved her hand dismissively, "Nothing, a welcome gift to my new friend Anna."

"Thank you. One more thing Thea, your other business, Martha asked me to get something special, for the Easter welcome ceremony at the Abbey for our two new guests. I have found nothing anywhere…"

The old lady, stood up, all business again, "Follow me."

She led them into another back room behind the kitchen, a stock room full of cloth and clothing, all clearly imported, exotic silks, linens and cottons in fantastic designs and colours. A single oil-lamp supplemented the little natural light filtering in from a small, dirty window, picking out the gold silks from the rich purples, blues, greens and crimsons. This was the Aladdin's cave she had been hoping for. Thea turned to face her, as if weighing up her colourings and figure.

"The skills of my homeland, desired by royalty and the nobility of centuries, my real business. Iltud helps me ship it into Logres, to the finest, most exclusive shops in London I believe, distributed through agents who rob an old woman by their commissions." She laughed, "Although I believe the prices they fetch make even some of the richest weep! Such artistry in such fabrics lives nowhere else. Now, Iltud, I think I have the answer."

She reached over and pulled out a bolt of cloth and unrolled it, struggling with the weight of it. Purples, golds, silvers, aquamarines, with strings of pearls sewn into the weave. "Some of my finest, take it, it is yours for your two new lady guests, there will be more than enough. I also give you sewing thread; I hope only that Martha can do it justice."

Iltud stuttered, embarrassed once more. "Thea, I just can't afford that, I'm sorry. It's probably much more than all the money we have."

Thea frowned at him. "Did I ask for money? I have a new friend, something worth far more, and Georgios told me of the girl… Pigs!"

Iltud and Sally both protested, argued with her, pleaded with her, but she was not to be dissuaded. In the end, only when they had refused the gift, offended her and had to apologise, did she relent a little and say she would take one thing in only payment. What? They asked.

"One golden guinea, and you" looking straight at Sally, "to come and visit me regularly, to cheer up a lonely old woman in a strange cold land. Now go, before my generosity ruins me any further!"

Bowson along with George Edward discharged themselves from the hospital mid-morning. Some of the medical staff were quite relieved to see Andy go, but not George who had been much more co-operative and was seemingly reluctant to return to duty just yet. He was back at the office just after 1:30pm, in time to see a miserable boss returning from a Home Secretary chaired update meeting which had proved something of a fiasco. The Command head was clearly in her bad books, and she bypassed him overtly, focusing on Dager and a couple of peers. A naïve person might have thought this a sign of career benefits to come, but not Dager and his colleagues. Her normal icy composure was now only masking a submerged molten magma stream of frustration that was threatening to erupt, incinerating anyone who stood in its way. Her career, ambition for progression, was on the line.

The weapons and cartridges recovered were effectively untraceable, although the FBI were now reasonably confident that the sniper rifle used to kill Amallifely was one of the batch of Barretts now believed to have been stolen, along with a terrifying inventory of other hardware, from the US Army. The few vehicles recovered were proving of little help, as were the charred remains of the house and the two recovered bodies. Trawling through witness statements, interviewing locals and family members of the suspected terrorists, had revealed little of value thus far. The posted martyr videos gave little away other than something of the subjects' narcissistic egomania and paranoia. The only survivor remained in a medically induced coma and was undergoing a series of operations to remove bullet fragments from various vital organs. His doctors were advising this situation could continue for several more days at least.

Ted Armstrong, irritated and insulted beyond measure at his by-passing, had then commented that given the state of border controls, or almost total absence thereof, he wouldn't be surprised if there were caches of terrorist hardware secreted all around the country along with hundreds, if not thousands, more terrorists waiting to come out of the woodwork. That kicked off a huge row, which the Home Secretary could only curtail by abandoning the meeting, swearing 'he's for early retirement as soon as this is over.'

'Henry' sat anonymously in the corner feeling much more cheerful and wondering if he should send Bowson some chocolates: on balance, probably not. Someone else present, for entirely different reasons, also left with a spring in his step.

"Mana, what have you done, that was some of our finest cloth? It's my business too now; you can't just give it away."

Georgios wasn't shouting, he knew better, but he was angry, that was clear.

"How dare you? You may be my son, my first born, but it is still my business. It will only be yours when I have passed on to join your father, perhaps a day that can't come soon enough for you. I didn't give it, I wanted to, but they insisted on paying, far more than my friend Iltud, my faithful helper, could afford. He's always there to help me when I need, unlike you who go off into the outside on your adventures, indulging yourself, leaving me, your mana, and your wife and little children, all alone to struggle on, a poor widow far from home."

Thea's eyes were shining brightly, with excitement rather than anger Georgy could see. The few customers in the café were looking stonily at their drinks, but he knew they were smirking inside; they knew the game being played out even though they didn't understand a word of the rapid Greek being sprayed around the little interior like machine-gun fire. The smile that was now playing across her lips, amused at her ability to pull the strings of his strong filial attachments, was there again. He couldn't stifle the laugh, these games they had played since his teenage days; she was still that wilful teenage runaway girl in so many ways, younger, much younger, at heart than him, teasing him like an older sister would her clumsy and gauche younger brother on the subject of girls.

"Hasn't everything I've ever done not been for you and yours, and for my poor loyal little Thea?" Middle-aged 'young' Thea, listening from the nearby kitchen giggled as usual as that stock line was wheeled out, as it must be twice daily when Georgy was about, besides his children were all well into their teens, almost of age.

He just looked at her, beaten in one move as always; she was his mana, his mum, he owed her almost everything. She held out her black sleeved arms to him; he bent down to embrace her, "Tell me again, my son, my first born, how you killed the Saracens, how hard they died…"

"Is she alright Mum?"

Sam's anxious face awaited Martha as she returned down the stairs. They had been up several hours, it was now mid-morning but there was no sign of the girl, her bedroom door remained shut. He had finally pestered Martha into intruding on the girl's privacy; there was no answer to her knock on the door. She opened it, the curtains remained drawn and the light dim, but enough to see a small and frightened face peeking over the pulled-up bedding covering her seated frame pressed into the corner of the small room. An uncharitable part of her thought that at least she was now only sufficiently fearful to be frightened into silence, no longer terrorised into mute catatonia. Perhaps that's progress. She put down the tray she was carrying which held some breakfast, water and hot sweet tea, and smiled. Just those dark eyes staring at her silently, it was quite unnerving.

Time to take the bull by the horns. She opened the curtains, fresh sunlight poured in, several hours ahead of the advancing clouds. Then she opened the window, vigorous Spring air to stimulate a tired body and soul she thought. And still those eyes followed her watchfully, mournfully.

She pointed at herself, "Martha," again "Martha," then at the girl, "You? You?"

Still no answer, no sound, just that silent stare. Perhaps time or the priest might elicit a response. He would be round before too long with the Doctor, and there was Sam waiting anxiously like a child with a sick puppy at the vet's, soft heart in a stone shell she thought; he's a strange boy, things touched him unpredictably, like this child.

"She's been through a terrible ordeal, goodness knows how terrible or for how long. Shock must be part of it; time will help with that and kindness will do the rest. Now let's get her a bowl of warm water for bathing and hope that Iltud manages to get her some decent new clothes."

The priest had come in with the Doctor at noon, and gone up with Martha in tow. The girl had eaten and drunk something at least, but was still there under the bedding in the corner, staring more fearfully now that there were three people in the little room with her. They all sat on the floor to appear less intimidating. Gillian opened her bag and showed it to the girl, took out a stethoscope, put it on and edged towards her: she shrank down, even smaller in the corner. Gillian backed away smiling in a resigned manner, "I can't force her to let me check her over."

Father Peran got on to his knees and edged forward, causing the girl to shrink back again, pressing against the walls as if trying to be absorbed into them. Then suddenly her eyes seemed to notice something for the first time, the Celtic cross hanging on his neck by a chain. "Aba? Aba?" She was pointing at him, at it, her slight voice trembling with fear and uncertainty as she looked at him anew wide-eyed. "Aba?"

Peran smiled and turned to face the others.

"She's saying Aba, which means Father in Aramaic, the language of the Disciples. She knows I'm a priest. You said he told Sam and Alan that she was probably a Yazidi Kurd abducted from her home and then brought to this country as a slave or worse? The Yazidi, I know a little of them, they are a pagan people that have adopted bits of Christianity, Judaism and Zoroastrianism, and are treated as Devil worshippers by Muslims. They aren't of course; at least as we would understand such a thing, they are just in grievous error. Many live in the mountains of Anatolia, often alongside Syrian Orthodox Christians, sharing the same churches, inter-marrying even, it's quite extraordinary really. The Syria Christians still use Aramaic in their liturgy and she must have some familiarity with it. She obviously assumes I am a Christian priest from recognising my crucifix and habit. Unfortunately, that's the limit of my Aramaic and I know no Kurdish; I fear no one else in the Pocket will be able to speak to her any more than I. Perhaps our friends from the Middle Sea will be able to help when they come, they may know more, or perhaps he can send aid in from Logres. It is in God's, hands but He has carried her away from Babylon, of that I am certain."

He got to his feet and took a step towards her with one hand grasping his cross. She just stared at him, poised between fear and wonder, as he made the benediction over her, stepped back and said "Aba. Aba Peran."

Martha noticed a tear running down his cheek towards the smile he was trying to wear for her sake. As if in sympathy, tears started to flow down the girl's cheeks, towards the faint smile of relief that framed her lips, as if to say that although she was still far from home and among strangers, at least they might be friends and she felt safe for the first time in years.

Time had slipped by, eased on by the old lady's story-telling and they had to set off at a brisk pace to be able to catch the afternoon train back to St Leonnorus, burdened by the now heavy holdalls and even heavier bolt of cloth. Too breathless to talk on the move, the inevitable questions Iltud knew would be headed his way had to wait until they were on the train. This time he was wishing Docco would come and discourage them by his presence, but his ever unreliable brother-in-law was busy elsewhere on the little train as it headed back slowly through the fields up the valley, the clouds now coming up from the Atlantic, shrouding the blue Spring day they had been enjoying, threatening rain.

Firstly, she had wanted to know how much the cloth would be worth so one day she could repay Thea and himself. He told her probably over twenty-five times, maybe fifty times, perhaps even more, than the price she had accepted in the end; how Byzantine silks, their designs, were highly prized in the fashion and luxury markets, people thinking them made by hand in small workshops in the eastern Mediterranean, to traditional patterns. The amusing thing was much of it was bought by wealthy Arabs as bedding and wall hangings, more than clothing. He helped Thea by overseeing its transportation up to the barrier whence it was taken by 'outside boys,' as everyone seemed to call them, to a trusted agent who ensured they were distributed selectively to the right merchants. It was neither a big market nor a huge income earner for the Pocket, but was growing, albeit slowly given the need for absolute security.

Thea had a real head for business and was now thought to be the wealthiest woman, perhaps even the wealthiest private individual, in the land. She had achieved this largely on the back of her connections with her homeland, importing such luxury fabrics and also by a small but even more profitable side-line in importing antiquities and extremely good reproductions made with the original materials and techniques, all sold into the shadowy dealers' markets for such things. She would only accept gold and silver coin, and some gemstones, nothing else would do in payment. She was always complaining about the commissions she had to pay middle-men and the export duties the Duchy government imposed, but had nevertheless amassed a large fortune. Who did Sally think had paid for the new Byzantine decoration of the side chapel, carried out so that she would have somewhere to remind her of home, she had said? She had had to bring over two highly skilled craftsmen from her home for two years and had donated the gold and silver in coin, the fabrics and altar dressings and even some of the icons; the remainder being a gift from her homeland's cathedral clergy.

If she were so wealthy, Sally had asked, why did she insist on running a tiny little café with all her family involved, and not live in a large house elsewhere with servants? He had laughed at that, saying several widowers had wanted to marry her, attracted by her wealth and vibrancy, but had all been driven off, sometimes at knife point. She wanted her family to work for their living, not get lazy she said, so they knew how it had been for her. She also gave heavily to the nunnery just outside the town, helping pay for the little hospital the nuns ran, which had treated her sick and dying husband so kindly, and to other causes as well. Iltud was clearly in awe of her, finding her completely overwhelming. Would she get in trouble for spilling the beans about her homeland? He laughed in answer, the Council wouldn't dare he confirmed, she was apparently too valuable and respected, besides they would just say it was Thea being Thea and make a joke of it, however even she knew where to draw the line.

How many "outside boys" were there, he had then been asked? Less than sixty, plus a few women called the same; she laughed at that. Only the most trusted, skilled and discreet, those who could fit seamlessly into the outside world and adopt its ways, chameleon-like and, at the same time, be resistant to culture-shock when confronted by the huge differences so close by. Some of the Pocket's inhabitants had little interest in the outside at all; they seemingly had had their horizons circumscribed by the barrier with the outside world, although this was becoming less common since the opening of relations with the Byzantines and the advent of growing immigrant numbers from Logres.

Could some of the outside boys get a message to her husband for her, tell him she and Josey were safe, they still loved him, try to persuade him to join them? He had smiled indulgently at that: it was apparently a common request from the accidental immigrants. He was sorry they couldn't help; it risked exposing their existence, their illicit dealings with the outside world, if they did it for her they would have to do it for others and besides would he want to come, just disappear from Logres one night never to return? Then the hammer blow of truth: anyway, he had understood she had left her husband, didn't want to be with him anymore. There were tears at that point, so many that the emotionally reticent Iltud had had to give her a hug and ask her to forgive him his clumsiness. She pulled herself together, if only for his sake, and then the questions returned. He was keen now to talk about anything else.

What did the Byzantines want? What were they like? Had he ever met any other than Thea? Who from the Pocket had gone there?

Trade, exchange, not to be alone any more he said. Composed, dignified, almost arrogant; he had only seen a small number once or twice at official functions, but none made an effort to speak to him in his own tongue, or even English, other than Thea. Only a very few from here were permitted to travel there: it was a long and difficult trip although the Byzantines had access to modern ships, and had quietly bought into two Greek family shipping companies and could now move goods and people around much of the world undetected by the authorities. He had smiled at that, wondering what she was thinking given her initial reaction to their own small scale local smuggling.

She sat back, once more trying to digest yet another, even more seemingly fantastic revelation. What was it that Churchill had said about Russia? She wasn't quite sure, something about it being a mystery wrapped in a riddle hidden inside an enigma or something like that; well Russia had nothing on this little place.

Then, at an intermediate stop, four well-armed and heavily laden men got on the train, sitting up the carriage from them. They had nodded perfunctorily to them, looking preoccupied and nervous, the result, Iltud whispered, of being an outside team headed into Logres on some errand or other. Their very presence inhibited her questions until the terminus, when the little carriage emptied and Docco waved them goodbye. As they set off up the lane towards the cottage she looked behind her, the four men were lounging about by the warehouse as if waiting to be met before heading off over the hills.

"What are they up to Iltud?" she had asked him.

"Just escorting trade goods out tonight most probably," was his answer.

She didn't ask why he wasn't going out with them, wasn't that part of his responsibilities, at least as far as the barrier? Later, when they had arrived back, and she had gone up to her room for a minute, she had seen four laden figures shrinking into the distance, on their own, moving up the valley hillside, no carts or pack animals in sight.

Chief Superintendent Dager had just finished briefing Bowson and two of his other subordinates on the outcome of the Home Secretary's steering group when someone appeared at his cubicle door; Bowson saw his face fall and sudden panicked realisation dawn. It was her; the HR Director with responsibility for senior officer development and such matters, his annual review with her was due shortly.

She smiled brusquely, oh boy, she seemed to conform to stereotype, severe blue suit, short brown hair, slim, no, skinny, angular, librarian spectacles, face composed in practised charm, thin gold chain around neck above white cotton blouse, sensible shoes. Feared by most officers, including a surprising number of the women, and trusted by even less, she was charged by the highest authorities with making the top echelons of the service more 'representative' and 'diverse' to reflect 'today's modern Britain." She was perceived to have the power to make or break careers, her influence more to be feared than that of one's direct line management. They at least had usually done a job similar to one's own on their way up and had some understanding of the realities of life for the officers below them in the chain.

He dismissed Bowson and the others and went to the door to ask her in, closing it behind him, explaining Bowson's injuries and return to work.

"He's not having much luck is he, nor with this critically important investigation?" was all she said.

The voice was even, almost mechanical, outwardly solicitous and sympathetic, inwardly… Try not to think about it he thought, focus, no wrong moves, words critical here, say the right things.

"Well Sheena, this is a pleasant surprise. We were scheduled to meet in another hour, is everything alright? I was just briefing the team on progress and next steps in our investigation."

"I'm here because there is concern," a sudden drop in room temperature to near zero, "shared by both the Home Secretary and Commissioner. This is almost certainly turning into one of the most important investigations into terrorism of the last twenty years and we seem to be making no headway at all, have no idea who is responsible, or what they may be planning next. Politically," her voice dropped even lower as if sharing a major confidence "the timing is most unfortunate, higher authorities are increasingly worried that the chief may not be treating it with the seriousness it deserves, and this may be being repeated more widely in the Command. I was wondering if you might agree that some changes in leadership style and tone might be required, perhaps new approaches from different perspectives…"

"I can assure you that we are all working hard, harder than ever, here and the chief is widely respected."

"Of course, I wasn't casting any aspersions at all, just thinking aloud, soliciting the views of one of the up-and-coming officers, one of those in the frame for future… advancement… Anyway, the reason I am here is that we have decided to postpone your appraisal until this unfortunate problem is satisfactorily resolved, see how the pieces lie afterwards, who's polished their credentials, who alas…"

The knife might be obscured in reams of cotton wool verbiage, but it was at his throat now, he could sense it, everything just slipping away before his eyes.

She smiled at him. "If you were to ask my advice, my help, I would say it is difficult for someone such as yourself, with your background, to fit easily the template of the future senior officer the service requires for today's challenges, given that the criteria have become so much broader. Unless of course one has people, support if you will, who know you for who you really are, who value your contribution and see it's not hidebound by past models that are no longer relevant."

The vocabulary might be tortured and obscure, but Dager was bright enough to see where this was going, in effect an ultimatum.

"I see from your record that you have not been making the time to attend some of our senior leadership programmes. That is disappointing, a disadvantage, you might be able to develop an appreciation of the qualities needed today if you were to attend, understand the things to demonstrate to be in tune with the future. It goes without saying that it puts you in contact with the right people, a developing alumnus you might say, people who can work together, co-operate for mutual good and that of the service, naturally. There are a couple of programmes I would recommend, run by our preferred leadership training partner, United Intent. Why don't you drop by my office tomorrow morning sometime and we can discuss it over coffee?"

The phone rings, he picks up.

"Ah. How did it go? Promising, but you'll know better tomorrow you say? Desperate is he, that far? Bit like today's meeting, shambles doesn't describe it. No, not a clue, leads drying up like a stream in the Sahara, that's what concerns me most. I think it's something new, different, unknowable for the present and therefore dangerous. She's in a head-hunting mood, so we need to be ready, make sure of our candidate and be ready to fill the hole she blasts. Don't worry; you're doing very well, I will be sure to inform the others."

The phone is replaced on the receiver. Hmmm, ambition's showing through, almost egocentricity. Useful though, very useful.

The mind wanders, speculates. It had all been going so well, still was, right people being moved into the right places, allies distracting everyone, pushing them into reactions that served others' ends, intimidating, curtailing dissenting thought. Now someone, albeit unknowingly, was stirring it all up, complicating things, unsettling their 'friends', who were unpredictable at the best of times. Who were they, what did they want? How to trace them? Money usually leaves a trail, who can help? That's one world in which we are weak.

It had all been going so well, so many years of almost uninterrupted success, encountering little and only spasmodic resistance; those resisting, having no vision, were just fighting uncoordinated individual battles, winning a few, losing most, foregoing the war almost by default; they were even arresting people in the street now for reading aloud from Winston Churchill's historical writings. Thatcher had worried them, at least for a time, but in the long run had proved to be a massive benefit. She had focused all the potential opposition's energies on money, the unending aspiration for more, no vision about what the silent war being fought was really about, had surrendered the institutions without a fight, not even realising it.

What was it Lenin had said about the capitalist selling you the rope to hang him with? So now we control almost everything that tells people how to think, what words to use, what they can't say, the universities, the Quangos, the broadcast media, the teacher training colleges, HR departments and increasingly whole sections of the civil service itself. But now someone's kicking back, targeting intelligently, upsetting our allies, clearly well-resourced, they must be a dissident group in the security services or tied to the military, no one else it could be. Well they've left it terribly late in the day, but we need to find them.

She went down to see if she could help Martha in anyway, help prepare supper, calm down an over-tired son who hadn't slept all day and had, she feared, hardly noticed her absence. Quick supper and an early night for him was what was required. Martha had heard the day's news from her husband, he had now gone up to the barn to check and feed the animals accompanied by the young man who had only recently starting to call him 'Dad.' She was surprised, but not shocked, by the disclosures and generosity of Thea, saying, but laughing as she did so, that the old woman undoubtedly had a soft spot for her husband and if Thea had been twenty-five years younger she might have had a fight on her hands to hold onto him. Well, Iltud clearly has a weakness for strong women reflected her guest later.

Her hostess examined the fabric clucking disapprovingly, unrolling enough to put it up against Sally, doubting her tailoring ability to do it justice, complaining about the extravagance, but smiling all-the-while and never mentioning the absence of the golden guinea from her purse.

"How did it go with the girl, and the visit of the priest and doctor?" she enquired.

Martha explained, "I said if anyone can get her to talk it would be him and I was right!"

After his departure, they had been able to coax the girl to allow the doctor to give her a superficial examination, trying to win her trust, and then to come downstairs for a little lunch. When she had seen Sam come in to eat, she had knelt by the table at his feet and tried to serve him, looking down at the ground. He had got upset and angry, and she had fled back to her room, Martha having to go up and persuade her, by means of smiles and gestures to come down again, sit at the table, Sam serving her. The girl had been shaking, on the point of weeping; Martha said it was one of the most distressing things she had ever seen.

They had taken the girl and Josey to see the little farm, the animals, the small village and church, the dirt lanes with their multitudes of spring flowers in bloom. She had taken it all in without a word. When they arrived back she had gone to her room with tears in her eyes.

"And there she still is," Martha said, "until we persuade her to come down for supper and give her the gifts you found for her in the town, show her she's welcome and secure; but that's when I am really worried her nightmares will start."

The atmosphere over dinner was fragile, just the five of them sat around the kitchen table by the warmth of the stove, a choice of plain foods, tea, water and some home-made apple juice from last year, no one knowing if the girl's religion prohibited anything. Sally could see Sam was miserable, ashamed of himself for getting angry earlier, trying to mask it with the pretence of jollity, something he did transparently badly. The other three just chattered about the day, the things they had seen and heard, the wondrous Thea, Docco, the simple trivia of a busy day, hoping that the girl, while not understanding a word, might sense the camaraderie, the familial buzz. They pointed at each other when they spoke, repeating their names, then, pointing at her, urged her to join in. Finally, she stuttered out, "Narin, Narin" and, just for a fleeting second, there appeared the gravest smile, then came the weeping, the wracking gulps of air, the shaking. The others watched helplessly, unsure of what to do until Sally reached across to her left, put an arm around Narin's shoulders and pulled her close.

Sam was mortified and started to reach over to the girl to comfort her, but caught Martha's discouraging eye and retreated. "Sam, my love, it's nothing you've done, nothing at all. You've done the most important thing, you've brought her to us where she can be protected and looked after. But men, some men, have done this to her, I don't want to think about what she's been through, but you need to leave this to me, Sally here, the doctor and perhaps the priest. Yes, I know he's a man, but something from her past means she has some trust in him. It will take time, kindness and endless patience, you need to be around, here, so that she knows you are watching out for her and protecting her, but not too close. Do you understand?"

He nodded, unhappily. "I wish I'd killed them myself, not let Georgy…"

His cold, flat killing tone, so matter-of-fact, was a greater shock to Sally than the words he had spoken. She had heard the circumstances of the rescue, but her mind had glossed over that part, finding it difficult to reconcile these kindly, loving people with such lethal actions. Now it was all too real confronting her across the dinner table in this little home in nowhere land. This boy and his comrades were killers, she couldn't, wouldn't, use the word murderers, but they had cold bloodedly killed a woman and a young man and probably others she didn't know about. Oh, the pair undoubtedly deserved punishment of some kind, life sentences perhaps, but to hear the naked truth here and now was chilling. Who were they really, what were they? Were they just dead inside, as she feared her husband was becoming? No, she felt they weren't, at least not Martha, Illtud and many of the others she had met, but they seemed to simply accept it. Furthermore, they seemed to believe she was becoming one of them. How wrong they must be, she hoped.

The other three cleared away while Sally sat there holding the girl, whose sobbing, slowly subsiding to a whimper eventually rested her head in her hands on the table. Sally looked helplessly at Martha who was watching from the kitchen door.

"Sally, my dear, could you go upstairs and get the things you bought her today, they're on our bed. Iltud, can you go up and get the cloth as well? I think now might be the time."

By the time they returned Martha had persuaded the girl to get up and go into the living room, where she sat on a rug on the floor, as if by habit. They passed the parcels, one by one, for her to examine, her bewilderment slowly transforming into wonder as she inspected each item of clothing, the house shoes and finally the rubber boots. These seemed to be the most amazing thing to her, running her fingertips over their seamlessly smooth outer surfaces, putting her arms inside trying to find something.

She started to smile and then Iltud unrolled the bolt of Byzantine silk; the light from the oil lamps, which had been lit to complement the now fading daylight filtering in through the small cottage windows, reflected off the gold and silver threads, picking out the strings of tiny pearls, distorting and emphasising the tones of the other richer colours of the heavy silk. Martha, using gestures only, mimicked making a dress from the cloth for both Sally and the girl; the latter's eyes and mouth opening in astonishment, her fingers exploring the cool, thick material, she excitedly emitted a stream of unintelligible vocabulary before throwing her arms around Martha, splashing her neck and shoulders with a renewed flow of tears.

Eventually, when she had been gently eased away from Martha and had subsided into a state approaching calm, she returned Martha's gestures of making clothing out of the fabric cutting, sewing, measuring; pointing to both Sally and herself.

Martha smiled. "I think she's saying she can help make the clothes, she's probably better than me, she probably learned the skills, as a child, at her mother or grandmother's knee. The challenge will do her good."

Sam smiled at Martha, much happier now, "Mum, you're a wonder, just like you did with me, you're magic."

What she didn't hear was his real thoughts, 'when he calls, I'll be there, outside, and this time, no doubts, no regrets, no mercy at all.'

Andy Bowson's heart wasn't in it this evening so he decided to tidy up his desk and make ready to go to the place he now dreaded, his home, or was it now just the house he lived in, bereft of its emotional investment? But he had to face it, keep it going for when, or even if, they should return.

Dager had looked lost when Sheena Ellison left his office, 'Poor sod,' he thought. Whatever she had said, or knowing her type, more probably implied, it appeared almost shattering for his boss. What was it that the spook 'Henry' had said in warning? To watch out for when Dager started spending time with HR? Well, if Dager started spending more time like he had just, he must have strong masochistic tendencies. He hadn't even come out of his office to parade about as was his wont most afternoons; giving little pep talks, showing his people managements skills as he thought them, or even berating those he deemed responsible for the lack of progress. Definitely not his normal self.

Andy packed up, said goodnight to his colleagues and then went home, hoping to confront his new demons by searching his house from top to bottom just in case he had missed any clues as to his wife and child's disappearance.

He had called to say he would be staying at home this evening, too much work to go through which he couldn't do in the office; she must know how it was, perhaps this weekend?

Of course, she understood, don't feel guilty. Well, maybe a little bit. Could she help in any way, come around; get some food for him, new pair of eyes?

No, no, nothing to do with her. Had she followed up any of his advice from last night?

No, too busy today, perhaps later this week.

She had promised him; tomorrow please?

Ok, will try. He would call tomorrow, the day after if not. Later that evening, when she arrived at her apartment, it felt less like a home than ever.

Eleven pm and still it felt like looking for a needle in a haystack. Most of the information, as was almost inevitable, was dross: wordy statements, communiqués, ideological frenzy, intelligence and planning for the fall-back mission by the NEC.

Fall-back, so what was the preferred target?

Birmingham New Street station and the redeveloped Bull Ring, including Selfridges: massive bomb attacks followed up by Mumbai style gun assaults, similar to the attack which had been attempted at the NEC.

The aim?

To bring chaos to the rail system while at the same time delivering a massive blow to the central business district of Britain's second city. All about instilling terror and economic disruption, making people wonder: which cities would be next, how almost impossible they would be to protect them from determined men happy to die for their cause? No wonder they went for the secondary target, losing their leader and his deputy like that, not enough experience or numbers left to go after the two primaries together.

So, what are we looking for: upstream contacts, logistics details, codes, caches, funding, numbers, addresses, other volunteers?

All of these, especially the upstream backers, managers, planners, along with any evidence of their thinking, strategy and objectives?

Too big for me alone and so very few, just a couple in fact, who might be able to lend me their trusted eyes, but they are too important in other ways to risk diverting on to this.

I know… Find and extract the juiciest bits and deliver the rest, anonymously, to the police. They have the resources to follow up the rest. Send to who though… a little chuckle… why not Andy Bowson himself, it certainly can't hurt his career?

Sympathy; that's probably the last thing he's bothered about now and, if it is, then I've misjudged him.

Nearly midnight, better get some sleep if I can, rest at least. Looks like I already know what I'm doing tomorrow evening. I hope Helena listened this time. She would come running to help if asked, but she had her job, jobs, to do, she was just too precious to suck in any further. She really was remarkable; she had helped bring in others over the years, even her cousin who was in her own different way even more surprising. "Our Father, which art…"

Tuesday

....

Sally was waking up with the light now, her body adjusting to the low-tech life style, seeking to squeeze every useful moment from the daylight available. So was her son, whom she could see watching her from the little bed alongside hers. At least he slept through here, the outdoor life clearly suiting him, although he did seem hungry most of the time. Poor Iltud and Martha, the trouble to which they were putting them, the expense; Iltud had not made any fuss of it but she was pretty sure the allowance they were paid for being hosts would not cover the gifts, and certainly not the cost of the cloth. She smiled at the memory of Thea. Almost a stereotypical Italian or Greek mother, albeit one who claimed the blood of long dead Emperors. Burning bright in her old age, like a Phoenix resisting the oncoming dark.

She and her son got up and dressed for the day, as they went downstairs, she, on an impulse, returned to her room and opened her case. Inside lay her little travelling jewellery box, the gifts Andy had bought her during the time when things had been warmer: gold earrings, a couple of gold bracelets, one with pearls, her engagement ring, a few other pieces and three strings of natural pearls. She loved the ivory iridescence of natural pearls, he always said they matched her colouring. She reached in and picked up one of the strings, stroking it fondly, the cool weight of the pearls sliding over the sides of her palm. She pocketed it, went to close the box then changed her mind, she was in a home of almost selfless generosity after all. She picked up one of the others and pocketed that as well, before closing and stowing away the box.

Martha, Iltud, Josey and the girl were already in the kitchen. Josey and Iltud unconcernedly devouring bowls of porridge at the kitchen table while Martha and the girl busied themselves, drinking tea and preparing the rest of the breakfast. Martha looked at Sally as she sat down.

"Narin here," she smiled broadly at the girl, "was already down when I came, cleaning the table and floor. It's not going to be easy to make her understand she's a guest, not a servant."

The girl sat there nervously, as if waiting on Martha's every syllable, hearing her name spoken amidst words she didn't comprehend.

Sally drew herself up. "Martha, Iltud, I realise I haven't really thanked you properly for taking us, complete strangers, into your home, or your friends for saving our lives, for bringing us here safe, or for your generosity." She looked at Iltud. "Don't try to convince me that's it's all paid for by the government, that cloth wasn't for a start and I'm sure there've been other things. I've been thinking about it: I want to see my husband again, make things right, but I can't just yet, I accept that now. I need to earn the right, to be trusted enough, to work, to support Josey and myself, perhaps be able to leave you in peace in your home before you tire of us. No, please don't interrupt, let me finish. I'll swear that oath, so I'm given support, but only once I've seen the Abbot so I can better understand to what I would be committing. In the meantime, I'll start to improve my languages as they asked, so I can be useful and help here, whatever you want me to do. But that isn't enough, not true thanks, I have little with me, little to give you in repayment for your kindness, but I have this for you Martha."

She held out her hand to her hostess across the table, unclenched it, the string of pearls once again spilling down the sides of her palm. Martha drew back, astonished tears in her eyes, looking at her husband; he nodded. Sally later learnt that such thing were rare in the Pocket, if they could be found they might cost over half a year's income for Iltud. Martha reached out and picked them up, fingering them.

"I don't know what to say, they're so beautiful, far, far too much."

Martha subsided into tears, taking Sally with her, Josey and the girl looking bewildered and mute. Iltud said something to himself in his own tongue, but all three women knew what he was saying by his tone.

"Women."

Martha showed them to Narin, who touched them in wonder, before placing them round her own neck, standing up to go and see them in the mirror in the adjoining bathroom.

"Narin," said Sally "I know you can't understand a word I say, but your presence here has helped me more than you will ever know, helped me find my courage. So, His Blessings upon you," Brother Peran has been getting into my head, "may you find your way safe back home and perhaps these will help you realise that there can be love in the hearts of strangers."

She placed the second string around the girl's neck and smiled at her, nodding. The girl's eyes widened in shock, marvelling. Then the tears came again, all three of them this time, leaving Josey even more bewildered and Iltud muttering anew.

A few minutes later, when they finished weeping and admiring themselves in the mirror, Sally noticed someone was missing. "Martha, where's Sam?"

"He was out before dawn with his gear. He said last night that the call would come soon, and he and the others needed to train, keep fit, that sort of thing. He seemed more determined than ever, but that's my Sam for you!"

Andy Bowson left home for work that morning unusually early, even for him. It had felt like camping in an abandoned tomb, old, echo-y, filled with imagined fears; he had found nothing, damnably nothing, that might help solve the mystery of his family's disappearance. So here he was, distracted but trying to concentrate, making calls. The local Devon & Cornwall missing person co-ordinator no longer really trying to mask the dying hope in his voice: they would be releasing resources back to other operations in the next forty-eight hours unless anything new turned up. He couldn't blame them, it was just the way things were done when resources were so stretched, but the grim news compounded the feel pervading the office.

The understanding was that things were going badly, no real progress, and the chief was out-of-favour. Dager appeared to be on the slide; the dark presence of Sheena Ellison in his office the previous day, along with the apparent cancellation of his annual review being seen as equivalent to the serving of a black spot on an errant pirate. Dager disappeared shortly after nine-thirty, his secretary gossiping that he had announced he was going to see the HR woman for a coffee. She would later disclose that he had seemed much happier when he came back, as if a deal had been done. Sure enough, later that afternoon a series of training appointments had appeared in Dagers electronic diary, something about senior leadership development she said; it appeared they had been inserted by Ms Ellison's office.

Lunchtime already. I need to go for a walk, get out of this place, grab a sandwich and juice nearby; I'm drinking too much coffee. A walk may help me clear my head, think things through afresh, I must be missing something, maybe we all are. He walked past a church; its front door was open. Well, why not, I'm all out of inspiration and, she would like it, I'm sure, me reaching out here, if only for her and Josey.

He found himself a seat halfway down the aisle on the left, wondering what came next.

He looked about, must be Victorian, simple and not too gothic, just a little. No one else about, so how does this go?

'Our Father, which art in heaven, hallowed be thy…'

It's no use, I'm sorry; I can't be a hypocrite, when I don't believe in you. I did once, long ago, before I saw the world as it is. I think they call it the problem of pain and evil. I know there are answers, good ones, but when you see the evil close-up, scrape its victims from the walls and floors, these answers seem all too glib. Sally didn't agree, she didn't understand, and he was glad in a way that she didn't, but it had become a wedge between them, hammered deeper and deeper by every argument, every incident he had to attend and every flashback. Well, if she's right and I'm wrong, look out for her please, she's not the one who should be punished in my place; you're supposed to be on the side of the little children, the innocent?"

Just silence, nothing, he was a fool, what was he thinking? He got up and walked out, into the daylight and dirty city air, contrasting with where his mind was, with her, up on the moor. She loved it there, had only been here for him, had hated the city.

He mentally shook himself; he had to stop using the past tense for them!

Mind clicking back into work mode, Dager and the bitch from HR to the forefront. Might as well give 'Henry' a ring, who knows, he might have something for me by now?

He was in the outskirts of Istanbul today, making sure that the logistics and recruitment pipeline, which began here and lanced through the bowels of Europe into those vital organs of the west; Britain, France, Germany, the Low Countries, before branching out beyond into the peripheries, was secure. The first three were the ones that really mattered though, that was where the wealth was and what remained of their moral courage, they were the ones that had frustrated them repeatedly over the centuries. Sure, Spain and Poland had had their moments, but they could not have stood without the others. The others, they were the ones who had inspired and supported the drives back to the Bosphorus and across the straits of Gibraltar; seizing the trade routes, bypassing them, and finally ruling most of the world for a time, spreading their blasphemous faith to its furthest corners. They were all but spent now, the British included. The values and energy that created the world's greatest empire extinguished, like a supernova, in a final blaze of glory, leaving only a diminished decadent darkened rump, an amoral gravity well, indiscriminately sucking in and corrupting whatever passed.

Mohammed Badr and his team were gone, martyred, but it was only the loss of a small advance party in reality. Others were already in place, distinct from Badr's brigade, located throughout the target countries, well dug in, with others still filtering in, weapons too.

That was the beauty of Schengen.

Once you were in you were in, free to cross borders at will, however it appeared the security agencies were still playing by the old rules. But perhaps not the British...

Of course, their government denied it, said it was a mystery who had killed the martyrs. Was it cowardice on their part or disingenuousness? The Arabs thought the latter, said they were unpredictable, back to the tactics that brought the IRA to its knees in the eighties and nineties.

He had not agreed at first, but was now coming around. They needed to be taught a simple lesson; what worked on the infidel Irish would fail against the true believers. Massive blows in their heartlands so that would make the IRA look like small town amateurs by comparison, encouraging our populations on the ground to become more assertive, accelerating the process of submission, making it clear to the Arabs who the real leaders were. The Caliphate had been Turkish for nearly nine hundred years; it was time for it to be restored.

Their allies wanted to talk, this was worrying them, an unknown force at work they said, they would have known if it were official. They had their uses, less so now, but remained helpful, mainly for intelligence purposes. Perhaps we have over-estimated their capabilities, they certainly undervalued ours. Well marriages of convenience rarely lasted; this one might not have much time to go.

How much could Badr have disclosed if he had been picked up and the rules had changed? Some, but not too much, he was a professional, cautious, experienced; most of what he knew was limited to the two aborted actions.

His wife and home? Well that was done to explain his death at the hands of the authorities. If he had given up anything they would have been rolling up the organisation, step-by-step, already, but there was no sign of anything, complete confusion, as if the authorities had simply run out of ideas. They could lie low, close it all down for a year as the Arabs wanted, wait to see if anything transpired. Their allies, on the other hand, were telling him the police and security forces knew very little. They wouldn't be expecting anything big any time soon and consequently their guard would be down, perhaps believing that Badr's team was it for the meantime.

Yes, push on, time usually works for the defender, speed for the attacker. Now to choose the date, outline missions were drawn up, detailed reconnaissance was underway, logistics were falling into place and foot-soldiers were no problem at all.

He picks up the phone, ah, it's her as promised, she sounds eager suppressing excitement at something well done, hoping to be stroked, praised.

"Pleased you could call, that's good news. The first step. He's signed up already has he? He's got the message alright; I thought it might be a bit harder than that, but he's desperate. He's seen his chief, his mentor, going down in flames, so what choice does he have? He's bright enough to realise what's good for him, you say? Well done indeed. The timing's good, very convenient, we need someone of ours even if still new and not fully one of us yet, because, as I said, she wants his chief's head. Yes, she's frothing, positively salivating even. Dager's our only runner in the succession stakes, an outside bet but with your help and that of some of our other friends, perhaps we can even the odds before anyone can notice. The Commissioner's always amenable to the right word in his ear."

"Yes, you've done very well, very well indeed. You know I can't disclose much about our allies, but I believe I can recommend that you merit more exposure to our thinking, could be a support to me in steering matters going forward. I'll be in touch, thank you."

Well, she certainly kept delivering, was keen and potentially loyal, one can never have enough devoted supporters; just because some of my colleagues have the same goals and motivations as I, doesn't mean they aren't rivals. Yes, see if we can get her a leg up, it would pay back.

"Hello, Henry, it's me; can we talk, when, where? Ok, I'll be there."

Better get going, half an hour only, meet in a coffee house round the back of Victoria Coach station. Yes, there he is, back to the wall, facing the door coffee already in hand. Cool as a cucumber, hasn't even acknowledged me. Get a tea; it's busy, no spare tables.

"Excuse me, Sir, do you mind if I sit here? Thank you."

"Have you heard, found any more about Sally and Josey?"

"I'm sorry, just vanished. We passed on everything we had to the local police, but they've got nowhere; I'm sure they've been talking to you. Don't worry; we are still keeping an ear to the ground for you. Sorry to hear about the explosion by-the-way, your maker seemed to be looking after you that day... Now your turn."

"Just as you warned, Dager and the cow from HR, he feared her, now they seem to be buddies. She's putting him on leadership courses, neuro-linguistic programming, that sort of guff, stuff he used to run a mile from. Rumour is the chief's upset the Home Sec really badly, maybe terminally, they might even be thinking about a replacement, office gossip for now, you know how it is, but you asked..."

Slight smile.

"Thanks, it's as I suspected; they're weaving their webs too."

"Who, who's web-weaving, what are you talking about?"

"Are these courses run by something called United Intent?"

"How did you know? Aren't they just the in-favour training provider?"

"Educated guess if you like, let's just say not all conspiracy theories are entirely groundless, rather exaggerated and misunderstood; sometimes the obvious enemy isn't always the most dangerous one. When something gets so big and bloated along the lines of our last little chat, nasty things, parasites, can get into the decaying parts of it and grow and spread happily, eating away the host from the inside, almost undetected. It's a common human terror, lots of science fiction films made about it; well the analogy is a good one in this instance. Thanks, very helpful. Here's a new phone, destroy the last one. You know where to reach me."

With that 'Henry' got up and left, leaving Bowson to finish his tea alone. What was all that about? This time, he thought he might be beginning to understand.

What had she been thinking of, handing over her US passport to them like that? She must have been mad; a weak moment was the best construction she could place on it. She was running out of places to go, out of friends, out of money, out of options really. She could try the embassy of course, but with her back story would they believe her, the police, with her record, skipping bail for low-level drug dealing, her family, huh, what did they care?

Now he and his friends were after her, she had fallen behind, hadn't really started at all, and now they wanted payment in kind, she knew what that meant. She had had to resort to that on occasion, but only for herself and when desperate; it had been loathsome, utterly hideous, and she had usually chosen who.

She was keeping out of the hostels as far as she could, just the Sally Army ones from time to time when she needed a bath and some hot food. How long had she been on the streets? Six or seven years now, on and off? Her Dad was a US serviceman based at Mildenhall; her mum had left him and gone back to the States to remarry. She had had a local boyfriend and hadn't wanted to go back to the States when her father was reposted. She had insisted on staying, ostensibly to complete her education, but had soon drifted to London to be with her boyfriend. Then, sans him, she moved from one to another, thing to thing, her visa long expired, slowing sinking lower and lower until she had started using more regularly, and dealing.

Now here she was, cold, homeless, afraid and out of options, apart from perhaps one.

One of her first boyfriends had been Matt, another lost soul on the streets, there one day and the next just gone. Didn't say where, there was nothing unusual about that; at least he had never maltreated her. Then, over three years later, he had suddenly come back into her life, turning up at the hostel, where she was staying, with a very well-dressed woman. She had questioned him: he had said he had found a new life, the lady, an unfamiliar word to her, and her man friend had helped him get clean, provided him with a new home and family, a job, and even a new name, Sam. He was just returning for old times' sake. His benefactor helped the organisation behind the hostel and he wanted to thank her personally. She had spoken to the 'lady' herself, wary of her as if still on foreign ground. She was clearly well off, smartly dressed and elegant, but she was sharp, very. She had given her a personal visiting card and had said, "If ever you have no one else to turn to Lena and you need the sort of help Sam got, call me."

Well, what other choice did she have? Stay in a poky flat pandering to vile men until she went mad or threw herself under a tube train? She had lost the card some time ago, but had scribbled the number and name on a bit of paper; put it in a little tear in her jacket lining. Ah, there it was. What was the catch, there always was one, but it couldn't be any worse than the one she was already caught on? Find a phone box and dial the number, hopefully she hasn't changed her number and remembers.

"Hello, hello, hi, we met, I'm Lena, remember, a friend of Matt's, sorry Sam's, at the hostel last year? You gave me your card and said if I had nowhere else to turn to call you? Well I'm in real trouble, completely screwed unless you can help... I need to get away, like you did for Sam?"

"Well I didn't for Sam, but I know what you mean. And yes, I remember you. Sam's okay by the way, very happy in his new life apparently. Would you like to meet somewhere, say by Gloucester Road tube station at eight tonight? Will you recognise me? Ok, see you there."

This meeting was the last thing she needed right now but it would be important to him, he was always stressing the value of individuals, one of the few things he ever seemed to get passionate about. Sometimes she was tempted to think of him as a bit like a rescue dog wandering the hills looking for the lost to bring into the shelter, and then she would think of all the other things and realise that no, he wasn't that at all. Work was crazy; cheap money was again flooding the markets, setting in motion a further speculative investment frenzy. She, they, had bought in a long time ago and were now starting to sell down. They could see the way it was going, people had such short memories, with no real feel for inherent value, monetary or otherwise, they just ran with the herd, but it meant things were full-on.

She would have to go straight from the office, couldn't meet the girl, Lena wasn't it, near her home, he was always quite firm about that. Sometimes she did listen, she smiled inwardly. Take her to a little café, somewhere quiet, see what she needed, try to gain her confidence. He said she was a natural at that, it must be one of the things that made her so good in her world; well tonight it meant there would be no chance of seeing him. She hoped Lena was worth it. Better get on.

By the time Sam got back, filthy, wet, tired and beaming from the day's exertions, the fragile atmosphere that had pervaded the house had relaxed at least a couple of notches. Sally explained to him the apparent breakthrough with the girl and that she had even been out for a walk with them around the village. She had looked in amazement at the sea freshened Spring countryside, the flowers, some of which sparked tears of recognition, as if they were uncomfortable reminders of her now long-lost home in the mountains. The little westerly micro-climate of the valley meant that the season was now maturing, with the hedgerow leaves starting to open and the white blackthorn blossom weighing down their spiky stems. The bay and sea, further in the distance were barely visible; the advent of a cold front dimming the visibility which had previously so raised Sally's heart.

The women had then spent the afternoon sketching out designs for the cloth, with Martha leading the way while at the same time realising the girl was far more expert than she. Her thin fingers deftly changing the lines, the cut, the placing of seams; Sally, the modern twenty first century western woman was completely out of her depth. Martha had clear views on what would be acceptable at a formal event on the island. With nods, shakes, gesticulations and smiles they slowly negotiated a consensus with the girl, whose face started to lose some of its lines in the intensity of concentration. By late afternoon Martha and the girl finally seemed to agree, showing Sally, who had been reduced to fetching tea and preparing dinner, she too smiling in agreement at what was put to her; it would be like nothing she had ever worn. It was all put away before the men's return, for revelation later, not that Iltud would be interested in the least, thought Sally. Sam might make some comment though, if only for the girl's benefit.

Martha had, as ever, clucked around him when he came in, making him wash and change, fetching him tea and homemade biscuits which he shared with Josey, the young boy seemingly in awe as if Sam were some hero from a nursery tale. Sam seemed to have a way with kids, Sally thought, watching Narin out of the corner of her eye as she peered at him nervously from the kitchen doorway, but didn't approach. He saw her and smiled, then frowned when she stepped back. Martha never missed a trick, at least where Sam's concerned, Sally saw.

"My love, she's had a very good day, much better than could have been hoped, but remember what we said last night? She may have a reaction, it's perfectly normal, but you mustn't get upset, please?"

They went into the kitchen to finish making supper leaving Sam in the living room with Josey and his tea for company. Ten minutes later Martha ducked back in there and exploded in fury.

"Sam, how many times have I told you not to clean those dreadful things in the house, especially with Narin and that little boy here. She's probably seen enough guns to last a lifetime and here you're rubbing them in her face. How could you be so thoughtless, and what sort of example do you think you're setting the boy?"

He just smiled sorrowfully.

"Sorry Mum, it won't happen again, but I might as well finish now I've started?"

Sally could see, on top of a large whitish cloth placed on the floor, some sort of broken down military pistol with a silencer adjacent along with a vicious looking assault rifle waiting to be stripped for cleaning. Josey was looking at her for permission, but his fingers were already stroking it in fascination, waiting for the rebuke. Scariest of all was the weapon on his lap which he had clearly just finished reassembling: it had an extraordinary looking telescopic sight fixed on top, and another simpler sort mounted on a spare barrel, also on the cloth. It had to be the largest rifle she had ever seen, clearly very heavy, with a bipod mounted on the fore-end under the barrel. Sally hated rifles, which she associated with deer poachers from her childhood by the moor, and latterly, and more personally, they were the things she feared would turn her into a young widow one day. But this was like something from a different dimension, matt black, broodingly functional: this clearly could have no possible purpose other than for the taking of human life at extreme distances.

"Sam," she said pointing, "what is that awful thing and why do you need it? Have you used it for real in the outside world?"

He nodded blushing.

"I'm sorry Miss, I was thoughtless, please forgive me. If you really must know it's a 0.5 inch sniper rifle from America. That's a thermal sight, it doesn't work here but sees targets by their body heat so it works at night and in bad visibility. It's the latest thing, the other one's for daytime. I'm good with it too…" he was showing professional pride now "and I used it on the people who kidnapped Narin, so don't expect me to apologise or be ashamed, because I'm not."

His voice had that flat tone she had heard last night, just matter of fact about terrible things he had to do; he was such a set of contradictions.

"I didn't mean to imply that, I'm just not used to such things…"

From the corner of her eye she became aware that the girl had re-entered the room, must have heard Sam mention her name and was now slowly inching forward towards the seated Sam as if fascinated by the weapons. Martha looked angrily at Sam again as if expecting some form of hysterical reaction to break out, but there was nothing, just silent intent moving closer to the cloth.

Narin leant down and touched the pistol with her finger tips, closed her palm over it, not lifting it, just cradling it where it lay. Turning to Sam she asked a question of him; none of them could guess what, but all caught the interrogative inflexion. He looked at her dumbly, almost stricken. She repeated it, whatever it was. He shook his head miming his lack of comprehension. She stood up straight and pulled her hand away from it, went over to Sam and, very slowly and gently, kissed the top of his head, turned on her heel and went back into the kitchen. The others had been watching spellbound, unsure of what to do, a state that broke only slowly.

"I'm sorry, but I think she recognised that we used pistols like that in the house where we found her, I think she was trying to say thank you."

Martha was the first to respond.

"Just pack them away my love, as quickly as possible, and you young man, come away into the kitchen."

Later, when they were alone she confided to Sally.

"I'm frightened, by him and her, what may be growing between them, and within them as well."

Eight o'clock, where was she? Better not be wasting my time. Seven minutes past, give it twenty, no more. A painfully thin, slightly unkempt girl approaches, hair lank from a few days without soap and water, clothes dirty and ageing fast, a small backpack under her right armpit, her eyes almost wild with suspicion, as if on the point of flight, expecting someone, something, to jump out on her. She smiled at the girl.

"Lena?"

The girl nodded furtively, as if frightened to admit it.

"We spoke earlier. There's a little eatery around the corner, is that ok?" She looks like she needed a few good meals. "We can talk there."

Fifty minutes later she knew the full story, another young life out-of-control, a bad break of luck, a couple of wrong choices and here she was pleading for help from a stranger, losing what few shards of self-respect she had left, if any. Two or three things, that's all it can take, the difference between her and I. Where would I be if I had made the same choices, not had a loving family behind me, urging me on? It was so frighteningly easy to fall between the cracks and so few seemed to care. Why did it always seem to afflict the prettier and brighter ones more? Too many opportunities to indulge their fantasies and their temptations perhaps; too easy when looks and brains make it simple, for a while anyway? This girl could have been not far short of stunning, she certainly wasn't stupid, but life on the streets, mind and body abused, had harrowed her, aged her at least ten or fifteen years. If she got clean, happy and settled some of it would come back, but not all, some was burnt away forever. What a waste.

"So, what do you want to do? Why do you think I can help?"

"I don't know… I just need to get away; start again… There's nothing for me here, nothing back in the States. I don't know where to go and haven't anything to get there with if I did. I can't spend the rest of my life moving from hostel to hostel, they'll find me eventually."

Fear was clouding her eyes now, hope just draining away, sensing that this woman was going to fall short, not be the miracle worker Matt had indicated.

"You haven't told me why you think I can help?"

"Matt… Sam said… said you and your man friend sorted it for him anyway, never said how. He seemed different, happier, said he had found a family, a place to live, somewhere to feel wanted."

"That's true, he's happy now, all those things, he's respected; we helped but he made it happen, got clean, never looked back, walked away from everything behind him. That's what making a new start means, leaving everything of your old life behind, even your name perhaps. Once you go, well, it's a one-way ticket and no returns."

"Matt came back, for a little while."

"It's rare, exceptional even; he could because of who he's made himself. I'm not sure you're ready yet, that I can help."

Cruel, but this could go on for hours, hours I don't have, and she isn't there yet, not quite.

Tears now.

"He… You, said you could help, I don't know what else to do…"

"Look, this is what I will do. But you need to think: do you want to go and leave it all behind? There's a hotel room booked for the next two nights, just around the corner; it's in your name, Lena James and it's paid for. Breakfast and lunch as well. The address is in the overnight bag by my feet below the table. There's a change of clothing in it as well, nothing fancy, but I think I guessed your size."

Her secretary who had bought the bag and clothes for her that afternoon knew better than to ask questions; it was a little secret, her unspoken philanthropy, she didn't want colleagues to think she was going soft.

"There's also a little money, twenty pounds," hopefully not enough to get into trouble with. "Rest, get clean, eat. Stay in. I'll meet you in the lobby tomorrow at seven-thirty and we can have supper, and talk. You need to decide, by then, whether you want to be happy like Sam. It means you have to follow in his footsteps, give this life up, no drugs, forever. Go where he's gone, try and get what he's got. Don't worry," she smiled, "you won't be trafficked, sold on, misused in anyway, but you will have to learn to work to support yourself, give more than you get. Do you believe me?"

The girl, Lena, was rapt now, looking at the last hand stretching towards her from the lifeboat before she was sucked under, her hardened distrust and cynicism acting like lead weights, pulling her down from that last despairing proffered grasp.

She nodded, uncertainly. Well at the least she had somewhere to stay and rest for a couple of days, a little money, new clothes, she'd see about the rest.

"Ok, see you tomorrow, I'll settle up and leave when you've gone. Don't forget the bag."

Ten o'clock, now we're getting somewhere. Names at first, some numbers to match, some names obviously noms-de-guerre, whatever those classifications meant if anything, allusions to imports, depots, a few account details. Hazard an educated guess: names only, probably just peripheral local help, not considered core, names and numbers, mainly local core volunteers, but not key leaders, nom-de-guerre and numbers, key people and contacts, some in the UK, others overseas, probably Europe, nom-de-guerre only, the leadership, backers, don't call us we'll call you types. Yes, that's probably it. Operation names, no details other than the resources that might be required, no intelligence details that might help… 'strewth, some of these operations are huge, over fifty people each, a number seem to be concurrent as well, here's another one of over eighty. They haven't got anything like enough names, but there seems to be a reference about people coming in from abroad. This is extraordinary, never seen anything like this outside the Middle East. No sign of dates though, nothing too imminent hopefully; that's a relief.

Need to start cross-referencing these names and numbers across the files here and also against those held at work to see if any are repeated. There's just too much chaff. Hmm. A few are repeated, mentioned in passing two or three times, likely important contacts. What had he been doing storing all this in one place? He must really have been convinced he wasn't on the radar.

Fatal mistake, for him.

Decisions, decisions.

Nothing imminent it seems, so have got some time. Use resources at work to find these repeat numbers, maybe some of the others, the people behind some of the names, not the low-grade ones though. Fortunately, there were ways of peering over GCHQ's shoulder into their data collection networks without them knowing, as long as you were selective.

Yes, I'll get on with that and go through the rest again tomorrow, decide what to pass on and what to keep for ourselves. If only there was someone else within at work to share the burden, I'm just so alone... Too late to bother her, I'm already leaning on her too much, can't impose. Get some sleep, be fresh for tomorrow.

"No, no, Jovanka, I didn't mean it like that, but it's heavy, so heavy when you're alone. I'm sorry, I'm sorry, please forgive... You know why... for you... your brother... all of us, those to come, those to come most of all. No, not in your name, in all our names, what else could I do, seeing what I saw, still see... No, not there, let me out, away."

A hospital bedside, no a hospice, single room, a young man and younger woman, little more than a girl, in the bed, wasted, semi-conscious from morphine, no one else, no one else interested really other than the staff and a few dutiful colleagues who'd done their bit. Hands clenched tight, holding on to prevent the final fall, no tears left to weep, just holding on, willing more life, more time, so many things still to do, to say. The relaxation, last strength to fight has gone, something's left, just him alone now. "Until I cross Jordan. I promised you, you were still there somewhere, in the room and you can trust me still, as you always did."

Wednesday

....

Another dawn start, but they were getting easier now; she was reverting to the rhythms of her country childhood so very quickly.

"Can I get up Mummy? I can hear them, Martha, the old man and Sam. He's nice, Sam."

"Of course, sweetie, get your clothes on and I will follow you down in a minute."

She needed to spend time with him today, had been neglecting him, not that he seemed to notice, everything else was much more interesting.

"One day, Mummy, when I'm bigger, like Sam, can I have a big gun like him?"

"Perhaps, sweetie, when you're much bigger, like Sam."

I suppose it's inevitable, the fascination with older boys, young men really, instruments of death, nature not nurture usually wins out in such things, whatever we do or say. I will have to have a word with Sam though.

Downstairs, the others are in the kitchen, finishing breakfast; Sam sitting next to Narin, whose fear of him seems to have thawed somewhat overnight. Martha looks at her in that way, yes, that's where some of it's gone. Sam and Narin are pointing at things, Sam naming in English, supplemented by Martha and now occasionally Josey, who thinks it a game, she repeating, trying to master the vowels, the syllables, the consonants, the intonations, smiling when successful, Sam even more.

Iltud just watching, quietly.

"If it's alright with you Martha, I want to get on with the washing today, it looks dry outside at least, spend some time with Josey and then this afternoon start looking at the language books I was given."

"That's fine Sally, Narin here and I will start on her dress this morning, when the light's best inside, keep her mind occupied and then get on around the house this afternoon. Sam will be helping Iltud out around the holding, won't you my love?" No dissent permitted there. "And then out training up on the moors this afternoon."

He nodded and so began perhaps Sally's first remotely normal day in the Pocket.

Just before lunchtime, her hands starting to get raw from manual clothes washing, learning to use a mangle for wringing out, hanging up outside, can't someone invent a steam engine powered washing machine something? Voices at the front door, it's Brother, or is it Father, Peran, never really sure what to call him. She dries her hands and goes into the front room.

"His Blessings on this house and its guests!"

His smile is infectious, the bonhomie bubbling up, raising the mood already. Narin and Martha are on their knees, at a low table, marking out cutting lines on the cloth in pins, trying to use every scrap of material; Josey near them on the settee looking at one of his books. He makes the benediction over them; Narin is smiling at him shyly. He beams at her, pointing to himself, "Father, Aba, Father Peran, Aba Peran!", then points at her.

She smiles more broadly now, "Narin, Narin," and then launches into a volley of unintelligible words, relapsing into silence when she sees his lack of comprehension. She tries to go forward on her knees to kiss his feet, but he leans down and pulls her upright, shakes his head and grins at her. She smiles back, less bashfully this time, and shocks him by hugging him fiercely; Martha has tears in her eyes.

"And now the news I carry!" he booms, "Narin here has been asked to see the Council on Monday, the Monday of Holy Week, a good sign of His promise to her, and Sally and this young man here have been invited by the Abbot himself to visit him at the Abbey afterwards, a great honour! I will take them down and guide them; perhaps he will take pity on me and lend me some more books! Martha, will you take the girl with Iltud to the Council, it may be frightening for her? Now, is someone making lunch and willing to share a little with a servant of the Lord?"

Alan breathed a sigh of contentment after his best night's sleep in ages, responsibilities and worries shed at least for the time being, home with his wife and children in his cottage by the bay. Other than the cold water and damp, mild winters it reminded him in many ways of his childhood home, south of Cairns in Queensland: was there anything more restful than the sound of the waves lapping gently on the sandy shore? Not in his view, certainly not today after the first full night beside his wife.

At least there were no nightmares or flashbacks yet, he had been warned there might be, especially after some of the things he had had to see and do. His wife, a local girl, fisherman's daughter, anchored him solidly, deeply rooting him in over fifteen hundred years of continuity, her extended family embracing him as one of their own, even more so after he had taken the trouble to learn the native language, a sign of respect and integration on his part. But they also had the sense not to ask those sort of questions, neither did his wife; they had just popped round after his return to catch up, invite him for a drink, just eminently sensible, practical wise folk. She, his wife, just looked at him and said if, when, he was ready to talk…

Stepping through the barrier had been harder for him than any of his team. For Art it was an adventure. As for Georgy, well he was increasingly worried about Georgy, and Sam, who really knew Sam anyway? He was ever the surprise package in the team. But he himself?

He had turned his back on the outside, its grasping, its shallowness, and by chance, well not by chance he now thought, had found what he was looking for here; it had been a complete surprise. Consequently, going back was perhaps the hardest thing he had ever done, but he had asked for him apparently, insisted Alan be the team leader, had seen something in him, so Alan had assented, if only because he felt he owed it to them and understood what was at stake a little more than most of the natives here.

He sat up, looking at the morning light streaming in around the gaps of the curtains until a soft voice whispered in his ear, "Alan, you've got nothing to do this morning, you're mine again…"

He was all business today, thought Elaine, working at high speed since a frighteningly early start, updates and memos all completed by nine. Then, other than grumpily discouraging visitors and answering phone calls, which he eventually diverted to her phone in exasperation, doing nothing but peering intently at two of his secure computers. He was methodically scrolling through lists of numbers, names and even maps with flashing dots, she noticed when taking him drinks; she could see he wasn't moving anywhere by choice. Among the calls she took for him was one from a woman, English, well-spoken but not posh, an assured voice, just asked for him by his first name, enquired of her how he was and could she make sure he call her? That was it, but she recognised a voice with real… affection in it… no stronger, warmth, so perhaps the office rumours were right, she hoped so this time; the voice was a nice voice and she wanted good things for him, he deserved them. She resolved that no one else in the office would learn she had spoken with her for the first time.

Most of the numbers were dormant, no message boxes registered, obviously pay-as-you-go, no data packages, just too obvious really, either not activated at present or discarded. A few were transmitting though, not broadcasting, but sending out "we are here", waiting. GCHQ and the NSA, at the heart of the old wartime five cousins communications intercept arrangements, had gone further than anyone outside realised in tabbing these sort of phones and numbers, huge databases constantly identified the markers of unusual patterns, listening into the more suspicious, monitoring and recording usage, even tracking them in real time, identifying new ones. He, like some of his more senior colleagues, had a direct feed into their systems.

There were things he couldn't do from here, such as switching on dormant phones' microphones or cameras. The American National Security Agency would go nuts if they knew, but they had people in Cheltenham who had set it up silently, maintained the cover, closed it down whenever security audits were rumoured. Some people still saw the bigger picture, putting other loyalties before those to their agency and now it could be invaluable, including today on this errand. His office was secure, unmonitored, those of all the key people were, it was one of the ways they did things differently.

Interesting, three of the numbers were intermittently active in what appeared to be the same spot, in a peripheral commercial street in Swindon, another two were likewise active together in a poorer residential side street in Reading, a few others were winking in and out around the country, London, Southampton, Midlands' towns, Bradford somewhat inevitably, and other similar communities in Lancashire and West Yorkshire. We can't go chasing them all, it's the concentrations that are most likely to indicate leadership or allies; two is as many as we can handle at one time, so few for this sort of work.

What have we got available? The base team is at the Cotswolds farm, gaining experience of the outside world, support ready only. The Beta team's just arrived there, ready but not experienced, put them on Reading, intel gathering only for now, but could be trusted to move in if required. Standby team not fully shaken down yet, back up and emergencies only, for the moment. The other teams, native boys, no incomers among them, simply not yet ready for aggressive deep penetration outside; they are needed to police the barrier, manage the outside trade. That leaves the Alpha team, just back. Alan and his boys were great, able to improvise, not panic, had two incomers which was very unusual, best sniper they had, Georgy was a natural… He had promised them a break though, you can't use up your best, you have to eke them out and keep your promises.

So, what to do, let it run a bit? What if I'm wrong about the lack of urgency and it costs lives? No, I don't think I am and staying our hand will give us more time to gather intel, rest Alan's boys, work up the other teams, maybe even let the other side expose themselves further before we start to close them down. I really want to get to the people behind them, their directors and these 'allies' they mention. I really need to identify them. So, get the teams already out to gather intel on the two clusters for now, and then start to look at the other un-clustered numbers.

What about sending some stuff we can't look into to my man at the Met? Yes, some of the volunteer names and perhaps something with a logistics angle: they must be bringing the weapons in somehow? If we can find out how and where, the police might be able to slow them down at least. And the bank account numbers, she might be able to help there; if not, send them in as well. But let's start identifying our suspects first in case they go to ground. I know what I'll be doing at home tonight.

Thanks Elaine for the messages. One from her to call her, great minds think alike, I wonder if she can spare an hour for lunch today or dinner tomorrow night? It seems a long time already.

She picks up straightaway; she guesses who it is, although it's very rare for him to call her at work. Thanks for calling back; he was going to call her anyway. How is she, has she started the things he had asked her, the deal she had accepted?

Errr, sort of started, packed a bag anyway, will tell him where when she sees him, no progress on the other, work's just mad and this girl phoned, had to meet her last night, seeing her again tonight. No time for anything else, understand?

Tomorrow, please, it's serious.

Alright, I'll try, I promise.

Can he see you for lunch?

Why, is something wrong?

No, nothing at all, just want to talk, nothing urgent, can wait a bit. Tomorrow for supper then?

Sure, no problem, come and stay over, no, you won't be putting me to any trouble, we can talk much better, you know, just like we said, you know how I like you staying over. See you then.

At least for another evening it will seem like a proper home, get something ordered in. He's onto something, could hear it in his voice, trying too hard to be measured, unusual for him. That small chink in his armoured skin she made has not healed over, at least not for her yet, the essence escaping warms her. How long can we keep this up before someone gets really hurt? He's giving what you asked for, just started: what more do you want now? I know, I think I always did. Back in your cell, now! Get back to work, making money I don't give a damn about any more.

Their allies want to talk, face-to-face, not good and too risky. Sound perturbed, yes, that's the phrase, not frightened, not panicked, but their balance has been disturbed, not so confident now, because of what has happened. Good, whoever is doing these things could actually be helping us indirectly, making our allies humbler and more dependent on us, Allah provides. So, we should refuse to meet them but hold something open for the future, perhaps next week when I am in Belgium checking out the other end of our land supply chain, our marshalling area for volunteers, pretty secure despite the presence of NATO and EU head-quarters; the Belgian authorities don't want the trouble, they prefer playing ostrich, so long as it's somewhere else. They can always come to Brussels or Antwerp to meet us if we allow it, to explain why they need us so much; he would enjoy seeing their pride being made humble.

Plans starting to shape up, five, maybe six concurrent operations, about three hundred volunteers, mostly intended martyrs, about sixty percent in place already, arms too, but big shipment by sea on route. Yes, we may need our allies' help ourselves, primarily intelligence, but this is stretching even us. Let's decide next week, the infidels' Holy Week, the irony amusing. It would have been nice to arrange something to mark their Easter festival, but it was just too soon. Hmm, religious dates, what comes next in the Christian calendar?

Time to think at last for you Andy Bowson, no seemingly connected incidents for well over ninety-six hours, forensics starting to yield what? Just the obvious really, two bodies in the ruins of the house, executed, hollow-tipped rounds, again custom made, fired from an unidentified military pistol, lack of gunshot sounds indicates it was silenced; expert shots like those that that did for our friend Amallifely. Gas left on, small detonation charge, homemade with alarm clock timer, petrol as an accelerant around the bodies, nothing unusual about it. No one saw anything, but it was a foul night in a divided and suspicious neighbourhood, so nothing surprising about that. Girl, believed to have lived there and now disappeared, remains missing and unidentified as do four of the terrorists killed at the NEC, almost certainly foreigners who came here illegally from some chaotic hellhole.

Plenty of weapons, old eastern block and new Chinese pattern AK47s from both sides, huge amounts of commercial explosives, where is this stuff getting in? Worst of all, the guys behind this, seems to be a minimum four, appear to know how to frustrate modern forensic science, gloves, probably hairnets, masks, disposable stock overalls almost certainly and shoes with stuck on soles, plastic coverings in vehicles which must have been removed before they were burnt and then all subsequently destroyed elsewhere. They will make, probably have already made, a mistake, we just need to be patient and spot it; the worst fear is that they go to ground, disappear for six months, a year, let the trail get kicked over then pop out again when we're looking elsewhere.

Some sections of the media, along with the usual agitators and community leaders, are demanding a public enquiry into what they are calling an Islamaphobic 'shoot to kill' policy and calling for the government to introduce more laws restricting liberty. Meanwhile, the opposite camp is growing stronger, bolder, saying the Muslim population is a threat and harbouring a growing number of murderous maniacs with international resources, a 'clear-and-present-danger'. How did that awful Yankee phrase get into our language anyway? The government, the state, seems paralysed between the two, instinctively on the side of the immigrants, but fearing the native voters' rising exasperation.

Maybe 'Henry' does know what he's talking about after all. And meanwhile Dager's shed the blues, strutting like the coming man again, no chance of that unfamiliar sympathy for him returning at the moment. She's always popping in to see him now, his PA loathes her, and the chief is no longer welcome at COBRA or the Home Secretary's sub-committee meetings. It's just pathetic.

What's happening to you Andy Bowson, have you just promoted yourself into a higher league of cynicism and negativity? She hated that, she saw it happening to you, changing the man she had married, but you refused to listen, you said it was just greater perspective, greater maturity. What was she saying now, what would she say if she could see you like this? Perhaps 'Henry' could help, he must have been through this, he was a senior spook after all, he would have experienced all this and more. Yet he appeared to have retained some balance, some sense of humour and detachment; he hadn't sensed cynicism in his voice, just acute perception. Yes, he would lean on 'Henry', after all there was no one else and he seemed to need my help too. Perhaps I'll give him a call later, suggest we meet.

He had had to move fast following his conversation with the Turk's contact man. He had never spoken with or met the Turk, just knew a little about him from contacts with his emissaries; he wasn't even sure if he was a Turk, but he was used to such obfuscation, indeed could teach their allies a thing or two. They seemed all for pressing on, a real sense of urgency and ambition, a drive for vengeance for their losses; the contact man hadn't been able to resist boasting a little about that, their resources, the unprecedented scale of what they were contemplating. He had tried to restrain him, advise caution, small steps in the long race, but the man's face just replied with an expression of distaste, even contempt, saying they would be in touch with a list of intelligence requirements. They were getting above themselves, becoming over-confident, it might be time to put some distance between us, after all their objectives were hardly compatible, but it needed talking through with some of the others.

They weren't an organisation as such, just a coalition of the like-minded, albeit with some loose structures and ways of working, but a few had a sort of emergent seniority. They were the ones who co-ordinated things if needed, discussed priorities, shared information and news, spotted talent, identified the resistant for undermining and isolation. Seventeen had made it at his short notice request to the meeting room above a pub in north London, an unusual degree of compliance; clearly, they too were starting to become worried by these unforeseen developments and had made themselves available. They had no leader, but the fact that so many responded to his call was encouraging, stimulating his ambition. Three from the broadcast media, very strong there, two from the print, not quite so there, two senior academics, another stronghold, three from the civil service including myself, two politicians of differing parties, one trade unionist, two from large company HR departments, the preferred entry point into a hostile world, and two from the entertainment industry, so-called celebrities, another sector of strength: they were all so insecure, anything to be 'on trend.'

"Thank you for making it at such short notice," he began, "your time is precious, and this shouldn't take long. As you know, one of the things I have been asked to oversee is our relations with our overseas friends, who have become unsettled by these appalling incidents in the Midlands."

They were just soaking it up, hanging on every word for their worlds were those of words and hidden meanings, incidents of action and decisive violence were things they saw only second hand and were therefore fascinating. "The security and police forces are hardly covering themselves in glory at present, have little idea as to who is responsible for these killings which may open up opportunities for us in the near future."

A murmuring now, like that of hyenas faintly scenting freshly spilled blood in the distance, suggesting better feeding ahead.

"Our allies seem to be taking it badly, very hard, and appear to be planning an unprecedentedly large response here, quite what they will not disclose. Despite their set-backs, they also appear to be growing in confidence, almost arrogance, as if they see themselves as the senior partner. They are quite unwilling to take our advice and are just making demands for information."

One of the media people interrupted, "It was always a massive risk working with these people, supporting them here; just because they share our enemies doesn't mean there is any commonality of interest at all. They're driven by benighted beliefs from the dark ages, are erratic and arrogant; how we thought we could use them over the long term I don't know, it's been a grave mistake…"

Here it comes, the challenge, ostensibly a fair critique of strategy, but she was ambitious too. Make a firm response. "They have had their uses, have been a big distraction to those we oppose, the consensus was, is, clear that on balance they have been helpful, but today I want to suggest we might need to commence considering a parting of the ways in the near future. After all we have made huge strides since we started to work with them. All things come to an end, but they may be useful for one more service, and then one day…"

The challenger backed down smoothly, biding her time, listening, "What do you suggest, you know them best?"

"Further major dramatics will be counter-productive for them; they are too blind to see that, but such events could serve our ends. New laws, further marginalisation of their support communities over here, a clamour that something must be done," he permitted himself a smile here, "which I am sure my colleagues here from the press and media will be able to make resound throughout the land, and which have always given us our best opportunities for advance. I foresee changes of senior personnel in the police and security services, which have proved resistant to us for the most part, that may favour us. Indeed, there may be a prospect of placing our candidate at the head of the Counter-Terrorism Command itself, which would be a major coup. Some of you know we have someone senior in the ranks of the Met who is working to effect this amongst other things. She has proven herself loyal and capable, and I believe merits inclusion here. Who knows, she may well be able to secure our preference for the Met Commissioner next time?"

"Please feel free to speak to me about her qualifications subsequently if you wish, and I can arrange for her to meet some of you if you would value that?"

One or two nodded at that, but the challenger didn't, he could see she was suspicious, but how could she argue against the promotion of another woman to this heavily male dominated body when she was always saying it needed to be fully representative of the people they believed themselves to be serving? That was the amusing thing; he sniggered inwardly.

"I conclude from your faces that we are leaning towards stepping back from our friends, not quite yet but perhaps after their next depravities. In the meantime, they can do us one more direct service. If the police are yielding, that leaves the security services, which are difficult for us. It is also likely that they, or some of them, are, in some manner not understood, behind these killings. The removal of some of their senior personnel may create openings for favourable new thinking in their ranks; it may merit us encouraging our friends to vent some of their excessive zeal in that direction, some names, addresses, that sort of thing, distracting both sides…"

Just nods, no dissent, he was pleased with himself, and she would owe him now, big time.

"Hi Lena, how are you?"

She had been a couple of minutes late and, due to constant demands from her work tablet for her attention, hadn't been able to prepare herself for what could be a tricky evening with a girl who was frightened and still a little jumpy. The girl mumbled something about being a bit better thank you. She certainly looked better, at least superficially, hair washed, clean, wearing the new clothes she had bought her, skin brighter from some regular decent food. Yes, she could have been stunning once, could be highly attractive again perhaps, if the skin improved, the black rings around her eyes faded, the metal perforations in her skin removed and healed over, at least she didn't seem to have indulged in the fashion for tattoos, ruining irredeemably the beauty that nature had given her.

The girl followed her out and down the street to a little Italian restaurant she knew, one of the old family sort, not a chain, dark inside, booth seating against the walls, discreet, wholesome food, just right for tonight. As they sat down, "By the way Lena, the rucksack is for you, more clothes, toiletries, a voucher for shoes from a place near here, a little more cash, a gift, whatever you've decided."

Let her talk, it was her decision, be firm with her, not soft, indulgence was not the way to help those like her, she had learnt that the hard way. They ordered food, soft drinks arrived.

"Thanks."

That was all, not a good sign.

The girl sat just looking at her, trying not to catch her eye, still thinking, not sure of her, or anything anymore, even herself. Just wait then, in silence, it's hers to break, the food arrives; it seems to cancel the spell over the girl.

"How can I be sure? I don't know you, anything about you, everyone's betrayed me, let me down…"

Giving in to self-pity now.

"That's true, you don't, but you did trust Matt, Sam, once?"

She nods.

"I, we, helped Sam. He trusted us and that meant we could help him, you saw that for yourself; we can't do the same for you if you won't trust us, don't want to make changes in your life, start a new one."

Silence again, just eating, slipping sly glances at me, thinking I don't notice, that I can't read her mind, see the debate within.

"I just need money, buy them off, set me up; you've got lots, can't you help, why won't you? They'll kill me if you don't, it'll be your fault."

Suppress the anger, be calm, it's just part of the process.

"Money isn't the answer, it never is, wasn't for Matt, he was bright enough to see that. Either you want a new life or you don't. If you don't I can't help you, I'm sorry."

Hopeless slient tears welling up, at least she's not sobbing.

"But what'll I do?"

She reaches across and grasps her arm, human contact, reassurance. The girl doesn't pull away, just looks in her eyes.

"It's up to you Lena; do you want to run forever or just one last time? To be free, secure, maybe loved, to make a place for yourself, somewhere you can be someone new, be who you really are inside, who you want to be? It's up to you. There are people there, others who have done what Matt's done; they can do the same for you, but once you are there, you're there, that's it."

She's desperate, she deluded herself that I could magic it all away without consequence for her, and now she sees there's a price: the nice lady isn't a fairy godmother after all.

"Can I have more time, take a little longer to decide?"

"Any longer, they might find you, you do know that?"

She hadn't thought of that, brain still sluggish from whatever she's been up to these last few weeks.

She nods, uncertainty, no escape routes any more.

"Would Matt meet me, help get me there?"

Breakthrough.

"If I can get hold of him and he wants to, yes, the last bit anyway. He's busy these days."

"Where is it anyway, you haven't said?"

"I can't, to keep them all safe and if I did you wouldn't believe me anyway. Dessert, tea, something else?" The girl nodded, she beckoned the waiter over.

"When?"

"A few days, leave it with me. I will extend your room at the hotel another night and then move you to another until we can get you away. Stay in, take no risks, understand, it'll be alright, I promise." Not easy, but alright anyway, the rest is up to you. "I'll walk you back to your hotel and then phone you there tomorrow sometime. Be there, okay?"

Lena nods.

"Good."

The best decision you probably ever made, I just wish I could be there to see the look on your face when you realise, and theirs' as well when they see you, their first black citizen so far as I know.

That night's dinner at Martha and Iltud's was Sally's happiest by far since she had crossed the barrier and, if she were honest, probably for months before that. Later, the guilt of that recognition twisted like a knife in her gut when she also realised that she had hardly thought of how Andy was for over twenty-four hours and then recollected, with shock, how few times Josey asked when they were going to see him. She would find a way, they would, but she had to be patient, determined and brave for her son's sake. The authorities here seemed very interested in her languages, her foreign office background; skills they had said could be invaluable to them. That might give her some negotiating leverage with them, perhaps she could test out the Abbot when she saw him on Monday, find out what they wanted of her, how far they might be amenable to help.

They had seemed particularly keen on her Italian and her Latin and had asked about her knowledge of the Vatican. She wasn't a Catholic, so they had been a little disappointed by her answer, as if only then realising then that she would have been too good to be true. They weren't just asking idle questions though; there was intent behind them. A theocracy; what would they want of a twenty first century theocracy whose authority they didn't recognise, saying it was less senior than their own? Theophano had mentioned the monks of the Holy Mountain, but had implied strongly they were Greeks, Orthodox at least, in long term contact with the Byzantine refuge. There was only one place she knew that fitted that description, Mount Athos, the Holy Mountain, home to Orthodox monasteries from Greek, Armenian, Russian and many other national traditions; self-governing, originating in ancient times, known to possess ancient treasures, manuscripts and other uncatalogued wonders.

Two theocracies then, one connected to the Byzantines… The other? Well there must be something going on, otherwise why ask the questions they had of her? If anyone could tell her it would be the Abbot, he seemed a decent and compassionate man, but she could also try Brother Peran on the way down to St Josephs, if she got him talking on such arcane matters, clearly, his first love after his faith, of course, his tongue might run away with him.

Gillian had come in to check on her and Narin, and pronounced her almost fully fit again, and Narin on the road to recovery. The girl had co-operated fully with her this time, letting her check her all over for almost an hour, smiling nervously, trying to use some of the new words she had learned that day. Before leaving, Gillian had confided that the girl was bruised all over, malnourished, undoubtedly brutally abused in the fullest sense of the word and would surely suffer prolonged reactions long into the future. For now though her recovery was remarkable, a triumph of the human heart and the love of others. Gillian had got quite emotional about it, she had even started talking like the priest at one point.

On the way out, Sally asked Gillian how could she bear to practise her trade here, when so many of the cures she was used to were unavailable: didn't it reduce her to despair to see people suffer and die when a few miles away, through the barrier, treatments were available that could cure them?

The doctor had smiled ruefully at that, answering that yes, at first, but then she noticed that some diseases, cancer, cardiovascular problems, asthma and dementia were much less common here, leading her to believe that they must be the consequences of modern lifestyles and were therefore less prevalent in the Pocket, where pollution, sedentary lifestyles and artificial chemicals were almost unknown. She had access to good medical drugs, especially antibiotics, brought in from the outside, which were critically important for treating people doing hard physical jobs who were far more prone to broken bones and bad wounds than on the outside. So yes, she could still make a positive difference, the nature of the problems were just different and, besides, here people seemed to accept that life had its risks and had to end at some point. So, no, she no longer despaired as she had done on the outside.

After dinner Martha and Narin had shown her the plans for the dress they were going to start making for the girl, and then for her if she liked it; Narin's eyes were alive when going through it with her. Later Sally noticed that they were equally alive when looking at Sam, something Martha didn't miss either. It was only natural they concluded, trying to calm their fears, given what he had done for her, she was still just a young girl after all, emotionally immature. They didn't share their surprise that she could look like that at any man given her suffering. Sam's eyes were hard to read when with the girl; he just spent hours with her patiently, teaching her words, smiling at her answers, nodding encouragement. If they had known that his real thoughts were over the moors and far away, they would have been mightily relieved, unless they had realised what he was rehearsing.

Thursday

....

The man he knew as 'Henry' was waiting for Andy Bowson in their coffee house of the day, already seated and drinking some sort of herbal tea. He looks tired, not quite as poised as normal, well we all are. The dispiriting lack of progress gets to everyone in the end.

"How are you Henry?"

"Fine thanks, you? Do you have something for me?"

"Just more of the same, you might almost think Dager and the HR bitch were flirting with each other."

"They are in a way. Is that all?"

"No, the chief's been cut out of the policy decisions; it seems to be the Commissioner's office and Home Office now. Heads are going down, it's not good for the investigation; whoever they are, they know how to minimise any forensics. But you must know all that, right?"

'Henry' nods. "It's now more political than policing, you can see that can't you? Doesn't it disturb you?"

"Damn right it does, I wanted your advice, to talk, there's no one else I can talk to. My wife, all this, I feel like it's all going to hell."

"Why me? You don't know me from Adam, they say I'm a spook; why trust me?"

"Just instinct I suppose, and I'm getting desperate about Sally, my son, it's going nowhere at all. You're the only one, other than the locals, who've tried to help, even if you do have your own reasons. And some of the things you said, warned me about the first couple of times we met, well I'm starting to see what you meant… You may be right. I'm just a career officer, catching baddies as my son says, this is all new. Oh, I've dealt with political cases before, but nothing like this, this is so much bigger and darker. My colleagues, some of them, ask me questions about it and I can't give them any real answers."

"So, what do you want me to say, to do? There's no more intelligence about your wife and child. I'm sorry, I wish there were. On the gang we're investigating, none of us are getting anywhere that's why it's getting political, being pulled into other games. Different people want different culprits to suit their own agendas. Some want it to be foreigners, CIA or Israelis, others native groups, others associates of our military or security services and quite a few want it to be other jihadis. Some others, perhaps like those cultivating your boss, want it all to go to hell so they can pick up the pieces."

"I'm starting to see that now, but how do you stand it, seeing the things that matter just gamed by others for their own ends? Or don't you care at all?"

'Henry' looked at him silently, intently, almost through him to somewhere else. He had never believed in providence until things had changed him, but now he did, but this, this was just too simple, too much of a come-on. Is it a trap or providential? It's too weird to be chance.

"I can't believe that this is the first time you've had these thoughts, that you're so naïve. Everything I've seen and heard about you says you are a dedicated and conscientious officer with a good future in front of you, but these things can't have come as any surprise, especially in your specialism. Why put yourself at risk by dealing with the likes of me? Why not just get your head down, play it safe?"

"Because half, more than half, my life has disappeared without trace on a moor and what's left is under a cloud of raining sh… Sorry. I just thought you might help and you seem to want my help in return."

I think you over-estimate your usefulness, but yes, you're desperate, I can see that.

"I knew a young man once, younger than you by a few years. He was working hard, but isolated, becoming disillusioned at what he found as he progressed: the higher, the closer, he got to the seats of power, the less solid it all seemed, the worse the people, not all, but most. He almost gave it all up, his promise, he felt powerless… Then one day something happened that helped him see things anew, that he had greater loyalties, responsibilities to those out there, those still to come. Perhaps he understood properly, for the first time, the oaths he had sworn and that he shouldn't give in to despair, that he would not always be alone in how he felt. That realisation still keeps him going, gives him courage when the odds seem insuperable, and others lend him their strength when he needs it, still to believe, keep trust, push on."

He paused, a deep breath.

"So, Andy, I can call you Andy? I don't know if I can trust you and you don't know if you can trust me. We could be at an impasse, but you seem willing to break it, am I right? Let me think, get back to you, but, in the meantime believe this: you, we, are not alone, very far from it. Be clear what you believe, the reasons why you do the dreadful job you do, where your real loyalties lie; just because so many others have lost these things, that is their problem, not yours. Lean on me when you need to and, I promise you this, I will not give up trying to reunite you with your family. In the final reckoning that's what this is all about, why we do what we do, to provide a safe place for those we love."

"Thanks, I appreciate that, I think I see what you're getting at. Keep me posted and I'll do likewise, ok?"

He leaves, Henry remains with the dregs of his tea.

'Far too soon for this one yet, but none the less tempting.'

At least Lena hadn't done a runner, nor did she seem to be having second thoughts, she had just lapsed into fatalistic passivity, as if having made this one big decision her life could continue without her steering it for a while.

She couldn't tell how long it would last; the girl was deeply troubled after all. It could take them months, years even, to straighten her out, assuming that she actually went through with it. Well, she was moving on to another hotel tomorrow, a transient one by Heathrow airport for a night then on to another, further out west, inching her inexorably towards her true destination, distancing her from the ruinous temptations of the big city without her even realising it.

Best of all though, he was coming, maybe staying tonight, bringing her his news, checking up on her. She felt some guilt there, but well, she could discuss the girl with him, strays with hard luck stories were irresistible magnets for him. Besides, it was his final decision whether to get her through into the Pocket, although he's never gainsaid you in the past. He trusts you, not in every way, in some things he's hard with you... Time will melt him, you'll see. That wasn't the deal, it was agreed, you'll spoil everything, all you really want. Get back in there, he'll be here any minute.

Ten minutes later, there goes the front door buzzer. It's him, don't hang around, let him in. She looks again in the viewer, dressed normally for him, briefcase, overnight bag, heart skips, another larger holdall, looks heavy.

"Come in."

In he comes, that usual two minutes longer today, by a few seconds, it must be the heavy bag. Don't leave the hall, wait for him. The doorbell rings, her hands fly to release the latch. There he is, he looks tired, almost stooping under the weight of the bags, been burning the midnight oil, but the smile is there.

"Can I come in or have you had a better offer this evening?"

"I'm sorry, I'm just... well, come in."

Losing it already, you've got two big deals on the go, lawyers and accountants sucking up to you, and look at you now. Shut up! He hands her his overnight bag, smiling once more, and brings the others in while she closes and locks the front door. She motions to repeat their little hallway entrance routine. He gives her his coat, same familiar weight, a little more reassuring now, but he keeps the others. "Same room ok for you?" He nods. "Go through into the kitchen while I put these away."

She enters shortly later; he's standing there, just waiting for her.

"On the off-chance that you were too busy to call the man I suggested, I called him myself and he's coming around at nine on Saturday morning, so you can enjoy a lie in, and whatever he recommends will be installed from eight on Monday morning, ok? Will you be able to square it with the other tenants, the landlord, or do you need me to have a word?"

I should be furious. "Sorry, I just didn't get around to it, thanks. And no, I'm the landlord; I own the other two flats below."

"I also took the liberty..." He opens the large holdall and pulls out a pistol and several boxes of ammunition. "I know you refused, but I insist, especially if I am going to be staying here. Don't worry, the paperwork's sorted. You can keep them in your safe. And this in your wardrobe..."

He pulled out a large black metal shotgun, followed by several boxes of cartridges, before she could react.

"Semi-automatic, I'll show you how later, but easy and ideal for inside. I assume you can lock your wardrobe?"

She nodded, stunned, "But I've never had... don't want such things. Perhaps the little one if you insist, but not that... thing, please?"

"It's not something I play at, my life, perhaps you didn't understand that. You told me you loved me in some way, that makes you vulnerable, means I have to take care of you, protect you, do you see?"

"But I don't want all of this, just..."

"It comes with me, I'm sorry. It's up to you. But if I thought you couldn't handle it I wouldn't even be here."

"But I didn't think..."

Just a smile.

"This isn't a game, this is just the way it is. I thought you knew, I'm sorry. If it's too much, I can go, cut my ties to keep you safe, or you can go, there, they would welcome you, you know, for what you've done, who you are."

"What about you, wouldn't you come too?"

A simple shake of his head.

"You know why."

So, what do you really want? Are you like that girl, just wishing, hoping someone will solve all her problems for her, not have to take a decision? No, not like that, I chose him, all of him, whatever comes. So, when did you get all so romantic? You know when, besides, this is a lot more.

"Ok, then I'm staying too, you know why. If you insist on keeping those things here, go ahead, but in return you must promise to take a key, stay more than two nights whenever possible."

Why not insist on more, don't be so weak?

"I'm glad I don't have to negotiate with you for a living, agreed."

The door buzzer goes.

"That's dinner, I'm sorry I didn't have time to do anything else. Could you please?"

Later, microwave going, music on, extractor fan whirring.

"Those sticks you so cleverly deciphered for me, there's so much there, some we can handle, but for some I may need your help, account numbers mainly. Can you find out who owns them, trace the funds in and out without exposing yourself to too much risk?"

He really didn't understand her world at all did he? She smiled inwardly, just because she's in finance, she must be a banker.

"I'm sorry, I just don't have the access, you would need a clearing banker, someone in the Bank of England or payments agency, or a forensic accountant and even then… Can't you go through your channels?"

"Not without raising questions, leaving a trail. Oh well, we'll just have to get it to the authorities anonymously along with some of the other things. The rest we're looking into, I can't thank you enough."

You could you know.

"How did it go with the girl, the American?"

"She just about got there; I still have my doubts though. She only really trusts Sam, insists on it being him who takes her there."

"Ok, I'll try to arrange it."

"Oh, and she's black."

"So? What's that got to do with anything? There's a Yazidi Kurd there at the moment, you know the brief. If she wants a new start, they can help her make the changes she needs, everyone changes there."

"Would it change me?"

"And why would anyone, me especially, want to do that?"

She smiled. "You say the nicest things sometimes."

See, what did I say? That's not what he meant! We'll see.

Sam was outside the girl's room when Martha came out on to the landing in the middle of the night. "Mum, she shouted out, and now she's crying, what should we do?"

He looked at a complete loss, her capable, tough adopted son. She beckoned him back into his room and gently pushed the door to.

"My love, the evil she's had to endure has to come out somehow, it's no surprise it happens when she's alone at night, it's part of the healing process. It could take months, years. If we could talk to her, we could help her recover more quickly, but now we just have to keep showing her she's safe, among friends. Perhaps Monday will help. Now get some sleep. If it gets too loud, leave it to me, you mustn't go in, do you understand?"

A nod.

*It pauses, Monday before Easter,
Holy Week*

....

An early morning start for the whole household, Martha, Iltud, Sally, Josey, Narin and an insistent Sam, who refused to be left behind; fresh clothes, big breakfasts, a stroll down to the station to catch the first train to St Josephs. What Narin made of it all they struggled to see; she had caught something of the excitement from them, but was clearly nervous, pressing in between Sam and Martha on the train seats for comfort and reassurance. Her progress in learning English was continuing, mastering many everyday nouns, some simple pronouns, a few common verbs, and she was now haltingly trying to put some together in rudimentary phrases. She was bright; they could all see that and very eager to communicate after years of isolation.

It was a sunny day, mixed with oncoming clouds, a freshening sea breeze tempering the air with its south-westerly mildness. Docco was fussing over them, employing a blissfully happy Josey as his assistant guard, helping to check tickets, wave the flags at the various halts, miming unrequested explanations to Narin who looked at him in bewildered amusement and then, in Josey's brief absences, watching the countryside rolling by, the little villages, churches, farms, wooded and flowered slopes rising above, the river at the bottom, occasionally asking for the names of what she saw. Two stops down the line Brother Peran clambered aboard, blessing the carriage and then filling half the bench seat opposite them, grinning broadly, telling stories of the sights they would see. The girl smiled at the sight of him and started to relax, clearly in her mind if he were going too it would be fine. He soon had them all laughing, even Narin and Sally, who realised that any chance to pump him for more information on this part of the trip was highly unlikely.

On arrival at St Josephs they walked up the main street to the Town Hall and then split up, Sally, her son and the priest headed down to the harbour to Thea's to wait while the others went to the Town Hall for Narin's interview, Sam muttering what was the point as no one could talk to her? Sally's party would wait for the Abbot to return from the Town Hall and then head over with him, by boat, to the island Abbey.

Thea's face lit up when Sally, Josey and Brother Peran came in, evidently regarding the monk as another island of culture and learning in her exile. Refusing all offers of payment, she ordered up small pastries, coffees and warm milk for Josey, joining them, asking how Peran's studies were going and why they had come to St Josephs, calling in her family to show them off. Even Georgy, initially sulky when he realised Sally was one of the recipients of his mother's earlier generosity, warmed up on learning of her friendship with Sam, recounting how they had rescued the girl and asking after her. He let slip that they had been warned they would be going back soon, more tasks to complete and so on, exactly what they were, he claimed not to know. Sally wondered how Martha and Narin would take the unanticipated early return of Sam to the outside, but Georgy seemed raring to go as if straining to complete unfinished business.

Thea though was not to be baulked of her desire to hold court for long. "I see," she said looking at Sally, and smiling, "that Anna here keeps her promises to visit a lonely old woman, as does my favourite priest Brother Peran, unlike that ungrateful Iltud… Tell me Anna, how is Martha faring with my finest cloth. Will she, you, do it justice, resemble a Byzantine princess, and become an object of majesty and beauty?"

"I still can't thank you enough Theophano," the old lady was delighted by this reverent pronunciation of her full name, "for your unbelievable generosity, I did not fully appreciate it at the time. It is a thing of beauty, but the most beautiful thing about it is how it has helped raise the spirits of the young girl Georgy helped rescue. Martha says she is a far more skilled needlewoman than herself and the task has helped bring her back to life, perhaps it's helped her realise that kindness and generosity can be found even when you are so far from home."

She could see her host was pleased by this little speech, as was Peran who was beaming exuberantly.

"When they have finished hers they will make mine, in time for the new arrivals Easter ceremony at the Abbey, I don't have the skills to help."

"Yes," Thea replied conspiratorially, "but you have others, or so I hear, even more valuable to the cause."

She caught Peran flashing Thea a warning look, and this time the little dynamo retreated a little.

"I'm sorry Theophano, what do you mean by my skills, my languages and what cause?"

But Thea would not be drawn any further and in any case the others arrived and poured out their news that Narin's interview had been just a formality, Peran's written character witness and Iltud's verbal summary settled the matter in five minutes, everyone smiling at Narin, a few with tears in their eyes, especially the Abbot himself. The only point of discussion had been her future, but the consensus was to wait for the Byzantine embassy, which was expected soon, and ask them, and likewise the mysterious unnamed 'he' everyone kept alluding to. Besides, it should be her decision, not theirs, and so they needed to wait for her to be able to speak with them well enough to discuss it if neither of the former could help. Narin was clearly completely mystified by it all, confused by the constant mentions of her name by strangers.

Thea had insisted she sat between her and the priest, and seemed to have taken on the role of her adoptive great aunt, offering cakes, anything, until Peran managed to convey to the girl by a mix of gestures and words that it was Thea who had given her the cloth. Tears flowed, hugs, almost prostration, embarrassing even the old lady, who insisted she follow her into the cloth room and see her stock, emerging fifteen minutes later with a fine white silk headscarf and matching waist band, the girl completely over-whelmed, Georgy just rolling his eyes in mock resignation. It was at that point that the Abbot arrived and came in to ask them to follow him to his gig for the trip to the island, but the thing that took Sally's attention was a brief sotto conversation in Greek between Georgy and his mother, her face conveying a savage desire, bright and hard, almost without limit. Then as she finally got out, having thanked her hosts effusively once more, she overheard a snatch of a muttered conversation between Georgy and Sam, their expressions composed into blankness, "now do you understand…"

The gig ride took about ten minutes to cross the calm sheltered bay water, coming into a little landing stage below the Abbey. The Abbot, Brother Winwaloe, was full of solicitous enquiries of her, Josey and Narin, her accommodation, hosts, everything other than what she wanted to know, jokingly enquiring of her if Brother Peran really took his parish duties seriously or did he devote all his energies to his scholarship?

Sally could see this was something of a running joke between the two of them. He told Peran he could borrow a further three books from the Abbey Library and to meet them in the refectory in an hour. In the meantime he would show Sally and her son the Abbey and a little of the island; Peran later telling her this was a most unusual honour.

The Abbey was clearly ancient, but newer than the Basilica and built in more typical ancient Celtic ecclesiastical style, albeit with what looked like a parish church sized, Romanesque bell tower at the eastern entrance. It was surprisingly small and simply furnished in comparison with the town's Basilica, white-washed rendered internal walls and all flagstone floored, other than by the altar where what looked like Byzantine tiles had been laid: small plain glass windows, gold and brass candelabra with carved oak seating in the two small side chapels only. The Abbot explained that the Abbey church was really only for use by the monks who lived there, about a dozen in total, who were the most scholarly of all and spent their time studying and practising the arts familiar from the Lindisfarne and other Celtic gospels. The only other regular congregants were the Duke's personal retinue, based in the ancient fort at the summit of the island about half a mile away, around a dozen guards and the same number of servants. The Brothers lived in a small cluster of cells with a library, wash-house, storerooms and workshops, situated between the Abbey and the southern shore.

He was in a mood to talk, to explain, needing little encouragement from her. The Duke was an old man now; reclusive since a bad injury and the death of his wife long ago, only indulging in state business on Easter Day each year, otherwise everything was run by the Council. Since the start of contact with the Byzantines, who apparently had an insatiable appetite for vellum books illustrated by the Abbey's Brothers, paying extremely high prices for them, and the advent of more immigrants from Logres, life in the Pocket had improved significantly. The population and the land itself were growing again, it was clearly His doing, confidence had returned, and they felt they were being directed to start to play a more active role in the world again.

Did he believe that stuff about the Pocket being set aside by God as a final refuge, an entry point?

Of course, wasn't it obvious, could there be any other explanation?

What were they trying to do, sending armed parties into Logres, attacking houses, killing people, rescuing girls like Narin?

Would you rather we hadn't and had left the poor child there?

Of course not, but that's not the point.

It is, it's the most important point, the protection of the weak and the freeing of captives.

Wasn't there some bigger goal?

To slow the spreading evil, only God could stop it, but slowing it down meant more innocent souls being rescued; what else could they do?

Surely though, priests, monks shouldn't and couldn't condone killing, violence?

Yes, so long as the cause is just, the defence of the weak, resistance against evil is permitted, indeed required; so long as it is not for gain, it is righteous.

What did they want of her, what were those questions for?

We all must make our contribution to the good of all in our own ways; you have been given gifts, talents, that are needed and the time for them is near, it is His providence undoubtedly that you are here.

But my husband… He wouldn't want us separated would He?

No, perhaps for a time if it serves His ends, but I am sure you will be restored to one another one day.

By now, they were on top of the bell tower looking over the eastern half of the island, just below the level of the walls of the fort on the slope above. Market gardens and orchards proliferated on the sheltered eastern side with a few gardeners, including monks, at work starting the planting of the Spring crops. To the north, near the edge of the island, was a graveyard surrounded by a drystone wall, containing low Celtic stone crosses.

He explained they were mainly the graves of monks, some Brothers at the Abbey in former times.

What about those in the far corner, they are bigger, laid out in an incomplete circle facing inwards, who are they?

Old non-clerical benefactors.

Why is the circle incomplete?

More may join them one day.

Then down to the library and scriptorium for her biggest shock of the tour. An old large windowed room, walls almost entirely shelved, with long oak desks running down the centre and little workshop alcoves between the windows and shelf stacks for binding, parchment preparation and pigment mixing. In a further room beyond stood a small old manual printing press, for functional books he explained; the others were hand-made for prestigious clients outside, including some at the Mountain by way of the Byzantines. But, the thing that truly stunned her was the locked basement level which contained a small lit wood-burner to keep away the damp along with thousands of books, ancient parchments, scrolls, each one in its own little wooden alcove with a piece of slate identifying it and, if it were loaned out, who had borrowed it.

Abbot Winwaloe explained that some of these were originals, manuscripts saved from the wreckage of Roman Britain, others brought by the Byzantines as gifts and exchanges, most were copies, some lost to the outside world, such as the full works of Diodorus Siculus, Pompeius Trogus, Hieronymous of Cardia, Ephorus, the lost works of Plato, and Aristotle's 'On Comedy,' among others.

"It's unbelievable. This is priceless; why keep it for yourself, this knowledge? Why not smuggle it into Logres, get it to scholars who can study it, fill in the gaps of our knowledge?"

The Abbot looked at her as a patient parent to an errant child.

"How many questions would be asked as to where they had been all this time, putting us at risk? Is any lost knowledge which can't change the future for the better worth that? We preserve and study it, as do the Byzantines, who have saved far more than us. Ancient histories, philosophies, religions, legends, sciences, poems, plays, wisdoms, the achievements of His creation, preserved as a remnant for the future, part of our charge from Him. Hello, there is Brother Peran, let us rescue him from his addiction and take him to the refectory for a Lent lunch. I hope you are not very hungry?"

His smile at his enquiry was simply a joke, she saw shortly afterwards. Lunch may have been simple, but it was plentiful, albeit only washed down with spring water. Both Peran and the Abbot seemed fascinated by her reaction to the library, which they appeared to consider their greatest treasure, Peran especially. Did he show her the basement volumes?

Yes.

Did she see the most precious treasures there?

The Abbot shook his head; there had been insufficient time, perhaps at Easter when she comes again.

What was it, this most precious treasure?

The Abbot grinned almost complacently, a first copy of St Mark's Gospel in the apostle's own hand, the Byzantines claimed to have the original, written within twenty years of the Ascension.

Why not release that alone, it would settle so many arguments, disprove so many doubts?

It would be too much, but I have to confess, I may have misled you earlier. We and our friends from the Middle Sea have placed a very few fragments from very early texts in the forgotten corners of one or two of the world's great libraries to help restore faith. Was she not aware that a few years ago a fragment of the Gospel of St Matthew, now dated by scholars to within forty years of the Ascension, had been found uncatalogued in an old box in the Bodleian Library in Oxford, how did she think it had got there?

Her jaw had dropped to full extension by now and was almost dislocated when this kindly man, eyes sparkling at her amazement, remarked casually that of course this was nothing compared to what the Byzantines claimed to possess. Original Epistles of St Paul, some from others of the Twelve who travelled to the east such as St Thomas, a letter from Thaddeus who found refuge at Edessa and converted its king very shortly after the Resurrection. Of course, he hadn't seen them for himself and the Byzantines were prone to exaggeration, after all they even claimed to possess cuneiform clay tablets dating back to Sumer and Assyria, a full undamaged Egyptian king list from the time of the Pharaohs, although they had now lost the knowledge of how to decipher them, so these claims could not be verified. Peran's eyes were shining too.

"If only I could be spared to study at Oxford to learn the knowledge of these tongues and to bring it back here, or could persuade the Council to kidnap some scholars and bring them back here to teach us, study alongside us."

Sally realised she was running out of time before having to depart, in danger of being swept away by their scholarly fascinations.

"What can you tell me about the Byzantines beyond the little that Peran and Thea have said? Will they be able to help with Narin?

Aren't they difficult to deal with, suspicious, quarrelsome, even a little arrogant?"

She could see Peran shift uncomfortably in his seat, waiting for the Abbot to respond.

"Less so than before and less than in their time of empire; their fall taught them some humility at least. You must recall that we were never part of the arguments over authority and doctrine that caused the schism between Orthodox and Catholic millennia ago. With our older tradition we had never accepted the Petrine supremacy of the Roman church; we allow our priests who are not Brothers to marry and have never adopted the 'filioque' clause of the Roman church which led to the schism. When they arrived and saw these things, their suspicions were allayed a little, that was the start at least…"

"Sorry, you've lost me, the 'filioque' clause?"

"One of the matters indifferent, adiaphorous, as I mentioned before."

Peran could restrain himself no longer.

"It relates to the Creed, the Western Church in early medieval times started to add a clause saying that the Holy Spirit proceeded from the Father and Son together, the Eastern still maintaining that it was just from the Father. It is a mystery of little consequence, unknown to man, to cause such a schism over such a minor matter of speculation…"

"It was the pretext Brother Peran, the cause was the desire for supremacy within Rome, the sinfulness of human pride working against His Will. In the end it led to Eastern Christianity being lost to the darkness, blows which have never fully healed: his judgement on our collective failure. We must all play our parts to further the restoration."

"So, yes, we have grown close to the Byzantines, not brothers or sisters yet, but cousins perhaps. We trade together, co-operate where we can, draw strength from each other, they have, these last few decades, even invited us to send emissaries from time to time, visiting us themselves each Spring after Easter. They even believe that other refuges may exist, are searching them out too, to bring hope, restore strength, make amends. But they must work by sea, the country beyond their barrier is alien, settled by their enemies, hard for them to build a presence in, unlike for us, but they have those of the Holy Mountain to help. Their wealth and that of their allies of the Mountain has enabled them to secure footholds in commerce in those lands restored to the Hellenes, contacts, influence, the ability to source what we and they need, to transport it where required, all the while moving quietly, hidden, unrecognised. They are a subtle and cunning people; that at least has not changed."

"The girl, Narin, can they help her?"

The Abbot shrugged. "It's in His hands. They have contact with some Armenians, descendants of those who survived the genocide of a hundred years ago, and previous attempts to exterminate them since their homelands were overrun. They believe there is an Armenian refuge on the southern coast of Anatolia somewhere, one that received some survivors of the conquest of their homes in Cilicia nearly a millennia ago. They say the Armenians may have contact with the Syrian Orthodox Christians who still cling on in the mountains of eastern Anatolia after over a thousand years of persecution; the Syrians are friendly with the Yazidi despite the latter's paganism, perhaps that is her route home. We will ask them; try to arrange it to help heal the wrongs done to her and her family. All things are possible in His Hands. Who knows? He may in His Wisdom have even preserved some of the Sabaeans of Harran, the Moon God worshippers, who the Orthodox in their mercy tried to protect from the persecutions of the Saracens before their own power was overthrown?"

Time was running short now; keep them off such matters of antiquarian speculation.

"People, Brother Peran here, keep mentioning a man who came from the outside fourteen years ago for a short time and was then sent back after discussions with the Duke and the Council, but never say who he was, what he's been sent back to do, why he was touched so quickly? Oh, and what's this 'touch,' can you tell me about that too please?"

He smiled once again, Peran looking at him carefully, as if trying to understand more for himself.

"It is not permitted to speak much of him, we do not name him to protect his work on the outside. It is not holy, it would be a breach of our promise to him. Of his work, I can tell you no more, at least not now, except that he saw the world the way as we do in some ways… He carried something within him we recognised and needed. He arrived in the early hours of a Palm Sunday, lost, on a walking trip he said, but we perceived that he had been found for us by providence and could not be passed by, so he was interviewed, touched and sent back the day after Easter."

"But some people say," she tried not to look at Peran, who was now ostensibly amusing her increasingly bored son, "he was someone from the past sent back, that can't be true can it?"

"We are Christians and do not believe in what the Hindus call reincarnation, we only have the one material life until the final day."

She could see she would get no further on the subject.

"And this 'touching': can I be touched so I might find my husband? Surely, it's not some sort of magic, is it?"

He smiled again.

"No, not magic, just faith, like baptism, a sacrament, a blessing from the Duke, anointing by me, the swearing of oaths on that Gospel of Mark, some other things, which part is efficacious is known only to Him, but it marks the one given it so they can leave and return through the barrier's gateways at will. Why some outsiders, such as you, are able to enter untouched is not known; some say it is when the barrier is weak, some because it is providence, His Will, who knows? Perhaps one day He will reveal His Will that you are touched, if so we will try to help you find your husband, but please do not raise your hopes unrealistically."

He looked at her, uncertainly this time, and then at Peran.

"Now, you must leave us or you will miss your train ride and the young man here would not forgive his missing the best part of his day."

"Father, one final question please?" He nodded that smile again. "Is there anything you expected me to ask which I haven't?"

"Plenty, but perhaps at Easter."

She thanked him profusely and left with her son and Brother Peran. As they were seated in the gig to take them back to St Joseph's, she realised there was one question she had forgotten to ask that maybe Peran would feel comfortable answering.

"Father Peran, there was one thing. You mentioned someone called Pelagius. Who was he?"

His answer was still going strong when they arrived at Thea's café to meet the others for the trip home.

When they were on the platform, starting to board the train, Peran took her aside quietly, urgently, "Forgive us our ways, we do not wish to frustrate you, mislead you, there is much I, even he" meaning the Abbot "do not understand. I, he I know, will try to help you within the bounds of our law, but this, after all, is not a theocracy so even we must obey."

Well, he had made the last train back from Brussels to St Pancras; that was one of the few things about the day to give him any satisfaction. Following the previous week's meeting, he had insisted to his contacts that the Turk meet him. Three times they had refused, finally relenting on Sunday afternoon and, even then, the Turk wouldn't meet him directly, but through a lieutenant in a non-descript suburban Brussels hotel, with the Turk in another room nearby and the intermediary conducting shuttle diplomacy between that room and the meeting room they were using. It was obvious they were trying to humiliate him, demonstrate who the supplicant was and who the granter of favours. So medieval, so primitive, so certain to be their ultimate downfall. That could wait until sometime in the future for now though.

They would not disclose what they were up to, security reasons they said, but it would be big: several actions of large scale, enough to rock the state apparatus on its heels, confuse the populace, cause them to lose faith in their government's ability to protect them. They weren't talking anymore of forcing a change of government policy, even a change of government, but the crippling of the state itself, its assumptions, and its economy, a seismic series of blows to the morale and self-belief of the country. They had never expressed their ambition quite so openly before, nor indicated their self-confidence or depth of resources. It was deeply disturbing, like trying to ride on the back of a tiger; the sooner they dismounted the better, but he had had one last favour to ask.

He had handed over a short list of names and addresses for their consideration, people in whom they might want to take a lethal interest, their common opponents so to speak. There was no reaction, no gratitude, just a demand for information in return. Odd, they just wanted a list of government and other senior figures who might be attending major events celebrating Whitsun: didn't they understand that hardly anyone bothered with such things anymore? But he had promised to do his best; he vowed it would be his last favour to them. Perhaps it was time to get our networks to press for rebuilding border controls, new restrictions on immigration, deportations of those not sufficiently subscribing to 'British values' whatever they were, new laws restricting religious expression and freedom of association. Yes, the primitives' boundless desire for blood could play right into our hands, so help them out one last time and give them the noose that hangs them.

Maundy Thursday, Holy Week before Easter

....

He sat back in his office chair, staring at the ceiling, stretching his back muscles, arms braced behind his head. Outside his door Elaine Ferris decided to intercept any calls and deter any would-be visitors; she knew him well enough to know that he wasn't staring vacantly at all, he was furiously at work in that eccentric way of his, thinking, making connections, twisting and testing all known possible permutations.

She hoped that he was thinking of the person behind that voice, but somehow she doubted it: he had said that the latest COBRA and other sub-committee meetings he had been obliged to attend were just going around in circles, as was the investigation, with ever rising proportions of successive meetings concerned with 'community relations' and PR issues. He had made a joke of it when she appeared worried by his candour, but the office gossip was unequivocal: little progress at all and whoever was behind these events had simply dropped off the radar without leaving a trail.

Yes, the lady behind that voice. It seemed things were getting serious; she smiled inwardly, well good for him. She had had to handle the paperwork for the issue of firearms and security equipment to the lady's apartment, classy, but not flashy, address, another box ticked on Elaine's checklist. She had a full name as well, the office gossips would have traded a lot for that, but none of them would ever learn it from her. He was taking the threat seriously; steel lined front door, alarms, sensors and a reinforced panic room too. Their trusted contractor would be in there for several days at least, but should finish sometime on Saturday.

Yes, his hunch, based on the data from the sticks and their follow up work was promising. Some of the numbers he had been monitoring had gone dead, either switched off or discarded, but others listed had been activated, and other numbers also appeared to be operating at the same cluster locations. Call traffic to and from them was staccato and brief, almost to the point, not conversational in tone at all, another indicator to raise suspicion.

The computer translations of the recorded conversations had never proved adequate substitutes for actual speech, missing all the tones and inflexions which provided so much context; nevertheless, it was clear that these two addresses housed people of some level of importance in one of the organisations they were up against. They used phrases that were obviously coded, indirect allusions, but they were planning something, marshalling resources, checking the willingness of others and, in doing so, inadvertently identifying for him the outliers in their network, the numbers of their correspondents and the scale of the group appeared larger than even he had thought. More interesting was a small cluster of numbers in Belgium that had divided into two, one staying on the move in the Low Countries, the other heading for Turkey. Tracing their call networks could be extremely interesting, but for now he had to focus, not get distracted.

Observation in situ had confirmed that the larger cluster was at a Bangladeshi restaurant on a tertiary arterial road into Swindon, the other lesser cluster in a residential house in an immigrant populated area of suburban Reading. The former was easier to watch simply by posing as customers, but more difficult to draw good intelligence from given the large numbers of staff, suppliers and diners coming and going. It seemed to have only one large family, including one Asian male, living in the flat above. The residential address was difficult to monitor given the surroundings, with few observations of residents, although the electoral roll gave one Asian male and two females as living there.

Here we are confronted by our greatest weaknesses: the lack of resources, our inability to just patiently monitor and analyse the identities of visitors, to unpeel slowly the network associated with these addresses. It would be so much easier to just pass it on to those authorities who had the resources and then to observe any progress from the inside, but that's not how we are going to find the bigger game behind all this, the allies they refer to, their backers. So, what to do? We don't have the capacity yet to operate outside the mainland which would allow us to pass any information on when we have found out their friends over here, their key links. So, what to do?

The Birmingham house job had been, in the end, a huge success: many of these people were paranoid, not true professionals; they had a tendency to keep sensitive information close to hand and were prone to crack under pressure. Could we handle similar jobs at both these addresses simultaneously? Go in late at night when only the residents were in situ, interrogate them, search the premises, bring anything of real interest away, burn the rest and eliminate anyone found there who seemed to be involved?

It would certainly disrupt anything they were planning, enable us to send on the lower level contact finance and logistics information we had already collected, so that the authorities could inflict further damage while we go after those further up the chain. Especially these so-called allies, perhaps identify those at the pinnacles of the power structures who must be associated in some way?

Hmmm?

With good planning we could just about manage it. Beta team to Reading, with back up from the base team. Alpha team to Swindon with support from the standby team; both teams move in straightaway. No messing, silenced weapons, extreme measures where necessary, minimise risk, straight back home via two vehicle changes and the base farm. That's the only way: a challenge, a risk, but observation hadn't indicated any active cells based there, just one or two individuals at most. Surprise and speed would be the key; we could get inside the restaurant disguised as customers, giving us an advantage. Ok, that's it. Get a note to the teams: be here for Tuesday morning after their Easter, briefings at the farm, final planning then go.

What to do this weekend? She would like me to stay, go away with her somewhere, especially as the contractors will still be there into Saturday now. Too busy though, too much planning, need to get away and join the base team, given the scale of what we're attempting. They might need persuading as well, given the ambition involved, the risks to so many; I'll need to spend some time at the farm as well if they want to talk. There's also the American girl, she needs to be taken to the farm for the final run home… I could kill two birds with one stone, pick her up on route, she could come that far at least to introduce me to the girl, Lena wasn't it?

Hopefully, Sam would be waiting to take her through the barrier; I've never understood why it will allow people in, but not out, if they are accompanied by someone who's been touched.

Helena will be upset and angry, she's clearly getting to the end of her tether, work stress, me, all of this, no longer in full control, that's probably the worst for her.

Smiles.

She is quite remarkable, a far better person than me, but she still doesn't really know what she wants, just what she doesn't. I'll make it up to her, stay Monday night, perhaps other nights too, just not Tuesday when the teams go in, I'll need to be elsewhere then, probably Wednesday too. I need to catch up with her cousin; what an amazing family, perhaps she'll have her over one night when I'm there. I just don't want to see either of them hurt, wish they hadn't got sucked into this. Wish I hadn't, sometimes.

Good Friday

....

Ten minutes from the farm, the sun sinking in the west, the American girl dozing on the back seat, at least she wasn't arguing now.

If Helena hadn't gone with him to meet Lena at the hotel in Hungerford, where she had stayed for the last three days, the girl wouldn't have come. Her time away from London, living in comfort, had revitalised her confidence, made her feel an illusory security again, buried the compliant desperation which would be her salvation. Like so many people in her position, she had no sense of perspective, no ability to step outside herself and think things through beyond the personal; such a pity, so immature and so impulsive, despite her years. But Helena had finally convinced her, had talked about choices, remaking herself, holding on to offered chances, love, friendship, trusting Matt and not looking back; at one point it had almost sounded as if Helena was trying to persuade herself.

He had held off telling her he would be away until Monday until the girl was safely in his car and they were parting; what a coward. He had expected her to remind him of his promise, say that she had made no plans for the weekend because of him, that she would be alone, to reproach him. She hadn't, she had just looked at him sympathetically, sadly, said she understood and in parting had kissed him softly on the side of his cheek, too close to the edge of his mouth for comfort, then turned and walked back to her car.

That was the worst of all; he would rather have had her anger than that.

He pulled into the farmyard behind the house and got a rucksack out of the boot. Things she had bought Lena to take with her, clothes mainly, Lena's own small backpack with her own effects and a bag containing suitable clothing and boots for the night hike across the moors. He smiled inwardly, she really was amazing, she thought of everything; he hoped the girl would be able to properly thank her one day. He woke Lena and took her into the farmhouse kitchen where hot food was brought out of the range cooker, marching food, no time to waste.

Mark the Seigneur was there with a couple of his team, discreetly armed, along with Sam. He explained they were going to take her to join a smuggling party meeting a lorry on the moorland road and join them for the hike through the barrier.

Mark was experienced, had done this many times, but was nervous too, looking at the girl as if doubting her mettle, her strength for what lay ahead, explaining quietly that the barrier was weak at the moment, the land was expanding, 'they' were becoming more of a threat. Such a large party should be fine, but was more noticeable; at least the weather was poor, blustery and raining, which should keep passing strangers away.

Sam was just talking quietly to the girl who seemed to have lapsed into that mute helplessness that had been her previous state of mind. He smiled at her frequently, reassuring her, explaining the upsides of his new life.

He asked Mark where he was taking the girl to stay.

"Well, she can't stay with Martha and Iltud, they have no more room, so it's either a choice between a couple in the next village who have looked after incomers with similar problems, or the nuns' guest house. She looks like she'll need a lot of attention, but I thought a loving family might work the best, at least at first. Besides, Sam will only be a little distance away, at least until he goes back. What do you think?"

"That will be fine I'm sure. Can you send this note to the Council when you get back? Sam, have you got a moment? Lena, good luck, don't worry, you're in the best of hands."

Seven hours later, the girl was out on her feet, her stamina long spent, wasted by her former life. Sam had supported her at first and was now carrying her for the final couple of miles along the valley floor; that was the trouble, these days every journey seemed somehow longer than the one before. But he was nearly home. How did he feel about going back so soon? He understood better now, things were black and white, he had work to do, wrongs to be avenged, enemies to be put down.

Easter Sunday

....

The apartment felt emptier than usual when she awoke on Sunday morning, like a vacant tomb, but at least the contractors had finished. Perhaps it was that analogy that had impelled her to go to church for the first time in twenty years, she couldn't think of any other reason. When he had told her he wouldn't see her again until Monday, at the earliest, it had been all she could do to retain her self-composure, not embarrass them both in front of Lena; he had enough on his plate as it was.

She didn't trust herself to call him, didn't take his calls, just replied by text. Petulance? No, it was more about the way she was in danger of dissolving inside. The more time she spent with him, the harder it got. Wasn't that what you wanted, wasn't that the deal? No, that's not it. Then break the ties before we both get hurt. Too late, talk to him again on Monday. Try not to be so needy, so selfish. No, that's not it either, let's see on Monday evening.

She considered herself as some kind of agnostic, not hostile; she just didn't see the relevance to her life most of the time. She had sat at the back, alone, while the service's Palm Sunday rhythms went through the gears; she was hardly paying attention, just musing idly, brain in neutral for once. She could see the appeal though, the promise of a new start, redemption, eternal unity with those we love, the coming together of people from entirely different walks of life, who would otherwise never meet, in a sort of community. Those things prized more than money and gain, things wealth could never buy.

He had never spoken to her about such things, she suspected they were so deeply internalised he had lost the power to discuss them; how could he even begin to share any of it after the things he had seen, had suffered, had lost?

Perhaps, one day, when they were somewhere away from all of this, content, she would raise it with him. Yes, that's what she really wanted. The realisation was like that beam of sunlight breaking through the window, picking out the polished brass cross on the white altar linen, just like those wartime photos of St Pauls in the Blitz, with the cross at the summit of the dome shining inviolate out of the smoke; dust, death and carnage all around.

She came to from her reverie, the congregation had gone, the sounds faded away. The vicar was standing beside her, looking down.

"Is everything alright? Is there anything you need?"

She smiled and shook her head.

"No thank you, but I'm clear now."

Thank you.

Bizarrely, Easter was the one Sunday a year when the trains ran, taking people down to the Abbey and Basilica for the festive highlight of their year, guests travelling at the Council's expense. They were all going, even Narin who, they had been told would receive special treatment, and an exhausted Sam, who had come in just before dawn. He had washed, breakfasted, changed and was now snoring on the seat in the corner next to Martha; the girl sat opposite him next to Sally, Josey already with his new best big friend Docco, playing trains.

Sally had been sent a small booklet, beautifully illustrated in the Celtic style, containing the oath she had to swear in Latin, Brythonic and English. There seemed to be nothing in it to which object, just items of antiquarian interest, allegiance to the Dux of Lethostow, Iltud explaining that it was the old native name for the Pocket, by the Grace of God etc. Narin's was different, written in very simple, almost babyish English, that she would never disclose the existence of the Pocket, its inhabitants, or act against them, sworn under whatever deity she worshipped, so no act of allegiance for her. Martha thought it ridiculous: how could she swear something she didn't understand, Illtud just mumbling that he was sure the authorities knew what they were doing and surely it was in her best interests?

A couple of stops down the line Gillian and Petroc got on board, sitting as close to them as they could in the rapidly filling carriage. Gillian came across to admire their long Byzantine silk dresses with fine, almost invisible silk thread stitching which Narin had largely been responsible for making. Sally felt ridiculously over-dressed, like something out of the dark ages, there was no doubting the quality of the materials, cut and workmanship, just her ability to do it, Narin and Thea the real justice they deserved.

Sally could see that all the women in the carriage admired both of them, casting bashful glances; such things were like hen's teeth in the valley, almost all being exported to the outside. Theophano had chosen well, especially for the girl, whose white silk headscarf and waist band completed her outfit along with the strings of pearls she wore in common with the other two women.

Sam had just stared at Narin in wonderment, at her transformation from a broken thin teenage girl into an attractive young woman, less emaciated, bruises largely faded and whose skin was recovering some of its youthful smoothness and vitality.

Yes, the exuberant colourings of the materials worked for Narins' darker skin tones better than for Sally's own, lighter English complexion. She could sense Martha's alarm bells were ringing fit to burst now, hardly surprising.

On arriving at their destination, they went to see Thea at the café to show off the results of her generosity. Thea and her family had already attended two services at the Basilica and would be returning, at dusk, for a service in the Byzantine side chapel where she had her own benefactor's seat. The little dynamo had clapped her hands, exclaiming in Greek, "kalliste, kalliste, most beautiful, most beautiful," dashing inside and coming back two minutes later with a sublimely fine silk cloth of gold headscarf and waistband for Sally, refusing all offers of payment, just arguing that an incomplete gift is no gift at all, and insisting they join her at the café on their return from the Abbey to tell her all about it.

Gigs were ferrying people to the island, their small sizes requiring Gillian and Petroc to go separately from them. The previous day and night's cold front had pushed on inland, leaving a cool but fine day before the arrival of the next front, coming in from the Atlantic to the west; fortunately, the bay water remained calm. On landing they were directed to the Abbey refectory, which was warmed by two large blazing stoves, to refresh until all the guests from the mainland had arrived.

Just before noon they were all led through into the Abbey church where they were sat on temporary benches arranged either side of the nave facing the altar, a low carpeted dais before it holding a small oak throne and chair. Their party filled an entire bench near the front, Sally and Josey sat down on the aisle end looking around as the Abbey filled with people; an expectant silence replacing the previous chattering hubbub.

Iltud had gone to the front to join the rest of the Council who had their own benches situated either side of the low platform. The Seigneurs, including Mark, dressed in some sort of antique Roman ceremonial cavalry armour on top of blue tunics and leggings, seated among them.

Gillian sat in the front row with her husband, looking extremely nervous. What was going on with her, she had already sworn her oath surely?

As the noon day bell's last chime was fading into silence, the choir, processing from the back of the nave, raised their voices in Latin plainsong.

Sally realised there was no organ or other musical instrument within the Abbey, all the music was the product of the human voice. Two dozen in total passed them, so they had clearly brought reinforcements from the mainland. The Abbot came behind the choir followed, in turn, by a very old man with white beard and long robe bearing a simple hazel staff, next came an ageing but clearly still active man in robes of purple, a sword by his side, white grey beard and shortish, military looking hair under a slim gold circlet, and finally the High Steward wielding a staff of office.

She turned to Martha as to ask the identity of the old man and if this were the Duke, but was waved into silence.

The new entrants sat down, followed by the congregation, the Duke, for it must be him, on the throne, the old man on the chair with the Abbot and High Steward remaining standing. Nothing was said until the Abbot welcomed everyone in three languages, the choir then breaking into a psalm in Latin. And so it continued, hymns and psalms sung by the choir in Latin and Brythonic interspersed with readings from the Gospel of St Mark and prayers in Brythonic and English until forty minutes later the singing subsided, whence the High Steward came forward to address the congregation, welcoming the new arrivals of the last year and inviting them forward to the front of the platform to begin the oath swearing.

Sally looked about, she was there with Josey holding her hand, silently wondering, hushed by the formality of the occasion for once, and about a dozen (she later learned fourteen) other arrivals since the previous year's ceremony. Most were middle-aged or older, men and women, but about a third were younger, teenagers or early twenties she guessed, but no other children. All looked nervous; scared of making fools of themselves. Their names were read out in turn in Brythonic and English, where they were staying, where they were from, their occupations. Each, other than Josey, was asked in turn to kneel and read the oath in three languages before the ceremony moved on to the next. It didn't take long, around 30 minutes or so, she estimated.

The old Duke then rose to his feet and gave, in Brythonic, a welcome to his new subjects and co-workers, which was translated by the Abbot. As they went back to their benches they were each given a small vellum book, beautifully hand illustrated, with their name, their date of arrival and copies of the oath in the three languages.

It also contained the first verses of St John's Gospel, the Creed and Lord's Prayer, again in three languages. Martha later explained that they were the Brothers' welcome gifts to all new citizens and each took a calligrapher a week to prepare.

As she sat down, she noticed that Gillian was making her way to the front of the dais where she knelt with nine other people, all but her young or fit looking middle-aged men. The High Steward introduced them all, Gillian last, explaining in the three languages that they had all demonstrated valuable skills and dedication in the service of the Duchy, were worthy of the highest trust and had been selected to be 'touched' so they could serve the Duchy in the outside if and when required. Sally looked at Martha, who was equally astonished at Gillian's inclusion, and then at Petroc, whose face was stony.

This time the Duke got up, followed by the old man, the High Steward, Abbot and two Brothers. One of the Brothers was carrying a cloth covered tray holding two golden vessels, the other a golden casket, all approached the first kneeling man.

Sally watched intently. The Duke had unsheathed his sword and placed it before the first man to kiss, then the next and so on until he arrived at Gillian; he then stepped back and held it before him, its dull steel blade notched from use. The High Steward did the same with a cavalry lance with a plain white banner hanging down with what looked like Greek chi-rho lettering on it. Next the Abbot, followed by the first Brother, anointed each in turn on the forehead, firstly with water and then with oil. Finally came the second Brother and the old man, each kneeling celebrant placed one hand on the casket, the other on an ancient looking scroll wrapped in crimson silk held by the old man, and then recited a different oath in Latin only, Gillian being the last. The kneeling supplicants were then dismissed back to their seats in the nave.

It looked as if business were done, the congregation's hubbub rose again until the Abbot was heard requesting silence, which rippled backwards through the Abbey until all was still. He came down from the dais and approached their bench smiling at Narin, holding out his hand for her to accompany him; she was frozen in shock and bewilderment. Sam started rising to his feet to argue, but was motioned down again by Martha, who looked equally surprised.

The Abbot, smiling still, beckoned her again, and then to Martha to accompany her. The girl relaxed, recognising his garb as similar to that of Brother Peran and stood up to accompany him and Martha back to the platform where she stood, looking so small in her riot of richly coloured Byzantine silks. Martha, standing beside her gestured to her to kneel but the Abbot countermanded her with a shake of his head, whispering an enquiry to her if she had the girl's oath to hand. She produced it. He smiled, and then the touching ceremony started again, the sword kiss, the lance kiss, the double anointing, but just one hand on the casket, no scroll this time. Martha spelled out the words slowly, one by one, nodding to the girl to repeat them.

What she made of them no one knew; they held their collective breath, some she clearly had gained a little familiarity with, others were still strange to her and her faltering tongue slowly meandered through them, the Abbot smiling encouragement all the while until she finished. He and the old man laid hands on her head and appeared to pray over her briefly, then he smiled once more and motioned Martha to lead her back to the bench, while the choir sang a final psalm and the procession reformed and headed back down the aisle and out of the eastern door.

A collective silence had held the entire congregation in thrall, broken only by the announcement by one of the Brothers from the open door that all oath swearers and their accompanying guests were invited to back to the refectory for dinner. As they made their way there, Sally realised that people were astonished that Narin had been 'touched' in that way, a radical departure from tradition; all were dumb-founded.

Entering, they found the room laid out with two long rows of trestle tables with another at the end where the Duke and his officials were taking their places. Purple and red silk hangings, again of what must be Byzantine origin, lined the walls now and similar cloths of linen this time covered the tables, along with glassware, crockery, cutlery, flagons of wine, water, cider and beer, and small loaves of bread. They were motioned to their seats and silence fell again as the Abbot relayed grace in Latin and then proposed toasts, to their new fellow compatriots, those entrusted to go outside, the Duke's continued long life and health, their cause and finally to the little lost lamb that had been found and brought back to them. Looking at Narin with tears in his eyes, he asked that God might return her safely to her family and homeland. Sally couldn't help thinking that he would have made the softest father she had ever known, and then noticed Sam's unhappy expression, and looked at Martha confirming that she had seen it too.

Lent had passed and consequently the dinner seemed to be a never-ending series of dishes, with no defined courses, consisting of meats, fish, shellfish, winter vegetables, cheeses, cakes and even preserved exotic fruits brought in by sea, apparently the most sought-after delicacies of all those presented. After the formality of the occasion in the Abbey it was delightfully informal, people just getting up and going to speak to others sat elsewhere, but, she noticed, no one approached the high table where it appeared that far more business-like discussions were underway.

After about two hours, people started drifting away as the serving staff began clearing; it seemed that the event had finished and the Duke and his officials were heading up to the fort with a handful of his guards and servants. However, Abbot Winwaloe was there, waiting outside the door for them when they emerged into the daylight, inviting them to one side away from the crush of the departing guests.

"Apologies, apologies for the surprise at the end, but there was no time to warn you, the young girl. It was only finally decided by the Duke just before the service that the girl, Narin," he smiled at her, "should receive the touch so she can leave for home, if God provides, before next Easter. We changed the ceremony a little, absenting the swearing on the Gospel of St Mark as we believe her not of the faith, but retaining the other things for fear that the touch would be invalidated if we left out too much. I had sent you a simple oath in case I was able to persuade my colleagues to make this exception, but it was only this morning that the Duke himself agreed: I had not wanted to raise false hopes by telling you what I intended beforehand. It is the Lord's Will I told them, this young man risked his life to free her from bondage," smiling at Sam, "how could we prevent her safe passage to those she loves? It would be sinful; laws are not made to frustrate the doing of good."

His face was so sincere that even Sam felt compelled to embrace him in thanks.

"Father, what were those relics she swore on?"

"Ah, Mistress Bowson, that is one of the questions I had expected you to ask me on your last visit! The sword is the Duke' own, a symbol of his sovereignty, the lance is that of Constantine the Great himself that he carried at the battle of the Milvian Bridge outside the gates of Rome. It was sent to St Josephs' Basilica by its patron, his mother the Empress Helena. The oil and water are sacramental and from the Abbey, representing divine majesty and baptism, and the casket contains the bones of St Joseph, they are normally held in a locked crypt beneath the Basilica. The Gospel you already know."

Before she could scoff or even ask a further question, he had moved on to Narin. "And now my dear child, you will have all our heartfelt prayers for a safe return home, this is a little going away present from the Brothers and a sentimental old man," handing over a small leather purse to the girl, blessing her and then heading off before turning back and saying, "And now I am late for business with the Duke, and so will you be for your train home, so be off!"

"Where's Iltud, Martha? Isn't he coming back with us?"

"No Sally, he's got late business with the Council tonight and will remain in the fort, returning later tomorrow. Now let's obey the Abbot one further time."

It was only later, after they had just made the last train home, that Narin had opened the purse. Within were twenty golden Sovereigns of recent years, some mixed silver coins of other nationalities, a small golden Celtic cross on a chain and a letter for Sally. 'My dear lady, the gold is for the girl to help her on her way home and the cross is a reminder of God's love for her. You will get your opportunity to ask yet more questions as you will soon be asked to meet the Council again. May He bless you all.'

She was in tears, passing it to the others. "Such love," said Martha, "such a good soul."

Narin, finally catching up, broke into sobs as well, Sam just looked embarrassed. Gillian, who was further down the carriage, headed their way. "Is anything wrong?" she said.

"Nothing," sniffed Martha, handing her the note, "what do you think of that?"

The doctor, sitting down with them read it and looked up.

"Nothing surprises me about this place anymore, other than the unrelenting saintliness of that man, Brother Winwaloe. I remember how he was with me when I first arrived. He had just been made Abbot himself, but nothing was too much trouble; I think it was he more than the fact of the place itself that made me start to believe."

"Gillian?" Sally had recovered herself and was not going to miss the opportunity. "I thought you didn't want to ever go back into the outside, so why were you there being touched?"

"It's true; I don't want to, Petroc doesn't want me to either." She looked anxiously down the passenger aisle at her husband who smiled back. "But I was asked only earlier this week, told there was no one else, with what's now going on outside they need a doctor in case one of our boys get hurt. They could hardly take them to a hospital… Someone who knows Logres, what it's like, won't panic. So, I had to say yes, I owe them that. But I'll only go when needed, in emergencies, and not too deep in."

"So, what are they up to there?"

"I can't tell you and I don't know much, just enough they said, but it's dangerous."

Sam was sitting stony faced in case he was asked next; he had already had to bat this sort of question away several times himself.

She changed her angle of questioning.

"What about what the Abbot said about those relics at the touching, that can't be true can it; you're a scientist after all?"

"If someone had told you a month ago, less, that there was a hidden British enclave in twenty first century England under some sort of special protection, that it was trading with a similarly hidden Byzantine refuge in the Mediterranean, making a living by smuggling into Britain, sending parties in and infiltrating the state, welcoming lost souls like me, what would you have said? It's not science, its fact. You can't escape it. So, if the Abbot, who is probably one of the most decent men you could ever hope to meet, tells you those things are true, then you'd need a pretty damn good reason to disbelieve him. It took me three months to realise that, and other things about this place, I only hope its sooner and less painful for you than for me."

Well, he and they had tried. He had felt that he had to go and spend Easter Day with Sally's parents; after all he had nowhere else to go other than work. He had driven down in the morning and would be heading back later. He just owed it to her really, to try to keep the embers of a family life burning until they could be reunited.

The search on the ground was winding down, the enthusiasm of the local volunteers exhausted by endless nothing, police resources required elsewhere. They would continue to be registered as missing persons; the posters would remain up until the weather did its worst. The park wardens and gamekeepers would keep their eyes open as they went about their work on the moors, but his local liaison officer made no attempt to disguise his hopelessness. Well he couldn't blame the man, they had tried, hard, but so many missing people were never found, just completely disappeared.

Her parents were in silent despair, their only child and grandson gone, so close to their home. They had attempted to make him welcome, seemed to appreciate his effort, tried to distract themselves by talking about the things he must be investigating, but her ghost was in the house, its mere presence paralysing every effort to have a normal day. They were talking about selling up, going far away, somewhere there would be no reminders; he had tried to tell them that's not what she would have wanted, and then caught himself using the past tense. He had brushed the tears from his eyes, excused himself and come away; he would call them every day, he promised. What state they were in after he left he couldn't begin to picture.

She opened the door and ushered in her cousin, embracing her. She was determined not to be alone for the whole weekend and had invited her spinster cousin over for dinner and to stay over if she wished. It was amazing they got on so well really, she herself was ten years younger, had been married, enjoyed the finer things in life, looked after herself and took pride in her appearance. Her cousin was a vegan, spiky, not interested in money, almost austere, never married, not even much sign of any close relationships, in another century she might have been an ideal nun in some puritanical order. They hadn't really seen much of each other until they were both working and living in London, but now they saw each other from time to time, talked about anything other than work, or politics, which would be sure to end in an argument: perhaps two lonely souls huddling up together for comfort. Lord, she was on a downer at the moment.

They were picking their way through some tasteless vegan ready meals from the local supermarket, she couldn't be bothered to cook such things herself, when her cousin smiled and fixed her in the eye. "So, where's your man-friend then, Henry? I thought he would be spending the weekend with you, at least today?"

Her eyes were sparkling with fond amusement at her younger cousin's spreading blush.

"It's not like that, can't be, you know... He's got things on, higher priorities."

"Higher priorities than making my little cousin happy?"

"Please don't joke about it, you know why."

"I'm not sure I do. I still can't quite believe he hasn't asked you to marry him or at least moved in with you. I never thought him a fool."

"It's not like that at all, it's not on the table, but he's staying here a couple of nights a week, he's got his own room."

Her face was burning now like a little girl asked out on a first date by the boy she secretly dotes on. "We're just best friends, no more."

Liar.

"Or is it just the lure of forbidden fruit, the fascination of the one you can't have? I'm not surprised none of your other relationships ever lasted, with him always just out of reach."

Helena just looked at cousin. Stricken. Mute. Skewered.

"Still, I can't believe he hasn't succumbed to your wiles yet, or have you had a change of heart?"

Tell her. No, I'm not ready, not sure. You were a few hours ago. No, no, not like that, besides I promised him. All's fair they say. Not with him, it's too risky. Back inside, leave me alone.

"I'm comfortable with the way things are, wouldn't want to jeopardise it, besides he's carrying too much, he doesn't need me as well."

A sympathetic smile, the amusement gone from her cousin's face.

"I'm sorry; I didn't mean to upset you. Just don't make the mistake I once made."

"What was that?"

A couple of hours later when they were packing up for the night, her cousin turned to her and smiled. "When, if, you do see him tomorrow, tell him we may have had a breakthrough, but I'll pass on more when I'm sure."

Easter Monday

....

That's another weekend you're owed that you won't ever get back. Exmoor farm, Cotswold base, drive-byes of the two target addresses, discussions and planning with the teams in situ, the remainder coming in tonight, on top of taking Lena to her transit point.

He knew he'd upset Helena, entirely understandable: she must be thinking he had already forgotten his promise. At least she wasn't arguing or causing a fuss, she'd just withdrawn, but not entirely: already becoming a larger presence in his thoughts.

The guilt comes.

Change your train of thought.

The restaurant closed late, even on Mondays, so Alan's boys would enter as the last customers, disguised without looking obvious, require kicking out and then get to work. The other customers would have gone, along with most of the staff. Take the place over, search it, interrogate those there and leave in a blaze of glory.

The house, that's harder.

They had debated it at some length. It had been agreed to co-ordinate the timing with the restaurant, so leave it until very late, perhaps one or two in the morning.

How to get access?

A break in would be too risky. Reporting a gas leak was the oldest and best excuse for disturbing someone in the middle of the night.

'Acquire' a white van, crudely re-spray the British Gas logo on the side, after all who's going to look closely in the middle of the night and then, in we go.

Alan's peer team leader, Tom, another outside stray, had been there over twelve years and was an engineer of some sort so would sound convincing. The other three were all natives; good lads like Art, but still lacking actual experience. This operation worried him more than the restaurant, harder to access, less capable teams, perhaps he should be with them? No, he would just get in the way, getting a bit old for that sort of thing anyway, besides he couldn't risk compromise. Helena would be furious as well. Anyway, they were ready to go without him so back to the day job and her.

Park up in the street at home, unpack, repack and over to her; he would have some explaining and apologising to do, should be there by eight, approaching seven now. Street parking, even with a resident's permit, was always a lottery and he'd had to walk almost four hundred yards from another street. Nearly there now, I'll sleep tonight for sure.

Hmmm.

A grey car is parked on the other side of the street, without a resident's disc, what looks like four men inside, but difficult to tell. Key's in the front door now, as the car doors are opening. Quick! The steel-lined front door was ajar and he was diving through it when the first bullet impacted on the surround above his head; that familiar sound of a Kalashnikov on automatic, whoever was shooting must have forgotten that they tend to pull high and left if you are inexperienced. The door won't close, my bag blocking it. Pistol out, click the safety off, all the while a rain of bullets striking the door and the surrounding brickwork.

Enthusiastic amateurs, must be, might have a chance.

Duck low, present a smaller target, fire four shots, two oncoming gunmen drop to the floor, hit.

Two more following up behind them.

Pull the bag clear and close the door, ah! Ricochet, below my left knee, blood everywhere, pain indescribable, it's hit the bone, must have. Four flights of stairs to safety, they haven't got long before help arrives, I've hit the panic button inside the door which should hold them a while. Three flights to make, I'm crawling now, two to go, the tenant on the first floor opening their door to see what's going on.

"Get inside now! Bolt the door, barricade it, get to the far end of your home and take shelter, call the police!"

Their door closes and locks.

An explosion outside, the building shakes, they've blown the door. Starting to tremble now, losing too much blood, adrenalin surging, got to make it inside, nearly there.

Boots racing up the stairs.

Too late, won't make it in time. Lie flat on the top landing, my only chance. The first one's bounding up, back open to me, reckless, excited by the chase. My hand's shaking now, vision furring. First shot misses, second topples him, third is the end for him, but the fourth shooter's past him now, firing wildly.

Damn, another ricochet, left shoulder, gun loose on the floor; it ends here?

He's gloating, exhilarated, levelling for the final kill.

Two successive explosions, that must be it, I've failed, utterly, at least I posted that stick to Bowson. Dark now, I'm coming, meet me at the river's edge…

Where was he? Over an hour late, no replies to texts. After her cousin had left she had spent the day working, then getting ready and then cooking something special for him, even getting out a bottle of wine, Chapelle-Chambertin 1998, good producer. They had things to discuss.

Ten o'clock now. No contact. It's not fair, he promised, I have my pride, my self-respect, after all I've done for him. Off to bed, early start tomorrow, what else is there now?

Don't leap to conclusions, something must have come up. He would have sent me a message if it had.

Tuesday after Easter

···

Nine o'clock, back at my desk after the morning meeting, there's a message on my personal number plus others on my work phone.

It must be him, to apologise, explain, promise to make amends. No, it isn't, it's his PA, Elaine, asking me to call her on a mobile number, echo-y institutional sounds in the background. Concern, alarm, even he wouldn't get his PA to call to make his excuses. Her call is picked up straightaway: real terror now.

"Helena, we spoke once before, I'm your fiancé's PA, do you remember?"

She let that pass, tell me woman.

"I'm at St Thomas', the hospital, a special ward, he's here, he's…" sobbing now, she's struggling to get the words out to her, "… he's been shot, last night at home, badly… Didn't you see the news?"

No, no, never hear it in the morning in case it spoils my day.

"He's unconscious; he's been in theatre most of the night. I've been here since eight but couldn't get hold of you. Do you want to come over?"

She's weeping hard now, poor Elaine; she seems really fond of him.

"I'll get them to let you in, there's armed police everywhere, he wasn't the only one either, two killed at home, one wounded, one got away, all in the… service… you know what I mean?"

"I'll be straight over."

266

She's racing for the door, coat and bag in hand, ignoring those staring at her from their work-stations. Numb, self-reproaching, no, self-loathing for her earlier thoughts, her selfishness. Stop that, that won't help him. What if I lose him, just as I was starting to? God, I'll do anything, give anything, please? Her assistant calls: what's the problem, can she do anything?

Damn, this taxi's taking forever in the morning traffic, cancel everything, family crisis, I'll be in touch.

Twenty-five minutes from her West End office to St Thomas', it's a joke, what's that clown of a mayor playing at?

Three armed policemen, flak jackets, machineguns, the works, stand in the hospital foyer. They check her ID and wave her through, top floor, at the back, a special secure ward. Ten-minute walk, she makes it in four, shoes abandoned in the drive for speed, three more policemen, one unarmed, two armed similarly to the three in the foyer, she's checked again and ushered through.

Last corridor, turn, another two heavily armed policemen, a uniformed Sergeant, and a fifty something little woman, eyes red-rimmed.

"Elaine?"

She nods, they check her again and Elaine leads her in. Small ward with barred and blinded windows, two armed police at the far end by a locked fire escape, two nurses, two drawn sets of curtains hiding the beds and their occupants, the rest unoccupied. She is taken to the far one; it's him, white as a sheet, sleeping, unnaturally still, one leg in traction, drips in his right forearm, large dressings around his left shoulder and lower left leg.

She sits on the chair beside his bed, her heart hardly beating, blinking back the tears. "I'm sorry Elaine, could you bear to tell me what happened please, how he is?"

His PA's tears were increasing to sobs, almost drawing a similar response from her, despite her best efforts. The older woman almost looked delirious with misery, incoherent.

"I'm sorry I said you were his fiancé, I had to, they wouldn't have let you in otherwise. It was just after seven last night, it seemed he was just unlocking the front door and a gang of four Muslim fanatics," she spat the words out, "jumped him. There was a gunfight, he must have killed two at the front door, but was shot and wounded himself, it appears. He was crawling to his flat when they blew in the front door and chased him up the stairs; he only had that little pistol while they had machineguns. He didn't stand a chance; he shot one on the stairs by his flat, but the remaining terrorist shot him again."

Comfort her if only to get the rest. She put her arms around the distraught woman, she's devoted to the point of love; how often does he have that effect on people?

"So how did he survive?"

"The man in the flat below, he must have been so brave, he came out and went up the stairs with some sort of shotgun and shot the last terrorist in the back of the head before he could pull the trigger. He had already called an ambulance, and he and his wife came back and tried to slow the bleeding with towels and string as a tourniquet until they arrived. The doctor here said they probably saved his life by that... I mean, without the shooting as well."

"Thank you. What else does the doctor say?"

She didn't have the nerve to use 'about his chances.'

"Too early to tell, so much blood loss, tissue damage, leg bone shattered, but it's the blood loss and trauma they're worried about. He was having transfusions all night until they could stop the bleeding and repair the worst of the damage. Don't you want to hear about the others?"

She really didn't care right now, but she could see Elaine was determined to finish it. She smiled a yes.

"There were four other attacks, all similar. One man got inside his home and held them off, another, a woman, was shot on her doorstep, as was another man, the woman in the bed there was wounded trying to drive away when she saw them, a bullet in the back, too early to say if..." No one would mention those words in here, at least not yet.

"How did they know who he was, they all were, where they lived? Someone must have betrayed them."

Elaine dissolved again.

"That's the worst part, there can't be any other answer, they were all senior department heads at least, he's even more…" She stopped herself in time. "That sort of information is highly secret, so it must be someone very senior. They've called a massive investigation, but you know…" She looked at her helplessly. "There's a COBRA meeting going on now."

Helena turned back to him, brushing his white face and leaned forward to kiss his forehead so gently. She whispered something so low that Elaine couldn't catch it, then turned back to Elaine.

"Can I stay?"

The woman went crimson with embarrassment, "I'm sorry, not for long, other service people will be visiting and they will be locking down this entire wing. I'll stay and make sure they let you in at the end of the day, I'll phone you with any news from the doctors, I promise."

She kissed his nose this time, hugged Elaine, took one last look back.

"Can you send me the contact details of the couple who saved him; I've a debt to repay, right now?"

"I'm not sure, well it can't hurt, but don't tell anyone, please?"

"Of course not," she said and hurried out.

She headed out for the entrance, better find my shoes. They were at reception, someone had handed them in, apparently it happened all the time. Just as she got into her taxi, she didn't know where to go, a text arrived from Elaine, the man's work address and name, a clearing banker in the City, well scrub what I said about drones.

Twelve minutes later she arrived outside his office, calmer now she entered the lobby, asking for him by name; they asked who she was, she told them and gave her company name for good measure. Three minutes he was in front of her, wondering what this high powered hedgy wanted with a middle ranking retail banker. He didn't look the macho type, but not a wimp, just a late thirties middle manager, grey suit and tie, short hair. She motioned to him to sit by her in the lobby.

Before he had chance to enquire if she had made a mistake seeking him out, "Are you David Holloway?"

He nodded.

"Then why are you at work after last evening? Where's your wife, your family? Do you have children? Are you completely insane?"

He could see she was forcing a smile.

"They're in protective custody, but I have a big deal on and the police said it would be ok."

So, she was wrong, there was a macho streak in there somewhere, it's the culture still in these older institutions.

"Well, I just want to thank you and your wife for saving the life someone very dear to me. I can't ever hope to repay you, but let me try a little at least. I assume you won't be able to live at home again, they'll probably change your identity as well." He hadn't thought of that she could see. "How big's your mortgage?"

"Why d'you want to know?"

"Just tell me please, I'm not in the mood."

"Just under £300k."

He was blushing now.

"Fine, I am writing you a personal cheque for that sum now. Please pay it in immediately, I'll call my bank. I'll also transfer another £200k later so you can move and not worry about the cost. I'm also going to call your chief executive and say how indebted I am to you and your wife, and how it is a tribute to his bank that they employ such people."

She knew the effect that could have on his career.

"Money is no thanks, but it's all I can do for now. Why did you have a gun with you anyway?"

"Well I shoot game," he blushed again, "and it had just come back from its end-of-season service. Two days earlier and I wouldn't have had it. Just didn't think really, didn't want to wait for them to come after us, instinct I suppose. My wife's furious, but this will help. Thanks, I don't know what to say…"

"Nothing; it's for me that words and money are not enough."

She had to get out of there before the tears started to flow. What would it do to her reputation?

"I'm sorry Ladies and Gentlemen," said the Director of MI5, surprising the other attendees of COBRA with the heat of his emotion, "but I don't think you fully understand the implications of last evening's incidents. Five senior department heads of various secret service arms have been attacked at their own homes, two are dead and two seriously wounded, by at least twenty terrorists carrying automatic rifles and explosives and acting in a co-ordinated fashion. This is a full-scale assault on our ability to combat subversion by a large and highly motivated terrorist force on our home-ground. Furthermore, it would appear that there has clearly been a security breach of significant magnitude to enable this to happen."

The PM dragged his eyes away from the headlines of the newspapers laid out on the highly polished table before him; it just didn't bear thinking about.

"Terrorist Murder Gangs on the Rampage in London"

"MI5 Under Attack"

"Killers on our Doorsteps" and worst of all, "What's Up PM?"

"I think we all grasp the implications Gerald; as I said, this is very serious indeed and we must leave no stone unturned. How is the investigation into the source of the leak coming along?"

"It's still far too early to tell, but that's what's so odd. One might think the five attacked had just been targeted at random from a senior officer directory, not targeted on any other basis. One was the head of SIS' China Command, one from our communications technology department, one the head of our remaining Irish operation, one the head of an inter-services operational review section and the other our head of finance. If you asked me to speculate now I would suggest that someone must have gained access to our secure payroll system which will have names and addresses, but no job titles, so they may have just selected five of the higher paid. We are of course making all the normal checks, but we also have a forensic systems team at the payroll centre while the employees there are all being interviewed, their associations followed up."

Someone in the room squirmed imperceptibly, that was fast. They certainly aren't stupid.

Ted Armstrong, head of the CT Command looked about him. The gravity of the crisis was such that even he had been asked to attend. The MI5 chief was a decent man, much preferable to that snobby git from SIS; he had worked with him closely over the years and rather suspected that he saw things similarly to himself. He certainly knew how he'd have felt if it had been four of his officers shot in this way, and here he was in a room of people for whom he had ever less respect, some of whom could hardly refrain from staring at the newspapers on the table.

"If I may add something Prime Minister?"

They all turned to face him, even the Home Secretary whose mask-like face could not hide her wish that he wouldn't say anything at all.

Stuff her.

"As you know six terrorists died at the scenes of two incidents, shot by two of the targets and a local resident. A further two were cornered a little way away and remain holed up for now, the others escaped, which means that there are at least a dozen heavily armed terrorists at large in London somewhere."

"My God, no one's safe."

Thank you for that contribution Minister of Defence, not even you could fail to draw that conclusion.

"Quite correct Minister. Of course, we have called up all our armed officers and are drafting in others from elsewhere in the country, but it seems those who undertook this violence are quite prepared to die. A sad truth we are becoming increasingly familiar with, already confirmed by the usual pre-recorded martyrdom videos which are now appearing on Jihadi websites."

"Of course, we're following up with the six identified dead ones' families, associates and so on, but I rather suspect it will be the usual very grudging and minimal co-operation, complete surprise and so forth. These though are just the demented foot-solders; there are many others behind them, brains, resources, armaments, money... This isn't following the usual pattern: a few maladjusted teenagers going to some Middle Eastern hellhole for a year and then coming back with the burning desire to start their own little jihad back home. This suggests infrastructure, planning and the ability to infiltrate our own security agencies."

The already sombre mood in the room darkened further, good; maybe you'll stop playing and start taking this seriously.

"Prime Minister, if I may?"

The Home Secretary could hardly believe that he of all people had given her the ideal opening.

"My department has been for some time considering additional measures which may be required to deal with the growing threat of Islamic terrorism," her departmental Permanent Secretary handed her a sheaf of papers, "new laws governing freedom of association, defining more tightly, freedom of speech, the prevention of funds from outside Britain heading to charities here, selective deportations, internment if required, immigration and visa bans on certain nationalities, more resources for the security services, bans on all kinds of face covering, religious slaughter and such things. Obviously said laws would have to be generic and not be community specific."

A stunned silence.

'Ho, ho,' thought Ted, 'now it gets interesting: is there to be an unexpected out-break of common sense at last?'

The Foreign Secretary was furious.

"This is not a policy forum! This is unacceptable: the impact on our relations with the Islamic world, our financial and trade dependence. It's like something out of 1984. I know they're going for that big brother stuff north of the border with their state snoopers for every child, but I won't be part of a government that goes that way."

Before the PM could intervene, The Home Secretary shot back.

"We have to be realistic, I know we don't like to admit it but many of those areas with large Islamic populations are slipping beyond our control, they've got their own parallel court systems, pay little tax, are separating themselves ever more from the wider community, FGM, need I go on? They only engage with our society to claim benefits…"

Their unspoken leadership rivalries were erupting before his eyes, and worse, those of their officials. He was looking weak.

"Thank you, Home Secretary; however, as the Foreign Secretary says these are policy matters for another occasion."

The latter minister smiled, presuming a battle won,

"However, I think there may be some merit in what you say Home Secretary. Can you please forward me a memorandum setting out those ideas that I may consider it at length?"

She smirks, me on points I think.

As he followed his boss out of the room Martin Dager was feeling cheerful despite all the serious faces around him. His boss wasn't much longer for this world, that was obvious; she hated him, that much was clear. He now had powerful new backers in the succession race, on his own he would have been an also-ran, still would appear that way to his competitors. He had been blind, hadn't seen the way things were going underneath, had been alone. Now he had been offered help, support, advice, a new network he hadn't known existed, influential patrons, all for using the right words, being on the inside. What had it cost him?

Nothing, yet.

They were on the road now, Alan and his boys, making their way cross-country by the unmonitored minor roads, slow and inefficient but secure, heading for the rendezvous with the standby team who had been maintaining a very loose and discreet watch on the restaurant just outside Swindon. There they would change vehicles for the van which the base team had procured the night before from a very used car dealer for cash. They'd given it a quick re-spray and plate change, the latter a replica of a local plumber's plates. Silenced pistols, sub-machine guns, a few grenades, plenty of petrol in jerry cans, hopefully they were ready. A bit under-prepared, but when would they ever have enough preparation for something like this?

Art was his usual taciturn self; Georgy was excited, full of jokes, almost too eager, but Sam… He thought he had got to know Sam a bit over months of training and preparation, but he was withdrawn now, talking more easily with Georgy. Something was different about him since they had brought the Kurdish girl back, he was harder somehow. When Alan had asked him how the girl was doing, he had just got more tongue-tied than usual, simply said she would be ok and that was all.

They were nearly there now. He hasn't called, normally does a few hours before an operation to wish us luck. Something must have come up. No worries.

The house Sam had left behind was subdued. He had just announced after Evening Prayer that he had been asked to go back into Logres on Monday night, something needed to be done; he would be meeting the other members of his team and Gillian at the little station. Martha had got upset, angry, saying it was too soon, he needed more rest; why didn't they send someone else?

There was no one else: they were all going.

Iltud had returned the following afternoon, walking into the icy bath of Martha's displeasure. What did the authorities think they were playing at? He said he was unhappy too, but he had asked, had written, saying it was vital, and they were all volunteers. The girl had only finally understood when she saw him packing his equipment by the front door, asking in the most broken English where was he going, was he taking her too? He had just shaken his head, tried to tell her he would not be long; she sat down and wept silently, seemingly shrunken again, Martha's arms around her, while he left to join his mates. She had gone into Sally's room to watch him head down to the station, be joined by four others, walk east into the distance until they all disappeared into the falling dusk. Silently she shut herself away in her own room. The others just looked at each other glumly until Josey asked what was for dinner.

Her day had dragged like no other she had experienced; she'd had a couple of quick calls from Elaine to say there was no change.

How was she keeping?

Probably not that much different from you by the sound of your voice.

Come over about four, all the visitors should have left by then and the doctor will be doing his rounds; you should be alright to stay for a few hours then.

She had nothing else to do, certainly wasn't in the mood to go back to work. She headed home and went for a long run, hoping the endorphins might counteract her feelings of helpless anguish, the guilt of last night's angry thoughts about him while he had been fighting for his life just a few miles away, almost bleeding to death on his front doorstep.

'Dear God, I may not believe in you but I'm pretty sure he does, something like that must keep him going, don't let him down now, please, it's not fair on him, all those who've come to depend on him. I meant it, that promise, I keep my promises.'

By the time she got back an hour and a half later, hot, exhausted, focused, her helplessness transmuted, she knew that where there had once been two beasts there were now three, the newcomer terrifying the others into quietude with its screaming, frothing savagery. Its name: vengeance.

Helena arrived at four on the dot. If anything, the checks were tighter, the looks more suspicious, as if the full seriousness of recent events were only now being fully appreciated. She had stopped to buy some flowers, a bouquet for the woman lying beside him, some King Alfreds for him, some grapes, the usual, her IPOD with his favourites sorted into his special playlist.

Elaine ushered her in.

"I felt so terrible, this morning after you left, before… I forgot to thank you for what you did for my husband and I… It was you, wasn't it? You don't know…"

"Pardon? Oh, that was him. He asked me, how could I say no? Besides, I can see why you matter to him so much."

That's it, be kind to the woman, it's not just about you and he. She's utterly devoted.

A brave smile in return.

"The doctor should be here any minute, do you mind if I stay to hear what he has to say, report back? I've been here all day and need to go back in to the office; I'll come back tomorrow morning if they let me.

Then a furtive glance around, head bent forward, voice basement level low, "The office word is that they are onto something, a way of tracking his betrayers, I pray they…"

The doors open and in walk two doctors, one clearly a senior consultant, with nurses fluttering about them like moths. They brush aside her attempt to question them, saying simply "Later."

They spend considerably more time with the woman in the adjoining bed than with him, surely that's a good sign? The consultant comes over to see Elaine and her, nervously brusque, clearing his throat. "Who are you? A relative? Colleague?"

Elaine spares her blushes,

"Helena's his fiancée."

"Oh, I see. Shall we take a seat over there?"

"How is he? What's the prognosis, just the truth please; your best estimate?"

"He was very lucky in a way. The leg should be fine; it may need a bone graft, but I hope not, just time and rehab. He's kept himself fit, that will help. The second bullet must have been a ricochet. It had broken up before it entered and had lost some of its velocity. It hit him at the top left of his rib cage, just below the shoulder, broke two of the ribs but didn't make it as far as his heart or other vital organs. If it hadn't been partly spent… Our worry is anoxia, oxygen deprivation to the brain, caused by his blood loss, especially the leg punctures. Those neighbours of his obviously knew what they were trying to do."

"What do you mean… when will you know?"

"We're keeping him medically sedated until we've got the physical wounds stabilised, his bloodwork has settled down and the trauma begun to subside. Maybe twenty-four hours, maybe longer, I'm sorry. But at least he's got a much better chance of a full recovery than that poor woman beside him. If you're here this time tomorrow, I'll update you. Don't despair. Just sit with him if you can, try to talk to him; some patients who've been in comas tell me that's helped, goodness knows why, but the workings of the human mind are still a mystery really."

A smile and then he heads away, probably endless more calls on his time. Elaine follows shortly after, relieved not to shoulder the burden of sitting by his still figure, not knowing where to start.

People have come in to visit the woman next door, must be family by the sounds of crying. Man pops his head round the screen, sees her and apologises, disappearing again. So how does this start? What to say? Is there anything recognisable left in there? Don't think it. I'm sorry, it just slipped out. So how does this begin? You were clear in the church, tell him really how you feel, what you think, your hopes, what you truly want… You've never really been able to before, not even that time, it always just seemed to go wrong when he looked at you.

Two hours later when the nurses changed shifts, one looked in to see how things were, saw a well-dressed woman, head bowed low to the patient's ear, hand on his right one, just whispering. Those were sometimes the best and worst moments of her job.

He's naked, walking across the desert scrub, feet not feeling the discomfort, and has started down the sharp scree slope towards the river below him, the hot air rising behind him, obscuring the view back. The desert runs right to the river's edge on this side but, on the other, there are faint glimpses of green and tree tops through the river mists. No bright lights, no feelings of transportation, just walking as if with a pre-programmed map in his head. The river seems familiar, but his thinking is diffusing, as if his memories were fading away in the arid wastelands behind him; he can't place it, name it. He looks back one final time before the drop to the valley floor hides the plains behind. In the far distance, is that another figure, blurred by the rising heat, coming this way, running even? Well if this is what he thought it was, there would be plenty more to follow.

He turns east again and heads downwards to the riverside. He hesitates before stepping in, the rushing sound of water falling downstream, plumes of mist and spray from large falls; it must be, difficult to judge distances here. He puts a foot in; the water's warm but fresh, delightful, sandy bottom too. He pulls the other one in. A young woman steps down through the mist on the far bank and steps into the water, her body and legs are indistinct, shifting, but her head, neck and arms are wonderfully, indubitably her. She smiles.

"I promised Jovanka, I'd join you one day, I've kept faith with you all these years. I'm coming."

He's halfway over, the water up to his waist. Her voice is in his head, clear, that heavy Balkan accent, that slightly husky lilt he loved so much. She puts out a hand to stop him, make him look behind. A woman's at the top of the slope, racing down, tumbling, rising, sliding in her urgency. He looks back to his wife.

"Why are you here? What do you want of me?"

He's puzzled, "They killed me, I'm coming home to you, as I promised."

"Why? Don't you have anything worth living for, them, her, those to come?"

"I'm done now, it's for others..." Fear. Uncertainty. "Don't you want me, aren't I welcome?"

"Yes, but not today, not now."

Crushing now, the water at his waist is strengthening, deepening, the roar from downstream rising.

"What do you mean?"

"You aren't finished there, not yet. You must return to them, those to come, her... She's there behind you, on the river bank, calling you, she can't enter, can't see me, just you. She's frightened, like you were with me."

"But I promised you, no others..."

"I know," she's smiling now, "but I never asked that of you, remember? Do you think I would want the one I love, who saved me once, to be unhappy all his days? You still don't understand, do you? Here all is unity, simplicity, like those Scholastic philosophers you told me about in the hospital thinking I couldn't hear; we'll still be one when your time comes to cross the Jordan. Now, go back, before it sweeps you away down there; that you don't deserve."

She turns solemnly, without even a farewell, and walks back up into the mist. The river is raging now, up to his chest; it's hard to fight the flow.

Helena's there behind him on the bank, hands outstretched, willing him back, tears in her eyes; he catches hold before he loses his footing and lies prostrate on the bank, exhausted, shattered, bereft.

He looks up. Helena's at the top of the slope looking sadly down at him, as if wondering, and turns on her heel and walks out of sight. He stumbles, crawls back up after her, but when he reaches the top there's no one in sight, just the desert heat obscuring the view.

The staff asked her to leave, nicely, but it was no suggestion. Almost six hours she had been there. A rambling, incoherent, discursive monologue; she would die of embarrassment if it had been recorded and were played back to her. Poor him, if he were still in there somewhere, don't say that, that might have tipped him over the edge. The staff explained it was better she take some rest, freshen up, perhaps return tomorrow afternoon, that nice older lady had said she would pop back in the morning, these things are often a marathon, not a sprint.

She left, got into a cab. She couldn't reach the others, didn't have their contact details, had only met that young man Sam a couple of times; they wouldn't know what had happened, the authorities were not disclosing the identities. Her home, wrong word, her tomblike dwelling, was draining her like a leech, the loneliness greater than ever, desperate for resolution. There's only one person I can talk to. Her cousin answers, sounds sleepy, must have gone to bed.

"What's wrong?"

"They shot him; in the news... He's badly hurt. They say he'll live, his body will recover, but... they don't know about his mind..."

"I'll be straight there, I'll stay. Filthy..."

She had never heard her cousin swear like that before, she was always so measured, in control; he must have got to her too.

Eleven o'clock now, all ready to go into town, park by the restaurant just before twelve, make sure there was beer on their breath, ham it up a bit so it would be just another tipsy boys' night out's last stop. Still haven't heard from him, a bad feeling, have tried calling twice, no answer, never any message service on his numbers. What if something's gone wrong and we're walking into a trap? Sam suggests they phone his lady friend in London, he's met her a couple of times, she gave him her number too, she was a bit free with things like that, just trying to help. If anyone knows anything it will be her.

Alan always tries to be decisive, prevarication just makes things worse, but this is matter of protocol. Sam and Art are watching him, wanting him to call, for Sam at least he has become something of a totem, solving problems, easing their paths, he's worried.

"You call her Sam, she's met you, but don't say anything about us, what we're doing, understand? Just about him, if she's heard from him."

Sam had memorised that number years ago, a possible lifeline if ever he were stranded alone again in an outside which was feeling increasingly alien to him. She's just got off the phone to her cousin and picks up right away fearing news from the hospital.

"Hello, Miss, its Sam, remember?"

"Of course I do Sam, what do you want?"

"News of him please Miss," he always called her Miss, it made her feel like a school mistress. "We haven't heard from him today when we expected to and don't know anyone else who might know something."

Oh no, I've got to go through it again, but not panic them, they'll feel out-of-their depth here without him watching over them. Hold it together, for him, them, just long enough. "There were some terrorist shootings last night in London, you might not have heard." He had but didn't know who was involved. "He survived, but he's wounded, in hospital, still unconscious. He should be alright they say, but it could be quite some time."

A second of stunned silence, almost as if Sam had thought him invincible.

"I'm sorry Miss, are you alright?"

"Yes, so long as he is. Are you alright; are some of the others with you?"

"Err, yes Miss."

"Well Sam, if you're doing what I hope you're doing, give them something special from me, won't you?"

"Of course, Miss."

The phone goes dead.

It's Alan's call now. Abort or go? Almost certainly not a trap then and Sam was pretty sure she wouldn't lie to him. Just terrible luck then, he clearly wasn't the only one targeted last night, must have been because of his official job. What a complex life he led: he had his own aims within an unofficial job inside an official one which was of itself supposed to be a secret. Well, somewhere along the line the subterfuge had faded enough to allow someone to get to him. Sam and Georgy were, if anything, keener to get on with it, Sam especially, Art was fine if they were. Well, we've come all this way, he helped set it up, let's do it as planned, but not tell the other teams until afterwards in case it unsettles them, we all need to be focused.

Then straight back home.

Wednesday after Easter

··

In the end Tom had decided to take his team in earlier than planned; the waiting was preying on their minds, feeling vulnerable as if every passing car or pedestrian could see through their van's sides and perceive what they were planning. It was about 11.50; traffic had been light and the streets dark; few people here seemed to stay up late, in the week at least. They had pulled up outside, at least the door had a buzzer rather than a knocker which could wake the neighbours. He fed some gas from the small camping canister he was carrying through the letterbox, the smell of which would prevent any arguments at the door. He rang once, twice, again, impatiently. Footsteps down the stairs, someone looking through the fisheye glass, sees his workman's overalls, holding what passes for ID, a tool box, smells the gas. The door's opened; it's an older man, well into his sixties, the resident male then, just awake.

"Excuse us sir, we're from the gas company, reports of a gas leak, can you smell it? We need to come in and check urgently. Could you bring anyone else staying here downstairs, but quietly; we don't want to cause panic, do we?"

He's bewildered, off-guard. He lets them in and goes off to wake the others and bring them down. By the time they're back, him, two women in their fifties, a boy of college age looking daggers at them, a younger sister, mid-teens, his whole team are in, the front and back doors locked and the rear checked. The residents are ushered at gunpoint into the back room, strapped ankles, knees, wrists and elbows behind, on their knees, gagged.

Two of the team head upstairs to check it's clear and commence a search, while the interrogation begins below. The bit he's dreaded, knowing what was agreed had to come: the importance of rapid success in saving many, many innocent lives, they need the evidence, the information. Nothing too direct at first; threats, knock him about a bit in front of the others, the fear in their eyes growing as the shock wears off. Fifteen minutes in, one of the men searching upstairs brings down three AK47s, a handgun, boxes of ammunition, a laptop, a plastic bag of mobile phones, a small leather bag containing a quantity of currency.

So, their information was right then.

Tom asks where the rest is. They're all wearing masks, hairnets, gloves; it's terrifying for their captives, something they've only seen done to infidels by their heroes on web videos. The man refuses. The son is shot between the eyes and then in the heart, just silently, no comment, no fuss.

The women are in silent tears, unable to make a sound, pleading with the man with their eyes to tell all, to save them. The gun is aimed at the first woman's head, six feet away, but he knows they won't miss. The first two guys have finished upstairs now, are searching the front room, the kitchen, while the man answers some brief questions about his contacts, numbers, plans. He's part way through and suddenly finds more resistance from somewhere, and stops in mute refusal. Tom's hand is starting to shake as the first and then the second women slump down. The girl is having silent hysterics, the man finally broken; he had never imagined this, pitiless ghost killers in the night.

Twenty furious minutes later, it's there; two pages of notes, names, places, outline plans, some more phones revealed hidden under the sofa, a single memory stick. There must be more? He shakes his head in resignation. If he's been lying, well they're taking the girl with them, does he get the idea? He does. The smell of leaking gas mixed with spreading petrol is now noticeable, he sees the future. The girl's pulled out to the hall and stunned, her father a lifeless corpse on the carpet with the others, their clotting blood pooling around them.

Nobody about in the street at all.

The base team have texted in the all-clear, the van's loaded with everything plus girl, front door shut and detonator set for ten minutes, by which time they are coming to the northern outskirts headed for the Chilterns and indirectly home. The girl's turfed out, still tied and gagged, into a field behind a hedge. She didn't really get a look at them and they didn't get into this to kill kids; there were limits.

Heading up the farm drive now, the van abandoned long ago, stripped and burning fiercely. Tom just feels exhaustion. First time after all. It had gone like a dream, but it felt like a nightmare.

Alan pulled the van up, just before midnight, almost directly in front of the restaurant. The two watchers from the supporting standby team, parked down the street, had reported that it seemed to be a quiet night and they had better go early in case the proprietor closed before they got in. They had decided to change the story: plumbing contractors away from home, working a late shift, just needing a late meal before hotel and bed, so in they walked in overalls, carrying large tool kits saying they didn't like leaving them in the van. He shrugged, it was late; there was only one other couple just finishing their coffee, better to have some trade after all, just him and the chef left anyway.

Food was swiftly ordered, with soft drinks: they had to work early again tomorrow apparently. The other couple leave and then, as the owner brings their first plates out, he's confronted by four masked men holding silenced pistols, one pointed at his head. Two of the men concentrate on closing the blinds, locking the door, putting up the 'Closed' sign and dimming the lights. The fourth man, dark skinned, steps past him and into the kitchen at the rear. As he obeyed the silent gesture to place the plates on the table he heard three whispered shots from the kitchen, two in quick succession, a sound like a body slumping to the floor, a third hushed whisper and then, the worst sound of all, a faint chuckle.

Alan heard it too and looked at Sam, who was impassive.

Leaving Art downstairs to check the remaining service rooms and commence preparing their getaway pyre – there was plenty of cooking oil and two large gas stoves – it should go up like Guy Fawkes' Night, the other three, with their prisoner, head upstairs to the first and only other floor. It's a rabbit warren, sub-divided rooms, office, stores as well as living accommodation. They soon gather up the other residents: a middle-aged woman, surely the wife, seven children ranging from an infant girl to a mid-teens son, an older woman, presumably grandmother or aunt, and commence the ritual of kneeling, binding and gagging.

"It'll take all week to search this place," growls Georgy, "it's like a flea market, full of crap everywhere, let's just get straight to the point."

"Hold them there you two; don't start anything 'til I get back. I'll check the office, that's the most likely place."

A few feet above them in a subsidiary attic specifically set aside for hideaways like him, Suleiman al-Libani heard the accented English-speaking voices. One sounded Antipodean, another unrecognisable. He had made it out of London after yesterday's successful attack. His team had split up, ditched their equipment, there was plenty more near at hand, he knew; he had been offered safety here until the next assignments came through.

Intruders, at this time of night?

He had a handgun by his mattress, just next to the hatchway which led below. There were Kalashnikovs up here, packed, greased, but he didn't want to put the light on in case it was spotted from below, nor risk the noise of opening the cases and readying them. Besides, in the tight spaces down there, a long assault rifle was too cumbersome, while a pistol with the element of surprise might suit him much better. Better wait and see before deciding whether to intervene.

Only a minute has passed when he hears another voice, unmistakeably English this time, with some sort of light regional accent. So, there's at least three. Big odds, but not hopeless; after all, he was a veteran. The sound of someone being hit, again, another, harder this time, a body falling to the floor, being pulled up. Filth, torturing faithful people like these.

His ear is pressed to the plasterboard between the rafters, straining to make out the words, demands for names, numbers, places, contacts. There's no answer, just silent resistance, true heroes to the cause. Should he wait or descend shooting? No more voices, just the three, one of whom has gone along the corridor and not come back? They're divided; this might be the time, creep to the hatch, try to lift it slightly without making any noise, at least to squint through.

What sounds like two moderated shots, little more than the leak of gas from a balloon, easy to miss, but the fall of a human body to the floor is unmistakeable: he had seen it, caused it, so many times himself. It almost made him drop the half-lifted hatch in his surprise. He could make out the voices now, but not see them without exposing his head. One was congratulating the other, saying the boy must have been of a similar age to the girl he was so fond of, then telling the man no more chances. He must be a champion, the little restaurateur, but of course he was really a key link in the chain, so much more than he seemed. He said nothing. Two more shots, another thud, followed by two more and then another. That first voice was happy, satisfied, asking did he want it to be three next time? If he was to do anything, it needed to be now.

Pulling out the hatch he dropped down heavily into the corridor, a masked man, back to him, half-turned but was too slow. Suleiman beat him to the draw, a rushed wild shot admittedly, hitting him right in the midriff, knocking him on to his back. Now for the other, he must be in here somewhere before the briefest of flashes inside his head as his body slumped lifelessly against the corridor's skirting board. The last sound he caught was of more shooting in the room ahead.

Alan put another two rounds into him as he stepped over his body, must have been in the roof space?

He jumped up, pulling himself through by brute force and looked about; no one else it seemed, must have been alone. They had got careless.

Georgy was on his front now, Sam applying a pressure dressing to slow the bleeding, he was breathing at least, conscious, not panicking. The rest of the room was like a charnel house, a sickeningly indescribable scene, so much so that Alan almost threw up. His phone rang, a call from the team outside on watch, it cleared his head, "What was that shot?"

"We're going to have to go, now, no time."

Art was in the room now, horrified.

"Art? Get Georgy into the back of the van now, start stripping away the clothing from his wound and fixing up the IV. Sam," the youngster he thought he had got to know and trust seemed a complete stranger now, "get his weapon, the bag I've been putting stuff in from the office and go with him, and tell the others to set up a diversion in the next street for five minutes and then meet us at the rendezvous." His eyes caught movement in the far corner, an infant, no a toddler, wriggling in its bonds behind a corpse, "And take that child as well, now!"

They were all in the van by the time Art emerged and shut the door behind him, less than two minutes later. The gas stoves turned on, petrol all over the death room, as he would always think of it; detonator set for five minutes upstairs, eight downstairs. Lights were on in the some of the nearby houses, one or two people were peering out of windows, a couple of doors were opening; in the far distance he could hear the sound of a siren.

They were almost half a mile away when the distraction, a small bomb under a parked car, went off. This was followed shortly afterwards by the detonator upstairs in the restaurant going off. They were almost in open country when, minutes later, the gas exploded in the kitchen, the detonator not being needed. By that time the police and an ambulance were at the end of the street, not entering, fearing that other car bombs were rigged nearby, until bomb disposal could arrive to investigate. The fire service couldn't approach either so the inferno, fed by the gas and liberal use of accelerants, supplemented by the cheap construction materials used, ensured that the building and its contents were well on their way to becoming powder. When the ammunition and grenades in the now burning roof-space started going off, it felt like war had started in Swindon.

Fifteen minutes later they were nearing the transfer point to abandon the van. It was going horribly wrong, no training could really prepare you for this and the inquisition as to what had happened in that room would follow later. Madness, complete insanity, but for now they had to get clear away. He was in the back with Art, who was only now finally managing to cut away the thin ultra-lightweight anti-ballistic under vest with a knife; it was putting up a hell of a fight and his struggles were hurting Georgy almost as much as the wound itself. Henry had insisted they use them, the latest thing he said, won't stop a nine millimetre at point blank range nor a rifle further out, but it would reduce the impact, although they couldn't see how far the bullet had gone into him. Well, it seemed to have given him a chance, perhaps one he didn't deserve right now.

Blood was flowing freely, but not as badly as he had expected, hopefully no arteries then, the pressure dressing should help for a while. Art at least hadn't lost his head, he'd rigged up the IV emergency plasma to Georgy's fore-arm, given him some morphine to still him whilst trying to cradle the little girl, he could see the gender now, in his other arm in a vain attempt to comfort the silently sobbing child, her face running with tears of hysteria, wrenching her little body about in its bonds.

"What'll we do with her Al?"

"No more deaths today Art, I promise. We'll take her with us, like the Kurdish girl we rescued, somebody will give her a loving home, she's young enough not to remember anything. What do you think to his chances?"

"Needs a good doctor badly and soon."

He shrugged helplessly, almost resigned.

"I'll warn the doc what to expect, get prepped up at the farm, if we go by the main roads we can be there in just over a couple of hours, it's up to him 'til then."

And You up there, of course, but I couldn't blame You.

Five minutes later they had made the transfer into another van, owned legitimately this time, and were headed south-west, pushing the speed limits on the empty night roads. One of the other team was in a hire car about half a mile ahead to alert them to any police traps, the others quickly stripping and cleaning the van, before leaving it a burning wreck and heading after them.

Gillian receives the call she's been dreading all night, it's Alan, his normally relaxed Aussie accent fraught with stress and anxiety. "Doc, there's been a problem; one of the boys is hit, top of the stomach by the lowest rib. We've slowed the bleeding, rigged up some plasma and sedated him, but that's all we can do until we see you, in about two hours. You need to get ready tonight. Also, can you prepare a sedative for a very young kid?"

That was it, the line went dead.

She had her part to play now, but she hadn't dealt with gunshot trauma for well over twenty years and even then it had only been as a duty registrar supporting a consultant. She didn't have a proper operating space, just the dining room table, some surgeons' tools, oxygen, blood of all types, plasma, anaesthetic and antibiotics, all the things they'd been able to procure for this kind of… mishap, but nowhere near what she might need today. It would be like working in a field hospital in a war zone. No nurses, just untrained helpers such as the farmer and his wife. She would be ok if it were a matter of cleaning up, repairing internal soft tissue damage, removing debris, even resetting shattered ribs if needs be, before closing up, but if any vital organs had been hit, or the spine, she would be totally out of her depth.

The choice then would be to see him, whoever he was, die painfully or take him to a hospital and, in effect, committing him to a life in a cell with the added risk of jeopardising them all, everything. Even her Hippocratic oath couldn't command that sort of price.

She had talked it through with Alan on the walk out: he was always the easiest with whom she could discuss things properly. He had just made light of it in that casual way of his, explaining that they all knew the risks and consequences of being wounded outside, they didn't expect her to perform miracles. He had then, almost as a joke to quash the subject, said if they couldn't take a wounded man to a surgeon, why not bring a surgeon to him?

She had only really thought about while trying to sleep in the following day's light, to be ready for the overnight vigil before they returned. Was there anyone she knew, trusted, an ex-colleague, someone with the skills she didn't have, whom she could persuade or, failing that, they could compel, to come if she fell short?

What then, if they refused?

No, they almost certainly wouldn't refuse to treat an injured patient but afterwards, what? Let them go, having seen her and the others? Even if they hid them from the location, it would still create too much risk. So, take them away to the Pocket, as a prisoner, a guest who couldn't leave? Far better than the alternative, she wouldn't condemn a life to save one, in this case it would be totally unacceptable.

To fill the time as much as anything while they were waiting she had, with the help of the couple's teenage daughter, used the house's internet to research some of her old colleagues from Frenchay. Some had disappeared, retirement or emigration she guessed. A couple were still working, but had moved to other hospitals, Edinburgh and Leeds, too far to be accessible.

There was only one, not long retired but still doing some part-time consultancy, David Kingsbridge, a specialist in trauma and micro-surgery; he had been a friend, as had his wife. No children, they couldn't, twenty years ago they had lived in a pretty house in the Chew Valley, she had actually been there on several occasions. The daughter tracked him down to the same house, using the electoral roll. On his own now; either his wife's left him, hardly likely, or more probably she had died. Search the local newspaper archives; yes, there it is, in the deaths section, two years ago, from an unspecified medical condition. So, if it's anybody, it's him. No, I couldn't do that to him, he was a friend. You might if it meant someone having to die painfully and slowly, far away from home. A good doctor was always prepared for any eventuality, they were counting on her, she owed them everything, her new life, happiness.

On the spur of the moment she rang Alan back. "Just in case it's beyond me, could you send someone to check if there's a David Kingsbridge at an address I'm going to give you, just south of Bristol? We might need to persuade him to come, but not until I've seen the patient, if you know what I mean?"

No worries. He rings off and calls the following van; they're on the A37, heading south through deepest Somerset, and are quickly turned around to head north again. They should be there well before Alan's vehicle makes the farm, which he should do with two and a half hours of darkness remaining.

At least the child's exhausted herself into sleep.

It was time to call Tom and share the bad news, hope to hear something good in return.

Last use of the phone before breaking the SIM and throwing it and the phone into a river, always mindful of what he'd been told about phone discipline.

It was bad, not inevitably terminal, but beyond her ability to fix properly. No trace of heart damage, but the bullets, as these modern horrible ones seem designed to do, had fragmented on hitting the lowest rib, puncturing his left lung and perforating a section of his upper colon.

Not too much damage lower down, seems okay, bowel too, but I'm so rusty. Blood loss was a problem, she could slow it further and they would have enough of his type for several manual transfusions for a day or two, but no more, and it was out of the question to carry him home over the moor.

They had spent the time until the arrival getting ready, erecting new lighting, cleaning every surface as it had never been cleaned before, disinfecting everything that might be required, whatever might do for Georgy it wasn't going to be a lack of hygiene.

She didn't know him well, other than as the talkative colleague of Sam and devoted son of Thea, everyone seemed to know her, but when they had brought him in her first reaction had been one of relief: at least it wasn't Sam, the impact that would have had on Martha, her friend, and of course the girl, it was impossible to tell.

She had done what she could quickly and without fully sealing him up: they needed to keep draining the blood away anyway. She washed up and went out to Alan. "That man, David Kingsbridge, are they still nearby?"

A nod.

"I'm going to need him, Georgy is, I'm afraid, otherwise… Can you get them on the phone, ask them to knock him up if they think he's on his own and then pass the phone to him so I can talk to him?"

At four fifteen that morning David Kingsbridge, eminent consultant surgeon, received one of the greatest shocks of his life, not being woken at an ungodly hour by two fit looking men whom, if they hadn't knocked and spoken respectfully, he might have thought to be intended burglars, but by a voice from the long past, the very long past.

"David, is that you? It's Gill, you remember, d'you recognise my voice?"

"Who is this, is it really you Gill? We thought you were dead, you disappeared without trace twenty years ago."

"It is, it really is, I'll tell you all when I see you. I was very sorry to hear about Mary. But you need to come with these men, a man's life is at stake and I'm in over my head, I need you. They won't hurt you."

"Are you alright? Is there something wrong? This must be some kind of trick."

"No, I'm happier than I've ever been, but I, he, needs your expertise right now. Please?"

"I'm sorry sir, can we come in? I'm afraid you don't have a choice."

And then the second big shock of the night: a pistol with what looked like a silencer fitted was pushed into his rib cage, forcing him gently back into the hall so the two men could shut the door behind them.

Gillian's voice was again in his ear. "I'm sorry David, we're desperate, we can't take a no, you'll see why later. We'll need your instruments, anything you've got for stomach and lung wounds, whatever's in the house really, any fine surgery viewing equipment, walking boots, glasses, outdoor clothing, any medications, a couple of cases of clothes. The guys will help you."

One of the men was already returning from checking the house, carrying wellingtons, walking boots, coat and hat, smiling at him sheepishly. It was strange, her familiar voice from long ago, urgently friendly, pleading, their smiling abashed demeanours contrasting with the cold threat of the weapons. "Oh, alright, but it had better be one hell of a good explanation."

In the office by seven and another early start thought Andy Bowson as he walked in the door where could see he was far from being one of the earliest. At some time overnight they had all heard the news. They'd been summoned, leave cancelled, contingencies for more resources, more people in other words, being put onto operational duty; the truth being that they were actually at breaking point.

The Birmingham enquiries had already consumed huge resources, not just the CT Command, to little effect, and now these London shootings. Sure, the two cornered loonies had died trying to break out, thankfully taking no one else with them, but the rest had disappeared, and a huge manhunt was spreading out from London into the provinces. Even the straitened military were having to post personnel to some sensitive sites.

There was nowhere near enough manpower though, insane government priorities had seen to that; some pundits were even talking about calling up the Territorial Army for God's sake. As if that weren't enough, last night had seen what seemed to be a car bombing and arson in Swindon and another arson in Reading, both sets of victims according to neighbours being good Muslims, pillars of the community, blah blah blah.

No one here gave that any credence at all, the parallels with the Birmingham house arson were just too close: no confirmed survivors, gas explosions and apparent liberal use of accelerants to minimise residual evidence. Maddening for the forensics teams, who were working really hard for their money but so far coming up with little of value.

It appeared though that something had gone wrong at Swindon; a shot had been reported, a neighbour had recognised it for what it was and called the emergency services, and then only when peering out their window had seen a figure bundling another into the back of a plumber's van.

Others had witnessed another man, heavily laden, get in and then, shortly after a fourth before the van drove away. Someone had even taken a couple of photos with their phone, but at night, under the dimmed street lighting and at distance it was poor quality, even after a digital clean up.

Nevertheless, they had the registration. A team was on its way to the registered owners now, but he knew in his bones they would be cloned plates, whoever it was just too professional. Eventually the van would be found, just like the others, dumped, cleaned and burned out.

The fire-fighters were still damping down the scenes so that the painstaking sifting process for forensic traces could begin. The Swindon site in particular had been levelled, almost consumed so that only dust and ash remained, the distraction bomb, clearly what it was, had kept them away long enough for that.

Everyone, the full complement except for those already on the streets, was in the morning meeting, getting their orders from the chief himself: Dager standing at his right hand looking composed, serious, even a little smug. What a change from just a few days ago. Given their recent injuries, not mentioning his family, they wanted him and George in the office, helping to co-ordinate and sift the torrent of material that was inevitably headed their way. 99.9% would be dross, but they had to keep trying to find the perhaps one golden key to it all. That suited him fine right now; he wanted to stay close to where 'Henry' could contact him: he was making a lot more sense than the rest put together these days.

Later that morning 'old' Ted left what was becoming part of his daily routine, another COBRA meeting. They were starting to get properly scared now, especially when he told them that the arson attacks were probably linked to the Birmingham incidents, that numerous casualties should be expected and that, so far, no useful evidence had come to light, other than that the plates identified were clones and the van used in Swindon had been found burnt out in a field. The Reading getaway vehicle hadn't yet been recovered but there were reports overnight of a vehicle fire near the Chilterns. Also, a farmer had found a bound Asian girl in a field a few miles away. She was now in hospital suffering from exposure and hypothermia; she'd clearly been out in the cold and damp night for hours. She would be interviewed later, when fit.

The press were on to it now of course, prompted by locals complaining about lack of security, racist murder gangs whom the police must be shielding, their rights to look to their own defence... All the usual, distilled and magnified by community 'spokesmen', agitators mounting a platform. But the thing that really scared them was the Met Commissioner's statement that the force was fully stretched, even with military support and would be hard pressed to deal with any widespread disorder which was now being hyped up on social media forums.

He was experienced enough not to be surprised by the emergence of an alliance between the Home Secretary and Defence Minister, arguing for massive new resources for the military, army particularly, and police, along with an even wider range of legal and other restrictions than she had read through last time. The Foreign Secretary and Chancellor of the Exchequer were fighting back, and the PM was wavering, there was no doubt about it.

If it wasn't for his people and the other innocents on the frontline it would be funny, not the nightmare it threatened to be. Well, for decades they had continued, without a by-your-leave, to shove ever more exotic ingredients into their stir-fry of a New Britain and were only now, reluctantly, starting to recognise the remote possibility that it might prove explosively foul. Well they could pour all the money in they wanted now, but all the signs were that the lid was about to blow off.

The best part for him had come on the walk out to the street, accompanied by the MI5 Director, their assistants keeping back a few discreet paces. "Well Gerald, what do you make of that?"

The MI5 man looked at him and dropped his voice, probably his normal work tone he thought. "This could bring them all to their senses, but it won't, all too wrapped up in personal ambition. But, if our people start getting tired, there are more incidents, well, that frightens me. Those being attacked are being specifically targeted by professionals. They seem to know more about them than we do and don't have to follow any rules, or care about the consequences. If we don't stop them, soon, well... And those being attacked, they aren't the usual small cells of nut-jobs, I'm convinced of it; there's a lot more behind them, organisation, resources. Call it a professional hunch, no more, but they got into us; that payroll clerk just disappeared, nothing in her background, no religious affiliations at all, all the background checks were fine. That's why I'm scared."

"I know. How are your people, the two in hospital?"

"Thanks for asking. They didn't even bother, did you notice? She's unlikely to walk again, young family. He they don't know, still in a coma, could be brain damage, I hope to God it isn't."

"What does he do anyway; I've never heard such a lot of mumbo-jumbo for a title?"

"That's the point."

And they left it at that.

Gillian followed David Kingsbridge out of the dining room into the kitchen to wash up, their whites, gloves, everything would be burned thoroughly she knew, the dining room cleaned and disinfected, and Georgy transferred to a room upstairs similarly sanitised. She sat at the kitchen table with him, smiling nervously, drinking tea and eating a cooked breakfast; they both looked at least twenty years older, but he was still just as professional, had just got on with it when he arrived, not complained about the lack of amenities, solely focused concern on the patient. It had gone reasonably, no more. Despite her earlier efforts there had been a lot of debris in there, a fragment she had missed even penetrating the liver, thankfully they were always the most resilient of organs. The bleeding had been stopped and his lung and stomach sealed, but he should never be quite the same again. Nevertheless, Georgy was fortunate, he was fit and active and, so long as he remained free of infection, not easy in a farmhouse, he should make a reasonable recovery.

They were both tired, nights up, long intense surgery, not getting any younger, shock at the situation. She might as well break the ice.

"Thanks so much David, we owe you his life. Please tell me what happened to Mary?"

Hard, she knew, but they had to start somewhere; tears were forming in his eyes, the wound still raw. Brain tumour, symptoms came too late to do anything, all over in four months as he was in the run down to retirement. No children or close relatives nearby, just friends in the area, so he had opted to continue to work a bit, stay local, try to keep going; what else was there at his time of life?

She smiled, didn't feel like it for a second, but then her emotions followed her expression.

"Far more than you know David. I found that out twenty years ago, so much more right under my nose, our noses."

He was looking at her quizzically, as if she had just declared herself a member of a cult.

"So, where've you been these last twenty years? The authorities said you were missing presumed dead, probably on the moors, or had somehow left the country."

As she went through it with him, step-by-step. She knew a couple of the lads were in earshot in case he tried to do something silly; the suspicion on his face was replaced with incredulity, outright disbelief.

"You may still be a doctor, but it sounds to me as if you've had some sort of break-down, at least you're not claiming to have been abducted by aliens. Don't you realise how all that sounds? Where've you really been hiding, who are these people?"

"I've just told you, more than I should have but we owed you that."

"You've got no proof at all!"

"Would you like to see the proof for yourself, for me to take you?"

He was going now whether he liked it or not, but at least she had to try to give him some sort of power of decision.

"You've nothing left here, after all."

"That's an awful thing to say. And what are all these guns for, the shot man?"

This was not going well, hardly surprising.

"Every country has a right to defend itself David, that's what they're trying to do."

"I've never heard such…"

He was cut off by the entry of Alan, Art and Sam, coming into the kitchen to cool things down. She looked at them helplessly.

"He doesn't believe me. I can't say I would in his position."

Alan and then Sam sat down and went through their own tales, explaining their origins; the huge Art standing casually by the stove, ready to make more tea should it be needed. By the time they had finished, twenty or so minutes later, their guest was starting to doubt his own sanity.

She squeezed his hand gently in reassurance.

"You're not going nuts and neither are we. It's the truth. You must have seen things in hospital, terminal patients who've suddenly recovered with no explanation? We all have, there's a lot more to this world than any of us know".

He looked about him.

"I assume from the presence of these gentlemen that I'm going to see this proof of yours for myself, whatever I say?"

"I won't lie to you David. They're never taken anyone there forcibly, only those found by accident or those who were invited. We rather hoped you wouldn't be the first, especially as we are so deeply in your debt."

He smiled, doubtfully.

"I had wondered what all the clothes and boots were for. Well, perhaps one last adventure, and once, long ago, I wanted to live beside the sea."

The tears, this time of relief, were running down her cheeks, she flung her arms around him.

"Oh David, you can stay with us, you'll see that it's all true and so much more."

Elaine had called her at eleven; she was back at work, what else was there now until the call came? Her cousin would be staying again this evening; she was really fond of him, like a sister admiring a bigger brother, feelings utterly different to her own. They hadn't stayed up talking too late, Helena's conversation with Sam had acted as a lightning rod for her excess anger, relieving some of the pressure, at least until she saw him again. She could be sure Sam wouldn't let her down; he was just so… solid. Elaine had said they were going to let him come around some time that afternoon and wondered if she would want to be there, be the first person he saw, it might help with the shock? Two o'clock would be fine, plenty of time; could be in the evening, it depended on him.

She made her way into the ward just before two, dressed more for him, comfort, than work today; his favourite royal blue, more King Alfreds too. It would soon look like a woodland floor in Spring at this rate, she reflected.

Elaine was there, fidgeting, saying the doctor was pleased, no reactions or infections, all stabilising, hence the decision. His colleagues would want to interview him, but not until tomorrow, assuming everything went well today. How was she holding up? She smiled in reply.

"Elaine, assuming everything goes ok and they want to release him some time, where will he go?" She had already decided the answer herself.

"Well his flat will have to go, it's not secure now, he's no family in this country, just a sister in New Zealand or somewhere and they're not close. I think they'll take him to a safe house somewhere outside London to allow him to get better and then set him up with another flat in town. They certainly don't want to lose him, especially after losing so many other leaders. They want him back quickly with everything going on, that's if…"

"Knowing him he's in there listening to us now, amusing himself. He didn't fight them off with his neighbour to go down that easily."

The conviction had come to her overnight: so that's what faith feels like, springing from her hours at his bedside yesterday and Sam's utter confidence in him?

No, not this time, this way.

"We can talk about the future when he comes around, but, in the meantime, can you get his personal effects sent round to my place quietly this evening, my cousin will be there. Please, for him?" For me. "It's for the best".

Elaine was looking at her uncertainly, as if torn between fear and longing.

"I don't know. I suppose it's best for now, until he comes out of here, but I'll have to let the service know and they may overrule me."

"I know you'll do your best. I'll call you as soon as there are any developments, I promise. It is for the best."

"I know."

And, with that, Elaine left.

She thought she could see why he might be interested in Helena; she was so indemonstrably strong, she was already sitting next to him, hand on his, head by his, just whispering quietly as the nurse from last night had described.

He was lost, could be walking in circles in this featureless desert forever, neither hot nor cold, no real sensations here other than the ones he felt in his mind, no perception of time at all. The river valley could be anywhere, mental satnav dissolved when I left it behind, just walking, hour after hour, until something turns up.

On the far horizon there was movement through the heat haze, someone waving, running towards him, he couldn't see who. He sets off towards them, tired now, tired of this. The distance steadily closing, it's a woman, it's her, Helena, it could only be, would only be… She's beside him now, her lips to his ear, her hand in his.

"Are you done here?"

"Yes."

His hand moves, just a fraction, in hers: his breath deepens; she sits up, not daring to hope, not speaking. His eyelids twitch, once, twice, then open, pupils adjusting to the move from darkness to bright light. She looks into those eyes that normally unnerve her, fearful; they start to focus on her, to make sense of what they are seeing.

She's desperate for that look of recognition, would sell everything, do anything, for it, seconds pass like eternity and then that faint smile at the corners of his mouth. She kisses his forehead lightly, "Hello, what kept you?"

Time to let the quacks know, but she has what she wanted, he's there alright. And we'll, I'll, make them pay.

The medical staff went into overdrive, moistening his lips, doing visual checks for responses, then audio, shining lights into eyes and ears, telling him not to speak, just to blink, raising the bed to a semi-reclining position, bringing mineralised drinks, more water, while she sat to one side of him, just watching him let them get on with it, that small smile was still there, just for her benefit. Thirty minutes later the consultant came in with another, clearly someone equally senior from another discipline, to join the doctor overseeing the response tests.

They introduced themselves, the consultant adding, "How are you feeling? Do you remember anything that happened? Start by telling me your name. Sorry, I'm not supposed to ask that. Errm, do you know where you are?"

That smile was broadening now.

"I was nearly in heaven, and you brought me back to this?"

Later the consultant couldn't decide whether he was more surprised by the answer or by a very well-groomed professional woman diving onto his patient, literally crying with laughter and smothering him with kisses.

"My dear lady, the patient's injuries, careful please, for him…"

She turned towards the doctors.

"I'm sorry, but you've no idea how much, how many, depend on this man."

Not just me, I see that now.

Later, they wouldn't use the word miraculous, but conceded remarkable. Given the injuries they had expected a grudging recovery, a slow restoration of memory and motor functions at best. She told them they hadn't known him before. She wasn't surprised at all, it was just him.

He would for sleep long periods, with shorter periods of consciousness at first, slowly recovering his strength and lengthening his waking spells. How long? A week, two, couldn't tell with him, could they?

They were smiling now, the whole little ward was, even the armed policemen, one small victory won. She now felt able to ask about the woman in the adjoining bed; Stoke Mandeville in a few days, but could be a lot worse, the shot was low down and they had learnt so much from the rehab of veterans from Iraq and Afghanistan, so who knows?

When they had left she stayed with him, late into the evening, talking at him really. Not asking those sorts of questions, not asking anything of him at all. His downstairs neighbours, who had saved him twice over, he said he would write, she told him what she had done; he thanked her and smiled again. She updated him on the other incidents, those connected to him officially, and those that followed her call with Sam; the press were reporting it all as certain now.

She hadn't heard any more from them, did he want her to try to pass on a message if they did?

Just go to ground, lie low until he could think, get home safely.

What if they had found something, say some more sticks?

Good idea, post them to her work, addressee only, nowhere else.

Would he want her to get them decrypted?

Please, like before.

No problem. She knew it was too soon, but had he given any thought to what came next?

No, just follow the thread where it leads.

Oh, by the way, she had asked that all his stuff be sent around to her place, just for keeping, in the meantime so to speak, was that ok?

He looked at her sharply, she blushed.

"Thanks for thinking of me. You know it was you that pulled me back in there, her as well? I wasn't really joking when I told the consultant."

"Tell me one day, when you're ready, about the other things too, what you can, so I can help more, in whatever way, please?"

"Ok, it's the least I can do."

"I mean where this is all headed? What you are trying to achieve? We've never truly discussed it."

He was just looking at her; ruminating inside, she could see.

Finally, "That's a question I'm not sure I can answer."

"Oh, and my cousin thinks she may have something for you soon. I've never seen her so upset as when I told her about you, is there something you're not telling me?"

She hadn't seen him blush before, his defences were low, her elation too high for him to resist then.

"Not that I'm aware of, but she is quite remarkable you know, you both are. I would like to meet some more of your family one day, see if you're typical."

I'll hold you to that.

"Have they said how long I'll be here?"

"No, but you'll need rehab, depends on your leg mainly. I could get a nurse in, physios, for the flat if you want to come out earlier, but it's up to you, and the authorities. Elaine tells me they want you back pronto, everyone seems to need you."

Shut up, not here, not now!

He smiled at that.

"I suppose it's better than the alternative."

His eyes were drooping; it was her better judgement that won out, she kissed his forehead and cheek again, slowly, brushed his hair back and said she would see him tomorrow, as soon as Elaine gave her the nod; with that she left and went back to her flat that was rapidly becoming something that again felt like a home.

The final post was distributed round the office and Andy Bowson was surprised to be given a Jiffy bag which had clearly been opened and ticketed as having been security checked and cleared. The postmark said Wiltshire, looked like second class, but with these new Post Office tariffs you couldn't tell anymore. A single unbranded memory stick, no covering note, no sender's details. The label on the front was just block capital printed, for his attention only. There were strict computer security protocols for this sort of thing, but a sixth sense about it, some sort of premonition, impelled him to take it himself to the relevant systems boys downstairs for a full virus and malware scan. He got there, regretting his instinctive prejudice about boys because it was a young woman who took it off him, smiling.

"Breakthrough?"

"No idea, but never received one of those anonymously before, how long please?"

She looked at him sympathetically; his near miss and the disappearance of his family had conferred a little celebrity on him within the building.

"Can't tell, depends on how much is on there, could be minutes, could be hours. Seeing as it's you I'll start straightaway. Tell you what, get me a white tea, no sugar, pull up a pew, and by then I might be able to give you an ETA."

By the time he returned and sat beside her he could see the virus and malware scans spreading across the screen. She turned to him and took the tea.

"Thanks, there's nothing so far, just script files, nothing special, a few pdfs, quite a few in fact, but little in terms of memory requirement. That was quick, nothing at all unless it's something we don't know about. Do you mind if I take a secure copy of it before we open anything up, it's standard procedure?"

"Of course not, thanks."

They were just finishing their teas as the copy was downloaded onto a cd for filing. "Let's have a look in here, the file names are just numbers, do you want me to start anywhere in particular, how about this Word file at the top?"

"Go ahead, take your pick."

She hit the cursor to open the highlighted file, revealing several pages in alternate Arabic and Turkish script with what looked like a clumsy English translation underneath. He read a little way and looked at her, a status report on local volunteers dated eleven days ago, names, dozens, even phone numbers and addresses of others over a couple of pages, it was obvious what they were, a fool could see that and the woman sitting beside was brighter than him, of that he was in no doubt. Her mouth was open revealing nice teeth.

"Is that what I think it is?"

"We'll have to check but thanks, I've seen enough. Can you start making secure copies on sticks and printing off hard copies of all the files please, start with twenty hard and five sticks? I can't thank you enough, and please, keep this to yourself." By then he was already heading for the stairs. Why me, why send it to me? The Security Services would all want copies; he would have to get one to 'Henry'. I'll call him later, but first there were channels to go through. People would be working through the night on this. In his excitement he never did make that call to 'Henry'.

They were walking back the five miles from the village where the new American girl was staying with an older married couple like Martha and Iltud, children no longer at home, who were paid by the authorities for looking after newly arrived guests. They had sent a message to Martha asking her to visit, as Lena was proving difficult, bring Sally too, as they knew that the girl knew Sam, the connection might help.

They had decided to bring Josey and Narin along; the girl was still withdrawn, her comprehension of English was improving, but she seemed to have given up trying to speak other than a few basic phrases. Hopefully Sam's return would fix that, but it might deepen further the thing that worried Martha most of all.

Lena's hostess had intercepted them on the lane to say that she was the most difficult guest they had ever had. She spent most of her time alone in her room, never offered to help, didn't want to do anything, said she wanted to go back to London, ate little and hardly spoke. They had been warned that she had been a drug user in the past, but the poor thing was a mess, couldn't settle, kept asking for Sam. Sally noticed that Narin started at his mention.

Sally, as a new arrival herself, had offered to go up to her room and introduce herself, try to find some common ground. The faded curtains were closed, Sally opened them to find the girl lying fully clothed on the bed, slumbering. That was her first surprise; she hadn't expected someone black or with such obvious beauty, even if currently spoilt by a lack of care.

"What do you want; I didn't say you could come in?"

"Hi, I'm Sally, a friend of Sam's," that was pushing it, "I've only been here a few weeks myself." Really, is that all it's been?

"I thought you might like to meet another recent immigrant or two."

The girl looked at her suspiciously.

Yes, nature had been kind to her in some ways at least. She was curious Sally could see, feeling isolated in a new world that must have been even stranger for her than it had been for Sally.

"Is that true?"

"Yes. Would you like some tea or coffee? Let me try to answer some of your questions, help you understand you're not alone…"

Lord, I'm starting to sound like Gillian did with me.

Whether the girl was still getting over whatever drugs had been in her system, or because of the loneliness she felt being in a house with people, however kind, with whom she felt she had nothing in common, or because Sally was a woman from London so much nearer to her in age, she seemed open to talking. After a while Sally went to ask for more tea and persuaded Narin to come up with her.

"Lena, I'd like to introduce you to Narin, who has only been here a little longer than you. She speaks very little English, but I think understands more than she admits."

Yes, she does from the look of surprise on her face, "but she helped me to get my head straight when I felt like you. Let me explain. Do you mind, Narin?"

The teenager looked at her.

"It okay."

Confirmed my suspicion anyway.

An hour later when they left, while it hadn't been a breakthrough, she could see Lena had been impressed, knocked out of her self-pity for a time at least, by the sufferings of others. It had felt exploitative using Narin like that, but the girl's example had lifted her, so why not others? At least she'd been able to deflect the conversation away from the subject of Sam, when Narin found out that he had once been Lena's boyfriend...

The girl had even walked out with them, promising to visit them for tea on Sunday afternoon. As they parted she had smiled a couple of times and thanked Narin. Definite progress. She thanked Narin herself as they walked back through the fading afternoon light, putting her arm around the girl.

"Come on Narin, I'll help you learn to speak English so you can talk to him properly when he returns, yes?"

The girl's face lit up, Martha, saying nothing, just kept on walking.

Not there, please not there, not after all I've been through...

A young man in an officer's uniform, standing alone by an open grave in a small windswept churchyard, hands pocketed, narrowed shoulders hunched, back towards the north wind, so little natural shelter up here on the Plain. It's all done, everyone's gone, vicar inside the church, putting it all away ready for another day, someone else's turn. A few spots of rain falling, failing, not having the heart to intrude too much; all seems ash now, the light losing its vigour, dark coruscating from the higher stones around, seeking to link with the black void of the pit in front to swallow all in its shade.

The emptiness within, up here, deeper than that below at his feet, the thread of a promise snaking up from below, entwining his legs, entering his marrow, infinitely elastic, seemingly unbreakable, trailing out behind him as he turns and walks to the lych-gate. He knows what comes next, so many times before, the driving, the motions, the wandering, the returns night after night, the burdens, the surprise.

But this time someone's waiting.

Thursday after Easter

....

People in the office were looking at him differently now; things just kept happening to him. He'd tried to make a joke of it, such a run of such misfortune had to end with something stunning coming out-of-the-blue to compensate, he said. Even Dager was trying to be pleasant again. Virtually everyone in the office had camped at work overnight and it was clear that similar levels of activity were being repeated in other agency buildings in London and Cheltenham. By mutual understanding the inter-agency sub-committee overseeing this investigation, or series of enquiries, had decided not to brief up the chain until they had had an opportunity to come to some conclusions and prepare actions. Only informing their leaky masters at the very last second, when ready to move. They'd decided to stonewall questions at that morning's Home Secretaries update; fortunately, the wet cold night across most of the country had dissuaded all but the most hardened troublemakers from taking to the streets, reducing the sense of impending crisis. It was forecast to continue until the weekend at least, good news for all concerned; perhaps their collective luck was changing for the better.

He was invited to attend the sub-committee meeting at eleven which would be trying to make sense of the plethora of translated files he had been gifted by his anonymous benefactor, a fact that would surely be the subject of some discussion itself. There were representatives from MI5, GCHQ, SIS, the Met of course, CT Command was heavily represented, the Serious and Organised Crime Agency, some regional forces where the bulk of the names and addresses identified were located, a couple of senior military people, and some others who he didn't know and who weren't identified.

He looked around, no 'Henry' though.

The Director of MI5 was in the chair, hardly surprising really, though one might have expected the Met to have claimed the right, but the Commissioner wasn't here either. I wonder if he knows? Naughty question, but he's seen as political within the agencies.

One of the MI5 'oppos' was standing at a projector screen, running through where everyone had got to so far, but apologising for the fact that things were still moving fast as they cogitated over the information.

The odd thing was that once the ideological waffle was cast aside, what was left was quite concise. Operation titles, names of individuals, some coded, eighty-two that weren't, some phone numbers and addresses, references to arms movements including one shipment identified as being on a named ship due shortly at Felixstowe, some bank account numbers and not much else.

Of the eighty-two identified names they already had addresses for over sixty and were confident that they would shortly have the rest. The unknown code names and phone numbers were already being cross-referenced with their databases and those of their key allies, the phones being traced and actively tapped, other addresses were being placed under covert surveillance. The bank accounts had not been frozen, but all payments in and out were being tracked up and down the chain. By the end of the day they should be a position to move and sweep up everything identified before it could melt away, but they could really wait no longer.

Two main questions remained to be answered: firstly, there appeared to be references to several very large terrorist outrages being planned, to take place concurrently and requiring hundreds of armed jihadists, but the identities of these targets weren't disclosed, and, secondly, where did this information come from: who sent it and why? There were no coding markers of any description to identify the computer or its owners, and the software was standard, available in its billions around the world. Furthermore, why send it to Chief Inspector Bowson who had survived two of the incidents in Birmingham? He felt himself blushing as everybody's eyes turned to him.

Yes, what's so special about you, what aren't you telling us?

The Director of MI5 took pity on the poor humble policeman and thanked his summariser. Had anyone anything useful to add? No, this was a serious business meeting, not one for pushing agendas. Did everyone agree on the need to act this evening, at say eleven o'clock? Could the military arrange to stop and board the suspect cargo ship this evening, and provide Special Forces back up, if required, to the police scheduled to make the raids? Yes, good. When would the accounts be frozen?

If large funds were about to be withdrawn, immediately, otherwise at close of play. Good. This sub-committee will remain in open session until the operation is concluded, but some of us better get over to see the PM and Home Secretary, but let's say after lunch? Don't want to spoil theirs. Sorry, poor joke. Sniggers.

The meeting was breaking up; 'Henry' was still not about. He picked up his things and was about the head away when the Director of MI5 caught his eye and came over, to be joined by Ted Armstrong. "Chief Inspector Bowson? May I have a word? Have you really no idea who sent you that stick or why?"

"I'm sorry Sir; I've been wracking my brains; all I can think is that my name got known because of my injuries in Birmingham and some local must have sent them to me because of that. Perhaps there's a split in their ranks, someone's got cold feet?"

"I hope so, I really hope so."

"May I ask where your man is? He's normally here, calls himself Henry?"

"He's not my man; he's 'ours', if anybody's." He seemed to find that funny. "Sorry, poor taste, I'm just tired. Didn't you know? He was one of the five; he was shot and is in hospital. He came to yesterday afternoon, should make a full recovery thank God. Why are you so interested anyway?"

"He's been at a few of these things and always made an effort to speak to me afterwards. I rather liked him I suppose. Can you pass on my best wishes please?"

"Of course; that sounds like Henry alright."

"Sam, I want you to tell me exactly what happened in there, while I was in the office."

Alan had decided to wait, let them all get some rest, regain some perspective, himself especially, get Georgy through the first twenty-four hours post-surgery. So far so good, no surprise there; someone always looked out for Georgy, must be on account of Thea's good works, her prayers perhaps. It certainly looked like it to him. Georgy might be the oldest of them, was certainly the hardest, maybe even the toughest, driven by some internal spring wound by Thea and the stories she had told him of his ancestors, iniquities inflicted, worlds lost, but hopes to come.

It looked as if Georgy's spring had unwound, all at once, in a mad uncontrolled outburst annihilating everything in its path, but that mechanism was now rewinding, recharging; the doctors pronouncing themselves delighted, almost amazed, by his early progress.

A very long way to go of course, but no sign of reaction, infection; he was conscious, talking lucidly, even joking and taking in fluids and nutrition through a drip, his eyes searching Alan's face, waiting for the questions. Don't give him the satisfaction yet, start with Sam; if anyone were tougher than Georgy it was him. I have to know before we go back, do anything else, begin to trust either of them again, and it'll need to be reported to the Council, but it would be his decision as to how it should be framed. He would want to know as well, if anything he would be more intrusive in his enquiries. He was all about looking inside people, turning them inside out to understand their fundamental drives and their default settings, how they would react in times of acute pressure, when all the learnt stuff boiled away, leaving just the inherent essence to continue, operating on instinct.

How was he doing anyway, they needed him now more than ever.

"What do you mean?" Sam's face was composed.

"You know, why you didn't wait, as I ordered, before starting the interrogation. Why you then started killing, even kids, do I have to say more?"

He was trying to keep his voice level, emotions in check.

"We all know the rules Sam: above all no kids and avoid hurting others not directly involved, wherever possible."

Sam paused, mute, weighing up whether to answer; he had always got on with Alan, that's why they had buddied up, two outsiders working together for the inside against the darkness. Alan though had come from a comfortable background, Sam didn't resent him that, but he didn't feel it in his bones, he didn't really understand the anger, the bitter helplessness, having to bide your time, revealing nothing until the moment came to strike out. He'd become Sam's friend as well as his leader, and he respected the Aussie's courage, his ability to take a decision under pressure.

Perhaps he owed him the truth: lies wouldn't help.

"We couldn't wait, needed to get started, that place was too big to find anything unless they told us where to look."

"But why start shooting, the killing?"

"He, they, wouldn't answer. Beating them up wouldn't do any good, they hated us, it was in their eyes."

"It was you that did the shooting, wasn't it? I checked Georgy's gun, just the three rounds used, that's what he used downstairs?"

"Yes, the oldest boy first, the heir. They hated that... Thought that might show them we were serious, but he just spat at us. Then the women, then Georgy was hit, fell down, so I shot the man... It was all going to hell, didn't want him to survive, the others, the kids started trying to get away. I don't know, it just happened, but I couldn't for the littlest, not her fault, she can be brought up the right way, not too late for her."

"Why Sam, those are reasons, not explanations? If it had been Georgy, I could understand it, be furious about it, but wouldn't be surprised, well not astonished anyway, but you?"

"Georgy's right, the girl, Narin, showed me that. I asked Brother Peran about her people, he told me. The attempts over hundreds of years to wipe them out, children killed and enslaved, women too, the men slaughtered. It's still going on, what that filth did to her, must have done to her family. It's not just her people either, dozens of other peoples, all over the world, blotted out, the Armenians and Greeks in their homelands for thousands of years, no one left, just them who've killed everyone, stolen everything. You can't spare the kids; they'll just grow up into more of them and want revenge as well. I did what needed doing, that's all."

He had never heard Sam speak like that before and certainly in nothing remotely resembling those terms, not even seeking to defend himself, as if he didn't see any need for any self-justification at all, it was just obvious what had needed to be done.

And terrifyingly logical.

Perhaps it was him, Alan himself or the leadership who were wrong, that it was about delaying defeat, winning battles, not aiming at a final victory given the odds? Perhaps they were confused by wishful-thinking, believing we shouldn't adopt the behaviours of the enemy to win? But no, he had seemed clear about the limits of what they could hope to achieve, small things which are of huge wider import because they were well chosen, thought through, not indiscriminate, so as not to risk forfeiting their souls.

"What do you think Brother Peran would say about what you did, or Martha?" He knew those were the two people that Sam cared most about in the world, they seemed though to be in the process of being joined by a third.

"Mum wouldn't understand; she'd be angry, but she hasn't seen it for herself. Brother Peran... I don't know, I haven't thought about it. He's a priest; he doesn't have to get his hands dirty. But if doing what I did helps stop what happened to Narin's people happening to those in England, I'm fine with it. I don't think I'll be condemned for destroying the darkness and protecting the innocent."

How to answer that? You can't, you know it's either right or wrong. Perhaps that's how the Byzantines think, looking through a barrier where only less than a century ago hundreds of thousands had been murdered outside, across a thousand miles of now alien landscape they used to call home. Perhaps, if instead of fighting defensively for eight hundred years they had decided to kill the snake in its nest, smash the eggs at source, whatever was required, as the Allies had done to the Nazis; not stopping until they got to Berlin, rooting them out wherever they were, men, women, even children, maybe that's what it was going to take. He had come to his little happy valley to get away from all of that, found somewhere safe, built a life he loved, other lives he loved even more, and yet the darkness always had a way of finding its way in, even through his friends' attempts to do what they thought to be on the side of the light. The darkness wasn't sometimes called the Deceiver for nothing.

"Well, I'll have to report it back, see what they want to do. At least we got the kid I suppose. I don't know what you'll tell Martha, but you can't ask me to cover for you."

"Will they stop me coming back, keep me from working here?"

"I don't know, there aren't many of us, but we're only useful if we follow the rules. Perhaps they'll ask him, assuming he lives."

That had knocked Sam off balance, he could see, at least for a while. He hadn't foreseen that possibility at all. What had he thought they would do, put him on bread and water for a month as penance?

"Speaking of him, why not give her a call and find out how he's doing?"

Alan no longer had the stomach for the conversation.

"And see if she knows what he would want done with the memory stick the other team found, apparently she was the one that got the others translated."

She was on her way back to the hospital when the call came. Elaine had got his personal things sent round to her place last night, she had arrived back just after they had started unloading them, something her capable cousin already had in hand. All his home things were still at his flat; there were surprisingly little of his personal effects in what she was already thinking of as his room. For now.

No, that's not it.

Books and clothes mainly, a few photos, mostly of his wife and family, a camera, some music, one or two nice but not valuable pictures, a few old prints, not much physical remembrance of him at all, but then he was always so... internal.

Still waters run deep they say, in his case there was hardly any flotsam, even on the surface.

They had put what they could away in 'his' room, the rest was piled in a corner of the dining room looking out of place: he could sort it out himself. Her cousin had had to leave first thing in the morning; Helena had come to St Thomas' first, a long detour, before starting work back at the office. He had been asleep, best thing for him they said, we don't want to wake him.

She would return later in the afternoon and spend the evening with him; she had taken the call from Sam on the way.

"Hi Sam, I didn't expect to hear from you today. Is everything alright?"

"It will be now Miss. Bit of trouble last evening, one of the lads got hurt, should be okay, but we'll be heading back home soon. It all went a bit wrong, but it's ok now. The other lads got something for you, like before; do you want it?"

"Yes, I'll give you the address; can you post it there for my attention only?"

"Ok, Miss. How is he, is he going to be ok?"

"He will be, gave us all a fright, but he's too much for them you know, he'll be back sooner than anyone thinks, I'm sure. He wants you all to go home for a while, 'til he's better."

"We did them hard last night, really hard, for him you know, like you asked. I might have a favour to ask of you myself, is that ok?"

"Are you alright Sam, is something wrong?"

"No Miss, just want to keep doing what needs to be done, for him, like you said. Just might need your help. See you."

He put the phone down and went to tell the others in the kitchen.

"She says he'll be fine, but will be in hospital for a while. But she wants the stick the other guys got and he wants the rest of us to go home until he's better."

Alan looked at the doctors, "Is Georgy well enough to be carried by stretcher for a few hours tonight?"

"If he must be, not advisable, but if necessary."

He felt better now, decision made, others could look to the rest for a while.

"Thanks. Everybody pack up, we're all going home, shutting it all down for a while, leave nothing at all. The base team can keep their ears to the ground for us, we head out tonight."

He focused on David Kingsbridge.

"Well, Doc, the next stage of your big adventure starts this evening. Are you fit for a hike? My guess is a lot of people will want to meet you, buy you drinks, not least Georgy here's mum."

Yes, he would have to be there for that.

Helena sat down at the bedside, handed over more grapes, a small bag containing some of his things, razor, tooth brush, that sort of thing. He was smiling at her in a lop-sided way.

"I understand that I'm now your fiancé, commiserations."

She blushed purple, how did he always seem to manage it, to shatter any control she might have when with him with such ease? His eyes were sparkling at her.

"Well?"

"I'm sorry, it was Elaine's idea, they wouldn't have let me in otherwise. She's very fond of you, you know."

"I don't know why, the trouble I put her to, including all this. She must have a soft spot for ageing Don Quixotes, a bit like you, no wonder you two get on so well."

"I don't know her at all really, but I can use my eyes."

"And what else can those baby blue eyes see?"

He really was already back with a vengeance, teasing her, almost provoking, where does he get it from, some deep well he hasn't disclosed to me yet? Get closer, find out. No, that's not the way. Play the game back at him, you came expecting to mother him a bit, enjoy being in charge, and already you're running to hold on to your dignity.

"Someone who's taken too much on himself, not shared the load with others who would help."

Not bad, it's a start.

"Someone who needs to learn when to ask for help, when to step back, when to listen to others who care for him a lot…"

Don't falter, keep going.

"Someone who needs a new home, and there's one right before him if only he would see it."

Keep going, you're on a roll.

"But someone's who's so stubborn, who's been on his own so long, buried things so deep, that he doesn't even know where they are anymore and needs others to help him find them again."

Why stop there, nail it now!

This is too big, this is big boys' games, it's his move, when… if he wants to, he knows that now.

He was looking at her now, not right through and past like so often, but more deeply, drilling away silently to find the seam he knew to be there. He spoke, that little smile reappearing on his cracked lips.

"That was quite a speech but perhaps that someone is frightened that those would offer their help would get sucked too far in, get hurt, and he would rather bear anything other than that?"

"Perhaps that's their choice to make, not his?"

"Perhaps. I think she approves of you, you know, even likes you."

I shouldn't be surprised anymore, I really shouldn't. Just when you think you've got him covered, almost cornered, he's behind you like magic, coming at you from somewhere entirely different.

"Why do you say that? I never met her, you know that."

"When I was there, at the river, she was there as well, and you were behind me. She sent me back to your side, for now."

What does that mean? He doesn't ramble, waste words?

"That must have been your subconscious, you knew I was beside you at the bed, trying to get through, calling you back." Are you sure that's all it was? Could be useful too, help him ditch the guilt. Don't think that, that's awful. "Whatever it was, I'm pleased, more than you can know. Anyway, I've been thinking."

"Am I going to like this?"

"That's up to you. I can never be sure what you're going to think, it's one of your…"

Stop right there.

"Anyway, Elaine said you're going to have to sell your flat, it's not secure. Why not stay at mine, it's secure now?"

He obviously hadn't thought of that.

"Come and go as you please and keep your promise at the same time, neat solution I think. Get your own place outside London, somewhere you like to be, maybe the West Country, secure too, unknown to anyone other than us. Somewhere we could both run to if we had to, somewhere where you, we, can go when we've had enough. You could just be a country friend staying with me when working in town, no more, I promise."

Too many 'we's' in there and why did you add that last bit? I know what I'm like, that's why.

He eased back into the pillows, smiling in surrender, but she wasn't fooled this time.

"I can see you've got it all mapped out, it seems it's dangerous to leave you with too much time when I'm on your mind. Alright, at least for a while, until the water clears a bit, but not permanently, understood? The bit about somewhere west might have some merit for other reasons, I'll think about it, but I can't stay here and will need quite a lot of rehab. What have you decided about that or are you going to let the Service do its worst?"

"That's up to them and your doctors, although we can easily sort out private rehab if you stay in London, but maybe getting you out into the country for a while, out of circulation, would be best."

That's not what I want! Hush, this isn't about me.

"This is also all too much for any one man, even you, you need others out here, not from there, people who can help, who believe as you, we, do, bring new expertise. I'll pack up work…"

"Not that, not unless you really want to, you're invaluable where you are, you've proved that already. But how the hell do you tell people, even if you think you can trust them?"

His voice was low now, just above a murmur, his right hand holding hers tightly; down the ward the armed policeman by the fire escape tried not to look, didn't want to feel like a voyeur, it was pretty plain to him what was between them.

"I told you because you caught me at a low moment, are expert in prising people open and I knew your feelings wouldn't lead you to turn me in. And your cousin was down to you again. There's no one else out here."

"There must be, people from your days in the military, some still in the service; they're not blind, they see what's happening, they must feel isolated, as if it's just them. Your trouble is you don't trust yourself and find it almost impossible to trust anyone else. There must be others."

He looked at her again, with even more respect than usual. She really was quite remarkable, it would be so easy to just relax, let her take the strain for a while, but not fair: she still didn't see the entire picture, hadn't seen for herself yet. But she was right in some things, perhaps he had become too set in his approach, compromising the possibilities, been too accepting of the limitations. She was undoubtedly brighter than him, sharper in her acuteness in some ways, had a different way of approaching complex problems, a greater willingness to take a risk.

He smiled at her, but there was something new in his expression this time, she shivered silently when she noticed it.

"There's always somebody, I'd start with Jonesy, my old and first Sergeant, he might be too old, late fifties, but he's fit. I bet he doesn't know I'm in here otherwise he would be banging on the door."

"Give me his details and I'll call him; anyone else?"

"A couple I knew from 22, maybe one or two from work, but not easy, that's why I've always held back, for fear of jeopardising everything. That's it I'm afraid."

He turned his eyes on her.

"Any more remarkable members of your remarkable family?"

She laughed, "I'm afraid not, but I'll think on it, but my world isn't one where people respect others' trust, it won't be a happy hunting ground. But another three would be a hundred percent increase, right? It'd be a start. Oh, by the way, Sam called. He said they found something for you; he's going to send it to me, so our tinfoil friends can get to work. He said they had trouble, you probably guessed from the news, but were alright now. I gave them your instructions like you said; he was very concerned about you. He said he might need my help but wouldn't say what with."

She could see he was starting to tire and felt her anger rising again, at them.

"Good, I'll need to get out of here to as soon as I can, it looks like it's your place, after all. The spares of the other ones are there you know, in that little bag I started to keep there, couldn't leave them in the office, the originals are hidden in one of my picture frames at home."

"They should be at my place as well then, I won't disturb them unless you want me to."

"I wonder what happened. He said they were all fine, did he? We've been pushing their luck too hard; a break will do us all good for a while. We need to keep following the thread though, something tells me we're a lot closer than we were and we can't let it get away again, but until I'm mobile we're stuck."

You are; I'm not.

"I should leave you in peace; I'll come again in the morning, text me and let me know when, then tomorrow, early evening. Let me know whatever you want, and thanks for Jonesy's number, I'll call him on my way home."

"I don't know what to say to you, but thanks for being here, just being you."

She almost floated home, it was all slotting into place, he would be there full time as soon as he could get discharged, she had no doubt of that, her friends from the Fens would be at her flat on Saturday morning, Jonesy would come down after work on Friday and stay with her overnight, head back some time on Saturday, he had sounded really upset not to know before, and a new plan was forming in her mind. Maybe Sam could help.

They were preparing to head out tonight, a dozen outside boys, one on a stretcher, Gillian and David Kingsbridge, and an infant carried by an Art who seemed to be trying to make amends for something. They were heavily loaded, personal kit and weapons, so would need to be driven to the moor road as close as possible to the barrier gateway.

Such a large well-armed party would be fine on the hike through, but would be slowed down by the stretcher and the two doctors. Alan was regarded as the senior man and was expected to organise and lead the little column once they had left the vehicles; the Beta and Standby teams would head out just after dusk to secure the assembly area then lie up and await the return of the vehicles with the rest teams just before midnight.

His main worry though was Sam, he seemed to have withdrawn into himself even more completely since their conversation, must be worrying about the reaction back home. What would they do with him? Sam's opinion, and that of Alan himself, would be listened to, but ultimately it was unknowable; they had not had to deal with such things before, so far as he was aware. They would surely be highly influenced by him as the leader on the spot.

In mitigation Sam was a young man in a highly stressful and unfamiliar situation, responding to the unexpected shooting of his colleague, primed by his hatred of what had been done to the girl he had rescued. But that was not the full explanation, was it? Sam was quite matter of fact about it, unapologetic. So, what would they do, suspend Sam at least, maybe imprison him for a while, ban him from outside duties as unreliable? What about Georgy, by far the far older man; he was equally complicit in his own way, but what had he done, other than start the questioning and not prevent three shootings which were, after all similar, to those which the Beta team had carried out in Reading and they themselves had done in Birmingham?

Perhaps it was partly his fault, leaving Sam and Georgy together in the room, both the playthings of their own histories, twisting and knotting them about. No; Georgy would get away with it, his wounds employed in mitigation, Thea's influence too, but Alan would do his damnedest to get him transferred off these duties. Sam shouldn't carry the can alone though, that would be unjust. Perhaps talk to Brother Peran; he might be able to advise him, perhaps a suspension, some serious penance, until they were ready to go back in? It might well have to be as part of another team; he wasn't sure he could ever trust Sam again after that.

The other teams set off while they finished packing up, getting Georgy ready, sedating the toddler and strapping her to Art's back, cleaning up behind them, preparing, nearly time to go.

Where's Sam? Anyone seen him?

Not for some time, his stuff's gone, his rifle, handgun, pack, a machine pistol, some explosives, no one's seen him for over half an hour.

The cars head out to check the roads, Alan and the standby guys split up and head out to the moorland around the farm, but it's hopeless, dark, he could be anywhere, and they had to get home. Where would he go?

Phone the base team in the Cotswolds; get a message to him if they can.

Try to track him down; he's taken phones, no answer, switched off. That's the last thing we need, a total screw up.

Where would he go? His old haunts, Bristol, London, maybe her place, damn, he's got the stick too? Only Sam had her number, it would have to wait until he made contact, get to her that way. Waste no more time for now, home.

They had left him little choice, well Alan had… It had all spiralled out of control and now he was walking away from the only real home he had never known, people for whom he would do anything: Martha, Iltud, the priest, and now the girl, Narin. Yes, her entry into his life had changed things, to have someone dependent on you, whose life you saved, had helped transform, that was the greatest responsibility of all. He would have to find a way to go back at some point, would have to make things straight. If anyone could make that happen it would be him, their mentor, Henry, when he had recovered. In the meantime, Sam would have to show them that he was invaluable, then go back and make amends. He had put a note for Martha in Art's backpack without him noticing, a message for her, and Narin, to wait, not listen to what they might be told about him, that things couldn't be allowed to stall.

He would return.

He walked east, over the Brendan Hills, the best way and then either London or Bristol, places where he knew the ground, had old acquaintances, could think things through. Yes, head for London; see if she would help, post her the stick himself for delivery first thing on Saturday, walk and hitch, no public transport, slip in invisibly, with cash you could hide, even in London. Helena would help, he was confident of that; he had heard the desire for vengeance in her voice. Henry must be bad, really bad, to want to pause things just as they were making inroads, but not her, not now. The others might believe in the cause, but they weren't owned by it, didn't have it coursing through their veins, only Georgy, and now Helena, had that. He would have to operate differently, less crash and bash, more hunt them down one by one, his natural metier; the Barrett was broken down in its nylon outer, from the outside it looked like a small tent, just another anonymous young hiker.

Friday after Easter

....

Four in the morning, ready to go, fifteen minutes to the target address in an East London street, a dozen armed police, flak jacketed with another unarmed team for back up. They were stretched thinner than ever: cross-referencing the eighty-two names taken from the stick with their own databases had expanded it exponentially, it now included known or suspected associates of the eighty-two, many of whom were on the radar but not regarded as high risk.

Simultaneous raids taking place in twenty-seven towns and cities across the length and breadth of the mainland, even a ship to be boarded by the navy and marines in the English Channel, hence the delay to four a.m.

He was leading one minor raid: a run-down terraced house. George and three others enter via the back, he and the three others through the front, smash the doors, the remaining four aiming at the windows and providing back up. Five adults believed inside, two of interest, brothers in their early twenties, Pakistanis.

He had made a lot of these raids over the last few years; violent surprise always overwhelmed latent resistance, concussion grenades were carried, but seldom needed. A tsunami of adrenalin carried him through the shattered front door behind the first pair, who swept through the ground floor while he and one other raced up the stairs, weapons screaming silently for targets. He could hear voices, surprised, shocked, rousing themselves, more racing footsteps on the stairs behind, reinforcements. A young man was on the landing heading for the back bathroom.

"Freeze, armed police!"

The man was turning, his hands moving upwards, a gun, some other threat?

"Freeze!"

Thank heavens; it would have been so easy to pull the trigger. The upstairs was full of police and waking occupants, wrists tied they were marched downstairs to the police van waiting to take them away, so the search could begin, two guys were already in the loft, "Bingo!"

If only they were all so instantly rewarding. He was exhausted, trembling as the adrenalin that carried him through that thirty seconds left him. All very well, satisfying, but this wasn't filling the huge hole in his life, one that just seemed to grow bigger by the day. Perhaps they would let him see 'Henry'?

Mark, Seigneur for the parish and its neighbouring Marches had met them by the barrier with a couple of his lads and escorted them down, talking with Alan quietly for much of the return journey. Hearing his report, shaking his head at the news of Sam, his wounding, the need to shut down for a while. Looking at the infant girl and checking Georgy who was stoically ignoring the movement of the stretcher over the rough ground, the two doctors trudging on beside him, not saying a word.

The cold light of the predawn was starting to pick out some of the landscape when one of the party caught sight of movement on the heather clad slope above them and called a silent halt.

What is it?

Someone, something, moving about up there, surely not them, this close in, can't be? Didn't move like an animal, more like a biped, look there it is again, moving up the slope away from us, disappearing into that shadow of a fold in the land. Mark spread a net of ten armed men, leaving Alan with the others to guard the rest of the party, but taking Art. They scaled the slope swiftly, stealthily, attempting to avoid being seen by whatever it was they were trying to follow; they were twenty yards apart, maintaining a hunter's concave drag line to encircle what was clearly a fleeing quarry now, definitely humanoid in shape and certainly not expert in moving over this sort of ground stealthily.

They've seen me, are headed this way.

Why she had sneaked out of her hosts' that night and decided to try to leave despite all the warnings, their kindness, Lena didn't know; perhaps it was all just too different or just an impulse? Anyway, she was soon lost and cold in the dark alien landscape. Keep heading higher, that's all she could do and then she had almost stumbled into that large party; only the light of their dim lamps had alerted her to their presence before it was too late. Now they were looking for her, covering the ground frighteningly quickly, but clearly not quite sure where she was.

She kept moving, another rise; head left along it and try to slip back through the cordon, she couldn't out-run them. There was a small gullied rivulet, down in the shadows, hide there, let them sweep past and then she'd be away again to see if this barrier of theirs' really existed.

She slipped, the ground loose and much deeper than she had realised, six feet at least, icy cold at the bottom.

A lamp was on the lip above her, he had heard her fall, looked like a giant up there in the half-light: it was the most terrifying moment of her young life so far. Then he was there, beside her, offering reassuring murmurs, putting her over his huge shoulders and hauling himself up the muddy bank, setting her down on the ground at the top, the oil lamp picking out the angles of his huge, fair features in the breaking dawn. She was wet, frozen, shivering, shattered, terrified; she looked up at him to thank him, his rueful smiling features, his gentleness, and the impulse to run was gone.

Dawn was at their backs now, cold but welcoming as they arrived at the little station halt at St Leonnorus. Mark took them to his house and base of operations, not big enough to be a manor house, more like a large stone farmhouse on the edge of the village, with exceptionally thick walls, very small locked and barred ground floor windows and a low tower at one end; to all intents and purposes a small fortress. Food was provided while they rested before joining the first train, due in an hour, which would take them all to their homes down the valley, apart from the team leaders whom Mark would escort to meet the High Steward and deliver the disturbing news.

They were all seated, in ones and twos, around the Seigneur's farmhouse kitchen table but even the tired and distracted Alan couldn't miss it; the American girl was pressed up next to Art, who was back holding the infant. She would go to the nuns for adoption by loving parents, hopefully to be raised on a diet of love rather than hate.

Georgy would go down to the little hospital, run by the nuns and monks from the monastery outside St Josephs, the two doctors travelling with him. They had been talking for much the journey, Gillian trying to answer, even pre-empt, his questions. How much he took in, let alone believed was hard to say, but he had marched better for a man of his age than Alan had expected. It almost seemed as if he were looking forward to getting there, was impatient to see if Gillian was really telling the truth.

For the first time since before the start of the mission he smiled, looking at Art and the girl, no, you couldn't help but notice: there was something about this place, if it could work for him and his wife, the fisherman's daughter, why not for them too?

Andy Bowson was back at the control centre by nine, starting to piece together the reports from the various raids around the country prior to a meeting with his superiors at tea time.

Days of painstaking follow-up work would be required, late nights and weekend working for him, them all, given their other enquiries were falling behind, they must be missing stuff despite all the additional resources now deployed. Of course, the media were having a field day, everyone could see something was up and recent events had drawn more foreign camera crews and reporters like honey attracts bees.

Three armed sieges were underway, one in Cambridge, of all places and two in Rochdale, the occupants heavily armed and more numerous than expected. Two coppers were being held hostage in one of them. In Birmingham another targeted group, again more heavily armed and numerous than expected, had shot their way out, killing three armed officers, injuring four more and had escaped: someone had messed up.

There had been sporadic armed resistance in four other raids, two officers injured, three suspects killed and two others wounded resisting arrest; nineteen of those they were looking for hadn't been found at the addresses raided, but overall it was considered a significant success. Over one hundred and fifty suspects detained, numerous arms caches recovered, and properties now being examined minutely. He and his colleagues still couldn't believe the scale of it; that the information was highly accurate and had come from inside their organisation was now beyond question. The previously subdued, even despairing atmosphere in the office had evaporated entirely, to be replaced with one approaching triumph. If only he could share it.

To all of this were to be added the preliminary reports from the searches of the burned-out premises in Swindon and Reading. Damaged assault rifles, handguns, traces of ammunition, grenades, military grade explosives, detonators, had all been recovered, major caches as well. Additionally, there were almost irrecoverably burned bodies, especially from Swindon, numerous bodies believed there; teeth recovered indicating adults and children, plus four from Reading, all adults, confirmed by the recovering girl, who had clearly been spared. Similar to Birmingham, although that girl had never been found, thought Andy.

The witness had been able to provide little help. They had been masked, European looking, all wearing overalls. They had pretended to be gasmen, come to fix a leak, had asked questions of her father, shot her family one by one and carried her away before abandoning her in the field where she was found. Had she known that there were illegal firearms in her home? She'd denied it of course, what else did they expect, that might change as the realities of life began to sink in.

He wished he could be a fly on the wall in the COBRA meeting scheduled for nine o'clock on Saturday morning. The press would be torn between rage and exultation, the politicians between preening and fear of a public opinion which was shifting rapidly towards fury. It could be amusing, but most of all he wanted to ask the Director of MI5 for permission to see 'Henry', to wish him well.

And to talk.

Saturday after Easter

....

The smoke was starting to clear after what was possibly the worst twenty-four hours of the Turk's life; it would be several days more before they could fully quantify the damage they had suffered. They were always prepared for losses, defeats even; that was just part of the war, one of the ways they wore their enemies down: just keep coming back with more: more martyrs, more resources, more ambition. But this was on a different scale, a long way from mortal, but a disaster nonetheless, 1683 all over again? He hoped not, they had to prove not, reorder, strike hard and quickly, show they weren't beaten, otherwise their backers would despair of them and move elsewhere. Good Friday the kaffirs called it, well it certainly had been for them.

They hadn't picked up that they had lost two of their key UK lieutenants in the Swindon and Reading attacks, domestic fires as they had been reported locally for several hours. Communications couldn't be regular, top down and need to know so far as possible, to prevent their enemies' listening ears identifying their local volunteers. Reading was still being officially identified as a domestic fire, although the local media were now saying it looked like arson with a racial motive. Swindon was being reported as having terrorist links: the police had recovered weapons and many dead bodies, what was left of them, from the wreckage.

It was clear to the Turk that some sort of UK government secret death squad was operating, had managed to extract information from those attacked, sufficient that the overnight raids, and the follow-up ones today, appeared to have wiped out over sixty percent of the organisation, including most of the local volunteers they had so laboriously set up there over the past weeks, months and, years. Even the Liberian registered coaster bringing arms and volunteers into the east coast had been intercepted, eighteen more operatives lost and for sure the authorities would be tracing its labyrinthine ownership and contracting structures through the world's shipping markets. They would relentlessly unpick that part of the organisation, stitch by stitch, unless his own government refused to co-operate when the enquiries reached their shores, as they inevitably would. That would test their mettle, their faith in the cause.

They still had resources in situ though, whole limbs that were entirely separate, known only to himself and those directly involved, including his four key lieutenants, two of whom were now gone, presumed killed. Everything was compartmentalised as far as possible so that if an operation and its resources were blown the others could continue unaffected. It appeared that, so far, the authorities didn't seem to have penetrated the other two networks already in place. Breaking up one wouldn't, couldn't, lead to the other.

He cursed himself for not having seen what was happening sooner, too complacent after Birmingham, that should have rung alarm bells. They had been too focused on striking back, too confident that their people would not betray them even if taken, their structures insulating them from local losses. He was missing something, assuming they had made someone in Reading and Swindon talk: and it had to be both, they were detached from one another, how else had they been able to move, in only twenty-four hours, to roll up over half the organisation so cleanly?

Not nearly enough time.

That's why most of those on the ground had stayed put, had reasoned that moving was riskier than staying where they thought they were safe. Bad decision after all.

Had their own higher structure been penetrated somehow, was someone betraying them? When one started thinking like that, it could all fall apart; that was after all how the Algerian military had won their dirty war against the insurgent FIA, GIA and others in the nineties: get them believing they were all betraying one another so that they turned on each other and began a process of mutual destruction.

No, if they had been betrayed at a senior level forty percent of the networks in the field would not still be intact. Now was the time for cool heads, regroup, use what is left soon before it can also be broken up.

They had been planning eight major actions, all Mumbai style; seven in London, all on their Pentecost Sunday and in their half term school holidays when London would be busy with tourists.

A major Christian festival underway, hence the planned attack on St Paul's Cathedral, highly symbolic, highlighting the weakness of their church, to hit what even the Nazis hadn't destroyed. Simultaneously, five attacks on major railway stations and underground intersections, Paddington, Victoria, Waterloo, King's Cross and Euston, paralysing the capital's transport infrastructure for days, destroying business and tourism confidence. A gun attack in the crowded streets of the entertainment district, Leicester Square and Covent Garden; sixteen teams of four gunmen, moving through the streets, causing panic, crowds fleeing from one group of martyrs and into the next. If the teams made it they could then target Trafalgar Square, within sight of Buckingham Palace, highly symbolic again, perhaps even penetrate the National Portrait Gallery with its idolatrous focus on representations of the human body. And the casualties would be immense, it went without saying, bigger than New York, but worse in some ways as well because it would be at street level, more personal, over an extended time and a wider area.

Finally, Manchester, that institution so beloved of and such a stronghold of their now distancing allies, the BBC in Salford Quays. A quiet day there, not ideal, but it needed to be concurrent with the other operations: truck bombs to flatten large parts of the buildings, suicide gunmen to kill those that survived. With a bit of luck some of their 'allies' would become casualties, showing them who were the supplicants now, but more importantly, bringing low one of the country's best-known institutions, taming them.

Perhaps it was our allies who have betrayed us, entirely possible although they know next to nothing about our organisation, but they could have marked us for their intelligence services, have been following us, eavesdropping, turning people.

No, you're getting paranoid.

We need to accelerate, reshape, fewer operations, two big ones, maximum three, don't disperse the impact. Definitely the BBC though, outside London, softer target, forget St Paul's; one station certainly. Go for a weekday, maximum impact. He looked at the sketch plans, obvious really, Euston, under-station taxi ranks are just too easy, it's also the main line to Birmingham and Manchester, ideal then. About forty volunteers for each, leaves a lesser number. Where, The City of London, too hard, too dispersed, Houses of Parliament, too hard, likewise Buckingham Palace; so, another station or the entertainment district? His puritanical soul cried out for the latter; there wouldn't be as many tourists, although a Friday in the spring would be close enough. Yes, that, and concentrate the remaining explosives on the other targets; after all they had been talking about demolishing Euston for years, let's show them how it's done.

Now, to work time is against us.

The conversation with Martha hadn't gone well. Alan knew he couldn't duck his responsibility, he could soften the blow by obfuscating his worst suspicions, explain that Sam had opted to stay behind on his own, not telling them his plans, ignoring orders.

They had brought a young child out, the injured Georgy back, persuaded a new doctor to come with them. But she had seen it in his eyes, the way they wouldn't hold hers when she asked for reasons, explanations. He related his suspicions about the way Narin's history had affected him, given him a reason to hate perhaps; she had sat bolt upright when he had said that, as if her worst fears were being confirmed. He had left for St Joseph's, leaving Martha and Iltud in their kitchen, Iltud comforting her, looking helpless as Martha cried a flood of silent tears.

Later she spoke to Sally. "What do we tell the girl, him not coming back with the others?"

"Tell her he's staying behind because he's got more to do, but he will be back at some point, there are others like her to rescue, like that little child they brought back. Not the rest, she might blame herself."

"Or be pleased."

"You don't know that, and could you really blame her if she was?"

Martha shook her head. "That's the worst thing about it, I couldn't, or him really."

"Then I'll tell her, one refugee to another. Besides, perhaps some time apart may help... diffuse things between them, make it easier for them when they work out how to get her home."

Later, when she had tried to tell Narin, the girl's face had remained a mask, impassive, but not from a lack of understanding, she got that well enough. Tears were around her eyes though when she said, through gestures and broken vocabulary that she was staying here until he returned, would help, would try to speak better English for him when he did.

Of course, absence could have the opposite effect.

And then the summons for Sally to meet the Council on Monday arrived, from the High Steward himself, to discuss her role going forward. Decisions would be required in advance of the imminently expected arrival of a Byzantine embassy. She could travel with Iltud and would be paid a stipend if she accepted. Iltud would not elaborate, saying only that she was being highly honoured, and it was her duty to co-operate; the annual Byzantine embassy was one of the most important events of the year.

Jonesy had come and gone, arriving late the previous night from Yorkshire, quick supper with her before setting off to see him in hospital and then back directly to his home. He was a spry little man, career military, finished as an RSM, and now doing people's gardens in the Dales to supplement his pension. She could understand how they became good friends despite the yawning differences in their lives, probably cemented by that one catalytic day in Bosnia. Jonesy hadn't wanted to talk about it, him either really, hadn't seemed comfortable with her, here; it must be a world away from his experience. He'd left first thing, shortly before the stick was delivered, and then they had arrived; father and daughter who left soon after lunch, pronouncing themselves disappointed. Two of the three codes were the same, only the third different and not up too much in their opinion. So, we've now two new decrypted sticks in the safe along with the two he had kept in his overnight bag, the others left untouched, and two more smashed pc's in the dining room.

I'll have to go to the bank and get more cash and order more gold coins in, as well; it's proving to be a very expensive few weeks. I can't keep this up too much longer, but no regrets, no, just one, his injuries, the scouring fear they had injected, the terror of mortality, being left alone, rudderless in a world that was increasingly alien. How has he become such a focal point for my life, an anchor, such that mine is lost? But he needs me more than ever, of that I'm certain, is even closer than before, needs protecting more than previously, and, she sniffs, I'm not without resource.

The plan: spend the rest of the afternoon and early evening with him, as long as he can manage, see how it had gone with Jonesy, update him on the stick.

He'll say, "You're all in royal blue again" and she'll smile: it was becoming instinctive when meeting him. Her phone rings as she gets into the taxi, a strange number, I never recognise the ones they use. It's Sam.

"Hello Miss, it's Sam. I've just got to London. How is he?"

"He's bouncing back, should be coming out in a week or two, thanks for asking. He'll be back in the saddle then I'm sure. What're you doing here, I thought you'd all gone back home? Are you alright? Where are you staying? Was it you who sent the stick?"

"Yes Miss. I don't know where I'm staying yet. We can't just stop now, it's not right."

"Are you in trouble Sam? Come and see me tonight, let me see if I can help?"

"Thanks Miss."

Helena could see he was perking up already, sitting up in his own room, the lady now taken to Stoke Mandeville for specialist treatment. Security was tight, but lower key, more comfortable; they also had privacy, although a camera on the wall meant only a little. Get on the front foot from the off, don't let him throw you this time.

"So how is the worst patient in London?"

They both knew it was a white lie, his smile and manner had long since charmed the nurses into compliance, just so typical she thought.

"Behaving himself. How is the blue bombshell?"

She blushed. "Full of worries and news," she sat in the chair beside him, handed over more fruit, "which do you want first?"

"Either."

His head leaned towards her for confidence, she responded, they were inches apart, it was intoxicating.

Stay focused.

"They decrypted it, it was quite easy apparently. Are you okay if I look through it, see if anything stands out as urgent?" He nodded. "They've all gone back home safely it seems, other than Sam, he's in London. I don't know why, I'm seeing him later to find out. I think something's happened."

"Find out, but please, be careful. It could be useful to have him around; he's the one who's most suitable for working alone here. There's not much on the news, he might be able to fill in more of the detail."

"How did you get on with Jonesy?"

"He's fine, but it could take weeks, recruitment is just about the trickiest thing, even of a good friend you trust. It's not like what you're used to at all I'm afraid."

She let that pass. Another time, how many had she helped bring in, Lena just being the latest?

"Any more on when they will let you out of here, what you will need at my place?"

He smiled, "Can't wait until you get me into your power eh?"

He stopped short, that had hurt her, he could see the stricken expression on her face.

"I'm sorry, that was thoughtless and unkind after all you've done."

He was only inches away, her attempt at self-control slowly being lost. He put his good right arm around her, he knows, pulls her close; she was shaking, her tears against his neck.

"I'm sorry, so sorry, all I've put you through these years, and still I hurt you. I don't know what to say... do."

She pulled herself together, just enough, but didn't move away, couldn't.

"It's not what you said, I know you were joking, it's just... You almost being killed... What would I do, what would any of us do? I'm tired of it all, worrying about you, doing my job, London... It sounds ever more appealing there, simple, but not on my own."

"There's nothing I can say, you know that. I can't lie to you, but if you ever want to go, just tell me but I'm not ready yet, you understand that better than anyone. I just don't want you wasting yourself on me; you could do so much better."

She pulled back and looked him in the eyes, hard, earnest, without playfulness.

"Never say that again, please. I know what I want. You know it. We're both grown-ups, understand the rules, have bigger things to do, just promise me we'll do as many of them together as we can, no secrets. You must trust me by now?"

"More than I do myself."

His temple was resting against hers again, they were drawing ever closer, not just here, over the months and years; it was just too easy...

"I promise and, one day, when we're ready, I'll take you there myself, if you still want to go."

She was leaning into him again, calmer now, even closer.

"Thanks. I don't want to put you under any more pressure, please understand?"

His smile returned, she could feel the inflexion as it rippled across his skin against her face.

"Stop talking, some things just can't be adequately said."

After some minutes, during which he didn't make the usual effort to extricate himself, "Why do you really do this, the real, inner reason, the thing that recharges you when you're out of strength, you've never really told me?"

He paused, a small sigh escaping his lips.

"A moment of singularity, there, standing in the main Basilica at pre-dawn, before I was due to cross to the Abbey on the morning of Easter Day; the Abbot had let me stay there all night. I was completely stripped down by then, by her, her leaving, the lack of anything to follow, blind despair you could call it, and then I stumbled on them, I was just walking to nowhere. They found me, nothing unusual in that, they took pity on me, the Abbot especially, but that night what was left peeled away in the dark, leaving me with just a sort of new baby skin, so sensitive as if I could feel, could hear, properly for the first time. I can't describe it, explain it at all, don't really understand it now, but everything became suddenly so singular, so simple and later that day, as they told me more, it became clear. I know I'm not making any sense; it probably sounds like mystical twaddle to you, but I was there, felt it inside my mind. It's never really left since that day, it just gets overlooked in the noisy busyness, but it's always there when I need it, that's all."

"You really are the most amazing man, I don't understand at all, but I can feel its echo in you sometimes, that's why I asked. Thanks… And where does all this end?"

He shrugged.

"I've no idea, but I had to try to do something, even if the ending is unclear. There they think it's just a holding action, buying time, doing what we can because we have a responsibility. They're right in some ways, but we are making openings, working our way in, disrupting things, saving lives, learning things. One of the things I found reference to in the first sticks was those they call 'allies', people over here, they seem to be in the establishment… I think we can guess the type, but it's the first evidence of active collusion. They've nothing in common other than hatred of the things we value, a desire to overthrow them. In some ways, I think these "allies" are the greater threat. They're like AIDS, attacking the body's own immune defences, inhibiting the fight against the invading virus, attempting to take over even if the attacking virus kills the host in the process. We've got to expose them, start cutting them out, and shift our focus in some ways from the other, more obvious threat, at least for now. Have you heard any more from your cousin?"

"No, other than daily questions about your health; all these older women worrying about you, our little boy lost; how do you do it?"

That smile, it's back, that's how, well, the start at least…

Later that evening she ushered in a dishevelled Sam, heavily laden with what looked a back pack, tent, sleeping bag, webbing.

"Thanks Miss."

He looked overawed, out of place in her restrained luxury, not used to seeing it from the interior, just gazing up at the towers of the alien rich from the unsparing streets below.

"Stay over Sam, at least for tonight. I saw him this afternoon; he, we, are worried about you. Tell me over something to eat, it's in the oven."

She helped him unburden himself, had a shock when she felt the tent bag's contents and looked in the top. He saw her reaction of dismay.

"Sorry Miss, but I might need them."

Half an hour later, they were seated at her kitchen table eating simply. He was tongue-tied still, frightened to make a faux-pas on foreign ground.

"Sam, what happened, why've you come here on your own and not gone back with the others?"

He'd been preparing himself for this ever since the conversation with Alan: if Alan couldn't understand, how could this woman inside her comfortable life? But then again, he trusted her, so perhaps he, Sam, should as well. He cleared his throat, nervous.

"It goes back to the Kurdish girl, Narin, who we rescued from that house in Birmingham, Miss. What they'd done to her over years, her family, people, others as well... and when we went into that restaurant in Swindon... There was one more in there than we thought. He shot one of us, wounded him badly. We were looking for more info, like that stick I posted you; we knew they were all involved, quite senior, your friend told us. We started to interrogate them, make them talk, but they wouldn't and then that other one jumped us. It all went wrong, we had to clean up, spare only the youngest, leave no witnesses, no other survivors, destroy the evidence and put the fear of God into others."

"But why not go back with the rest?"

She wasn't horrified, perhaps she should be, but what would she have done in their place? This young man, she knew a little of his background, was trying to make things right in his own way, as they all were, and it had all just slipped out of control, ended up doing things he had never intended. That girl, Lena, she had seemed to look to him for strength, protection, perhaps he was in some few ways a little like that wounded romantic lying in the hospital. That young girl he had rescued must have exerted a fatal compulsion to protect, defend, avenge.

Vengeance, the word broke into her consciousness now, no longer in the mist just beyond its periphery, the tool for its implementation put into her hands... By what: luck, circumstance, providence?

"What're you doing in London; have you got any plans?"

"I'm not sure if I can go back, they'll blame me. They don't understand what it's about, it's not knights in shining armour, it's total war, like against the Nazis. I thought if I could see him, your friend, he could tell me what to do, how to keep going at them, perhaps one day he can make things right for me at home. They would listen to him, I know they would."

Such a touching, naïve faith in one man from such a hard case, but then again perhaps she was no different.

"He's not going anywhere for quite a while, so you're going to have to stay here for a few days until he comes out. Have you got money?"

"A bit".

"Don't worry, that's one way I can help. Can you disappear for a while if you need to?"

He smiled.

"That's the easy bit in a place like this; the hard part is where to put these... tools."

"They'll be alright here for a while, but not too long. Why don't you rest up for the next couple of days, while I go through what's on that stick you sent me, see if it gives you anything to do until he comes out."

There wasn't much on the stick at all, a few brief files, some street plans of that area of central London around Leicester Square and Covent Garden with some handwritten scribbles on it in a script she didn't recognise, Arabic it looked. Arrows, starting in a ring and moving inwards to the centre, with a couple diverting towards Trafalgar Square and on to the National Portrait Gallery, lots of arrows and a thick ring. It presaged evil, of that there could be no doubt. Likewise, the sketch plans of Paddington, Euston and Waterloo stations, similarly marked up in hand written script and obviously scanned in as a pdf. No dates, nothing.

In another file was a map reference, or so it seemed, nothing else. She web-searched it, up in the Chilterns, on an estate owned by a private holding company; this was her world now, her appetite whetted. The ownership structure was opaque, must be deliberate, tax reasons perhaps? Well she was getting as far as she could here, would need to use the greater resources at work on Monday. They were well used to penetrating even the most masked ownership structures and as a partner no one would even ask why she was interested. The estate itself was well back from the roads, a long drive, a couple of small private valleys, ideal game shooting, one public footpath crossing one of the outer quadrants. Satellite imagery showed a large house, well hidden from public view, a farm on the edge of the estate, some estate cottages likewise, but most of it was completely cut off, only serious wealth could buy that so close to London. What was really odd was that there was nothing in the local press at all about the owners, no tittle-tattle, no disputes with neighbours. Nothing, just a passing reference to the wealthy Gulf based owners, not named. She called Sam over.

"What do you make of this? One of the files just refers to a grid reference in this little valley on this estate, completely isolated, even from the large house."

"Do you want me to have a look Miss?"

"I think it's owned by rich Arabs, don't know who yet, but will find out on Monday. Why don't we drive up to the area tomorrow, have a look around the fringes? Then decide."

Sunday, a week after Easter

···

They drove to the Chilterns early. After parking in the nearest village, dressed as hikers they would walk through the estate using the public footpath, taking photos as they went and then move onto the public roads skirting the perimeter as closely as possible, exploiting any vantage points to look down into the little valley referred to on the map.

Six hours later, on the way back to London, it was clear that the little valley was well chosen if someone wanted to be discreet. Even with the early Spring trees being largely bare of foliage, with only the hedgerows showing signs of re-born life in the blackthorn blossom and scattering of flowers along the verges, it was an ideal spot to avoid prying eyes. A security presence was visible all around the perimeter, high stone estate walls capped with barbed wire, even the footpath lined either side with high wire fences interlaced with brambles and thorn bushes, with cameras mounted on wall pillars at key points, moving as if on a programmed setting, but there was no sign of guards patrolling the grounds. The gates, on the front and back drives to the main house were similarly solid, high wire topped and camera monitored, and flanked by lodge houses that were clearly inhabited.

"What d'you think Sam, could you get in there, get close, lie up, see what's going on?"

"Child's play, Miss, unless there's patrols with dogs, no signs of electric trips or other sensors in the trees; that wire fence's a joke, less than a minute to get over that, that's the way in, off the footpath, track away from the house and overlook that little valley. If there's anything else more sophisticated, it'll be nearer the house, an inner ring; the outer perimeter is just to keep nosey parkers and trespassers away, it's too long to do anything more. Old Hendricks and your friend taught us how. Go in at night with my thermal and NV goggles, find a hide, blend in and settle down for as long as it takes, could be days; that was part of the training too."

"Oh, I thought you'd set up a camera, come out and monitor it remotely. And who's Hendricks, I haven't heard of him?"

"Old American contact of your friend, ex-forces, Ranger I think, fell on hard times. Your friend took him there over ten years ago, died last year; he was our main instructor."

"He never told me about him." But then why would he?

"The camera won't work; it needs to be someone who can move about quietly if needed, find a better spot."

"Are you sure? Won't it be dangerous?"

He nodded, "I'll take my kit, make sure I'm more dangerous. I'll head up tomorrow, be in there tomorrow evening. I'll get some supplies in the day. Miss?"

"Yes?"

"I might need a lift out in a hurry if I have to make a break for it; I'll just text you three z's, no more."

"I can be there in just over an hour, just let me know where."

"Here, he marked a spot on the OS map they had been using, "unless I say otherwise, ok?"

"If you're sure."

"Yes. I can't tackle the house on my own, but one man can watch unobserved in the woods better than a team."

Monday, second week after Easter

....

The car had met him at the airport and was taking him straight to a villa away from the city, by the coast, nice and quiet, almost certainly the opposite of the impending meeting to which he had summoned from him from his home in Ankara the previous evening. He had been expecting it of course, had even considered refusing to attend, but that would have been to put personal pride before the cause, something he could never do.

They were disturbed by the news from the UK. Hardly surprising, the media was confirming almost three hundred arrests, with more expected as the authorities widened their net, whole families were being taken into custody, many with no connection to his networks. But the real damage to them was what he had most feared: a major shipment lost, most of the local volunteers and many brought in from outside, a kaleidoscope of nationalities, arrested, weapons confiscated, safe houses blown and even some bank accounts frozen, tens of millions of dollars lost.

This last deeply worrying fact only becoming clear with the morning's reopening of the banks.

Someone in their organisation had been stockpiling information against all the protocols and somehow the authorities had got hold of it; maybe they had turned someone in one of the blown networks, maybe both. Would they have enough information to bridge across into another cell, rip that apart as well? Hopefully not, besides the later arrests were largely people with no connections to us at all, other suspect figures, but not ours, suggesting that they had largely consumed all their quality intelligence and were now becoming indiscriminate, hoping to stumble across something by sheer volume of effort. No, the two remaining networks in place were intact according to the leaders on the ground. Besides, there were very few locals involved; they were largely from overseas, brought in specially, people likely to be unknown to European security forces.

We have remained organised and will respond quickly: three major attacks, large enough to ring down through the ages, the effect of such things was cumulative after all. His Arab masters, as they liked to think themselves, would not pull the plug yet, they would sit there conveying their disapproval, making threats, taking a vicarious pleasure in his discomfiture, but would still support the reorganised plan.

After all what else did they have? Their own people had consistently proved themselves unreliable, undisciplined, hard to control once the blood had started flowing, unlike us with our centuries of iron Ottoman discipline. No, let them talk themselves out until they are satisfied, what could they do if he ignored them? It was no longer even vaguely their organisation. He would be home tonight and back to work. Those fools, their allies as they called themselves, trying to convince him it wasn't the authorities, well recent events proved otherwise to his satisfaction; they must be playing both ends against the middle. He would make them pay.

It had been an early start, nothing unusual about that for Abbot Winwaloe, but the news that Alan had brought back from the outside was more than a little disturbing for them all, their first real setback. Him wounded, Georgy Tredare shot, Samson disappeared, suspicions about both of them, certainly a disregard for orders. On the other side of the scales: a young girl had been recovered, many lives in the outside saved and a highly skilled surgeon recruited. Yes, God in His infinite mercy had not entirely deserted them.

The rest of the Council was divided, some wanting to send parties to find Samson, drag him back; others excusing him, wanting to sit tight, withdraw for a while until he had recovered, build up their strength, prepare more teams for the outside. The High Steward was cautious, wanting to take advice from the hopefully soon to arrive Byzantine embassy. This was to the frustration of some of the Seigneurs, the equites, so named from the old Roman knightly class. Increasingly they were all looking to him to try to bring consensus from disagreement, his length in office meaning that he was almost the longest serving on the Council, highly trusted by the Duke.

Sitting there, listening to them question Alan, debate the way forward, it seemed a life away from his vows renouncing the secular world. How little he knew of the world outside, all from books and the stories of travellers, so constrained was he.

Poor Alan, a good man doing a task he found distasteful out of a sense of loyalty to his new homeland, a refugee asked to return to that from which he had fled. That was why he had insisted on him; it wasn't an adventure or a mission of revenge for him, that kept him balanced, proportionate, calm under stress. He had done well, never panicked, tried to avoid unnecessary ruthlessness. Now they would need Alan more than ever, couldn't allow him to resign his role, as he wanted. Yes, give Alan time to recover, spend time with his family by the sea, all of them, and having heard from the Byzantines, send an envoy to him, asking his advice, select and train up some more outside teams; there would be sufficient volunteers, and pray to Him for guidance and moral strength.

Now the lady Sally was before them, Iltud beside her, Brother Peran too; he, they, had grown fond of her. It was hard not to, the reports were good; she was stronger than she realised, sympathetic to those less fortunate than her, like the poor Yazidi girl, stable, asked mostly the right questions and didn't rant when the answers were inconvenient. He smiled; she still didn't really understand where she was. She had some things they needed if the Byzantines' reports were true, His ways were mysterious and He had a way of providing, and it would be a boon to have another female voice at their counsels.

There were only three women on the High Council, all elected Stewards. It had taken him over ten years to persuade the Duke and the rest to allow women to be elected; it was a recent innovation but if they were to undertake the work in the outside world they needed to draw on all their collective wisdom and strength, consequently he had prevailed in the end. The Seigneurs, a military caste, would remain exclusively male, as it should be, although they were now training some women for outside work, much to the horror of some of the more conservative Councillors, but it seemed to be His will.

His thoughts wandered back to the discussion.

"Mistress Bowson, the last time you were before us you said that you would help us, use your expertise for the good of all, does that remain the case?"

She had grown in confidence it was obvious; she knew they needed something which only she could provide.

"Yes, it does, but on some conditions."

Iltud squirmed beside her, Peran smiled briefly; they could guess what was coming.

"And what are those pray?"

"Firstly, you actually try to help me get my husband here, not in the fullness of time, but as soon as is practicable."

"That would mean abducting him, by force, he would not believe us if we tried to persuade him, surely you see that?"

"I understand, I don't see how exactly, he would come if he could see for himself, I'm sure."

Why was she so sure? She didn't know, but the conviction had been seeping through her, like the sap rising after a long winter's hibernation in the roots, over the last few weeks. Just as their separation had clarified things for her, had shown her what was really important, she was utterly convinced it would do the same for him; things had become not broken, but distant between them, that was all.

"My husband would be a huge asset to your work, which brings me on to my second condition."

Iltud was red with embarrassment now, a recent immigrant making demands of the Council, it was almost unprecedented.

"I want to know what you are up to back there."

She chose not to call it home, knowing it would weaken her case.

"You've been evasive, but men with guns, people coming back wounded, missing like Sam, others brought back, people killed, it's a whole lot more than smuggling isn't it?"

Brother Peran whispered to her while the Council debated in Brythonic so she couldn't understand. It was clear from the faces, the tones, that many were angry, insulted.

"Don't worry, be firm, leave it to Him and the Abbot, they will prevail; they need you more than you know. After all, why else did He bring you here?"

The argument must have raged for a quarter of an hour, slowly calming before the previously silent Abbot had weighed in, more direct, energised, than she could have imagined, but still smiling. Finally, they seemed to reach a consensus of sorts, although some were still muttering, but it was clear that the Abbot had the High Steward onside, probably had before they even started. The High Steward spoke up, in heavily accented English again.

"Our work is, as you say, more than smuggling, more than rescuing a few unfortunates, although that is important in itself. We are trying to help those in Logres who are fighting the darkness, providing resources, a refuge, trying to help the few there who see as we do from going the way of the Byzantines and so many others. The darkness has been stopped before, at Tours by the Franks of Charles Martel, at Vienna twice by the Holy Roman Emperors, in Italy by the Normans, Spanish and Germans and now it is returning, as it always does but so few on the outside see, sunk in their lethargy of possessions, forgetting the lessons their ancestors learned. But there is hope, more are awakening, and we here, privileged by Him, must do our duty, quietly, secretly, because we are few. Our work is slowing the evil so that more may awaken in time and trying to protect the innocent where we can. We do not take life indiscriminately, but where we have no choice, and hope that He in His infinite mercy forgives us our presumption."

"But where do you get all these weapons? Who is working with you in England? How do you know what to do?"

"The Byzantines, I think you already know, have control of two Greek shipping lines, access to other countries. Together, we have been quietly establishing ourselves in America, accessing their resources; there are more there who see the evil for what it is, want to resist, but do not trust their own government, its compromises for the sake of money. Very few there know fully, only a handful, but that is enough. Many more are sympathetic without fully understanding and we are deepening our positions there, gaining more access to funds, arms, technology, hopefully even intelligence and eventually we hope, volunteers. Perhaps, in time Australia, Canada and others will join us as well."

"But what of those in England, this mystery man you keep referring to?"

"He alone is perhaps our greatest gift from Him in the struggle. His position enables him to pass on information, guidance, direction, even funds and recruits such as Samson, whom you know, but he is almost alone; recruitment of others has been almost impossible for fear of betrayal. He has met your husband you know, believes him to be a good man, who may, one day, join us."

Andy, they had access to Andy, her heart leapt in hope.

"Then you can get him here, if he sees for himself, he may join us," that's it, use us, not you, show them you're on their side, "you've no excuse to wait."

The Abbot spoke up, "If you do as we ask, without further condition, we will try to reach out to your husband, but it must be our decision how and when, and you must be patient, better to wait and be successful than rush and miscarry."

"Then, if I agree, what do you want me to do?"

353

He was smiling now, joined by the High Steward, and some of the others, they could see she was on the hook. "Word has reached us from the Byzantines that they have learnt, through the offices of the monks of the Holy Mountain, that the Vatican, or some at its heart, may be receptive to a secret approach. Our goal is to work together, put aside old quarrels, to face the common threat. The Papacy is under new leadership, more humble, regretful of past arrogances and it is used to keeping secrets, working quietly over decades; they may even suspect our existence, who knows with their hidden records? With their addition, we would be much stronger, be starting to reunite Christendom as it should be, not by authority but by true communion. We will need to send envoys alongside the Byzantines; your languages will prove invaluable, you can understand the local tongue and others, Latin we know already."

"But when… my son… I can't leave him behind?"

"Not until next year, after Easter when you would need to be touched, when further enquiries have revealed whether our hopes are true. Your son could not go, it would be a difficult journey, undertaken in secret and he will be safe here with Martha. Stop! I know what you are going to say! By then, we will try to bring your husband here, but if for whatever reason we cannot, you must still go, but you have my solemn promise, and that of the Council, that we will do everything in our power to bring him here short of forcible abduction. Do you agree?"

Peran was smiling at her. The Abbot had it all planned beforehand, he'd foreseen her demands, worked out how to get her onside, the rest of the Council too, without making a hard commitment that may be beyond their power to achieve? Everybody said he was a saint. Well, if he were he was one of the old school, those who had converted barbarian kings and nations by force of argument and personality, dragging a continent back from the edge of irredeemable ruin in the space of a few centuries by persuasion and example.

"Well Mistress Bowson, do you consent? We can offer no more."

This place just kept getting more extraordinary, amazing things kept unfolding before her at almost every turn; international reach, ambition allied with modesty, vision even… They could all be mad or deluded of course, but of that there was no evidence. They were serious, Narin was proof of that.

"I agree, thank you."

What else can I do, but you knew that didn't you?

On the way out with Brother Peran she passed Gillian coming in with the new Doctor, David Kingsbridge, who introduced them. She tried to reassure him like the veteran she was already starting to feel, asking him how he was finding things. He laughed, but didn't speak before being summoned upstairs for his interview.

"Meet you at Thea's afterwards?" said Gillian, "She's commanded us to join her for looking after Georgy, and you can't possibly head back without dropping in."

He was strolling along the street with George Edward to get some outside air, hardly fresh in central London, and a sandwich. George had seemed unusually keen on accompanying him, had insisted he pay and that they find a table rather than head back to the office. It was clear the younger man had something on his mind, hardly surprising given all that had happened over the past weeks.

"Andy, can I talk to you as a friend, rather than a colleague?"

Friend?

That was pushing it a bit, but they did get on well, their injuries had only furthered their mutual confidence.

"Sure, what's up?"

"We, a lot of us that is, are worried about you, Sally, your son, Birmingham, all of this. Are you sure you're alright?"

How to answer that, why not truthfully?

"I'm not sure. I've been so busy that I haven't had time to think about myself."

Liar, you've been running away from it, the void of absence. Is that it, what he really wants to talk about? No, I can see it isn't, he's nervous, summoning courage, dare he trust me?

"Ok Andy, just let me know if anyone can do anything, right? Some of us have been talking, about things, the case, how we feel about it?"

Here it comes, what's up, he's really fearful of telling me something.

"I'm… err… thinking of resigning, some of the others too, going private in some way."

"Why on earth would you do that? You've got a good career ahead of you, being blown up can only help you know."

The feeble attempt at humour didn't even register.

"Well," he hesitated, a last-minute prevarication, "I think I can trust you. It's just that I'm not sure I want us to catch these people behind Swindon, Reading and some of Birmingham; a lot of us feel the same way. They're doing what we should be doing; the scale of what we're uncovering is terrifying, you must see that, and no one wants to tackle the causes, just the symptoms. We all know the government, the establishment, is being bought and sold by the sort of people who want to end our way of life: they own half of central London now. Now at least, someone's starting to do something… They're on our side, sort of, they could have killed us easily, but made it harder for themselves by sparing us and those young girls. They must have sent that stick to you, it couldn't be anyone else… They must have found it in one of those addresses."

I wish I could say I'm shocked, but I'm not.

"Do you know what you're saying? We're here to maintain the law whatever we personally feel. You'd be disciplined, maybe even charged, if someone reported you to Dager or HR."

"I know, that's why I'm considering resignation. Anyway, what future do I have as a white Englishman, we're the last they want to promote? Even Dager has sold out, it's as plain as a pikestaff, that cow from HR is smoothing his path. I don't know what it'll cost him, but I don't think the price is worth paying whatever it is. You must see it too, feel the same, lots of us do, even the women officers; most of them hate HR more than the men, they don't want to be promoted just because of their body parts. Try telling me I'm wrong Andy, I hope I am in some ways, it would be easier."

Well, is he? What happens when the law is twisted into a weapon to attack those it's supposed to protect, when those who sustain it start to believe it no longer relates to justice anymore, when they come to despise those who remake the laws to suit hostile interests? That's when it starts to break down or otherwise becomes a tyranny.

"How many of the others feel the same?"

"Can't tell, half at least, some are talking about going a bit slow, missing a few things, turning a blind eye to whoever is taking the loonies on."

"And you?"

"I feel the same, that's why I think I must resign."

"Don't, just do your job. I understand your feelings, sympathise, I wouldn't be human if I didn't. Don't worry, I won't turn you in. If you find anything, let me know first, yes, so we can decide together what to do? Also, there's someone I know, you met him once in Birmingham, he was one of the ones shot. I think he's highest level Security Service, but I believe we can trust him. I'll talk to him, mentioning no names, get his advice. Tell the others the same, but not about our contact, that's for you and me only, understood?"

The younger man nodded, relieved he could see.

"As for Dager, he's a fool if he thinks he can trust the likes of her and her colleagues. And let's hope we don't catch them before they finish the job, eh?"

I shouldn't have said that last bit, but it's the truth.

Sally and Brother Peran were at Thea's awaiting the arrival of Gillian and David Kingsbridge following his interview. Thea had just returned from the little hospital by the nunnery where her son was being treated. Sally could see the strain evident in her features, her normally bright, exuberant expression suppressed. Nevertheless, she still seemed pleased to see them, explaining her son's wounds, his steady recovery, lauding his heroism, but when the two doctors arrived she was back to her old self, determined to put on a show. It was clear she had met David

Kingsbridge at one of her visits to the hospital, but had not been able to talk to him properly. Sally could see the older, slightly shy man was simply overwhelmed by her fierce joy at his presence. Gillian just smiled.

"So, the two wonder workers to whom I owe the life of my son have joined us, no charge for anyone while they are here!"

She summoned the rest of her clan to thank the doctors, commanding near obeisance and that drinks and dishes of food be prepared and brought out, commandeering a table she demanded they sit either side of her. They were both blushing deeply now.

"Thea, we're both just doing our jobs, and those who brought Georgy back here, found David, they deserve equal thanks, Alan especially," Gillian vainly protested.

"I know. I will repay my debts to them too, but without you, the master surgeon gracing my little establishment with his presence, all would have been in vain. He, I understand, gave up his life, his home, in Logres to save my son; how can my family repay? We cannot, but we must try. You Gillian, choose anything you want from my stock room, the best, the finest, anything we possess, it is yours!"

"Thea, that's incredibly generous of you, but I don't need... I already have everything I want; this place has given me that..."

"Nonsense, don't insult me! We will talk later about this, I will make you see. But now I must speak to your colleague, the master surgeon."

The doctor was almost crimson by now, fearing public embarrassment in a new world. The other customers, Thea's family, were all grinning at him as the force of her personality unfolded like a huge scented bloom, filling the air in the café with a heady aroma that assaulted the senses, dazzling them with its vibrancy.

"You gave up everything for my son, his family. There is nothing that can repay that, only Our Lord Himself, to whom I will dedicate new offerings in the Basilica, the hospital, on Georgy's behalf, yours too... How to repay such a man?"

Thea was smiling craftily now, that keen calculating intelligence amusing itself as she went through the almost ceremonial rigmarole of debt repayment. Sally suspected that she had thought it all through, had done her research.

"That good man Alan, my undeserving son too, both told me things about you. And so, this is my decision, to refuse would be a mortal insult to an old woman near her departure: a thing not to be borne by one as weak as I."

Yes, Sally could see, she was on stage now, thoroughly enjoying herself.

"I give you a new home for your life here, a beautiful cottage with a little garden down by the sea which I own, only a short walk from the hospital, where I understand the Council has offered you a senior position already? Yes?" News travels as fast as ever here. "We will furnish it with our finest things, someone will clean it for you, and you can eat here with us whenever you want. Is there anything else you would like? "

"I don't know what to say, it's just too generous, too much. You don't need to at all."

She looked at him in triumph. "But there is one thing I believe?"

"I don't see how that can be done, but yes, my wife's body. It probably sounds odd, mawkish…"

"It is entirely possible: it was done once before for an incomer like you, someone we needed to believe that this is really their home. I will speak to the Council, they will listen. Leave it with me, but be patient, He will provide."

The doctor was looking at Gillian helplessly, no was not a word Thea seemed to recognise. Later, as they came away with Sally and Brother Peran, Gillian promising to return to choose her gifts, David asked them about the girl they had found on the moor. Sally felt obliged to tell him.

"She's a troubled runaway, drugs, that sort of thing. One of her old friends who came here years ago helped persuade her to come here, but it's been a shock, hard for her and the people looking after her. She's just mixed up; although" here she permitted herself a smile "I hear she has formed a strong attachment to Art as he has to her. It's remarkable, but, as I'm learning, so typical of this place; the more I find out the more I wonder. Things just keep unfolding, I'm sure I don't understand the half of it yet."

Gillian just smiled silently to herself, so little do you know, and even I know only a part.

She left the office for St Thomas'; Sam was making his own way to the Chilterns, and now she had to see how her other man was progressing. She was supposed to be working in the cab, but found it impossible for thinking about him, worries about his long-term recovery: was he now a marked man, needing to retreat into the shadows even further, reduce his contact with her? Sam too, that young man, almost entirely alone again, having exiled himself from the place he had come to call home, dependent almost entirely on her. Was she guilty of manipulating him, twisting him into inflicting her desire for vengeance on those who would destroy the happiness she increasingly felt was finally coming her way?

So many years alone, even when notionally with others, then seeing and wanting, settling for friendship at first and then the rising tide of longing, ignored for years by both of them, but now at flood level due to recent events, almost drowning in it. The panic when Elaine had told her, the elation when he returned from wherever he was and now the rage that someone had done this to him, to her. It had brought them closer, far closer than she could have envisaged, but she needed to be careful, he was frightened for her, had been for some time, that was obvious now. He needed to see she could take care of things, not just through money and brains, but take some of the strain off him, not let progress slip while he was out of commission, so don't tell him everything, try not to worry him, let him know when they had something for him. Brush off any enquiries about Sam too; focus him on his own rehabilitation.

She opened the door into his room; he was sitting up.

"I'm surprised there isn't a pretty young nurse cooing round you in here, or has she ducked under the bed?"

The smile he gave her made it all worthwhile.

There were eighteen of them tonight, in a room above another pub in Islington; so convenient for so many. The usual mix of backgrounds, some the same and others different from the previous meeting. It was ever thus, informal, a loose network, never an organisation. Of course, there were other such networks like theirs both around the country and internationally, working towards common goals, most of the members not really being much aware of the others unless considered one of the leaders. This though was one of the most, if not the most, important in the UK, if only because of its strength of presence in the national and international media and central government. Yes, he liked to think they were increasingly the pre-eminent group, the others starting to fall into orbit around them, and of course he was emerging as one of, if not yet the, most important among them.

Today he would introduce another to their leadership circle, his disciple Sheena Ellison who had been accepted by the others without too much cajoling on his part. Yes, she owed him now, another voice in his choir, blending with the others to establish the predominant harmony, written and conducted by himself of course.

He had reported on the incomplete success of their allies' attacks on the list of names he had given them, only partial of course, and their consequent increasing arrogance towards them. Yes, the consensus was now for a parting of the ways, a loosening of contact ending in permanent divorce. She had not shown any emotion when she realised they had sanctioned deadly attacks on five individuals, had said nothing as befitted an ingénue. A test passed. All very satisfactory, and then on to the usual business, such unpleasantness swiftly forgotten, no blood on their hands at least.

As he had predicted, the fence was the easy way in, the various cameras had plenty of blind spots among the trees and would have little capability in the dark anyway. Sam's main concern was the weight of his load: Barrett, night vision and thermal imaging kit, handgun, ammo, claymore mines and detonators, provisions for five days, shelter. Heading to the referenced valley was easy, no signs of trip wires or sensors; the time of year meant the shooting season had finished and it was still too early for next season's birds to have been put out, so not much in the way of keeper activity, even if there were any here.

First thing was to establish his hide, just below the lip of the slope facing the little valley, scraped in under the carpet of leaf mould and bramble, home for the next few stiff days and nights. Second, establish his escape route out to the perimeter wall, cutting the wire but leaving it in place, finding a large log to help him scale it if the time came, then arraying four claymore charges along the route to buy time if pursued, hiding them under leaf mould at tree bases so they would shower, on command, ball bearings across a shaped 120° arc at any pursuers. Finally, setting the remaining four, two on either side and just in front of the hide to discourage anyone trying to outflank him if he were discovered. All this he and Hendricks had taught them, conceal your position, establish your route out, defend it if possible, and then worry about observation and attack. Move only at night and then sparingly, daytime was stone time, leave no trace.

His NV scope and goggles were the latest US digital 3+, giving him good night vision to over 400 yards, he could see down the slope, into the trees and then into the narrow clearing at the foot of the valley before it rose again on the far slope, which remained a mystery although the thermal goggles would give him advance warning of any living mammals moving over it. His own camo shelter was insulated and foil lined to impede any opposition use of thermal imagers, not perfect, but he should see them well before they could see him.

As dawn scraped its way across the valley, scouring away the lingering darkness, he switched the Barrett's NV scope barrel to the day scope, already zeroed, and started to site key features, using the range finder to establish aiming points, check potential bullet falls, establish clear shot paths through the trees and undergrowth, monitoring wind direction and speed. He had chosen well; the whole valley would become a killing ground, even the top of the opposite valley side, it being just lower than his own position. He could even aim right down the valley's exit, over three quarters of a mile. As long as he wasn't sleeping when, if, they came, he would be in command of the terrain until sheer numbers started to get around his flanks, and, so long as they didn't inspect his portion of the hill side closely, his mission of observation should be entirely uneventful.

Tuesday, second week after Easter

....

He had permitted himself a few hours' sleep as things were so quiet, just the usual night time wood sounds: owls hooting, the stealthy movement of foxes, deer, rabbits and stoats; the more obvious rooting and blundering of badgers pursuing their age-old trails, supplemented by the silent twisting shapes of owls and bats in flight, briefly visible in shafts of moon and star light, all signs of an environment with little nocturnal human presence.

Tomorrow night, if all remained quiet, he would move forward to the top of the opposite slope for a couple of hours to survey the next valley and place the house under distant observation. For now, it was all about remaining as invisible as possible as the woodland started to awaken and, potentially, the local human population too. He stretched himself again, took a sip of water and ate a carbohydrate bar; better be sparing, don't want to be caught short in daylight, over twelve hours to dusk.

Four hours later, he heard voices in the distance, coming up the valley, accented English, a sizeable force. His scope was on them now, dressed in camo gear, small backpacks, AK47s, carrying what looked like cartridge boxes, sixteen, no eighteen, twenty, walking purposefully up the track from the entrance to the valley. Most looked Asian or African, one or two Caucasian, mainly bearded; their Kalashnikovs had small wired boxes attached and it looked like they had sensors on their torsos, so laser training equipment, but clearly live ammo too. Bingo, looked like a shooting range at the bottom just to his right, but the training kit suggested they would be practising fire and movement in the woods around him, bad news that, but not necessarily a disaster if his luck didn't desert him.

The escape message to her was already on his phone, pre-dialled, there was enough signal up here near the top of the rise. She had said an hour, hopelessly optimistic, maybe at night if she took risks; he was budgeting at least two. Evading back to the perimeter wall, fighting them if necessary, would take at least an hour, heedful flight less than fifteen minutes. He was watching the men on the valley floor intently; these looked largely experienced, the way they moved, conversed, handled their weapons. They were on their knees now, praying, so he scanned the hillsides all around him, no, no one else about, back to them. No obvious leaders from their clothing or even behaviours. How many could he get before they worked out where he was, started to respond? Four or five, maybe six, depends which way they went. Don't even think about it. His silenced 9mm pistol was by his right side, nine rounds in the magazine and one in the chamber, plus two further spare clips beside it and one more in his tunic pocket; if they stumbled on him that was his best bet, preserve the element of surprise.

They were up on their feet again, moving up the track to commence a static live firing exercise, laying, kneeling and standing, single shots only, no automatic. The sounds rattled round the valley as if it had its own little thunderstorm, but the site was well chosen, the surrounding woodland and hill sides would muffle the noise of the shots. A keen eared listener by the boundary wall might hear the sound of distant shooting if the wind were right, but that was nothing unusual here, gamekeepers after the vermin or pigeons, if they couldn't tell the difference between a shotgun and rifle cartridge.

He watched them closely through the scope. Yes, for the most part they knew what they were doing, bracing themselves against the kick, rounds striking around the target, some direct hits. They then moved on to fire and movement, working in pairs and fours, rushing, covering, shooting at the targets. They clearly didn't have to pay for their ammunition. Two hours went by, they were taking a break, water and a snack, rifles slung over shoulders, standing talking. Hopefully, they were nearly done. Twenty minutes later, no they're not, they're breaking up into two teams of eight, while the remaining four are back on the targets.

Can't move, just sit tight. One team of eight is heading up the slope to my right, the other up the opposite slope, both running. It looks like they unloaded their weapons and have rigged the lasers for further practice. They're behind me now, I can hear them moving beyond the top of the rise, spreading out to commence the exercise; having them behind me where I can't see them is the worst of all. Pick up the pistol, pull the Barrett further back under the camo sheet; if one treads on me by mistake I've no choice.

They're working their way down the slope now, intermittent rushes from tree to tree in pairs, one covering, one moving, either side of me thank heavens, about a dozen feet only on the right. Breathing has ceased, the most dangerous moment, they're level with me now, still working their ways downwards, scanning for the opposing team somewhere on the opposite slope. Yes, it looks like three pairs strung out to the left further down the slope, the furthest about a hundred yards, the nearest pair to my left, about ten yards and growing longer now. Permit myself to breathe again, then the tunic sensors of the nearest go off: he's been hit, he falls to the ground and sits there watching as the exercise hots up. His partner is down now, and one to the left; the opposition are on this slope below me, sweeping right to left, catching this side in a pincer movement. Twenty minutes later, it's all over; they break off, the casualties standing up, heading back up their respective slopes, but not in groups, just straggling any old how this time.

The nearest pair is almost on top of me, talking in some lingo I don't understand, could be anything. They stop two yards below me; one voice sounds in the interrogative, takes a step further up the slope. And drops, two bullets planted silently in his chest, followed by the second. Couldn't risk it. Where're the others? Coming this way, the nearest pair at least, calling the others who are now on route to a well-deserved Hell. They're twenty, fifteen yards away, can't believe they haven't seen the bodies yet, their camo gear must be working, twelve yards, no further. Four more silent bullets planted, two more corpses in the leaf mould. No, one's gurgling, trying to move, not now, final shot sees to that.

New magazine inserted, start reloading the empty, two, three, four, five rounds in, damn another pair coming in to sight on my left, twenty-five yards out, twenty-two... One stops, raises an arm to point, he's seen one of the corpses, exhale slowly, reduce your heart rate, long range but shouldn't be a problem for you, wrist braced by the other hand and the ground beneath it. He starts to say something, the first round takes him in the mouth, the second in the heart; the second man half cries out, reaching for his slung assault rifle, but drops down with two rounds in his chest, the cry squeezing out in a gurgle.

The last pair call out an enquiry, accented English this time.

"What was that?"

They're running over, hard targets, wait. They see the bodies and scramble to a halt twenty yards away, calling loudly, but briefly as they drop to the ground, going the same way as the others, but one isn't quiet, he must have moved just a fraction before the rounds struck him, somewhere not immediately paralysing or terminal. Eight dead or dying targets within twenty-five yards of me, what to do? The others down in the valley or on the other hillside are calling out now, not getting any replies. Big trouble, only a couple of minutes to decide.

Movement too risky, twelve against one; if I move I lose the advantages of surprise, my defensive position.

Need to reduce the odds before I make a run for it. It's gone to Hell so quickly, can't believe it... Quickly crawl out a yard, grab the nearest Kalashnikov and a couple of clips: he won't be needing it, I might later; back under the camo sheet, send the SOS text to her, it's a count-down now. Two hours to survive.

Scan the opposite slope and valley floor. There's been a shouted conversation between the two groups, with the upshot that the four on the valley floor are heading up the slope from my right, moving from tree to tree, not sure what's going on. They haven't seen anything yet, but are wary, calling out to one another, their missing comrades. Movement on the opposite slope, the other group of eight are assembling there, waiting to see what the group headed this way report. Let them get close as before, try to do it silently, or use the Barrett? They're five hundred yards away, moving only slowly, the others will know I'm here if I shoot?

I've got to confuse them, keep them away, buy time. The other side of the valley is an easy shot for the rifle, the acoustics of the shot in this little valley would be confusing, difficult to identify the round's direction of travel and trace it back to its point of origin. The four are now three hundred and fifty yards down slope to the right, exercising ever more caution. Time to put the cat among the pigeons, you were taught to be decisive, take the initiative.

The eight on the opposite slope are looking across the valley, incautiously clustered, make the most of it. The Barrett screams out, the sound of the round shattering the valley's peace, echoing around and around, two men are down, one dead, one wounded badly by the bullet emerging from the first. Reload, observe, they're in shock, falling to the floor, looking out panic-stricken, one calls out to the other group, who've frozen, are turned around, calling back. Don't make it so easy, will you? One of the four rocks forward down the slope, torn asunder through his back, another is too slow in reacting, diving full length, and it's done for him, lifeless on the slope.

They're jabbering away to each other now, trying to get a fix on where, how many, what to do. The surviving pair on this slope must be flat on their faces behind the trees, awaiting the arrival of the other group of six who are now rushing down the slope from tree to tree. Don't be impatient; your best chance is when they emerge into the clearing on the valley floor. But they're not complete fools, they're not just going to rush across heedlessly; some are laying down blind covering fire, joined by the two lower down this slope, bullets landing any old where on this slope, even over the top. Ignore them, you'd be damned unlucky.

The first rushes across the clearing, I didn't have time for the shot, the second too, same again, but the third is not lucky today, his thigh's shot away, he's screaming, he's out of it, leave him. Movement to my lower right; they're starting to work out roughly where I might be, they're moving away to my right, trying to outflank me, crawling on their bellies, sheltered by the trees and uneven ground, heading into Hell nevertheless.

Two fronts, too much to focus on, two more have made it across the clearing now while I was distracted, the final one must be there, not as courageous as the rest, hanging back, the others are impatient, working their way up the slope in front of me and to my left, two there trying to outflank me from the other side. Switch back to the right, that's the bigger threat for the next couple of minutes, they must be near the furthest claymore mine by now. Yes, there's a stirring of movement just below. Remote detonator is armed. An explosion, a shrill shriek cut short, another shout, a wounded man trying to roll down the slope away, just away, today's not your day sunshine. The Barrett barks again, fully reloaded in the interval, the movement ceases, all that remains is the clearing smoke and smell of cordite, and a low murmur from the other man, too injured to contemplate flight.

Back to the others, can't see, had the fifth one crossed?

No.

There's a gun barrel peeking out from behind that tree on the edge of the clearing. The four this side have gone still, calling to the others, but there's no answer. The two in front resume their random covering fire, single shots only, trying to avoid giving away their positions, keep his head down, while the other pair circle further left, away from the first claymore, but just within range of the second outer mine. It explodes, sending high velocity ball bearings and shrapnel across its front just above ground level. Both would-be out-flankers seem to be down, wounded, but not dead, calling out; one's well enough to start laying down covering fire. That leaves two in front of me, and the one on the other side of the clearing. Let them make the first move.

Fifteen minutes pass; the moans to my right have faded away, one of the wounded men to the left is calling more urgently in another language, pain and weakness enfolding his voice. The cover fire has slackened; they're trying to conserve ammunition and position. There's another sound, the crackle of radio static, they must have called for more help. How many more of them are there? How long have I got?

The one on the other slope has disappeared, movement above his last position, he's climbing the facing hillside, hoping to get the advantage of height or withdrawing. Turning your back, bad mistake, there's too little tree foliage this early in the season, and the steep slope is taking its toll, he's slowing as he nears the top. A round from the rifle stops him dead, good shot considering he was lurching upwards unevenly, looked like left shoulder blade, his inner eye could see Hendricks approving smile.

But the three down this slope have a better fix on my position; shots are striking within twenty yards now. Time's no longer on my side, how long's passed, unbelievable, over eighty minutes.

Where did that go?

Time to move then, break down and pack away the Barrett, can't bear to leave it for them, drop the pack, rig a small charge underneath it to ruin its discoverer's day, hand gun in pocket with clips, AK in both hands, start wriggling away to the right and then up the slope, ten yards gone, fifteen, round a tree, then bullets start striking it, poor old beech, must be nearly two hundred years old. They've seen me, looks like one is trying to move parallel up the slope on my right, the other inching forward below me, loosing off the odd shot. They're game, I'll give them that: ninety percent casualties and still they keep coming, except for that one that got going, it didn't help him either.

Can't let that one on to the right get up the hillside before me, he must be near that remaining mine on that side. Detonate it, a cry, thanks Uncle Sam, near the hill summit now. The sound of vehicles racing into the valley floor, three, four, assume at least sixteen armed men then. Time to scoot, but a shot to the right reminds me I'm not alone on the slope. Where is he? The call of radio static has betrayed him, by that tree about sixty yards away, he's talking to his mates down in the valley. Hurl a rock just to his right, he's startled, moves away on instinct, into the path of four rounds from the AK47. When you're on your own, Hendricks taught me, continuity of concentration sorted the living from the dying, too bad for you. Now scoot for the boundary wall, just hope she's nearby,

Through the woodland hedge into the open field beyond, sprint like crazy, you've got at least five hundred yards and a steep slope's head start, just pray they haven't sent anyone ahead around you. Over the barbed wire fence into another strip of woodland, through that, another fence before an open field, this and more woodland, down the hillside to the perimeter wall.

Seven or eight minutes have passed.

His phone goes off, a text message, from her, twenty minutes away, is he okay?

One word answer, 'yes', then one more, 'hunted'.

The hunter becomes the hunted, nothing new there, he'd felt hunted most of his young life, until the past few years at least. Have to buy time for her, time for the prey to turn predator for a while.

He was crossing the last open field now, the worst moment, where were they, his pursuers? An explosion away behind him, must be his pack booby trap, that's one less then, perhaps more. Might as well use the last front-line claymore, another explosion, who knows if it achieves anything? No, it would, it would force them to move more slowly, more cautiously. There remained two more in the previous strip of woodland, and two here, in this last strip, both sets just inside the wire fencing, aiming backwards in his direction. You've got a nasty, cunning mind, you know that, no wonder Hendricks liked you, get them from behind as they pause at the fences. Any intense shooting here, this close to the perimeter, or explosions, would be sure to attract attention: how long would it take the police to arrive?

He settled behind a tree just inside the last strip of woodland, about one hundred and eighty yards below lay the perimeter wall, he would need a clear minute from here. Movement in the woodland opposite, can't tell how many, wait 'til the first ones start to climb the fence. Here he comes, point man, dead man, three rounds fired, one strikes him, crude these things, four hundred yards and it becomes a lottery. Bullets coming cracking across now, single shots, two, three minutes, odd; are they trying to encircle me? No signs of movement either side? Hold them here another fifteen minutes at least.

Time passes, then the sound of vehicle engines, from the far left, yes, there, two pick-ups entering the field through a gate, going straight for his woodland side, aiming to get men behind him. The fire from in front intensifies. Clear that away, both claymores go off, perhaps I should have waited, but the fire ceases… No just one or two left shooting, very slack though. Aim at the first vehicle, automatic, no choice now, a full clip brings it to a halt, one survivor takes cover behind and starts shooting back, the other pick-up crashes the fence while I'm is inserting the final clip. Move, no time, sprint for the wall, pull the wire away, over we go, down the other side, peek over the top. Voices in the trees above, moving swiftly from tree to tree, they can't let him get away.

A car's coming down the road, more of them, he points his weapon, heart sinking, no it's her, a couple of minutes early.

He turns back, sees one of them half way down the slope, head poking round a tree, tough luck, he's down, but they know where I am. He's racing towards the car, crouched low behind the wall, motioning for her to turn the car around. She does, she's twenty yards away… Pop up and look back over the wall, there's one, eighty yards away almost behind the wall, a burst settles him, she's got the door open, starting to pull away. One last burst into the woodland, drop the weapon and in behind her as she accelerates away; trigger the last two mines, why not, can only make them put their heads down for a second or two?

They're around a corner now, accelerating away.

"Thanks Miss. That was a close one. By the way, how did you know to do that, pull away with the door open after turning around?"

She's in shock, face strained and pale, but smiles.

"Old spy films, what else? Are you hurt?"

"No Miss, the thing with the number plates?"

"You noticed? Just masking tape, should be able to stop soon and take it off. Is there any sign of pursuit?"

They were three miles away already, heading deeper along the small lanes and into the hills, away from the gathering sirens converging on the site of the recent battle.

"No Miss, I think they've got their hands full right now."

"What did you find out, anything?"

"A whole lot of gunmen training, well over thirty, perhaps forty, assault rifles, the works. I was lucky to make it out in one piece. Are you going to tell him, I think the police will know more than us shortly?"

"He'll know soon enough. What happened in there?"

"I almost got trodden on, had to shoot my way out, left my pack behind, but there's nothing there to trace me. Well, maybe some DNA, that's all."

"Tell me about it later, on we get back, so I can go and tell him this evening. What do you want to do now, go home?"

"Not yet Miss, not until he can speak for me there. Do you want me to disappear?"

"No, but you'll need to be elsewhere when my cleaner and other people come around on Thursday, just for the day."

"No problem, Miss, and thanks again, I owe you."

How many was it, at least twenty-six, probably over thirty, that's a start at least?

Later, when he told her the number, recounted events, she didn't know whether to hug him or recoil, but he was the one to do the job for her, of that there was no doubt. Yes, providence it must be.

Later that afternoon, at the same time as she was leaving her flat for the trip to the hospital, Andy Bowson was arriving at the estate in the Chilterns. In the convoy of vehicles were the Command chief, Dager and a plethora of other officers. The first police to arrive at the scene had been shot at suffering casualties, three serious, before heavily armed back up had started to arrive, followed later by soldiers and armed helicopters. There were now hundreds of men at the site with more arriving all the time.

A siege of the main house was underway; several armed men were in situ with seemingly no shortage of weaponry or ammunition. The estate grounds were being combed in an effort to contain the situation, prevent escapees. Over thirty dead and dying men had been found, dressed in camouflage gear and suffering from gunshot and blast injuries. There were assault rifles and spent cartridge cases scattered about in profusion and the remains of detonated explosives. It was a war zone alright; the question was: whose?

Andy went across to a couple of ambulances in which body bagged corpses were being placed, unzipped a couple, a massive gunshot wound to one, the other looked more like handgun rounds.

It was the first he lingered over; he turned to Edward beside him.

"Are you thinking what I'm thinking? This looks eerily familiar, he's almost been torn apart, just one shot by the look of it. We've seen something like this before, heard it in fact."

They backed off while the medics re-zipped them, glaring disapprovingly, and closed the doors.

"From a back street in Birmingham to a super-expensive country estate in the Chilterns, what's the connection? Other than a number of dead and dying murderous Islamic lunatics, some with bullet wounds that make it look like they were hit by a cannon?"

"Don't know boss, but I can't say I'm sorry. Whoever's done it has taken on an army and it looks like they got away, again. It's got to be part of the same thing, can't be coincidence."

"I think you're right. Only this time they must've left something behind for us, and one or two of those wounded gunmen may live long enough to tell us what happened."

The politicians are going to go loopy, this place was apparently owned by super-rich Arabs, very well connected diplomatically, a supposed ally, and here they were hosting a major terrorist training base. With friends like these…

His assistant looked at him squarely in the eye.

"I hope they didn't leave anything behind. I hope they just keep going as long as they avoid harming the innocent."

George was challenging him, trying to see if he would turn him in, to provoke a reaction which would show his hand, which way he would jump if it came to it?

"I didn't hear that, let's get on with the job."

I hope I'm not forced to decide.

No point going back to the office, I'll head off to see him. Helena opened the lobby door and entered, followed by Sam, closing it behind him; a large bunch of narcissi was sitting there in the hall, with a card. She didn't really need to read it, but couldn't help herself, 'Thanks for all you've done, from the new John.' That threw her, she could have sworn it was from him; she took them upstairs and let Sam into the flat.

"Will you be alright here? Get yourself cleaned up, something to eat, you must be starving, just don't answer the door or phone as you're not here, right? I'll be back later."

He stuttered his assent as she was already heading back out to catch a cab, carrying that little card. It couldn't be anyone else, what did he mean by the 'new John'? Was it some new game to keep him amused in hospital? How was she going to explain about Sam's adventures, what they had found on the stick, why she had delayed telling him? Would he be furious?

You should have thought of that earlier, the impact on his trust in you… Well, was it worth it?

She was ushered into his room after some confusion, the guards purporting that no one called Henry was there. Fortunately, Elaine had left a message for her to be allowed in.

"John is it today?"

He was smiling now, "Sorry, I'm told I've been reborn, new identity, the lot. Say goodbye to Henry, he died apparently, to no one's great loss."

She chuckled; he was indeed well on the road to recovery.

"I don't know, I think I'll miss Henry, not sure about John yet."

She sat beside him, craning forward as his voice dropped to a murmur, staring into her eyes, holding them steadily.

"I've a confession to make; I was never really Henry either. I just never got around to telling you, but I think I owe it to you."

"I wish I could say I was shocked, but I can't, nothing much about you surprises me these days. Are the other things you told me about yourself true, her for instance?"

He nodded.

"Sorry. It just becomes a habit, you stop thinking about it. Henry was just my service name after a previous episode."

"So, what should I call you now, really, I mean, when we're alone?"

He told her.

"How apt, and I much prefer it."

There, you see, he's opening up to you, bit by bit, don't blow it now. She embraced him.

"I'm sorry, I'm not sure you like that, but I needed it after today."

He was smiling. "Sometimes you're too much, you know. So, what's happened to ruin your day?"

She told him; the data on the stick, the research, the estate, the annotated plans of sites in central London, Sam's reconnaissance, his need to fight his way out, the subsequent news reports.

He lay there, staring at her thoughtfully as if seeing her anew; she really was quite exceptional, he had been so right about that, new dimensions kept being revealed. She was looking nervous now, scared of him, of what he might say.

"Helena," his voice was level, calm, but not cold, "what possessed you… to put yourself in danger like that, without telling me first? Do you know the risk you were both taking, without any back up? I should be furious…"

"I'm sorry, it just got out of control, but we didn't want to let things slip with you being in here and the others encamped at home. Sam'll need you to speak for him, make things right at home. I'm sure he hasn't told me everything that happened, but he's earned it, near thirty of them on his own. Please say you're not angry, I couldn't bear it."

Stop playing the weak woman, don't lose his respect.

But it's true, I couldn't.

"I don't think I can ever be truly angry with you, but sometimes you frighten me with your willingness to take risks you don't comprehend. I lost her; I'm not going to lose you. You must promise me, no more risks like that?"

Her new tears were those of happiness at what he had said, who he had compared her to. In his consternation at her reaction, he didn't press her to promise.

"I'm sorry, I didn't mean…"

She stilled his lips with her fingers, smiling through her tears.

"Hush; that was probably the nicest thing you've ever said to me, I just want to enjoy it for a minute or two, please?"

Anyone surveying the room through the security camera on the wall would have seen two mature adults, a battered male patient and an elegant younger woman gazing at one another, one hand clasped in another, statue still. They wouldn't have detected the unspoken communication wrapping its bonds ever more tightly around them, binding them ever closer together.

She broke away first, much to her own surprise. "Will you help Sam?"

He nodded.

"I want to speak to him first though. I'm worried he's crossed a line, may not be the only one. I know things happen in the heat of the moment, intense stress and fear… He's so young and inexperienced. What you say he did in those woods, it's almost unbelievable, not just the courage, but the detachment, the ice-cold nerve, the concentration. I just want to make sure it's not something else, something that would disqualify him. You mentioned that young girl they found in that house, they've grown close, hardly surprising. I just hope that's the explanation."

He took a breath and adjusted his position in the bed.

"The authorities are all over it now, you certainly stirred up a hornet's nest, hurt them hard, and the diplomats won't be happy, very embarrassing. I'll find out more from my colleagues later. These plans of central London and some stations you say? It's pretty obvious what they were intending. Hopefully what Sam started the authorities can finish, but can you post a copy of the stick anonymously to Chief Inspector Andy Bowson at New Scotland Yard. It's beyond our resources to do anything else at present. Leave no trace, nothing, wear gloves, that sort of thing, please?"

She nodded, silenced by the sweeping tide of relief washing through her.

"Now what have you brought me, something special I hope?"

"What do you mean? Did you want something?"

"I'm sorry, I shouldn't tease you, but I'm so bored here, I need to get out. My rehab's started fine; I won't need a bone graft apparently. I'm as tough as old boots according to the consultant. But I need to be out and about, doing things, keeping you on the rails for a start, that's probably a full-time job in itself."

There's only one way you can do that. Don't think it; it's not on the table. Yet.

"Give me a date, what they say you need, I'll get it set up at home. You're still coming, aren't you?"

"I don't have any choice, do I?" He was almost laughing, "Lord knows what mischief you'll get into without me looking over your shoulder. I'll ask them and let you know; what would I do without you?"

She was soaring now, her spirit rising up and out through the window, into the shining blue, over the river and away, wheeling and dipping, borne upwards by the warm draughts of contentment promised and sighted.

"Says the man in the hospital bed; pot and kettle I think. Anyway, I'd better go, make sure Sam's ok, work out what to do with his tools."

Her farewell kiss was far too close to his mouth, but he couldn't pull away.

Their mobile command centre was off to one side of the long drive up to the main house, out of sight of both house and road. Intermittent staccato bursts of gunfire, mainly from the house could be heard, answered by the single rifle shots of military snipers. Those inside, how many they hadn't a clue, weren't making demands, saying anything at all, just trying to kill, not even trying to shoot their way out. Must be waiting for darkness, he thought, not that it will do them much good.

Ted Armstrong was in charge, although plenty of other big-wigs were in evidence, the local Chief Constable, a Brigadier, a special forces Lieutenant-Colonel, and a plethora of assistants and other officers, dealing with 'helpful' calls from those in London issuing advice, instructions, do's and don'ts, mostly contradictory. The world's press was gathering too, vultures sniffing at the flesh feast, appetites made ravenous by the smell of blood, real and political, being kept back by the cordon which was now trying to seal the entire estate off from the outside world.

Andy Bowson was on the edge of the group by the communications vehicle, eavesdropping on the impassioned debate about what to do, the police largely wanting to contain and negotiate, the military wanting a full-scale assault led by the pair of Apache gunships landed in what he would always think of now as the Valley of Death.

Thirty-one corpses had been recovered, plus three injured, one mortally, the other two in the balance. The Brigadier was arguing for missile strikes from the drone circling high overhead. Their political masters were almost paralysed, reflecting the developing split in the Cabinet, the Home and Defence Secretaries demanding a decisive assault, the Chancellor of the Exchequer and Foreign Secretary demanding a softly-softly approach, the diplomatic and market implications. The estate was owned by a Prince of a key Gulf ally after all.

Not much he could do here until they could gain access to the house; the prisoners were already being interviewed by specialists, their wounds being treated at the same time, a clear breaking of protocol, not surprising given the circumstances. Transcripts of the initial interviews would be available shortly, but the best news was a shredded back pack alongside two corpses at what clearly seemed to have been a hide, just large enough for one prone man. It contained the remains of water, food, some 0.5" and 9 mm ammunition that matched the spent cartridges scattered around the hide, some clothing, stimulant tablets, the hide's cover, not much, but it should be enough. All of this had already been sent to a forensic laboratory for examination, including the spent and live ammunition. It had told him what he wanted to know though; he was almost certain that this was the same sniper, same weapon, no signs of another. Thirty-four casualties on the other side though and only one man?

He caught the eye of the Lieutenant-Colonel.

"Sir, I don't want to jump to any conclusions, but I would stake my mortgage on it being the same gun as that long range shot in Birmingham, the same marksman too, but how's that possible, one man against over forty, accounting for at least thirty-four of them, and seemingly getting clean away?"

The military man looked at him keenly.

"Could be, seems certain that there was only one sniper, used claymore mines to cover his flanks and escape route, silenced 9 mm pistol and 0.5" sniper rifle, highly proficient with both. He made bunnies out of this lot for sure. It's been done in the past, wartime and so on, but not to my knowledge in so a short time and so confined a space. I wonder if he was one of ours, or a Yank or Aussie, possibly Israeli or Russian? There aren't many others good enough."

"I think he's native, the way he, the rest, just disappear. Do you track your veterans when they leave?"

The Colonel bristled.

"What do you mean by that? Of course we do. We'll check through, but may not just be ex 22, could be one of several others, SBS and so on. May not even be one of ours; could just have been trained by someone with the background, less likely, but not impossible. Damn good job from a professional point of view of course."

The Colonel turned away, irritated by his inadvertent self-disclosure: coppers trying to pin the blame on the military as always, pussy footing around with the bad guys and kicking down hard whenever a serviceman put a foot out of line. Just typical, can't even take a decision now with bullets raining down around the English countryside.

Bowson wandered back to join Edward.

"Pretty clear to me, whether the evidence tells us anything useful is another matter of course."

"Chief Inspector Bowson?" A civilian, early forties was by his side, "Can we talk privately please?" They wandered back up the drive a way, out of earshot, Edward's gaze following him.

"Forgive me. Gerald, our director, whom I believe you have met, wanted you to know that Henry passed away yesterday in hospital."

He felt shattered, he hardly knew the guy, and yet it hurt surprisingly hard.

"I'm sorry, terribly sorry, to hear that."

"I understand. Thank you for your concern, but the Director wondered if you wanted to meet his replacement, his successor, so to speak, his name is John, perhaps tomorrow sometime? Ring this number if you wish to arrange something. I'm sure you appreciate the need for confidence."

He handed him a corner of notepaper with a number on it.

"I don't understand, why would his successor want to see me?"

The man was smiling broadly now.

"Henry may be gone, but as others have found, he's not so easy to finish with: he always seems to come back somehow."

"I see, thank you. And what are your organisation's thoughts on this episode?"

"They're classified of course, but, speaking purely personally, I can't see why anyone would be surprised at all. Our friends in Hereford and Poole deny responsibility vehemently of course, and I'm sure they're telling the truth, which one might say was a pity of course, speaking purely metaphorically. Good bye Chief Inspector."

He wandered back to Edward, "You know what you didn't say to me earlier? Well, a lot of other people aren't saying it either."

George Edward just smiled.

The Turk was watching the live satellite news feed, alerted by an angry call from the Gulf. A disaster was unfolding before him. It was the safe house and training site near London; they'd been using it for the past six months, ramping up training, there were over forty operatives at the site.

Fleets of ambulances were taking away the dead and injured under police escort, armed police and soldiers everywhere said the press, with over thirty casualties according to police reports. A full-scale battle was in progress, military helicopters and drones flying overhead, the whole place sealed off. The UK authorities were denying an unprovoked attack of course, saying they only responded to reports of heavy gunfire and explosions at the estate, coming under attack themselves when they arrived. Liars, who else could it be? He would contact their allies, not much hope there, but they might know something.

In the meantime, the whole organisation in the UK was being dismantled, annihilated, piece by piece. Another network this time, most of the one allocated for the streets of central London. His lieutenants were trying to establish which of them were still free: could something be saved from the wreckage? They were now left with just one intact network, plus the remains of this one, but for how long?

The Arabs were furious, not just the loss of their estate, but rather the establishing of a direct link to terrorist activity on the home soil of a notional ally; their sycophants and dependents in the UK media and political circles were going to be hard-pressed to explain that away.

They would try of course, there were far too many snouts too deep in the trough; the banks and other businesses would be lobbying behind the scenes for a calm response. Yes, he could write the script already. But more of the somnolent populace would wake up, joining the other Islamophobes in their cacophonies of blasphemy, intensifying resistance, not just there in the UK, but across Europe, the US, elsewhere.

The pressure was intense. For the first time, he, the others, felt as if they were losing the initiative. Well, they had to wrest it back, accelerate with the resources still at hand, ideally in the next seventy-two hours. Twenty-four to assess what was left, twenty-four to re-plan and reallocate men and equipment, twenty-four to deploy and execute: after all the reconnaissance was complete. The challenge was the number of missions. They had been going with three, looked like they were down to two now, but it could still be enough if done with maximum ferocity. When all this was over, he vowed to himself, he was going to hunt down their 'allies', and make them into their servants on pain of, well, just pain actually.

Later, when his key contact among their allies didn't respond to his agent's call, he upgraded his plans for them to death.

Brother Peran, he seemed to prefer to be called that rather than Father, saying he was still a scholar-monk at heart, was at the door beaming, holding forth an envelope, hand written, made out to 'Sally Bowson, Mistress'; she couldn't get used to the formality of the address. She let him in. Iltud was there in the sitting room, playing with Josey who had grown fond of the older man, calling him Uncle, to his obvious delight. Martha came through from the kitchen followed by Narin, attracted by the sound of his voice. The girl's face lit up when she saw him, she went forward to kiss his hands, he was beaming at her, blessing her, all of them.

"The Byzantines, their embassy, arrived today, the Exarch of the West himself, momentous news indeed. The High Steward has summoned all the Council, you included Iltud, and you too Mistress

Bowson, to confer and greet them, hear their news, share ours, the progress of our work in the world, our successes against the darkness, all in His name of course! And you too, little Narin, they may be able to help you return to your family, your land, do you understand?"

The girl nodded, but didn't smile. She understood, her English continued to improve, certainly her comprehension. The others were all watching her, awaiting the reaction: no sign of joy, no sign of emotion. But what awaited her there anyway, had her family, her village just been wiped away like so many others, expunged from their ancestral homeland?

"I go he want, when Sam come. He go me."

They were astounded; she had never shown so much of her ability to speak to them before, Peran especially. Martha recovered first, "But Narin, don't you want to go home, to your family?"

"Family dead. I see. Them do."

Sally was weeping silently now, all were mute, but Martha.

"But Narin, other family, your people?"

"You no want me, me go?"

Martha was upset now, she should have foreseen it. Iltud stepped in.

"Narin, you can stay here as long as you want. We want you here if it's what you want, do you understand?"

She nodded, tears riming her eyes, shaking slightly, but the fear that had seeped away was back, trying to take hold once more, security gained threatened with renewed loss.

"But Narin, we don't know when Sam will return. It may not be before the Byzantines, our friends who can help you, have left."

"I wait, I work, wait. Then talk. I…"

She went no further, whatever she was going to say being washed away in a tide of deep emotion; she was shaking, sobbing now. No one knew what to do; she looked so small again, almost broken. She had grown in her time with them, her skin refreshed, its lines fading away, the bruises gone, even the scars fading. Girlhood was being replaced rapidly by young womanhood as her body, frozen in stasis by mistreatment and malnutrition, responded to its change in circumstances, as if determined to make up for lost time, but now it was seemingly shrinking again in her misery.

They looked at one another helplessly, and then Sally's young son, uninhibited by adult reticence, went up to her and hugged his arms around her knees, trying to comfort this girl in her distress. It was enough, it broke the ice, released the tension with one person's simple act of spontaneous empathy for another. Martha recovered herself.

"Narin, you're welcome here. Wait for Sam, see if he can take you home, but we will see if our friends can send word to your people, make a road for you to go home if you want. Until then, be one of us, please?"

Later, when Martha and Sally were alone in the kitchen, she poured out her worries for Sam, her fears for the way he was changing, his bond with Narin, the future.

"What if…".

She couldn't bring herself to say the words, but what if Sam chose to return there with her, stayed there? Martha, the normally capable resilient Martha, her love for her adoptive son was her Achilles' Heel, thought Sally.

"Martha, I used to torture myself with imagined fears for the future, it almost cost me everything, and then I found this place. If I've learnt one thing here, it's to travel into the future hopefully and with faith, so long as you are surrounded by people who care for you, like you all do. I think she's frightened that we might take that away from her… He's become a sort of saviour figure, a symbol of a better future for her. I'm not sure she sees him as a flesh-and-blood young man; she might start to if he were here."

"And Sam?"

"He wants to strike out at those who hurt Narin, others like her, protect you all here, others in Logres like that American girl. He'll return when he's ready; he loves you like you were his mother. I don't know how he feels about the girl. He wants to protect her, that's clear, make her safe, happy again. There may be more to it, but I'm not sure he's aware of it if there is. We just have to trust it's all meant to be, that we're gathered together here for a reason, and to get on with it, supporting one another. As for Sam, if there's one man who can look after himself in the outside, it's him, especially if he's angry."

Martha hugged her. "Thanks for coming here, staying, being our friend. Stay here as long as you want, please, and we pray every day that the Council will be able to reunite you with your husband."

Wednesday, second week after Easter

....

Ted Armstrong had been summoned down to London overnight for another COBRA talking shop. The estate grounds were still being combed, but the evidence of a fight was confined to just one part of them and around the house itself. That siege still floundered on. The house was sealed off now, even its residents could see that, and were making no sign of a move, just occasionally firing from a window or two. The army marksmen were claiming at least three hits since its start, but there was no way of confirming that until they could gain entry, and that increasingly seemed to depend on the strength of will of their political masters.

He entered the meeting with low expectations and came out with an even poorer opinion of how decisions were being made, or not made, at the highest levels. The Home Secretary was bickering with the Minister of Defence about how much force to use, and when, while the Foreign Secretary and Chancellor quibbled about the need for discretion: the impact on our allies in the Arabic world, especially the Gulf states, one of which seemed to be hosting a major terror facility a few dozen miles from Downing street itself. The PM wavered one way, then another.

Pathetic.

He looked about the room at the others, the servants: the Directors of GCHQ, SIS, MI5, a few other more obscure agencies, departmental civil servants, his boss the Met Commissioner, the Chief of the General Staff, noting the various expressions of disquiet, even dismay, on their faces as the discussion circled round and round. He even found himself slipping glances at the newspaper headlines scattered on the table, 'Get a Grip PM', 'Invasion', 'With Allies Like These, Who Needs Enemies?' Demands for drastic crackdowns, almost martial law, exacerbated by reports of rising civil disorder in Muslim dominated localities, some native residents firebombed from their homes, churches vandalised, police cars burnt out.

Around and around they went, repeating the shibboleths of modern political and cultural discourse like a ritualistic mantra which would make everything go away: 'community relations', 'de-radicalisation', 'preventing a backlash', 'containing Islamophobia'. What was that story, the emperor's new clothes? They're not interested, wouldn't even understand if I told them, even if supported by the others. They're just playing their games, hoping it isn't going to blow up on their watch, derail their careers. Yes, I'm getting too old, but then looking at some of the other faces; I'm not the only one feeling like that today.

Finally, he's had enough.

"Excuse me ladies and gentlemen, Ministers, PM. The situation in the Chilterns… We need a decision. We just can't string it out without a strategy. We either starve them out, hoping they haven't enough supplies to hold out for months, or we ask our military colleagues to settle it decisively. You should know though that we're already stretched very thinly. A prolonged resource intensive siege is a huge distraction from our other enquiries, which you are aware have uncovered an unprecedentedly large conspiracy against the state and its citizens, hatched and supported by someone we believed to be our ally. We need to roll them up, not get tied down. It's my belief that holding back any longer won't enable us to find any additional evidence in the house to support our enquiries; those inside are almost certainly destroying it as we debate."

The Met Commissioner and the Home Secretary were looking at him in shock, that's not what they thought he would say. Why had he changed his mind?

He was tired, fed up: strike at the snake, kill it.

Hadn't they learnt by now that these people don't change, just keep coming at us? Be done with them; change the law to enable it… I don't want any more of my officers on the receiving end of their malice towards our way of life.

He looked at the others, beseeching support silently. Gerald, the MI5 Director nodded to him, cleared his throat.

"I concur with my colleague: end this now, free us up to go elsewhere. The debate shouldn't be about this, it should be about how to respond to those supporting these maniacs from abroad, how to crush those already here."

The SIS man, the General too, they were nodding, body language pressurising the PM. The Minister of Defence, the Home Secretary too, seeing the way the wind was blowing, were positioning to be on the winning side. The Foreign Secretary beat a tactical retreat, withdrawing from the fight, the Chancellor was overwhelmed, the PM capitulated.

"General, how quickly and when? Have you everything you need?"

"Yes, Sir, just need clear rules of engagement. I don't want my people being taken to court afterwards by some muckraking lawyer. Declare martial law for a mile around the house, a full legally water-tight indemnity for all service people involved, the police as well."

"Ye Gods!" The Chancellor flickered back into life, but slumped again.

The PM assented, turning to the Attorney-General.

"Do whatever needs to be done, right away please."

On the way out, Gerald came up to him with the GCHQ Director and Chief of the General Staff.

"Well done, it'll be harder for her to move you on after that."

He shrugged. "Where did it all go wrong? It just seems to have crept up on us."

The GCHQ man, normally so reserved, smiled bitterly,

"Setting aside Adam and Eve, after the First World War if anywhere. We drew the wrong conclusions, that the values that had made us great had caused a terrible war and so needed to be discarded, their opposites embraced. The fact that the new ones led to an even more terrible war twenty years later no one seemed to notice; neither the fact that it was those older values that had won us the first world war, and then what was left of them, the second." He blushed, "Sorry bit of a hobby horse."

They broke up in the lobby, the General looking grim as he entered his car; it would his boys and girls that did the dirty work, exposing themselves to correct the follies of others.

Four hours later, two drone launched Hellfire missiles entered the upper stories of the house, at the same time shoulder launched anti-tank missiles blew in the front and rear doors and several windows. The Apache gunships provided covering fire with their cannon and rockets as the assault teams rushed for the house sides, entering at ground floor window level. By then the heavy weapon barrage had done its job, setting the building ablaze, bringing down ceilings and floors, shredding the defenders, leaving only a few stunned and wounded survivors incapable of serious resistance against the highly trained troopers storming through the remains of the building, shooting them out of hand.

The General's orders had been clear, no risks to our people, to hell with the rest; he would have deployed heavy artillery if he could have got away with it. Only two severely wounded survivors were dragged out; later sixteen corpses in various states of preservation were recovered. Sifting through the rubble for shreds of intelligence was not his problem, he had written enough letters to grieving families during his career.

Andy Bowson was back in London, going through the reports of arrests, interview records and evidential analysis. Yes, the rifle was almost certainly the same and the pistol had been used in most of the Swindon killings. Why killings, not murders, why that language, a whole family died there?

So, a small group then, working their way methodically through a seemingly huge organisation, sending us the evidence we need, things they can't deal with, as if they are our cutting-edge, our spear point. So, is it some dark arm of the State, playing by its own rules? How to find out? Do I want to? I think most of my colleagues are hoping it is. The scale of military weapons and explosives being recovered from the estate was terrifying, enough to fight a small war, enough people too. What the hell was the Border Agency playing at? Be fair, they're overwhelmed, it's not their fault, at least most of them. It's those above them, like the HR bitch, Dager too, following other agendas, other paths.

I'll give that number a call, arrange to see him, soon as I can.

"Hello, who's calling?"

"I was given this number by one of the Director's lieutenants, to call if I wanted to visit John in hospital. My name's Chief Inspector Andrew Bowson."

A woman's voice, quite ordinary.

"Ah, yes, I was told to expect a call. He's still in St Thomas', would five o'clock be convenient? I'll make arrangements at reception, just say who you are, they'll show you through. I know he'll be pleased to see you," for the first time a hint of emotion in her anonymous voice, "but you may not be able to stay long; he's more knocked about than he pretends."

"Thanks, I'll be there."

"Post for you Chief Inspector."

Lots of eyes turned to watch him receive another small Jiffy bag with a security cleared sticker on the front; he had form for receiving helpful surprises recently. A simple printed white label. Well, if it were what he suspected, it would be thoroughly analysed; not that it would do much good, after all the previous one was a blank. Yep, just another single memory stick, major high street store, little chance there then. Retrace my steps to Systems for analysis, go and talk to my new lady techie friend, she's smiling at me as if expecting more goodies from that poor old copper, boosting her kudos among her colleagues.

"Hello again, got something nice for me?"

The others, her colleagues, were watching, smiling at some perceived innuendo.

"Well there's over two hundred wannabe and actual murderers behind bars partly down to you. You brought me luck, thought you might be able to repeat the trick again?"

"Well then, tea as before, okay, while I get started?"

Twenty minutes later, all clean, some London Street and station plans, annotated in handwriting requiring translation, map grid reference corresponding with the estate in the Chilterns, no lists of names or numbers. Was it a disappointment? Perhaps, but that it came from the same source, was accurate, he didn't doubt for a second. The young girl, woman, was looking at him, eyes full of questions.

He smiled, "You're becoming my lucky charm. Thanks, I owe you."

"You can buy me a drink sometime then."

"Err, okay." Consternation, confusion, no, can't be. "Can you make copies as before? Keep it to yourself as well please?"

"Sure, give me a few minutes… Tell you what; I'll bring them up to you."

Why had she done that? He was nice, polite, not pushy, looked beat up, hardly surprising, most of them were well past fraying at the edges by now, but he was still pleasant to her despite everything. He probably just needed a friend, some company away from this place, his personal tragedy, that's all. At least for now.

Dager was in the Chilterns, overseeing the evidence gathering. The incident was still leading the news, over forty dead, dozens of weapons recovered, the biggest battle on the UK mainland since Culloden. The press were baying for blood, the government's approval ratings crashing through the floor, low level clashes on the streets becoming more widespread, fire-bombings too, all police leave was being cancelled. Dager, the man on the spot; hopefully he'll mishandle it, wreck his prospects...

Why now so bitter about the man Andy, he'd almost seemed decent a few weeks ago? Well, a lot's changed in that time, everyone's comfortable illusions are being shredded by reality, the naked flame of burning truth erupting through the crust of complacent, woolly thinking that they had all assumed to be so solid. In times like these you make choices that show your real persona, all constructed artifice blown away, and his boss had made his choices, that much was clear. As for me, perhaps I don't have the imagination to do anything other than plod on, talk to those I think I can trust, and hope, pray, that she, they, will be found.

His real boss, the Command chief, had just got back. He went straight to see him, was waved in, offered a drink, asked to sit down; how was he, any news of his family? Old school, his own people first, no wonder even the younger ones liked him.

"Chief, I've received another package, a stick like the other, in the post. There's a reference to that estate in the Chilterns, annotated plans of the streets around Leicester Square, also Paddington, Waterloo and Euston stations. It's our mole alright. Ah, there she is."

He waved his Systems lady in, who handed over the copies and originals without a word and departed as soon as she could, just leaving him with a smile. His boss looked at the hard copies, face set, short whitening hair showing up against his darkening skin tones as his circulation responded to the gear changes in his adrenal glands.

"Someone likes you, don't they?"

"Haven't a clue, Sir. It's got to be someone on our side."

"Well, we'll reconvene our little sub-committee straightaway, but keep this quiet for now, understood? If it is, we're not in the loop, and neither are most of the other agencies, so I struggle to believe it. More like some ex-service people have had enough; hardly surprising really."

Two hours later they were all there, the agency chiefs although again the Met Commissioner was missing. A collusive camaraderie was evident, the absence of politicians and their civil servants liberating the atmosphere, rivalries put aside for the moment in the heat of the chase. Gerald Clifford, the MI5 Director, was in the chair again. The discussion was short, to the point, consensual.

"In summary, ladies and gentlemen, do we agree that this latest intelligence is almost certainly genuine and from the same source as before? That these annotated plans are clearly references to major atrocities planned for central London and are linked in some way to those whom we encountered in the Chilterns?"

"That we cannot be confident that the events in the Chilterns have ended the threat to one or more of these intended targets, given our discoveries about the apparent scale of the organisation planning these attacks? And that therefore we must meet the PM and other Ministers to propose a major security increase in central London, particularly its transport hubs, but, given our lack of knowledge of timing, a full lockdown is impracticable and so we need a more sustainable and less heavy-handed approach?"

"To include closing the in-station taxi ranks, securing other service traffic access, closing most of the exits, with security on the rest, increased armed patrols and a discreet twenty-four hour military presence both above these stations and in key government buildings across the capital, yes?"

Nods and murmurs of assent.

"That we four major agency heads head over now, after first seeing the Met Commissioner to cover our friend's back?" Chuckles all round. "Anyone want a lift?"

Andy Bowson headed over to St Thomas'. He wasn't needed for a while and could be spared while the chiefs tried to talk some sense into higher authority. So why so low now after the exhilaration of another breakthrough, another positive in his service book, a step up in his reputation? That young woman from systems, she felt sorry for him, that was it, trying to be nice, cheer him up. She wasn't unattractive in a way… How can you think that?

Perhaps Henry, no John, could help clear his head. There was no one else; she wasn't here, how he missed her, his son, he'd never really thought about it before they went. Dear God, things will be different if, when, she was returned, I promise. We'll make the most of our time together. The chief was too busy, Dager, well, enough, the others looking to him or otherwise too preoccupied. Few real friends, little family that would understand, just someone he hardly knew who changed names like a snake shedding its skin.

He was shown in; it was him alright, sitting in his chair, perspiring from recent effort, sipping some water, he looked up.

"Chief Inspector, this is a pleasant surprise; I was told you were planning to look in. Pull up a chair."

"How are you… John?"

"Something like that. Making progress, the rehab is a pain, and this place a bore. You can only watch some news reporter speculating in a loop for so long. Were you there?"

Straight down to business I see.

"Yes, not at the end though, really a job for the army and forensics, it's all grunt work now, following leads, interviewing witnesses, suspects, that sort of thing. The day job, no glamour, we leave that to your sort."

Just a smile.

"I hear you've got yourself a tame mole, something like that could put a huge boost behind your prospects?"

"You've heard? Lord knows who or why, but thank heavens for it. How many lives must it have saved up in the Chilterns?"

"Quite a piece of work that was. Any leads?"

"Little enough, hopefully some DNA on a hide, ballistics, no more, they think that just one man inflicted over thirty casualties on armed men and then vanished without trace, just as before. I'm starting to wonder if he, they, are more than human. Our military are denying it, as are your lot, everyone really."

"So, what did you really come here for?"

To the point, that hasn't changed with the name anyway.

"Honestly, I don't know. I don't know why, but I think I might be able to trust you; there's no one else. Not my boss; his chief has got too much on his plate, many of the others are looking to me for leadership, certainty; lots of them are having doubts, sympathising with those taking the fight to the jihadis, however they do it."

"Entirely understandable. What do you think about it?"

Inches or yards, which is it to be today?

"Increasingly I don't know what to think, I suppose out of habit or duty. I just trust the chief, uphold the law."

"Commendable."

Inches only today, obviously.

"But quite a few are thinking about packing it in, resigning. They don't believe in it any more, the leadership, the lies; it's got me wondering."

"What do you want me to say, everything's fine and dandy? It's not; you can see that, some of your colleagues too by the sound of it, I certainly can, people in the service as well. That's why we have consciences, free will. It's how we frame them, our choices, which makes us act for good or ill. Chief Inspector, I said before that I think you're a good man; I'm certain now that I was right about that at least. What does that good man inside tell you?"

The strain on the younger man's face was evident, poor sap. Like so many others, trying to do his best, a stoker still feeding the fuel into a sinking liner's engines, focused entirely on doing the duty in front of him, not looking around, and then suddenly he's got no choice and is well-nigh overwhelmed, confused, terrified. Well, I was there too, and then someone, something, helped me, perhaps…

"Focus on the actors, not the reactors, keep people going I suppose?"

"Tell me, have you ever read any scholastic thought, Thomas Aquinas, Aristotle, that sort of thing? Teleology? Ends, causes and consequences from alpha to omega?"

"No, why would I? Sally liked some of that stuff; we used to argue about it when she started getting all religious. Why?"

"Oh. Hardly surprising, I suppose. It helped me to make sense of things. How things are directed towards an end. Our actions are just part of infinitely complex chain reactions, but our choices can determine the ways they flow, potentially devastating like that quantum butterfly. You need to think about your choices, not just repeat those set before you by others."

What is he on about, has his near miss made him all mystical?

"I'm sorry; I don't see how that's relevant?"

'John' was smiling.

"I wish I could make it easy for you, but one thing you learn is that the higher you rise the harder the choices, if you wish to retain your integrity, your humanity. Those around you, the good ones, can help you do that. If they're uncomfortable, conflicted, shouldn't you be too? Don't confuse the current denizens of the establishment with the interests of the state, let alone the country. Ask yourself: who are you there to serve, to protect? Talk to friends you trust, a priest, colleagues, I don't know, but when you're clear come and talk to me."

"Is that it?"

"No, not by a long chalk, but I can't decide for you, even make you see. We're all floundering, out of our depth; we just need to hold on to the things we know are true, proven over centuries, no matter how unfashionable, how sneered at by the powerful. I always try to remember that I do it for my old squaddies, their families and people like them: what would they say if they could see? It may prove to be surprisingly simple when you get there, the truth usually is."

"Thanks, I think. When will they be letting you out?"

"Thanks for asking. A week at most, probably sooner, then rehab and light duties. Let me know when you want to talk again, the same number, I can't be of much use to anyone else right now."

As Bowson was opening the door to let himself out, 'John' added; "Oh, by the way, I rather think I would like your wife from what you've said. When I get out of here, I promise to do all I can, use all my contacts, to help you find her. Don't give up hope, please?"

On the way out he passed a well-groomed lady dressed in blue hurrying the other way, another visitor maybe? She didn't even notice him in her preoccupation; he would have to go home tonight and look up what the hell 'John' had been on about.

"Hello, how's your day been, made lots of money?"

"Someone's feeling better then?"

He was smiling at her; it was like a sunray lamp on her soul, warming, relaxing, cheering.

"The quacks say they may let me out on Monday, if I'm a good boy and have somewhere nice to go. They've given me a list of conditions, exercises, potential physios, that sort of thing. The service has offered me somewhere safe, but you seem quite determined?"

"What do they say about recovery time? And yes, I am determined, and you could get on with things much better at my place."

"I know. About twelve to fourteen weeks for the leg, bit more than ten for the shoulder, depending on how hard I work them, but should be out and about well before then."

"Good, give me a copy and I'll get it all set up, and I'll see the consultant as well. I'll also arrange some weekends away, beside the sea. It'll be good for both of us. Anywhere you like particularly?"

"Surprise me, you always do."

He was in a good mood today.

"Why so cheerful?"

He beckoned her close, ostensibly to embrace him, but really for another whispered conversation.

"Hope for the future, more people awakening, that huge boulder we've been trying to move these past years just rolled a little this week, and thanks for your deliverance from folly, Sam's too, I'm alive, you're here, lots of reasons."

Strike while the iron's hot, he's opening wide to you.

No, no, I promised.

"I've been thinking again I'm afraid."

He chuckled, muffled because his head was against her shoulder, her hair spilling over him.

"If you won't stay at my place permanently, have one of the two flats beneath that I own. I can break the lease of the one below in a couple of months, you can have it."

"I expect I couldn't afford it, how much?"

She told him.

"I'm sorry, that's way out of my league and I won't take your charity; you've done too much for me already."

"It's a recovery gift, that's all, a contribution to the cause, with the bonus that you could keep an eye on me without compromising your principles. There's no knowing what I may get up to next if you don't."

"We'll see. I just don't know why your ex ever let you get away."

I was never really his, you still don't see that do you? She shook herself, this was too distracting.

"What do I do about Sam, what's he going to do all day? He can't, won't, go back until you're better.

"We'll find something for him to do when I'm out of here, observation, gathering intelligence; these allies of theirs, we need to find out more about them. Also speed our recruitment up. You're right about that, as in so many things. Can he stay with you a bit longer?"

"Yes, he can, but we need something longer term for him."

"And how's your cousin?"

"She's fine. She really wants to talk to you about something; I was going to suggest the evening you get discharged."

"Good, intriguing, something to look forward to, beside you."

There's lots I'm looking forward to.

Sally's letter had asked her to attend a meeting the following day at the Civic Offices in St Joseph's. She was to be accompanied by Iltud in preparation for the start of business with the Byzantine Exarch on Friday. The visitors, who were staying in the Ducal fort on Apple Island, were having a day to rest. The letter explained that there would be a formal reception at the Abbey followed by a series of business meetings and other less formal functions over the subsequent five days. It went on to say that she would be required to attend all of them; overnight accommodation in St Joseph's would be provided. She was in two minds whether to refuse, unhappy at having to leave her young son with Martha if she were away overnight, no matter how happy he might be about it.

He was spending more time with Narin now, enjoying having a sort of older sister figure while being an outlet for the girl's pent up reservoir of affection with Sam away. We really are becoming an unconventional extended family, she thought, hurled together by providence. He was talking about his father less and less, although it seemed to come and go in waves; he was just accepting the new familial arrangements as normal. She found herself wondering if it were the modern family that was dysfunctional: cousins, grandparents and so forth scattered around the globe, distant from their close kin, even parents increasingly distanced from one another by force of economic circumstance or preoccupation with individualistic self-gratification. But she couldn't refuse; she was in their debt and without their active support a reunion of their little nuclear family was impossible.

She had duly arrived, along with Iltud and Brother Peran on the first train of the morning. All the monks had been summoned to stay at either the Abbey or monastery in St Joseph's to participate in the various religious and other ceremonies being organised. Neither could answer many of her enquiries about what would be expected of her, saying that her role today would be mainly one of listening and learning more about relations with the Byzantines, before meeting them in preparation for her potential involvement in a mission to the Vatican. They reassured her about their response to a woman's involvement, even in a junior capacity. Apparently, the Byzantines had an ancient tradition of according women great influence in their counsels, right back to Justinian's wife Theodora in the early sixth century, with many having significant influence, even exercising regency powers at times. They would be much more concerned to ensure that she followed protocol as a newcomer, not yet fully deserving of trust.

She and Iltud were ushered through into the Council Chamber while Peran made his way over to the Abbey. She could see almost the entire Council were there, missing only a few of the younger Seigneurs, including Mark, who were required to continue patrolling the barrier. Several monks were present at one end of the table, clearly the clerical contingent who helped run the Pocket's small civil service, with the Town Clerk and Georgy Tredare's sister Thea, who was there, Iltud explained, as a bilingual speaker to help one of the monks record any Greek spoken by the visitors. Iltud smiled at the older Theophano, who was seated just behind and between the Abbot and High Steward, again for her language skills and intimate knowledge of her homeland: she was having to stand in for the injured Georgy. Sally was directed to take a place by the younger Thea to just observe and learn, not speak unless asked.

Mainly out of consideration for her, the discussion was in English. She really was going to have to learn Brythonic if she wanted to spend the rest of her life here fully accepted by all, although apparently the Byzantines were increasingly conducting their foreign dealings in English as the modern world's lingua franca, and would do so on this mission. Brythonic was seen by them as too rustic and Latin as too redolent of their historic disputes with the papacy. It soon became clear to her that foreign policy was decided outside the Council by a loose inner circle of the Duke, Abbot, High Steward, a handful of the more eminent Seigneurs and one or two of the longer serving Stewards; today was about consultation and consensus.

The High Steward led the discussion.

"Our visitors bring us momentous news, such that the Exarch of the West, one of His Imperial Majesty's most trusted officials, Alexios

Palaiologos, has come to confer with us himself, along with the Archimandrite Anastasios from the Holy Mountain. The Council will receive them formally tonight at the Abbey and dine with them there as well. Discussions will begin tomorrow morning and continue for three days to agree common policy on several matters."

"Firstly, they have noted our activities in Logres, the direct interventions we are undertaking there as previously agreed with them. They are pleased and wish to provide more resources and encouragement for us to deepen and expand our activities. They believe that Britain, England and Wales in particular, is the most promising land in Western Europe to strengthen the awakening, lacking a presence in the other lands as they do, bar one possible exception. We have explained to them our recent set-backs and advances, but they wish to invest more resources in us here."

"Second, the exception is in the Latin lands of Western Europe. They increasingly believe that a small enclave, protected by a barrier similar to theirs and ours, may exist on the coast of Hispania somewhere. A refuge granted to the Visigoths when the darkness overran Iberia in the seventh and eight centuries after Our Lord. They have not yet located it and it may take many years as it did for them to find us. The existence of this enclave was suggested by a reference in some memoirs of a Visigoth refugee who sought sanctuary on the Holy Mountain in the eighth century; that is all. But as we know, they are patient."

"Third, their tentative relations with a small and secretive group at the heart of the Vatican continue to progress. They have not revealed themselves fully, nor we at all, but they aim to do so later this year and undertake an embassy with us next spring. As you all know, they have been progressing this for several years now, very cautiously, but believe that the time cannot be long delayed as the hierarchy of the Roman church is more receptive and humble at present; more anxious about the oncoming darkness. Like the Byzantines and ourselves, they have long memories."

"Fourth and finally, after over four decades of searching they have established relations with the Armenian refuge on the southern coast of Asia Minor, in the ancient land of Higher Cilicia, which they had long believed existed. An Armenian envoy, the Archimandrite Krikor, has travelled here with them to open relations with us. It seems that the Armenian refuge was established as the same time as the Byzantine enclave, when the darkness overran Anatolia, but remained small, until the persecutions grew in ferocity, finally culminating in the attempt to exterminate the entire Armenian people at the time of the second cataclysm, when tens of thousands of fleeing refugees were guided there by His Hand."

"Their land has continued to grow ever since, such that there are now nearly half a million souls there, but they have been isolated, their lands outside resettled by the denizens of the darkness. They are fearful and remain distrusting as where we, when first found. But our allies believe that with their numbers, their diaspora in the outside world, the fragment of Armenia that survived because it had become subject to the Third Rome before the genocide, many new great possibilities are being opened to us by His guiding hand. Perhaps contacts with the Syrian and Assyrian churches, the Maronites, the Copts, all of whom continue to suffer at the hands of the darkness, perhaps, as we have learned by the Kurdish girl's arrival here, even the non-Christian victims, the Yazidi, Mandaeans, Zoroastrians… Who can foresee?"

"They wish us to join with them in these policies, to extend our reach around the globe, to find those who truly see, to strengthen our resources and to develop our presence in Logres. To penetrate its institutions, defend its people, extend our position in America, gain recruits and new resources and establish ourselves in the other English-speaking dominions of Australia, New Zealand, Canada."

"They believe that it was His Hand, directing the English speakers, which secured the defeat of the darkness in its other guises during the first three cataclysms, broke what may have been the fourth during what those outside called the Cold War, before it became fully manifest. Now the English-speaking world has become decadent, increasingly faithless and rootless, heedless to losing its homelands to the returning darkness. We must help to rouse them, that is, they say, our role."

"I, like many of you here today, find it ironic that those same pagan Saxons who drove us here, conquered Logres, then became His instrument three, four, times, to defeat the darkness in various guises, may still do so again should Our Lord will it. Our enmity is past and should now be finally forgotten. The question is: should we accede to our allies' pleas, seeing in them His Will for us, to risk ourselves more greatly? Should we reach out further, prepare more people to go into the outside? That I leave to you, but would say that this news, the Armenians, the Papacy, removes my final doubts."

She was astonished, the High Steward had previously struck her as a diffident man, surely intelligent, but not eloquent or passionate, so different to today; looking around, it occurred to her that she was not the only one present to react similarly. There was a pause as people digested his news, the murmur of quiet conversation between those sitting next to one another. The High Steward looked nervous, as if fearing that this was too much for his audience, might they choke on a surfeit of revelations? But the Abbot was smiling gently, confidently. Always watch him Sally told herself, I'm more and more convinced it's him behind the scenes, the invisible directing hand, weaving the pattern so well that no one can see any trace of its maker.

Finally, one of the parish Stewards spoke up.

"High Steward, is this the will of His Grace, the Duke?"

There was a new tension in the air, why? The High Steward hesitated, but the Abbot was there, seamlessly before him.

"Yes, it is. As you know His Grace," how did that English form of addressing a Duke establish itself here she wondered idly, "spent his vigour, his health, fighting the darkness: how could he say differently now?"

Bingo, thought Sally, I'm even more certain it's more him than anyone now, what a clever answer, assuming it's true. The Steward nodded, apparently satisfied, but one of the Seigneurs spoke up. "High Steward, we are few, very few for the outside work, how can we increase our efforts? One of us was injured badly, as was our ally, and one seems to have left us, the first time such a thing has happened? Yet you speak of extending us to other countries, continents, when we are already too few here? What are these extra resources our allies promise?"

The High Steward, his face flushing at this apparent disagreement about something that was clearly close to his heart, almost tumbled the words out, fighting his natural reticence to do so.

"What you say has merit, but lacks faith, in our capacities, of those in the outside who are increasingly waking, our allies old and new, our friend's guidance and most of all that of Our Lord Himself. This cause may well still be in its infancy when we have left this world, but we have travelled so far already, after centuries of torpor, how can we lose our courage now when new allies are being found? Our work in Logres has saved thousands of lives, inflicted defeats on the darkness out of all proportion to our resources. Our ally and Georgy Tredare, will soon be recovered, and I am sure the young man will be found, may perhaps be only criticised for an excess of zeal and devotion."

That's one way of putting it thought Sally.

"Do you doubt His Will?"

The Seigneur was embarrassed; this unexpected eloquence from someone who was once just a glorified parish steward, albeit personally chosen by the Duke himself.

"Forgive me. I do not mean to doubt, I just wish to ensure that we are methodical, patient, calculated, avoiding excess risk."

Sally glanced about the room, it looked like that was it, a consensus had been achieved, the Abbot was smiling, he even winked at her. Yes, you know, don't you?

He came over to her as the session broke up.

"Mistress Bowson, how are you, your son, the Yazidi girl? Are you still content where you are staying? Have you been studying the books I lent you?"

"So many questions at once."

He smiled again in apology.

"Yes, everything's fine, and yes, I am studying as you asked. I still worry about my husband, and about Sam too now, but thank you for asking."

"Good, good. One of my brothers here," he gestured to one of the nearby monks, "will give you your stipend for this month; I hope it is fair recompense for your labours for the commune. He will also spend this afternoon with you explaining the protocols of such events as this embassy. We will keep your duties to a minimum, just those in the daytime so that you can return each evening to your son. You will mainly be attending the open meetings with the envoys, just listening to the discussions, being introduced to them, so you gain experience of their thinking, their attitudes, understand more about their approach to the Vatican. They are not as formal, dignified, as they sometimes strive to seem, but please wear those beautiful robes with which you graced us on the day of Our Lord's Rising, they will be pleased. And, also, please bring the girl Narin on Saturday. I wish her to meet the Byzantines and Armenians, to raise the subject of her safe return to her people with them. If He himself can be troubled with the fate of a small sparrow, how can we not be by that of a young girl?"

"But Father, may I call you that? I'm not sure she wants to go, she may refuse until Sam returns. She has grown very attached to him, Martha fears for it, them both. Narin says all her family are dead, and she will only go if Sam takes her."

"His Will is ineffable and shall prevail. If it be so, it must be, but even so she must see her homeland again for, if she stays here, in time she may grow to regret it. It might eat away at her and whatever happiness, a new life, she has built here. We will consider this. You say Martha worries what is between them now? But she is still a young girl, fearfully abused by men, what can she truly know of such things?"

"Father, I'm sorry, but you may not understand the mind of a girl becoming a young woman. That she is very determined you must know by the fact that she survived at all and she is learning English so she can talk to him. I and Martha believe she knows her mind and the more we oppose it the stronger it will grow. I know she is not of our faith…"

He was smiling again.

"I stand corrected in my ignorance and presumption of wisdom in such matters; thank you for correcting me so gently. As for the faith, if she stays how can she not believe when it is all around her? His Will is evident by our very presence, the existence of our allies. He has spared her for a reason, that is clear, fortified her; it is not for me, for any of us to doubt. Her people may be in error, but they are not the enemies of our faith; they have lived alongside Christians for over a millennia, intermarried on occasion, they are not of the darkness no matter how outlandish some of their beliefs. Do you know they undergo baptism? Perhaps that is enough; it is for Him to judge. If she wishes to return here after going home, I will bid her welcome, support her, as will the Brothers and Sisters. In the meantime, we must find young Samson, make him realise his sins can be forgiven. He should not think himself an exile; if there is any sin it is more on we who sent him, myself, for not seeing the risks we asked him to bear on our behalf."

"Father, you amaze me sometimes."

"Why my child? I listen, I observe, and then I consider, that is all; that takes no special wisdom? This land of ours, of His, sometimes it surprises me still, how new possibilities for joy emerge from two young refugees from different sides of the world thrown together in the most brutal circumstances. After all, even that troubled American girl seems to be finding happiness and peace with that young fisherman who dragged her out of a moorland stream in the middle of the night only a few days ago. It reanimates my old, dry heart sometimes, reminds me why we do what we do."

"Thank you, Father."

As she followed the hovering Brother away, she overheard her own sub-conscious, 'Old dry heart, my eye. I feel entirely better just because of those few words of his. If there's anyone here who will get Andy back for me, it's him, not a shadow of a doubt.'

Out in the bay on his family's small fishing smack Art lay back against the stern, one hand on the tiller, listening to the sound of the low swell lapping against the wooden hull, calm waters restoring his mind from the horrors of recent weeks. It was lovely out here, reminding him of his boyhood on the boats after school, hard lives, but somehow peaceful. Sometimes over recent weeks he had wondered silently why he'd volunteered to step into the darkness and dangers of working in the outside: had it just been a young man's bravado? But now he knew why; those they had brought back, given a new home, that's why Sam was still out there he was sure, still fighting against them, for the others who needed them. Well he would go back to help him when the time was right.

She was watching the huge young man, just easing back there, so at home on the water. Lena had never lived by the sea, London was just a land-locked metropolis to her, and she was still adjusting to the constant motion of the water. He didn't use many words, but then, over the years on her own, she had lost all faith in them so it wasn't much of an absence to be missed. She had come down to live in St Josephs with a younger couple, more at home for her than that old couple's village and nearer to him. He had come around to see her, invited her to dinner with his family who lived in a warren of interconnected cottages on the shore. He had his own small annex almost, but ate with his parents and extended family. They had welcomed her, fitted her in somehow and not asked too many questions. He'd then offered her a trip on the boat around some of the islands the following day, and here she was.

This place was only just starting to sink in; it overturned all her assumptions, if even half what they had told her was true… Her old life was already starting to feel distant, as if belonging to someone else she had once known quite well.

Now she was getting used to the swell, she was relaxing, it was just so easy; he was so at home here. What to make of him? On pure impulse she came and sat on the stern bench beside him, his steady grey eyes were on her, no words, she was getting used to that now. She reached out and touched his curly blondish hair, he smiled, just looking at her, she smiled back, and that was it, if not before.

Later, as they sailed back to the shore, he went red and looked at her, "You'll have to marry me now, you see?"

"I guess. Happy?"

His grin was answer enough. She was home.

She put the phone down from talking to her cousin; the usual questions about his health, state of mind, and yes, she would love to come around on Monday for supper if he were discharged. What was she so keen to tell him? Hesitation, revelation, shock, and then, as the handset touched the receiver, the third beast was howling with fury, foaming at the mouth, its prey identified, the hunt could begin.

"Sam, can you put the kettle on? We need to talk?"

Helena would tell him after the event; this was personal.

Thursday, second week after Easter

Curse them, just one network remaining intact and the shreds of a second now being reorganised. How long before those captured at the training base began spilling out names of those not taken? We've relocated those still free, but even now they might be being followed, traced. Use it or lose it. And those cursed allies, filthy atheists, weren't taking our calls, were clearly cutting us off suddenly and totally. We're almost blind and deaf. Well we can still speak; shout out loud with our deeds.

The news feed was full of it: the continued arrests, the civil disturbances as fights between the natives and our people rumble on, the aftermath of the Chilterns and revelations of the arms found in the ruins of the Swindon and Reading addresses, and now a huge upgrading of security at the main central London transport hubs, stations especially. They knew, they had to: taxi ranks were closed; service accesses tightly guarded, minor entrances sealed off; increased armed police presence, military as well, if rumour were to be believed. The dozen or so left of the network intended for central London would be entirely ineffective in trying to undertake a major attack on Euston as planned; sure, there would be lots of casualties, but nothing like the scale originally intended.

So, use them elsewhere, but where? Somewhere different, perhaps connected to the other major attack planned for the fourth network.

Something that had the elegance of hurting their ex-allies hard at the same time. Yes, the London centre, while they still hit the provincial base. Sixteen to twenty intended martyrs could create mayhem there, their deeds would resound around the world, inspiring fear, maybe even submission.

He had an idea, had considered it before, perhaps it was time to resurrect it, but change would mean delay, maybe until the following week. Yes, Monday. Yes, you could even book a tour, well that would take care of reconnaissance and the insertion of an initial team; they're making it easy for us. The more he considered it, the more he wondered why they hadn't seen it earlier, the beauty of simultaneous and symbiotic northern and southern operations. Yes, divert eight from the north to the south, leaving over fifty for the larger operation in Manchester: it should still be sufficient and twenty or more in London would cause carnage. He picked up the phone.

The day of the first formal discussions with the Byzantines was scheduled to start with a service in Thea's Orthodox chapel in the Basilica at ten, followed by a meeting between a small group of delegates from both sides which would probably continue through to mid-afternoon. It required an early start for Sally; the first train of the day, sitting there feeling foolish and self-conscious in her Byzantine silks covered in her old country coat given the dampening weather. Fortunately, Martha had decided to travel down to St Josephs with her, bringing Narin and her son along as well; time to give the girl a change of scenery she said, lift her mood, show Josey the bay and harbour, introduce him to Thea and her clan. The girl was distant still, but at least trying to speak English to them again. Once Sally caught sight of her looking out of the carriage window, a single tear on her cheek; Martha noticed it too and glanced anxiously across at Sally. No more needed to be said.

"Narin, have you met any Armenians? Some have come here with the Greeks for the first time; they want to meet you on Saturday."

"No, all gone, Turks do, like my people."

That single tear was now being joined by others.

"Many live still, in a land like this near your people. We want them to send a message to your people for you."

She shrugged, as if it were not her concern.

"When he come back?"

Sally and Martha looked at one another, how often were they asked that question each day? Sally spared the older woman the pain of answering once again.

"When his work is finished, then he'll come back, see us all, you as well."

Narin didn't respond, meaning a solemn journey, broken only occasionally by the laughter of Docco playing games with Sally's son. She was glad to head to the Basilica leaving the others to visit some of the little shops in the main street on the way to Thea's café.

If the journey were somewhat sombre, the Orthodox service, conducted by the Byzantine Archimandrite in accordance with the Greek rite, was a thing of solemn beauty. The Pocket's diplomatic team were all there: High Steward, Abbot, Mayor, three older Seigneurs, Parish Stewards, a team of clerical support staff, the two Theophanos and herself.

The darkness of the sparsely windowed chapel was beaten back by the illumination of dozens of candles reflecting on the golden and metallic pigments of the roof. The candelabra, the vibrancy of the eastern silks and cottons, the heady smell of the incense wafting from the Orthodox censers, the unaccompanied chanting of the priests, combining for a bewildering, captivating spectacle light years from her minimalistic Anglican experience. Her heavy-lidded eyes eased, closed as Lethe like lethargy spread through her, relaxing and losing herself.

The extravagance of the atmosphere filtered throughout her body, brushing past conscious mind, stroking and caressing her subconscious, gently pulling her free of her material impulses, enfolding her in a speckling warm mist, sweet scented – was that lillies? – opening her wide, suppling her soul, her being dissipating, that still small voice penetrating the sensory moment, a hint of frankincense now, a salty minerality on her tongue, the sound of a rustling breeze, the radiance of imminent heat, stoned light on her face, then a tingling loosening, building gently to overload, the drowsiness falling away, a glow of inner sunlight seeping through her, pushing back the fatalism, the despair, the fear, burning them out painlessly so new life could begin, seeding and growing, pollinating, fruiting hope, strength, conviction, clarity, courage, smell, touch, tasting so good, sacred rose scented, lavender honeyed sweetness, delighting, satiating, then, as if of the season, shrinking back, withdrawing slowly, teasingly, the image of a thorn tree retreating to its roots, the echoes of falling leaves, a musky myrrh in the air, the shadow of a cross on a dusty hill, a hot breeze from the East, the lightest pressure between her shoulder-blades as of an unseen hand steadying her, a shaft of a risen warm Sun on her face, its presence allowing her physical senses to register once more, to intrude their noise into that preternatural calm, like a diver returning from the deep ocean, depressurising her, forcing her eyelids apart, her breath returning slowly, light bursting in on her, seeing and hearing again, evenly, deeply, finally.

She looked about.

The Abbot's eyes were on her; he was smiling and then turned his head to his front once more. Him again, what does he see in me?

Service over, Sally followed the others, in procession into the cool outside, the contrast with… what was it… her internal experience… was too much, too profound to take in, sharpening her, chilling through her, as they covered the short distance to the Council chamber. A small crowd watched them silently as a dozen Seigneurs in their antique ceremonial armour and uniforms marched either side until they reached the Town Hall.

The functionality of the chamber was even more stark now, its sounds hard from their reverberations on the wooden floor, masonry walls and glazed windows, bringing her finally back down to earth, that ethereal moment now faded completely other than in the well of her memory. Hot drinks were served, but all was still formal, the assembly were gathered around the table, High Steward opposite what must be the Exarch, the Abbot facing the senior Greek cleric, three uniformed Seigneurs in front of three uniformed Byzantines, three Stewards opposite three older men robed as civilians, then what must be the Armenian Archimandrite, a couple of aides, one a monk or priest, then other aides, both secular and clerical, Greek and Brythonic arrayed respectively behind, the older Thea just so, the younger with the junior annotating staff and Sally herself.

Both sides – no. three, she later realised – started with the introductions in their own tongues, Greek, Armenian and English, progress slowed by the need to translate everything; no wonder they needed at least three days for any discussion she thought. The High Steward was leading the speaking on behalf of their side, recapping their news, summarising progress and set-backs. Much was new to Sally; the scale of some of the violence and that prevented was appalling, so at variance with what she had seen and heard here, the natures of those she had met. The attempt on the life of their mystery contact in the outside, his survival, the early signs of awakening in a growing segment of the population of Logres, the further revelation of the scale of what they called 'the darkness', their determination to persevere, push harder, invest more resources in the struggle, her own fortuitous, nay providential arrival, those of others, and now the news of the Armenians, further signs of His Blessing.

Then the Exarch spoke of things: the finding of their Armenian brothers and sisters and the joy of it, the continued growth of their trading networks, now into Australia, Canada and Russia with investments already made. The intention to build a significant organisation in the United States, beginning with the Greek and Armenian communities, setting up businesses and securing supply lines for money, arms, intelligence and recruits. The acceleration of progress, the doubts and debates about whether to establish a presence in other European countries, the starting of a search for the believed Hispanic refuge, the hopes and fears for the Papacy, the desire to invest more effort into their work in Logres, the imperative that he, their bridgehead into the security services, survive. The always unnamed 'he' being their means to find others of like mind, not just in the UK, but elsewhere. Most of all though he spoke of the Armenians: their diaspora, their own country, its intimate relations with Russia, its closeness to the fractured Christian communities of the Near East, the Copts and Syriacs and from them maybe one day, others, the Druze, the Yazidi, Zoroastrians, even Alevis perhaps. Finally, the growing confidence of the Emperor, his decision to further develop their networks on the Greek mainland and in Cyprus, providing succour and hope to the many despairing there, more small steps on the longest journey back.

The Armenian cleric then addressed the assembly: wishing all His Blessings, proclaiming their joy at finding themselves no longer isolated. The initial shock of it, the need to adjust, not shrink away, to trust Him, them, have patience, give us time to still our fears, discern our own path, so much to take in and learn, but yes, they would start to reach out into the Armenian diaspora, initially through the Armenian church, and yes, they would join any embassy to the Vatican. They would need the support of their new allies to upgrade their homeland as was being done here, but it also would take many years as it had here. They were many in number and growing quickly, so was their land, but this meant food was scarce sometimes, new land took years to become fully productive, to be settled, so please be patient.

It was clear that an agenda had been agreed in advance; much was routine, trade matters, market potentials. Was tobacco still the best earner? Yes, unlikely to change, sales were still growing but antiquities were also seeing rising demand, also reproduction icons made with traditional techniques, they were in great demand, increasingly fashionable. The routine business discussions continued, with a break for lunch in the adjacent dining room. The parties didn't mix she noticed; all was formal, diplomatic, three, no four, languages being spoken. She felt very much the spare wheel, had aimed to head for the older Thea, but was intercepted by the Abbot, smiling once more.

"How progresses your understanding, my child?

"Well Father, I'm not sure though that I am of much value here."

"Have patience. These are but the formal steps; the real discussions will begin later, after dinner this evening, preparing the ground for tomorrow, all must be seen to go well. They see you are here, are trusted by us. They are watching you, how you behave, are you impulsive or reliable, indiscreet or confidential? That is why you are invited today and for the days to come, but surely your three days of torpor have been made worthwhile already?"

"Pardon?"

"In the Basilica… Such moments are precious, a gift of grace, unfathomable, so rare. Do you think that I did not notice, have not been so blessed myself? I won't enquire as to details, but your face showed something of that within; truly we are right to trust you, be thankful for your presence among us."

"I… I can't explain, words can't…"

"No, they cannot. Which is why those who live by them solely are lost for all their knowledge; wisdom, sofia, as our Greek friends call it, passes them by. In finding the garnet they overlook the ruby, a truly human failing. So, think on it, try to remember its essence, and trace its path before you. Will the girl Narin join us on Saturday? I wish to raise her future with our friends tonight at dinner."

"I believe so Father, she's here in St Joseph's today with Martha, but she won't leave until Sam returns."

"So you said. Then we must ensure he does. I will write to our ally to see if young Samson has been in contact with him, ask him to persuade him to return, to bring him back himself if he can. I will enclose a personal letter for Samson offering him our understanding, a future here for him, our continued love for him as fellow sinners, and speak also of the girl, her need for him in a strange land. Will that be sufficient do you think? The Council is not in a mood to be vengeful as I said before, we share the blame too, must ask His forgiveness."

"I don't really know him well enough, but I'll ask Martha tonight. I'm sure it will help though."

416

"Then let me know tomorrow when you return. Now back to work, look wise, but tomorrow will be much more interesting, our and their plans for Logres, America, the Vatican."

Later that evening when she relayed his thoughts on Sam to Martha, the older woman broke down, confessing her fears for her adoptive son: the soul tarnishing effect of killing for any cause, the girl's adhesion to him, his desire to provide recompense, to punish evil at almost any cost to himself, the limits of any individual's capacity to carry so much before breaking. What could she say to that? But Iltud was in St Josephs; it fell to her.

"Martha, just as I'm increasingly sure I'm here for a reason, so Sam must be as well even if we don't understand it or like the ways he travels. His arrival here was providential; you must see the good he has done, saving that girl's life, perhaps inspiring her to love again. These things aren't small miracles, they're of huge value. If it should be providence's will that they be together, how can we be unhappy?"

"I know, I'm being foolish, but he is my unlooked-for son… He was lost and was found for us, the thought that he should be lost again…"

"Martha, just as I trust Abbot Winwaloe to find Andy, perhaps you should trust him likewise with Sam. That he should bother himself so much with such things when he has the Byzantines and Armenians here, everything else on his mind, well, I'm not sure I would in his position."

"I know… I know you're right, but what is he doing there, on his own?"

But Sam wasn't on his own. He was with someone else, close enough, but not so close that that someone knew he was being followed, to the station, up the line, out of the station and then a ten-minute walk through the streets to what was clearly his home, which Sam walked past, round the block, and back again, taking secretive photos, pacing the distances, timing various sections, noting the vacant spaces where one could loiter unobserved. Then back to his hostess to report, and a late supper. He had never seen her so animated as when she told him what she had in mind, pleaded for his help, explained why. After that, he didn't hesitate for a moment.

Abbot Winwaloe finished the final blessing in the sleeping Duke's bedchamber and turned for the door. He was accompanied as usual by the Chamberlain, but this time, as a special mark of favour, by the Exarch and the Armenian Archimandrite, both keen to see if the stories held any truth. They looked on in surprise at an apparently active man entering old age, sleeping deeply, both offered blessings in their own native tongues, and then preceded their two companions out, to be conducted to their rooms by the Chamberlain.

The Abbot knew that the guard had been increased for the duration of the embassy: two were patrolling the battlements above, two on the landing and stairs, including one of the younger Seigneurs, and two more were patrolling outside, around the walls of the fort itself; all fully armed.

He sighed, whispering a private prayer that the guards would not be needed, for those in the outside still, for Samson, their ally's recovery, as he made his way back to his cell. To have seen her caught in such a moment in the Basilica was a faith renewing gift, helping surmount his latent doubts about what they were doing. Yes, if anyone bore the moral pollution it was chiefly himself. But she had seen a glimpse, no, not seen, felt. His few remaining doubts about her had been dispelled, she would do. Who knows how far she might go in their… His… service one day? Further than she could envisage he suspected; she was not ambitious, just focused on reuniting what fate had sundered, as she should be.

Yes, the Exarch, Alexios Palaiologos, of the imperial family itself, wasn't what he had expected. In private he was engaging, not formal, so unlike previous envoys, willing to debate openly, speculatively, ask advice. He had wanted to come to see for himself he said, to visit some of their other developing bases of operation, accompany the embassy to the Vatican. He had energy, a man in his early forties perhaps, real vision, charisma, but also the humility of true faith. He had revealed more of his people's hand in a couple of days than all the other envoys of recent years; they had been sending volunteers to live in the Hellenic communities of the USA, Greece and Cyprus for some years now, intermarrying with locals, recruiting more, even bringing some home. Their presence in America was growing steadily, by dollar value it was approaching billions, mainly in legitimate businesses now, over one hundred and fifty souls there, some even in the US military and a couple in junior positions in their intelligence services.

It was their intention to do the same in Australia, Canada, South Africa, maybe others, but he had explained that the Greek émigré communities could only carry them so far. The Armenians in time could help take them further, maybe in France too where so many had settled after the genocide, but that would be a decade or more, and the darkness was spreading too quickly. He was urging them to accelerate their recruitment efforts in Logres, to send volunteers to America, the old dominions, where so many were awaking to the threat. The Anglophone world was pivotal, why were they so slow in spreading their presence in Logres? They had taken the challenge, explained their small numbers, their ally's caution; they could not do everything they wanted, but they would reflect.

He was in his cell now, making ready to sleep. Big pictures, vision, were all very well, vital in such matters indeed, but must be balanced against the value of individual souls, their lives. He would have to confer with the others in the morning before the next session, weighing up the greater good. He sighed again; how far he was travelling from those early days as a novice. Have mercy on me.

Friday, second week after Easter

....

She was starting to feel like a commuter again, on the first train down to St Josephs, this time alone; her mind wandering back to the events of the day before, ludicrously over-dressed once more.

At least the weather was dry today.

How was Andy? Since the others had returned she had heard nothing of the latest events in the outside world; the last news had been appalling, he must be in it up to his neck, probably in real danger. Today was the heavy lifting day she had been told, most of the important business would be covered, with Saturday for tidying up loose ends, Sunday for ceremonial and goodbyes, and then departures on Monday.

And so she sat there, mute, listening as the subjects were discussed in turn. She was stunned by the discussion about America, the developing presence there, the already successful procuring of arms, more shipments on the way along with more trade goods, the volunteers needed from this place to serve there. No, it can't be; the Exarch called it Lyonnesse? It's the Pocket, or what was it Iltud said was the archaic name? Lethostow? Must have misheard. Lyonnesse was the mythical land that sank beneath the waves in the Dark Ages, between Cornwall and the Isles of Scilly. And then on… Australia, Canada and so forth.

The High Steward was answering, face flushed, they would consider preparing a small team for America, would ask for volunteers; would their friends be able to get things set up for them? Their resources were small, increasingly committed to the fight in Logres. They were urging him to accelerate recruitment, train up more teams for the outside, but they needed to buy more bases, a farm near London, a base near the centre, one in the north as well, perhaps Wales too, such things were very expensive. No matter, the Exarch replied, funds would be made available to buy one such each year; the other details should be of no concern: they now had people in the US immigration service.

They broke for lunch and she finally cornered the Abbot.

"Father, I thought I heard the Exarch call this place Lyonnesse, that can't be, surely?"

He smiled at her in that way of his; she recognised it well now.

"I'm surprised you have not asked before with your fondness for questions. That is the Norman French name for our original native name of Lethostow; nowadays people just call it the Pocket, reflecting His favour to us. The English adopted the French name, which was a faint memory of an old land suddenly lost long ago. Neighbours telling stories that it must have sunk under the sea in a single night, presuming it was to the west of Cornwall. That is all, no great mystery."

"But the old legends Father, Tristan and Iseult, are they true as well?"

"Some, in part; the lives of Tristan and Iseult are well attested, they lived before Lethostow was taken away, one day I can show you their grave if you wish, it's by the Basilica. But these things are not for today; this afternoon is about the embassy to the Vatican. They may ask you some questions, be prepared."

But they didn't, it was almost an anti-climax. The discussion about the Vatican was focused on their understanding of the inner workings of the Papacy, those who would prove receptive and the ones they needed to win over, given their influence over policy, how and when to make the initial approach, later this year and, following that, when the embassy should happen. April, it was agreed, following the Byzantine embassy here after Easter. How much to disclose? Not too much until we can trust them, this is just an introduction, nothing more.

On the way out, one of the Brothers intercepted her.

"Mistress Bowson?" He was thin, grey haired, bespectacled, scholarly looking, "Abbot Winwaloe wants you to know that the Exarch and Archimandrite wish to meet you tomorrow morning. Please don't be alarmed. The Abbot will be alongside you, as will the High Steward; they just want to understand you better, your suitability for the mission to the Vatican. You are aware that it is not as open to women as our society is, or that of the Greeks?"

She nodded, said her goodbyes and then raced away: she wanted to catch Thea so the older woman wouldn't think her rude. She overtook her on the stairs, embraced her to the delight of the old lady and her daughter.

"Theophano, forgive me. How is Georgy?"

Her face clouded, a stab of bitterness, anger, thrusting out and withdrawing in an instant.

"He will make a full recovery, thanks to the doctors, his comrades, Our Lord; sufficient to return and strike down our enemies once more. He is walking again and will return home in a week they say. Thank you for asking. You like all this?" She made a dismissive gesture back up the stairs, "All this talk? When they should be fighting back?"

The younger Thea rolled her eyes at Sally; this was obviously a regular complaint.

"Well, if it helps the cause. I think I am just here to learn, there's so much I don't know."

"Will you come with us to visit Georgy?"

"Not now Thea. I must go for my train; thank you once again for these beautiful robes."

Thea laughed.

"Be careful, one of those young Byzantine men may try to steal you away to his home, make you his Greek bride."

Sir Kenneth McCloud, Permanent Secretary to the Home Secretary, hoped that he had finished for the week. He made his way out of the station into the streets, which in eleven brisk minutes of walking would take him to his front door. He was late, it was dark and, as it was Friday night, there were people about, headed out for the evening. His mind was full, not just with his day job; she was a demanding creature, slippery with ambition, but also their ex-allies and their unknown assailants, destabilising understood dynamics, making events unpredictable, hard to plot ahead.

The police and security services seemed to be making major strides, due to an unidentified internal source they said, breaking up a huge organisation piece by piece. He had never suspected the scale of their allies' resources, cutting their ties was well overdue. His boss was almost orgasmic; it served her purposes, the media were ecstatic, working as her outriders for ever more outrageous security measures, expanding her following, whetting her appetite for a move on a PM she so clearly detested. Yes, serving her well could get him the top job, Cabinet Secretary, head of the Civil Service. That would make him undisputed leader of their loose network, so he was driving his underlings' hard, preparing policy measures, option papers, making himself her indispensable right-hand man.

No COBRA meetings were scheduled for the weekend, not even her little sub-committee: the security forces seem to think they were getting things under control, even the street disorders seemed to have stabilised to a level at which the press would soon start to lose interest. Nevertheless, he was uncomfortable despite everything; this unknown force remained unfathomable, had made almost no errors. Perhaps the recovered fragments of DNA from the Chilterns, analysis promised for early next week, might give them a name; nothing else seemed to be yielding anything of use. He sometimes suspected some of the security personnel felt something akin to respect for them, whoever they were, and his latest disciple, Sheena Ellison, was reporting that some of the police were showing signs of covert sympathy. Furthermore, the service chiefs seemed too cohesive somehow, too prepared when they came to their masters with recommendations, their rivalries less apparent. Yes, he increasingly suspected they were behind this new force or at least knew more than they were letting on.

He was striding along the most deserted part of his way home, a small side street, almost an alley really, intermittently lit, large pools of darkness jostling with flourishes of amber light. An attractive woman was hurrying towards him as if headed out for the night, well but casually dressed, a patent black leather bag clutched under her left shoulder as if fearing an attempt to snatch it at any moment. He was passing a parked car, blackened windows as he neared her, she stumbled, knocked into him, apologised.

"Are you alright?"

Before he could react he found himself staring into the muzzle of a handgun, some form of silencer attached, as a door of the car beside him opened and a dark clad masked young man pulled him inside, sitting beside him, covering him with another silenced handgun. It had all happened in three or four seconds, he hadn't even had time to register what was occurring before the car was pulling away, driven by that same woman.

The man beside him in the back seat stared silently at him, masked and beweaponed, he instilled terror with his unwavering concentration. The man handed him a large plastic tie and gestured to him to attach it around his ankles.

He bridled. "Who are you? You've no right… Do you know who I am?"

The woman's eyes strayed to him in the rear-view mirror.

"We know exactly who, what, you are. Now comply please. We won't ask again."

It was an educated feminine voice, evenly toned, calm, no signs of stress unlike his own wavering tones. The man's handgun was at his chest now, he could see what must be the safety sliding forward to the off position, it was no more than nine niches from his eyes.

"Ok."

The gun retreated as he moved to bind his ankles before removing his watch in response to another gesture, next a black cloth was handed to him, another motion to place it over his head, fear building now: he complied. Was it them, that mysterious new force, the dark arm of the shadowy state? Then he felt his wrists bound forcibly, tightly, he felt his phone taken from his pocket, heard it be switched off and opened, no doubt for the SIM to be withdrawn, then a sharp command from the female. "Silence, now!"

He was pushed low down on to the seat, his knees sliding into the foot-well. There he remained for what seemed hours, the feeling in his legs ebbing away as the circulation faltered, straining for any sounds that might convey something useful to him, but there were none. Only the road noise, the sound of the indicators, braking, accelerating, and finally nothing, the engine ceasing along with motion, a car door opening, a large door closing, his ankle bindings being cut roughly, a stinging sensation in one leg as the knife blade overshot, being dragged out, up-righted, the hood removed. He was inside an unlit garage, the light from an adjacent room's open door allowing him some vision.

The metal feeling of the gun was back, pressing against the rear of his neck, forcing him to walk forward to the open door and into the light. The room was small, blinds pulled down, a utility room. He was pushed through another open door into a small cottage kitchen, again blinds pulled. On then into another room, what looked like an old beamed dining hall, all curtains drawn, four other doors leading off, one opened onto a low staircase. He was pushed up it, onto a low landing without windows and through another door into a small bedroom. Again, the curtains were drawn closed, the low sloping ceiling told him this was an old hall cottage somewhere in the country. The woman was back, masked now; he was thrust onto the bed, hooded once more, shoes removed, ankles and knees bound, secured to the bed's headboard on a short chain, his wrists unbound, jacket and tie removed, wrists rebound, elbows too, pushed flat.

"I need the bathroom."

The next few minutes were some of the most humiliating of his life, dragged out, no concessions made to his bindings, trousers cut away, then dragged back to the bedroom. Her voice returned, almost honeyed with tender menace, the sense of burning emotion barely restrained, truly the female could be deadlier than the male he thought, what does she want?

"Now Sir Kenneth, tell us what we want to know, no evasions, no hesitations, no resistance. You will hear no threats, get no second chances; it will just be the end, a painful one, if you don't comply."

That horrible metallic pressure was back, pressing on his heart, almost as if slavering for the life blood circulating there, a slight tremble conveying its thirst. "If this is a case of mistaken identity, it can be resolved. If you are from some part of the state, you must know my position; I'm on your side."

A risk to say that, but he was feeling the panic spreading through his nervous system now, the adrenalin surging in response to the stress hormones being released into his body. They must be something shadowy, she was English, the man seemed it too, definitely not their ex-allies, some branch of the state which was slipping the leash then; while they might be ruthless in dealing with the Turk's lot, they must be more circumspect with someone like me.

Her voice was clear, precise.

"Yes, an arm of the state," she didn't say which one, but he was past noticing that now, "dealing with the mess people such as you have created. We want names, contact details, those in your little network." She started to read out a list of names, other members of their senior circle, their network. "Others of the same persuasion, start now; we know others, will know if you are lying or withholding anything."

The feelings of energy and strength that the adrenalin had been fostering turned to bile in an instant, like an addict coming off a high, replacing them with shaky exhaustion. They knew then, had quoted over a dozen of their names, they must have turned someone very senior: perhaps one of his rivals had betrayed them in a fit of pique.

"I don't know what you're talking about, I recognise some of those names, they're public figure, that's all."

A gag was stuffed under the hood into his mouth, then the most appalling blow on a knee, excruciating pain, he tried to scream, but the gag sank deeper into his mouth on the inhale, threatening to suffocate him.

"I'm not sure that blow broke the knee cap," her loathsome voice was back, "we will try harder with the next, perhaps a sledgehammer. Let's try again."

The gag was removed, he moaned, the pain while still fierce was dulling now, digging in for the long haul.

"Alright, alright, I'll talk."

The first ones were easy, confirming those quoted to him, then a few more, rivals and their supporters; maybe some good could come out of this if he survived. That thought caused him to falter, "What will you do with me if I tell?"

"Well your family will survive, we haven't decided about you. You will certainly have to resign, confess all to the authorities; we'll decide after."

"What do you mean, my family?"

"Your wife, grown up children, their families, how far do you want us to go?"

If what had gone before was horrific this was worse, the flat way this attractive, elegant and educated woman uttered the words that completed his disintegration. Insults, threats, promises, he knew he was wasting his breath; there was something diabolical about her, something hidden beneath. Not just a professional doing a job, nor even a fanatic on a mission, but something else. The names, their details, all spilled out; she told him to slow down, she didn't want to miss anything.

Sam looked at the woman he called Miss Helena. She had been a revelation, focused, clear, decisive, icy nerved, had even insisted on taking the lump hammer. There was something slightly terrifying about her, such intensity, even Georgy displayed nothing like it. He looked back at the man; the kneecap was black and purple, distending and swelling, must be at least a partial fracture. He was broken now, had never experienced anything like this up close, was clearly just used to telling other people to do his dirty work, hiding in the shadows, never having to see it with his own eyes, hear the sounds, carrying its echoes with him for months, years, afterwards. Well, the biter was bit, almost certainly fatally if her mood was anything to go by.

The prisoner stopped. She looked at the list, forty-two names, almost a dozen of some public recognition, but she had expected more. She picked up the hammer, gagged him, he tried to scream again as the blow fell, was cut off by the gag. Well, he wouldn't be walking out of here Sam thought.

"The rest, now."

She pressed the weight of the hammer against one of the damaged knees, he gasped as the gag was withdrawn.

"Okay, okay."

Nine, twelve, seventeen names, squeezing out slowly like toothpaste from a tube, his most loyal supporters: it was the end of his power base; even he, in his shattered state, could recognise that. These fiends and others like them would see to it, of that he had no doubt. More chains were attached to him, securing both legs to the bed, and the gag bound into his mouth so he had to fight for every breath, exhausting him still further. He heard them leave the room, the distant murmur of voices, one set of footsteps descend the stairs, returning quite some time later, but exactly how much he had no idea.

The hood was removed along with the chains and ankle bindings, the room light had been turned off; the woman, still masked, was pointing a gun at him while the masked man pulled him down to the floor and into a sitting position. From there they dragged him out of the room, down the stairs, back through the ground floor and into the garage, in which a single low power bulb now shone. He was struggling for breath against the gag, but noticed that a corner of the garage had been covered in plastic sheeting supported by a rickety frame, forming a sort of fully lined cube. What now? A taped confession, the sheeting designed to hide his surroundings? He was dragged in and the sheeting dropped behind him, just cracks allowing the light to filter into the semi-dark space. He was forced to sit in the corner of the plastic covered walls and left alone. He heard another muttered conversation: what were they discussing out there? His heart rate was racing, restrained only by his lungs' inability to supply enough oxygen because of the gag; he felt light headed, on the edge of blacking out, poised between terror and the passivity of despair.

Light surged in as the plastic sheeting was pulled back a little, just a couple of inches. Her voice again, damn her, it was as if she were filing his nerve endings.

"Kenneth McCloud, you ordered a murderous attack on five people, servants of this country. Two died and two were seriously injured as a result, one of them someone more precious to me than anything. He would have died if it were not for the bravery of a neighbour."

Her voice was calm, low, petrifyingly so, but emotion was there, pressing like hot magma up against the stone cap of the volcano, her hand holding the handgun was trembling with the tension. So this's how it ends, into the blackness of the void of nothing, no God to save him, just a humiliating termination, for he knew with iron certainty that was what she intended. He couldn't speak, couldn't plead, restrained by the gag, couldn't move. She wasn't gloating, he could sense that, was just watching him, steeling herself.

"You are a traitor, a murderer, a coward, you tried to kill someone so much greater than yourself; someone so selfless, who has given me, others, so much but asked nothing in return. Public trial and conviction wouldn't be justice enough; your friends would mitigate it, even stymie it entirely, and so it's down to me and this young man. But I want you to know one last thing before I send you to the Hell I fervently hope exists for you: that the person who betrayed you is my cousin, Sheena Ellison, and with your confession we will now take apart your little conspiracy traitor by traitor. Why did she do it you are probably thinking? Because she still believes in truth, virtue, freedom, all things you seek to destroy. Give my regards to Lucifer."

The first round sprouted red in his chest, as did the second, but neither was vital: she was a novice. He slumped to the side; her tension released in part, the next two penetrated the side of his head, ending it instantly, the blood pooling on the plastic sheet floor, little drops running down the internal sides of the cube. She stepped back, turned and handed Sam the weapon, and leant against the car.

"Oh, Sam, I never imagined such a thing until she told me; how do you stand it?"

"It's for them, Miss, those who need us to protect them from the darkness."

"Is it that simple?"

He simply nodded; it was that way for him since he had carried Narin away from that place, over the moorland hills and saw the change in her eyes, who needed more?

"Leave the rest to me Miss. I'll clean up, sort him out. Why not make a hot drink, sweet tea, get something to eat, light the fire, think about what we do next?"

She left him to it; she didn't want to see it for herself. The plastic sheets, timbers and clothes would be burnt tomorrow; the ashes dumped elsewhere, he would take care of the body, he said and then deep clean everything. She would never feel the same about this place again, hardly came here anyway after her divorce, their little country retreat. She would put it on the market next week, priced for a quick sale, the car too. Sam would remove the false plates tonight and put back the real ones. He just knew what to do, how to do it, such a capable young man; she was starting to understand the events in the Chilterns, how he had walked out of the maelstrom without a scratch.

The beast, the third beast, was exultant, sated for the moment, retreating back to its lair to digest, to rest. The others raising their heads, looking at her accusingly: how would he react, would he be angry, distance himself from her? He can't do it all alone, someone has to watch his back, hold him when his strength fails, who else is there? The third beast opened an eye, there is no need to justify, they tried to take him from me after so many years of fruitless search; no one does that and not pay the price.

Helena had come to see him at lunchtime, briefly, saying she was busy tonight, so much to catch up on, would probably not be in tomorrow either. Sure, he was still receiving a trickle of visitors, mainly colleagues, Elaine most days, but her absence left a huge void, far larger than he had expected. She had been distracted he could see, trying not to show it for his sake, not wanting to talk about whatever it was, had just held him even closer than normal, asked how he was getting on, explaining her cousin would be there on Monday evening; was he still expecting to be discharged then? A physiotherapist would be in every day, a nurse had been retained to help in the daytime, Sam would move out early on Tuesday morning, disappear until needed or a solution was found for him.

It was all in hand, nothing to worry him, leave it to her; she was smiling at him, but he could see it was forced, she was suppressing something. They would have to talk when they were alone at her place, settle things, not leave them to drift on, creating more complications.

But what do I mean by that?

I don't know, but she worries me: her desire to be close, shelter me, expose herself to things so alien to her on my behalf. Even her farewell kiss had been different, timid almost, her smile strained; as she closed the door behind her he had realised that she had taken part of him with her.

Then she called, very late, past eleven. She sounded tired, even more strained, apologising, asking how he was, telling him she missed him, apologising again. He asked her what was wrong.

Nothing she replied, just tired, too much on, everything would be alright. Goodnight.

Yes, she was not her usual self, most unlike her. They needed to talk.

She put the phone down and tried to get some sleep. Sam had reassured her that the body was dealt with, just needed them to take it to a place he knew, one of their bases here, where it could be disposed of, about an hour's drive through the Cotswolds. She hadn't dared ask what he had had to do. The guys there were friends, they would try to persuade him to stay with them of course, go back home, but almost certainly wouldn't compel him, especially if she were there. Burn everything else first thing in the morning, including some of the carpets, his clothes and the bed linen, and drive over later, then back here for deep cleaning of the house and car. He was just so matter of fact about everything, but it wasn't lack of intelligence she was sure, there was a streetwise wit there, a cunning imagination; she wondered what Sam might have been with a formal education.

She was feeling shaky still, drained by her switchback roller coaster ride of emotion; she just lay in the dark attempting to sleep, trying to move her mind on from recent events. She thought about him, how to approach him, the risks of having him live with her, his exposure to the mundane practicalities of her daily life, his potential disillusionment, his recovery. Her mind started wandering, free-wheeling away from her direction, images of tracing his scars, his wounds, with her finger tips, bringing him so close to her, beside her…

Don't torture yourself.

Perhaps just this once, it's better than the other images, those lurking just on the edge of visual imagination.

Don't look.

A tiny red dot growing into view, obscuring his fading image in her mind, blotting it out, a giant reddish orange hand, disembodied, fist clenched, just the index finger pointed straight at her accusingly, the tip of that finger expanding into the living picture of a bound and huddled man, pleading with her silently, stricken mute eyes communicating his terror, the flexing of her index finger, the recoil travelling up her wrist, once, twice, three times, four and finally the red spreading circles on his chest and head, something leaving him, reduced to an inanimate collection of dusty materials, blank eyes boring into her until she could stand it no longer and turned away, out-stared by a corpse. The end of that index finger extending, lengthening until it almost reached the bridge of her nose. She couldn't retreat, was held frozen, helpless, like that man whose blood was coagulating around the shiny black plastic tomb. She was shaking, trembling under the effort to break its hold, get away, she was in the shadow of that hand now, swollen to monstrous proportions, beckoning her, and then he was there in between, breaking the spell, freeing her to move, but he was carrying another burden now, buckling under the strain, crimson with effort. She woke, bathed in cold sweat, tears coursing down her cheeks. As she sat up, almost retching, she pondered: just what have I done?

Saturday, second week after Easter

···

There, it was done, at least as far as he could manage; the execution was down to others now, a triumph of flexibility, reorganisation and improvisation. The reconnaissance completed, Monday it would be, late afternoon, when the number of those working at the two sites should be at its peak but when people were tiring at the end of the day, less alert hopefully. Twenty-four volunteers for London, fifty for Manchester, all that were left unless he waited at least another month to bring in more from overseas, but that was too risky. Weapons and explosives aplenty, over half those directly involved had previous experience, the outline plans devised, timings scheduled, but not too tightly: be prepared for the unexpected. He reached for the phone, time to inform those who thought themselves his masters what the plan was.

The four of them travelled down together, Sally, her son, Martha and Narin, the girl being almost certainly needed today; at least someone else on the train was as ridiculously over-dressed as she was. She found herself wondering if they had a decent dry-cleaner here for these gorgeous silks: of course not, she would have to ask Martha. She had tried to explain to Narin last night that the envoys might want to see her, learn how they could help. The girl had just nodded; looking resigned and then made them promise she wouldn't have to leave if she refused. That promise had seemed to relax her, she was much more voluble afterwards, trying to speak in more expansive English, showing more interest in what was going on, and then the questions about Sam, how old was he, did he have a girlfriend, was he a soldier?

Martha just shrugged, answering truthfully. He was twenty-three, no he didn't, he was in a way, she had never really thought about it like that before now. Why was he away when the others had come back? They didn't know, it was a secret, his job. She seemed satisfied with that. Martha anything but, Sally could see.

It was clear that today's business was being conducted in a very different manner, with specific issues being discussed, agreements secured, and plans formulated in small groups, just like Parliament's committee stages back in Logres she thought, before coming up short: she was no longer thinking of it instinctively as home, had her loyalties shifted that far already? She felt like a spare cog even more than before, just sitting there by the group discussing the embassy to the Vatican, unable to contribute. After a couple of hours, the Abbot came over and asked her to follow him out and up to another room on the floor above.

"Is the girl Narin here?"

"Yes Father, as you asked. She wouldn't come until we had promised that she wouldn't be forced to leave. Is that alright?"

"Of course, no one is forced to leave. Now, my daughter, the Exarch wishes to meet with you for a few minutes with his translator, just to ask some questions, nothing you have not already been asked a hundred times since you joined us. And yes, I haven't forgotten about your husband, that rash promise you extracted from us."

He was smiling though.

In the room were the Exarch, a Greek translator, a couple of aides, the High Steward, the younger Thea, much more diplomatic than her mother Sally suspected, and one of the Abbot's monks. She curtsied self-consciously, the Exarch laughed, asked her through the translator what she was doing. She blushed crimson with embarrassment, feeling a fool, explained it was an old mark of respect in her country. He smiled, thanking her, again through the translator. Then the questions, as the Abbot had said, nothing she was not now well practised at answering, then, out-of-the-blue: how did she feel about the Roman church, its pretensions, its schisms with other true Christians? He understood she was an Anglican?

How to answer that? It was like trying to navigate an unmarked minefield: we should focus on the future, not the past, what unites us, not the faults of our ancestors, overlook matters adiaphora, thanks Brother Peran for that, the Exarch's eyes widened in approval, remember what the faith is for, try to forgive, unite whenever possible.

He looked at the Abbot as if asking whether she had been coached; the old man shook his head, beaming. The Exarch asked how she felt about leaving her young son for weeks, months, to end up serving as a minor aide in a world run exclusively by men who might not respect her.

His questions were the result of a sharp mind she realised, here was danger: if they refused to take her the Council's promise about Andy would be void, she would be trapped here alone, forever.

She would do as she were asked, directed, by the Council in the interests of the greater good, a few slights were of little importance in the scale of things.

The High Steward smiled at that, the worry sloughing off him, the Exarch nodded, said that was all, she would do; they, He, had chosen well, and would she bring those beautiful robes with her to Rome? Had she others? She said she would, but that was all she possessed, a remarkable gift from Thea's mother. No matter he said, more would be provided, she must be clothed to reflect the respect she is due as one of us, those who will forge a new alliance, repair old rifts. Moisture was in his eyes she could see, he really believed it, he wanted to mend history, heal ancient wounds.

The shock of what she was being asked to work on finally broke through, flooring her: no, she wouldn't let them down. Later, she reflected, if there was one moment in which they had finally won her allegiance that was it; if they could get Andy here, there would be no pining to go back.

What about my parents, other family, can we get them here too? Just focus on the art of the possible, be practical.

That seemed to be it, the tension gone.

"Father, before I go… Narin? Can they help?"

"We had not forgotten child; she has been summoned."

Five minutes later in came the Armenian Archimandrite and an aide with another Greek translator; everything would have to be relayed from English to Greek to Armenian and back again. Narin entered then, looking about her fearfully, eyes alighting on Sally and the Abbot, she sat by them, shimmering in her Byzantine robes, giving off a presence out of all proportion to her slender frame. Sally looked at her objectively for once; she would be a lovely young woman soon, that's why Martha's so afraid. It was her courage though that Sally found most impressive, such strength of will to survive all that had been inflicted on her, to still want to live, to love, and not to surrender.

She puts me in the shade.

The Exarch smiled at the girl reassuringly; Sally could see he was a kind man for all his status and dignity. They had been told of her, her sad history, what did she want of them? How could they help her?

Narin looked at him gravely, listening to the translation only slightly overawed, but before she could answer the Armenian aide spoke in another language, somewhat falteringly perhaps, but surprising them all, shocking Narin most of all. She replied in what must be her native tongue, her features conveying astonishment. There was a rapid conversation, two, three, minutes, no more, her face melting into smiles at what must be her own tongue, here, so far from home, so unexpected. The Armenian translated for the others and then via another interpreter: she was indeed a Kurdish Yazidi, family murdered when her village was overrun, she and her elder sister taken to serve their enslavers, separated, then she was brought to this country by one of them, as a servant, concubine, then freed by people from here, brought here, given sanctuary, friendship, love.

But how?

The translator smiled, his grandparents were Kurds, another native sect, who fled the genocide of 1915 with Armenian friends, came to the refuge, eventually converted, intermarried, but some like him learned their ancestors' tongue.

What did she want?

He became hesitant, directing more questions at the girl who was now fully engaged, almost passionate in her response, gesticulating energetically, he was struggling to keep up in a language he knew more as a theoretical exercise than as an everyday tongue; he was flushing pink with concentration.

She wanted to stay here and would only return if Sam would go back with her. Could they find out if any of her distant relatives had survived, or even her sister? She was afraid her sufferings would bring shame on her and her community, that she might not be accepted back home: this had been the case with others. If he wanted her, her life was here. Thank heavens Martha isn't here Sally thought: what she wanted was utterly clear. That the girl's mind was really that of a woman was apparent now; she had had to grow up fast, and not break in the process. I hope Sam knows what's headed his way, but, somehow, I doubt it.

The rest of the room were just looking at one another, wondering who was going to break the ice. To Sally's complete lack of surprise, it was the Abbot.

"She," he smiled at Narin, "has made her wishes plain, we must abide by them. I did not anticipate the fact that she might be considered shamed by her compatriots, even unwelcome, but perhaps her fears are exaggerated. Will our friends send a message to her people to find out if anyone who knows her survives, whether she can return, if only for a visit, to explain her story?"

The Exarch was nodding, as was the Armenian cleric, the translator explaining in Narin's language for her benefit; she was smiling the broadest smile Sally had seen her give, lighting up her whole face. Yes, Sam had better watch out, but she wasn't going to warn him, or Martha.

On the way out of the room Narin insisted on kissing the hands of all the clerics; if she had needed to convince them any further to grant her wishes, Sally could see that had sealed it. She squeezed Narin's hand as they left the room, descending the stairs to the first-floor landing with one of the aides; she then kissed her cheek in a brief goodbye, whispering well done in her ear, then letting the aide escort the girl, no, young woman, back down to Martha and Josey in the waiting room.

Returning to the Council room she could see that the various committees were winding up, hers had dissolved entirely; people were milling around, drifting out to the dining room where food and drink were being laid out. She followed them, trying to find someone she knew well enough to talk to, feeling entirely alone until the Abbot appeared at her elbow.

"Well done, very well done! He, they, liked you and I think he quite wants to take a woman or two into the depths of the Papacy. He's a surprising man in many ways, quite imaginative, and I think sincere. The girl too, and she also seems to know her own mind." he chuckled, "All these strong women, such a blessing to His work. If you wish, you may leave now, meet your friends, travel back home, there is little more to do, just tiresome formalities, ceremonies, before they leave on Monday. No one will take it amiss if you should go, or stay if you prefer. They will return at the end of the Summer, September probably, to confirm progress, prepare the finer detail. You will need to attend then, and, in the meantime, meet the Council when summoned and continue to practice your languages, improve your Latin too. Oh, and I believe the Exarch is arranging with the redoubtable Theophano for you to receive some more formal robes and other items so that you are not outshone in the Vatican. As I said, he is quite imaginative, and the Armenians were a blessing, understanding the tongue of that young girl! They asked me to give you this for her, a New Testament in her own language, the translator's own apparently, so that she may have something of her home with her here."

"Thank you, Father. How can we repay your kindness to her and to me?"

"Just keep doing what you are doing and having faith that your family will be restored. That letter I promised has been written and will be carried into Logres tonight for posting to him."

With that he blessed her and turned away to join the other senior figures in the room as she hurried to get her coat and race down the stairs to join Martha and the others.

Narin appeared completely exultant, her first conversation in her own tongue for many years, shattering any remaining sense of isolation, if only temporarily. Then the gift, something of her own land, if not faith, but that didn't seem to matter in the least. That she could read was swiftly clear, the book was old, nineteenth century probably; perhaps they didn't have printing presses in the Armenian refuge? No, they must do; the knowledge of them must have entered with the refugees of 1915 and the years after. She was holding it tightly, saving it to study while alone, trying to converse with them, expressing her thanks to them for their kindness, the others, the Greeks, the Armenians. Her tears were running freely, moistening her smiling lips, wetting Martha's hands as she kissed them, promising to work harder for them, learn their languages faster. Later, when they were home and it was just the two of them in the kitchen, her hostess got angry with herself for being so fearful of the girl, for having in part blamed her for Sam's disappearance.

"Martha, you do know the Abbot is very fond of her, says she can stay here if she wants? I'm sure he wouldn't stand in their way and I think Sam is much more likely to hurry back if she's still here."

"I know, I'm not being fair, you know why though…"

"I was in the meeting Martha. She was trying to find reasons to stay here, not go back. But the Abbot's right, she must return at least for a visit, to decide whether she really wants to make a life among strangers or among her own people, only then can any decision to be here be secure, without deep regret…"

"But Sam?"

"You must let him go with her if he wants to, but he'll be back. This is his home now; he loves you as his mother. I'm not as close to him as you, so perhaps I can see better, but it's for the two of them to decide for themselves."

"I know, but it's so hard, the not knowing where he is, what he's doing."

"The Abbot told me he has written to that man you all seem so in awe of, asking for his help about Sam and Andy; he seemed quite confident."

Leave her with what I have, hope.

He was turning into a sad old stick, but so were many of his colleagues. Working through another weekend, attacking the pile of evidence that continued to amass, following every lead, conducting hundreds of interviews, searching more addresses, cross-referencing more names and numbers with the databases of other agencies, both British and foreign.

Two hundred and eleven suspects had been remanded in custody, over one hundred and sixty already charged, this number rising by the day with more charges being added. More suspects had had their passports confiscated, told not to leave their homes without first notifying the authorities and more were being swept up all the time, along with a veritable arsenal of military weapons, mainly Kalashnikov variants, grenades and explosives.

His colleagues were cock-a-hoop, but the mood was fragile, a stratum of fear lying close to the surface, the other investigations into those almost certainly responsible for the breakthroughs had been effectively put on ice, resources diverted elsewhere. They were pretty much counting on the DNA they had recovered from that warzone in the Chilterns; the bullets had told them nothing they didn't know already. If that gave them a match, they would at least be able to open another line of enquiry. Perhaps it were better it didn't: the culprits seemed to have shut up shop as if, having broken the investigation for the authorities, they felt that their work had been done, at least for now.

George Edward came over to him carrying a sheet of paper.

"Thought you should see this boss. The head of the civil service in the Home Office never made it home last night, left the office as usual, got off the train at his normal station and simply vanished; name's Sir Kenneth McCloud."

"I'm not sure that's got anything to do with us, that's for the uniformed boys surely, just a missing person enquiry? Perhaps he's shacked up with his mistress, wouldn't be the first time."

"I'm not sure the Home Sec sees it like that. They want a full team on it; they think it may be connected to this case, a terrorist angle. No demands made or anything like that yet, but it's still very early."

"We're at full stretch; we've got no one to put on it now, perhaps on Monday…"

The younger man looked with sympathy at his boss. He was driving himself too hard, powered by the fear of an empty home, determined to achieve a successful conclusion in one facet of his life as if in compensation, almost obsessional with it, resenting any distraction or impediment to reaching the goal.

"Tell you what boss; let me deal with it until Monday, okay? Just make the usual enquiries, that sort of thing, liaise with uniform, keep them happy?"

"Thanks a lot George, you're a star."

Sam had kept an eye on Miss Helena, as he still insisted on calling her, all day. She was tired, uncommunicative and clearly hadn't slept; he had thought he heard the sounds of crying during the night, hadn't known what to do. Hardly surprising, she must be in shock, wasn't trained for this sort of thing, hadn't really prepared herself.

They had spent the morning burning everything the dead man might have touched, methodically, piece by piece, in a metal dustbin. They'd bagged the ashes up, cleaned the bedroom, stairs and landing, the rest could wait until they returned. She had driven them to the farm on autopilot, hadn't even left the car when they arrived. The others had helped, of course. They had tried to persuade him, but not too hard, and had let them go when he explained who she was.

The body would go the way of that of the terrorist previously disposed of; nothing would be left by dinner time tonight. They had driven back to her cottage, neither saying a word, cleaned the car out thoroughly, then the garage and other rooms, made and ate some dinner.

She hadn't wanted to go to bed, even though she looked exhausted. He tried to talk to her about it but got nowhere, it was just something she needed to get through herself. He talked to her about him with more success, asking her about him, how they knew one another, why she was helping him, but the deeper his questions, the shallower her answers became. They were friends, nothing more, best friends she supposed, but there was lots she didn't understand about him, she just helped him because, well, he had asked her to, she couldn't say no to him, that's all there was to it. He needed help, couldn't do it all himself even though he tried to pretend he could.

Sam had given up shortly afterwards; he wasn't much of a skilled conversationalist at the best of times, but knew when he was getting nowhere fast.

Eventually she had had to let him go to bed, had tried to stay up, watch some late-night television, gave up after ten minutes, not worth the licence fee these days, can't concentrate anyway. Now she was just lying here, fearful of sleeping but her body compelling it against the wishes of her mind. The hand returning, larger than before, more demanding of her, more insistent, paralysing her and then there he was again, shielding her, placing his body in the way, that poor broken form, wrestling with the hand, slowly losing. She couldn't move to help, was distraught, failing him again, calling for somebody, anybody, to help him, he was almost on the ground now, at its mercy and then

443

someone else was there, a man she didn't recognise, didn't know at all. He was forcing the hand away, his back to her, pushing it into the distant darkness until they both faded from view, as did he, leaving her alone, crying for him, wishing he had never met her, no, never that, rather that she had made different choices.

In another bedroom at the other end of the little landing, someone else was talking to Sam in his dreams, burning through the darkness with the flaming light of hope.

Sunday, a fortnight after Easter

....

'I'm not sure why I'm doing this,' George Edward thought to himself, seated alone in a little cubicle scrolling through video tapes and digital memory sticks of security and traffic cameras in the vicinity of the disappearance. The locals were knocking on doors, interviewing transport workers, family, friends, while he and one of his junior colleagues were all that could be spared on a Sunday morning for humdrum duties like reviewing hours of camera footage.

They had an approximate time: the station camera showed him leaving the platform at 19:02, so he should have been home by 19:15. There were no signs of him visiting any of the local shops, nor of him dropping into a pub or bar for a drink; he wasn't the type anyway, people said. Sometimes, when you read the transcripts of people interviewed about someone to whom something terrible may have happened, you just got the impression that they weren't liked, not hated, just left people cold. No one was saying anything bad about him, they rarely did in such situations, it's just that their statements were somehow measured, trying not to say anything disparaging, but not able to say anything that was heartfelt.

So here he was, trudging through hours of footage for anything, but the footage from the residential streets was generally a blank, few cameras, none on most: they were largely confined to the main commercial streets which he would have left behind in a minute or two. Again, they were generally poor quality, low resolution at night time, flared by the street lamps' stabbing fluorescence, not continuous, more single frame shots every second or two. His colleague had found an external camera shot from a shop with the missing man walking by, seeming to turn into a residential side street, the quickest way home. Helpful. He took those cameras on the direct route home for himself, leaving his assistant to look at those in the various side streets that branched off. He only had three to review himself, one digital memory, and two tapes. The digital hard drive one was on the man's home's front wall, covering a thirty yard stretch of the road. There was very little to see in the ten or fifteen minute period: a few cars, impossible to read plates even with enhancement, a couple of groups, largely younger by the look of it, heading out for the night. He printed them out for subsequent identification and interview, but they were very thin pickings. The next camera along from his house, near an intersection one hundred yards away was an equal bust, some of the same groups moving along, vehicles too, but less, some must have turned off in between.

Then the last tape, meant to cover the little side street, almost an alley really, but wasn't set up right so part of its field of view covered the pavement immediately in front of the house, but not the road itself, so no moving vehicles.

Hopeless really, he thought, but for the sake of thoroughness…

No one at all, no, wait, what looked like a young woman, hard to make out in the faint black-and-white image blurred by the street lamps' glare. What looked like a shoulder bag under her arm, skirt, coat, well dressed, looking ahead at the pavement, must be walking quickly, only in two frames, but going in the right direction to meet him if he was coming home the direct route.

He glanced at the street plan; this street was the darkest, the narrowest, a pinch point: if he were going to kidnap someone, it would be here. He looked back at the woman's image, no face really, looked like fair hair, white, well dressed, professional, alone, her manner suggesting someone on the way to do something, not just out for the night. His intuition was ringing bells now, no evidence, just gut feel. He scrolled on through, nothing at all, returned to those frames, but only one would have any value, the other was of her disappearing back.

He reached for the print button, the duplication button, but his hand pulled away almost on its own volition. Think. Pause. Think. Add it up. If you're right, what does it come to: a white woman, well dressed, skirt, probably not a loony then. So, who, the others? They're British, pretty sure of it, probably some shadowy state element, must be. So why pick on him, a pillar of the establishment, someone very senior in the Home Office? Well someone senior had betrayed those five security people with deadly effect. Andy knew one of them, liked him.

Sure, a payroll clerk had disappeared, but everyone seemed to think someone much further up the chain had been involved, had passed their details on to the loonies, so sympathetic to the enemy. A traitor maybe, possibly even a murderer. Then he disappears, no trace, no fuss, on a short ten minute walk home in the very spot he would have chosen himself.

Experts then, professionals.

Might be entirely wrong, probably am, but what if I'm not, just one frame really? What did Andy say, talk to him first before reporting anything? Yes, he felt the same way, things were bad, terrible, someone was doing something about it at last; there were hundreds of them running around, they needed to be stopped and someone was trying. So, whose side are we, am I, on? I know that already. So, don't tell the boss, he's enough on his plate.

Eject the tape. The frame's exposed. Just a small cassette, fits easily into my pocket. Evidence tapes go missing all the time; it just turned up in a bag with all the others, not even inventoried properly, someone taking short cuts, result of over-tiredness. Time for a breath of air, get a sandwich, take it apart in my pocket bit by bit, some in bins, some in drains, all gone. Hope I know what I'm doing. Those rooms aren't monitored, pretty sure of that, anyway, too late now.

Good luck whoever you are.

Alan Dare was sitting in the Basilica with his wife, watching the spectacle of the Orthodox rite playing out in front of him, along with Art, what now appeared to be his girlfriend, the American runaway, the other members of the outside teams and their families; even Georgy was there in a wheelchair with his mother and extended family. They were there at the express invitation of the ambassadors who wanted to meet those operating outside the barrier; apparently there was going to be a reception for them afterwards. It really wasn't his sort of thing, this formality, but he had promised, didn't want to let the others down by not turning up. He didn't understand much of it, neither did the others, just tried to look outwardly attentive while his hand sought out his wife's and his thoughts strolled away.

On his return he had spoken to the Council, unburdened himself of his suspicions about the events in Swindon, his concerns about Samson and Georgy, his desire to retire from this horrible work. That had shocked them, no doubt about it. They weren't naïve or fools, certainly not the Seigneurs, neither the Abbot, but they didn't really understand the outside world, its pressures, its confusions. They had said they would consider what to do, then recalled him after the arrival of the Greeks to meet privately with the Abbot, the High Steward and two of the senior equites.

They had hit him with a charm offensive, stressing his importance to the work, his irreplaceability, the fact that he had been chosen partly because of his strong moral scruples, the progress of their plans with their allies, old and new. His suspicions were not proof, however reasonable, of what may have happened; if anyone's, it was largely their fault, not his. Georgy would be stood down from operations in Logres for the foreseeable future, might be sent to the Vatican or one of their new allies, perhaps to escort the Kurdish girl: he would need to demonstrate improved reliability before entrusted in Logres again. Sam, well he deserved understanding, forgiveness, a young man, troubled past, perhaps excessive zeal, and his relationship with the girl; if he returned he could be recovered, perhaps sent out to escort the girl home.

As for Alan himself, he was essential, their most experienced operator on the outside, his moral sense vital if their work was not to go awry, further mistakes made. What did he need to carry on, more time at home to spend with his family? No problem.

More resources? Agreed: they were going to train up at least four more outside teams; they needed him to oversee this, if nothing else, the other teams were nearly fully ready now. Additionally, the Greeks had sent four volunteers to train beside them, get experience of operating outside, become proficient in English, the Armenians had also sent four, with more on the way to train and learn English.

More money, armaments, technology, were already on the way, the first consignment had just been landed, more bases to be bought and established in Logres too. They needed to find more trainers, experts from outside, like Hendricks, but they needed his help for this, to oversee it all. They needed clear operational leadership for the outside, Logres, too; there was no one else they trusted sufficiently, other than Alan himself. Would he refuse them, abandon the progress he had helped deliver, those he had helped rescue, the happiness of the lost he had found and helped restore, the Kurd, the American, those to whom they had become close? How many more out there could they reach out to now, doing His work?

It was unfair he thought, to put him under this pressure, but subtle, not even mentioning his debt to them; he knew they were confident they didn't need to. He had spoken of it to his wife, her family, Art, the leaders of the other outside teams, asked their advice, explained his reservations. All, even his wife, finally, had urged him to accept. Yes, even she, the one who had most to lose. He had even been to see the Abbot privately, explained his fears for his soul, his doubts. As ever the cleric had listened, then explained that the burden fell chiefly to him, the one who asked him to do these things. There were no simple answers, no automatic absolutions, but they needed to think of the consequences of stepping back from the conflict, how many lives had they already saved, innocents rescued? It was a fallen world, no course of action was perfect, but they had to do their human best, defend the defenceless, combat the wicked. He knew it was easy for him, the others, to say these words to Alan and the others, safe as they were here in their homes, but the moral risks were even more on them, sending others out to do their work. Would Alan think on it further, there was time, perhaps take up the offer at least until someone else was ready to take his place?

He had looked deeply and questioningly at the Abbot, but he knew he had no choice when it was put like that, what would his fellow citizens think of him if he stepped away? What was it President Kennedy had said at the start of the sixties, 'ask not what your country can do for you, but what you can do for your country?' From there it had all gone wrong; that decade's attitudinal revolution had been really all about self-indulgence and self-gratification hidden beneath a mask of idealism: hypocrites. Then along came the consumerism of the next decades, selfishness raised to an art form and to hell with the rest. Yes, he had to say yes, at least until another could take his place.

Brother Winwaloe had embraced him, thanking him profusely and then said they had decided to appoint him to a new position, Seigneur for their operations in Logres, temporary until confirmed by the Duke. Why had they not told him before he asked? The monk smiled, they didn't think him the sort to be bought by promotion, they wanted him to do it for the right reasons. So here he was with the other dignitaries, dressed up, feeling a fool, his wife so proud beside him.

Afterwards, along with the others, he was presented to the Exarch and the other envoys, their volunteers whose training he would help oversee. Pretty speeches were made, oh, he was bored already with this formality, and then they were presented with gifts, small exquisite ikons in gold frames, bolts of Byzantine silk cloth for them and their wives, things unaffordable to all of them, as a mark of the Emperor's appreciation. He had looked at the High Steward who had nodded his approval, it had been agreed, and then they had left, the ceremonies continuing with other guests. On the way home his wife had whispered how proud she was of him, and other things that made what he must do all the harder. Following behind, Art and the American girl, it was unavoidably obvious now what had grown between them; at least she had her wedding cloth. If he needed any final convincing that was it.

At the Town Hall, for yet another lunch and final discussions, the Abbot couldn't wait for it all to finish, time to get back to being just a Brother again. He was starting to feel his age, 'Lord, give me strength to serve for sufficient years to prepare a successor, perhaps Brother Peran, so like a younger me, so unaware of his potential in Your Hands.' Another thing to worry himself about; it was always all about people, individuals precious to Him, never forget that.

Sunday morning, clean, clean, clean. Sam was obsessed with it, the car, the house, their clothes, at least those he couldn't persuade her to burn with his own. Get the place sorted in time for the estate agent, who was coming to value it and prepare details for a quick sale, while a decorator would be there the following week to repaint the cleaned rooms. They were even going to dump the bedroom carpet and mattress at the local tip that afternoon. He was also insistent that she sell the car after another full valeting: she would take it in to the dealer this week.

Then back to London tonight. She would work from home tomorrow, make sure everything was ready for his arrival; the firm were going easy on her, one of their star assets, but she couldn't afford to take too much leeway, create doubts in their minds, at least until she had decided her future, had talked to him again.

She wouldn't make it to the hospital to see 'John' today either, would have to make do with calling him. Perhaps when he came over she could talk to him about the nightmares, how to get some restful sleep; he might know, be able to comfort her.

Stop being so needy, so weak. He's got enough on his plate, getting better; with everything else he doesn't need my little concerns as well.

But he was concerned about her, it was obvious when she called him, apologised; he was all about her, not himself, nor even Sam. How was she? Was something wrong? Had he offended her in some way?

Is that why she wasn't visiting? Was she having second thoughts about him staying at her place? It was no problem if she was, he would understand, could go to a service place they had found for him.

No, no, no, the words had stuttered out, it's not that at all, just pressure of work; want to spend time with you next week. She didn't like misleading him, but wasn't going to let him off the hook this time; besides he seemed to have accepted things, at least for now. Don't mess it up.

Sam keeps stealing sly glances at me as we drive back to the big city; he's concerned, almost worried, but not sure how to broach the subject, trying to summon up the nerve. Divert him.

"Sam, I think you should go home when you've seen him. I've spoken to him; he wants to talk to you, help you straighten things out. Your family must be missing you, friends too. See how Lena's doing, that girl you rescued? It sounds lovely there, peaceful, simple. I know it's harder in some ways, got its drawbacks, but you need time to recuperate."

He started, anxious again.

"I know Miss, it depends on him, what he says, but that list of names we got, someone needs to look into them, deal with them if necessary."

"You can't put the world right on your own you know, he can't either. None of us must make the mistake of thinking that we can."

He didn't answer, has just lapsed into silence once more, almost brooding.

"Sam, I didn't mean you to think you can't stay at my place, you can as long as he thinks it prudent, or we'll fix you up somewhere else. It's up to you, but it's a big hostile city, especially given what you're trying to do. Just don't turn your back on those who care for you, please?"

You're turning into his big sister. Sheena was right though, don't squander those who want the best for you, don't be too proud to keep love alive. That's one thing I've learnt these weeks and months anyway. I see that now, with all the clarity of that sunbeam through the church window.

Later, just before bed, she called him again. He must have been asleep, but sounded happy to hear her voice. When she was sleeping, the hand, the face, returned, but this time he was there, but stronger, and the other man came sooner; she didn't see his face, but something told her she knew him from somewhere. It retreated, disappearing with them again. He would be here this time tomorrow; the nightmare was less intense, she slept better, she couldn't wait.

The lights were on late in a suburban villa in Ankara; he was already working on the follow up. Isolated attacks, no matter how dramatic, how successful, were less influential than a sequence of almost continual lesser attacks. His agents on the ground were reporting greater polarisation of local populations, a steady drumbeat of reciprocal abuse, minor arson, vandalism, assaults, even people moving address: good, success. Keep stirring the pot, but don't let it boil over too often for fear of provoking a fundamental response from the authorities or natives, rather leave them poised between making concessions, temporising, and cracking down, as they had done for years. The Arabs were right in some ways about that, but we need the headline grabbing attacks to cement our leadership, side-line the Arabs, inspire our immigrant populations there and intimidate the weak-willed.

Yes, tomorrow would terrify the media crowd and pay their ex-allies back for their disloyalty.

Meanwhile, the press was reporting that their main contact among their allies had disappeared on his way home, no explanations offered at all. Perhaps somebody's saved us the trouble, who knows? I'm pretty sure it wasn't our side. Perhaps his treachery had been discovered, could be a problem, but he doesn't know me, only an intermediary who is already on his way back here and who'll be given a new identity. Well, it's too late for them to stop tomorrow now. I wonder whether those who are going to die tomorrow enjoyed their extra weekend of life after the postponement?

So, what next? Volunteers already training, a new network being established on the ground, new arms being delivered, safe houses procured. Western Europe was a rich breeding ground for them, almost too many wanting to help, join, support in any way. In three months they would be ready for a new round, with another successor network already germinating, sending forth new roots, seeding others for subsequent waves. Relentlessness would win out in the end. So, choices, almost too many options, what to do for the next waves? Lots of small provincial targets to convey the feeling that no one's immune, or a few big spectaculars to damage the key organs of the state and economy?

She stayed in the church long after the others had gone. St Leonnorus' was almost dark in the oncoming evening dusk, a few candles still lit; even Brother Peran had gone, bidding her a good night, and Martha and Iltud had left, taking Josey back home. She needed to be alone, to think of him, to try harder to bring Andy, his image, to the front of her mind. It had been getting shuffled back into the pack of her memory with each new revelation and experience here, getting fainter, less frequent when she closed her eyes. The human tendency to forget things, even those vital to us, to slide forward into the future, was frightening.

Her eyes were screwed shut, part of her praying for the freshening of memory as well as his safe recovery to her, the other fixing his portrait in her mind, bringing it forward from the back of the pack. The peace of this place helped, erased the distractions, clarified her thinking, just like this whole little land had eradicated the selfish worries that had made her so miserable in London, had revealed once more the things that really mattered: her love for her husband, her son, the timeless values that embraced them, making a life together.

She blew out the last candles after lighting her oil lamp, closing the door behind her. The stars were out; it was a clear, crisp night, all the more beautiful for that. There was virtually no sign of artificial light in the valley at all, but the night sky, the glistening moonlight, were all the illumination she needed. She was getting used to a world without electricity, electronics; there were compensations and the stars were one of them. As she headed down the churchyard path the corner of her eye caught sight of that Orthodox looking gravestone picked out in the moonlight. She wandered over through the moistening grass and bent before it, holding out the lantern to read the simple carved lettering. It was in English unlike the others, almost freshly cut from granite by the look of it. She bent closer, trying to make out the lettering. 'Jovana Meynell, 1979-1997.' And then below, 'God is Gracious'. That was all, just a space below sufficient for another inscription.

Jovana, sounded Slavonic, fitting in with the eastern cross, she would have to enquire of the Abbot: if she wanted a real answer he was her best bet. Meynell though, sounded French or English. Odd, well nothing about this place surprises me anymore… What would they do for Narin if she made her life here? She found herself increasingly hoping she would, and that Sam would return; Josey wasn't alone in missing him.

Monday, third week after Easter

··

He took the phone call shortly after another hospital breakfast, hopefully his last. He would hear this morning if the consultant thought him well enough to be discharged today. Her flat, even with a physio and nurse provided, simply wouldn't have the rehab facilities available elsewhere, didn't even have a lift. The doctors disapproved, as did the service, but he needed to be somewhere private, somewhere he could start to pick up the reins again, keep an eye on her, talk to Sam. They said he was at least a fortnight away from being able to get about using crutches. His shoulder was mending nicely, but the muscle would take weeks to rebuild, the ribs weren't moving about either and the leg was still painful, plastered, but would bear some weight in a few weeks. Perhaps it was too soon, another fortnight here or in a service house, but no, other things were higher priorities. Helena. Sam. Helena…

At least he was working from his room now, his team leaders coming in most days, Elaine too; he was plugged back into the network again. Those sticks recovered, decrypted, had been worth their weight in diamonds, had resulted in breaking the largest terrorist conspiracy in history, at least in the West. They justified, or at least compensated for, what they had had to do, even Sam.

His colleagues were delighted, but the more thoughtful ones, the MI5 Director included, those in the informal inner web, were worried by its scale, its penetration, the facts on the ground, with some local areas seemingly under ever less secure government control. Some were even starting to become pessimistic, muttering about the current establishment, state structures, even cultural assumptions, being fundamentally flawed, unable to surmount the challenge.

Some were saying there was a scent of Weimar in the air, civilisational breakdown, cultural decadence and materialism generating a state and populace psychologically and morally ill-equipped to win through. A few were despairing, although not Gerald, yet. Was this how the Romanised native populations felt when the empire finally crumbled before the barbarians, too exhausted to drive them back? Or how the Christian populations of the Near East and North Africa, the Zoroastrians of Persia, the Buddhists of Afghanistan, felt when their homelands went down under the Arabic Muslim invaders in the seventh and eighth centuries, their governors too enfeebled to offer effective resistance?

He had tried to cheer them up, but not too much, was encouraged himself by these musings. He'd been there long before them, had despaired at what he felt alone in seeing, like Thucydides understanding the pattern of history which he knew would bring low his native Athens in its war with Sparta. He however had been restored to belief, if not optimism. They who were starting to ask these questions of those they trusted, challenging their fundamental assumptions, repeating perhaps his journey: they were the recruits of the future. How much more would it take for them to be ready? Some not much, especially those in the deeper circles, a few more attacks, more ground compromised away by politicians, more lies told to the native populace would be enough, surely?

But this internal conspiracy, for that's what it must be, these 'allies', if exposed to his colleagues, that alone would be sufficient for most. That must be their next priority, to expose the rotten heart of the setup, to challenge people who still cared to look within, transforming their assumptions, helping them value again things beyond selfish concerns, to worry about what we leave for those to come, what those who went before struggled to build and sustain for us… All things now disparaged, the inter-generational contract, the cultural inheritance, abrogated, squandered in just a few decades of self-gratification. Then he thought of Helena, her home… Yes, time to begin again; besides, something told him there was more to come, those memory sticks hadn't told the full story. He needed to be free to work unobserved. There was nowhere else.

He looked up; a nurse was opening the door, mid-thirties, Caribbean extraction. He had become one of her favourites he knew; she would talk to him like a friend, was becoming one, take some of her lunch breaks in his room, had told him she would miss him when he left. No matter, he had said, come and have dinner with us. He found himself already thinking of it as his new home. He caught sight of the photograph of his wedding day, Jovana in his arms smiling straight out of it into his eyes, his heart, as she always seemed to, warming him through, but no regrets today, no loss, one day, one day, I know that now for sure, the waters of the Jordan will part for me.

His personal phone rang. He picked it up and answered. Celtic accented voice, innocuous code word as he asked for him: they had a letter for him from his father, the Abbot then.

How, where, did he want it?

Straightaway please, my new address will be with you later today, good, make it out to her please, thank you.

Inspector Angela Griffiths took the call from another officer, who muttered, "Another weird one, but it might be related?"

It was the Churchwarden of the church in the village of the missing man, Doctor David Kingsbridge, "I'm sorry to bother you with this, but given you're looking into Doctor Kingsbridge's disappearance, I thought you should know that his wife's grave was dug up sometime last night and her coffin's gone. No one here saw anything. It's awful, like some evil curse has fallen…"

The woman was in tears, she gave her time to re-gather herself.

"Thank you for letting me know, we'll be over shortly, can I have your number and meet you there?"

She put the phone down, the doctor's disappearance was odd, but many of his clothes had gone, and his bank accounts were untouched, so had not been made a high priority. This would make it one though, very creepy… They would need a closer forensic examination of his house and the churchyard for sure.

They were in the Counter Terrorism Command's main conference room, the chief, senior officers, Andy Bowson himself, other colleagues and a couple of forensics experts. They had apparently worked through the weekend on the materials recovered from the hide in the Chilterns, a few human hairs, done the DNA analysis, had a good match against police records from seven years ago. A Matthew David Williams, English-Welsh Caucasian, educated in Bristol, twenty-three, arrested a couple of times for petty crime, no convictions though, apparently just another troubled homeless youth, then nothing for the last five years.

"We need to find him, talk to the people who know him, where he's been, how he could pick up the skills to kill over thirty heavily armed terrorists. Andy, can you pick this up? The Bristol force will help, someone else will take on the missing civil servant case; we'll get you three or four other officers from the Command, some uniformed bods as well, this is second only to rolling up the fanatics. Thank you."

He picked up the details; they had kept this very quiet over the weekend, must have wanted to be sure of the identification before spreading it wider. Why me, perhaps because they think that I've the extra incentive, was he one of the masked men in that house in Birmingham?

Can't tell, it's never dull around here these days. I wonder how Henry, no, John, is doing? If I ever get a minute, I'll get in touch.

Abbot Winwaloe, along with the rest of the High Council, bade farewell to the envoys after lunch and walked with them down to the quay where a fleet of fishing smacks and gigs were unloading the last of the goods from the ship that had brought them, which was now waiting off-shore, just beyond the barrier. The cargo now being delivered had been unloaded last night onto the smaller native vessels; he saw it was mainly trade goods for Logres, other supplies, foods, construction materials, medicines, clothing, tobacco and cigarettes. The more sensitive imports, weapons, military supplies, money, gold and silver, antiquities, had been unloaded immediately on the envoy's arrival and were now either in the town arsenal or in the Duke's fort.

They had been staggered by what had been unloaded, far more than ever before, with more on its way in the next few weeks, before the nights got too short. The Exarch and their allies were serious then, had asked them to build a training barracks and camp for two hundred volunteers immediately. In some ways he was glad to see them leave, to allow us time to digest it all, make sure we were not just being swept along. He blessed their departing gig and headed back to the Town Hall with the rest of the Council, questioning himself more fiercely than ever.

The private ambulance pulled up outside her house just before three; she was waiting and opened the front door, wedging it wide, her smile of welcome even wider. He had been wheeled in feeling like a complete fool. Looking around he was pretty sure some plain clothes security had him in view; there, a fit looking female pedestrian, almost certainly wired to a vehicle around a nearby corner. The retained nurse was present as well, he could see Helena left nothing to chance, the nurse supervised his half carrying upstairs, leaning on one crutch and the driver, while the other ambulance man brought up the chair and Helena his bag, closing the door behind her; Sam must have been banished until the evening.

Ten minutes later he was seated in the living room while the nurse ran through the usual pointless tests, put his leg up, checked his dressings, Helena smiling quietly in amusement before letting out the ambulance men and putting his bag in his room. On her return to the room she found him looking at her in despair, supplication: she could see how helpless he looked and felt as the nurse gently scolded him for daring to complain. She struggled not to laugh, said she would make some tea, get on with some work in her office. Clara, the nurse, a Filipino, would be here during working days from eight to six to keep an eye on him and help the physio with his exercises; the dining room had been converted into a rehab gym, keep him in order, help him bathe. Helena burst into laughter at that point and fled into the kitchen.

Helena had been working with Sam early that morning, starting to trace some of the names the late Permanent Secretary had disclosed and now here he was walking around parts of central London, jacket hood up to screen himself from the hundreds of spying cameras everywhere; fortunately the day was damp and cool, so he didn't stand out.

Three of the people identified so far were in the media, two of them senior in BBC management based in Broadcasting House at the top of Regent Street, another a celebrity presenter also often to be found there. The dead man had seemed to regard the BBC as the redoubt, a core of their conspiracy, so what else to do but go and hang out in the vicinity for a while, pretend to be a tourist, conduct a preliminary recce in case we need to get in, then back to the flat later in the afternoon when the nurse had gone? Then tomorrow, targets identified, start following them, find where they live, their daily patterns…

Sam was nervous: how would he respond? He wouldn't be as easily satisfied as Helena, he would want to know everything before he helped him return home. Well, at least the walk will do me good, he thought; I'm not getting anything like enough exercise since I came to town.

Abdul Al-Benazzi finished the prayer. There were eight of them in his van, heavily loaded with automatic weapons, ammunition, explosives and enough rations in their packs to hold out for forty-eight hours; there was another van just behind them, similarly loaded. Making up the numbers a third vehicle, driven by two more of them and laden with over a metric tonne of explosives, was close behind. Six were ahead of them, on foot, two booked on a tour, the other four posing as backpackers walking towards the front entrance. None of them expected to come out alive, better to stay to the end and obtain martyrdom's reward.

The aim was to finish the job thoroughly then take on the security forces as they raced to the site. Security at Broadcasting House was expected to be light; most of the armed police were guarding government sites or major transport facilities. It would take them time to respond cohesively and with sufficient force, even here, in the heart of their capital, ten minutes at least, sufficient to get well inside, start sealing off the exits, penetrate the heart of the building. They didn't understand the layout of the building well, reconnaissance was sketchy, but they had numbers, surprise and ruthlessness on their side.

15:26, the two booked on the tour would be in reception by now, carrying only pistols and small plastic explosive charges: their job was to deal with any security then start to blow the lifts. His team of eight and two of the six on the street outside would then blow in the entrance lobby doors, neutralise any remaining lifts and storm the stairs to the top floors to isolate the senior management, leaving the two of the advance party to start to deal with those on the lower floors using the weapons brought by his team. The remaining four on the outside of the building would blow any obstacles preventing the final van moving onto the forecourt between the building's two wings and then break through one of the side fire exits, working their way to the news room. If he should survive this he would want to see tapes of the BBC news channel's reporters wondering what was happening and then cringing as they realised, hearing the shots and explosions getting closer.

The second van's complement would enter by two more fire doors to the left of the old part of the building, blowing the stairs behind them and then working their way up floor by floor. Finally, the pair in the last van would park by the shattered front entrance, just inside the lobby, detonating its payload as the police raced to the scene, before holding the remains of the entrance hall as long as possible, retreating through the ground floor. With luck, the sealing of many of the exits and the demolition of the front of the building, accompanied by the outbreaks of fires, would panic the hundreds of staff working there, trapping them long enough for his martyrs to deal with them, plant and detonate more explosives, wreck the building, wipe out the management and journalists, and then fight it out with the arriving security forces. They would probably be reckless, racing in to try to stop the slaughter, unsure how many of his fighters awaited them. He and his men could hold them into the second day he was confident; they had enough ammunition and food. They also had night vision goggles so would not be vulnerable in the dark and would, if necessary, hold some of the mainly female junior staff hostage to drag it out longer, maybe even negotiate a way out.

He looked at his watch again, 15:28; he nodded to the driver to make the final run in from their side street. The teams in Manchester attacking the same organisation's base in Salford Quays, two sets of offices and the studios, would be simultaneous. More complex, more volunteers, but similar modus operandi; oh yes, he was western educated, hence his hatred of their decadence. He had originally been tasked to lead the force attacking the main office on the waterfront, twenty of them, with two vans packed full of explosives with a similar team, but of sixteen, assaulting the second set of offices adjacent, a further sixteen the nearby studios.

Their instructions were to bring the organisation to its knees, intimidate other western media into silence, and strike at the heart of the British establishment.

15:30, they were pulling up now at the intersection of Langham Place and Langham Street, the "leave behind" charge would go off in ten minutes, long enough for everything else to be well underway, taking out security people, escapees from the building, so-called good Samaritans. They were racing for the front door, through it; the first four of the advance party already there shooting, putting explosives in the lifts, sending them up and down with thirty second fuses. He paused to look behind: the team outside were planting charges to blow the obstacles, the final van would be here in two minutes. The lobby door bombs were set to blow in one minute just as the obstacles were demolished, all to plan, blood and bodies in reception, footsteps racing up the stairs, the sound of explosions in his ears as the charges in the lifts, front doors and outside went off, automatic weapon fire, screaming, bodies falling on the stairs and landings, hell on earth. One of the new men was stopped on the second landing, throwing up, first time, he kicked him, pushed him on, shouting to him to shoot at a group of people in the corridor, keep him moving, no time to think, to freeze.

Sixth floor landing, his phone goes, it's the reception area team leader reporting all lifts disabled, the van in position, have shot two unarmed police outside, alarms and sirens starting up around them, have brought in the spare ammunition and explosives. Somebody comes onto the landing below him, he fires, they fall, others, not in view, retreat.

Seventh floor, five of the team leave the landing to start clearing operations, more gunfire, grenade explosions, screaming. He and the other four enter the eighth floor, people milling around, dropping, running, others coming out of meeting rooms, offices, fleeing, falling, some of his men are exultant, laughing, firing, reloading, he shouts at them to stop wasting ammunition, semi-automatic only, they'll need every round they carry, round up the younger women, shoot the rest. Some are running, others trying to surrender. It makes no difference.

Half of the top floor cleared now, he details two of the men to the roof, some will be hiding there, trying to get away, make them jump for it he shouts, then engage any security forces arriving, hold them back. Some have shut themselves away in offices, meeting and store rooms, but such impediments present little challenge to determined armed men.

A large explosion, the first van bomb has detonated; he looks out of a window.

Yes.

Flames, carnage, shattered glass and twisted metal everywhere, other vehicles thrown across the road, bodies clearly visible, some trying to move; back to work, no, observe, don't lose control, more police arriving, sealing off the road.

He starts to call the other teams for updates, leave the other two on my floor to finish the job, their weapons still firing, though now more disciplined.

Sam, at the corner of Great Portland Street and Langham Street, heard the initial explosions and bursts of gunfire ahead of him; as he was heading into the latter for another pass of Broadcasting House. He instinctively started to run towards the sounds, his hands reaching for the SigSauer 9mm and silencer in his jacket pockets; he always travelled armed in the outside these days, he felt naked and vulnerable if he didn't.

Twenty rounds including the spare magazine, that's all, silencer screwed on now in the hoody's front pouch pocket, people running his way, screaming for him to get away, he ignored them, shouting "Police".

Within seconds he is nearing the Langham Street side of the BBC building, four men appear to have broken down a fire escape door, entering, carrying automatic rifles, Asian looking. One catches sight of him, starts to raise his weapon. Instinct again, thirty yards say, two shots to the chest, the man goes down, his weapon spewing on the floor, another turns, two are already inside the building, climbing the stairs, Sam shoots him as well, the man's heavy pack falling loose into the street. What to do now?

The adrenalin was saying follow them in, you can deal with them. More gunfire to his left and from the building ahead, explosions too, alarms everywhere, the sound of police sirens in the distance, checking him, causing him to think. This place will be crawling with police in seconds; it sounds like a real battle... You're out of your depth, get away, call Helena, him. Martha's voice it was, get away, come home to us... He turns, hesitates, picks up one of the fallen assault rifles, some spare magazines, turns back again and heads into the building, people in there need him, the enemy are here, must be dealt with, for me... Narin's voice now.

Andy Bowson was on the way to the coffee machine when the first call came in. By the time he had returned the whole place was in uproar, a live feed from the newsroom of Broadcasting House registering the shock of explosions, people shouting, milling about, the camera just rolling on remorselessly, the producers hooked on their central role in the developing drama, torn between flight and film. His own offices were in ferment, phones ringing, people dialling out, others spilling out of meeting rooms, jostling with one another to see the television screens. A huge explosion, the camera shaking, then they heard it, gunfire within the news room now, what sounded like grenade explosions, an armed man with what looked like an AK47 ran into view, firing left, right, ahead. He could see still and writhing forms on the floor, others bent below desks or fleeing.

The chief was at the Home Office, Dager up country, he found himself shouting, "Everyone who's firearms qualified stand to at the armoury for weapons and body armour, then head for the vehicles." That's it; get them focused on doing something. He dialled the Command head, "Boss, Bowson here, Broadcasting House is under attack, armed men inside shooting, explosions. We're getting ready to go but I need your authority."

"Do it, I'll take command from here until we can get organised," he paused, someone was talking in his ear, "Andy, there's another attack underway at the BBC's offices in Manchester, that's all I know I'm afraid. By the time you get there we'll have established a chain of command. Somebody'll call you then, but take orders from the senior officer on the spot until you hear from me."

He got into the van, George beside him, struggling into his Kevlar vest, the vehicle was screeching out into the street, ten, fifteen minutes at this time of day. Just when they thought they were starting to get on top of things…

Al-Benazzi and his men were in danger of becoming bewildered by the size of the building, the number of people there, the plethora of stairwells and exits. They were quickly using their pack explosives up, hadn't been able to carry enough. The top two floors and the roof were cleared, a couple of dozen female hostages taken so far, locked in a meeting room. His problem was avoiding tripping over the bodies and upturned furniture as he headed up to the roof. He could hear the helicopter overhead, well they had a surprise for them: a shoulder-launched SAM, an old Russian model, but should be sufficient. He hefted it, crouched on the steps just below the roof, locating the target, he could hardly be seen, yes, the target had been acquired; it was only six hundred metres away, no time for evasive action. Two seconds later it was a flaming fireball dropping onto the roof of the Langham Hotel along the street, his comrades on the roof were whooping like Yankees, celebrating. He shouted to them to lie down, stop exposing themselves, but that would keep them away for a while; they wouldn't know it was his only missile.

He headed back down to the sixth floor, leaving just one brother on the top floor guarding the hostages and one more on the seventh. The rest would work their ways down floor by floor, wing by wing, until they met the other teams coming up. The helicopter was a stroke of luck, it would keep the infidel back long enough for them to finish securing control of the building. He and one other comrade headed for the newsroom: that was the highest priority now that the Director-General and most of the other directors were dead. He had dealt with the former personally as he cowered under his desk.

The television was on, set to Sky News while her laptop was streaming the BBC news feed direct from Broadcasting House news centre, the cameras still viewing and broadcasting: it was like the Marie Celeste, no one in charge, all just automatic. The sound on both was turned off so they didn't have to listen to hysterical journalists' speculative blather. They had seen two gunmen roaming the room on occasion, what looked like bodies everywhere, then another two enter, confer with the others, then head up the stairs to the balcony where the camera was sited.

He was on the settee, the nurse on a chair silent, mouth open, her nice white teeth clashing with the expression of horror on her face. Helena was sitting beside him, putting her hand in his without thinking, not even noticing, taking comfort from its warm grip around hers.

They were silent, his face set grim, eyes moist, but she could tell he was calculating, trying to understand what was happening, the deeper, larger, unseen events and the intentions behind them. These were the moments when she knew him least, his experience in such situations, his years of training, preparation, the ability to divorce himself from the immediate drama, to think clearly, analytically, shouldering aside the distraction of immediate emotion. A taxi had been ordered for the nurse, she needed to get away from central London and home before the transport infrastructure locked down; Helena had insisted, against all protest: it would be here any minute.

A masked and armed man was in front of the camera now, reciting what seemed a prepared statement in English, short and to the point, a blow to punish the idolaters, the enemies of the true faith, to show how powerful was their arm and the length of its reach, both here and in Manchester. No demands, no claims of attribution, no more.

He stepped out of camera shot, leaving it running on empty, almost addictively compelling, just the occasional shot now as the wounded were despatched, and the echoes of more distant shots from other parts of the building.

By the time Bowson and his colleagues had arrived, the emergency services were establishing a loose cordon around the building; all roads were sealed off, armed police and some military entering adjacent and over-looking buildings, which were simultaneously being evacuated. Snipers were heading for roof tops, fire engines and ambulances trying to deal with the now fiercely blazing hotel without making themselves targets for the gunmen, who were firing the occasional shot in their direction. They debouched into Cavendish Square which was becoming the emergency services' base on the spot, the Command chief calling him as they stood waiting for the last of the team to arrive.

"Andy, I've just arrived at the Cabinet Office emergency centre, a full COBRA meeting's been called. How many officers have you got with you? Fourteen? Armed? Good. The senior officer on the ground is Anita Stanley; find her then take your people where she wants to reinforce the perimeter. The military are on their way, are already planning an intervention, the longer we leave it, the more the casualties. I'll get out there as soon as I can."

Ten minutes later he and the others were in two buildings overlooking the bottom of Portland Place, across from the north-western corner of Broadcasting House, spread out over a couple of floors. They could see the two shattered side exits used by the terrorists to enter the building, demolishing them behind them. Gunfire could still be heard from the interior of the building, now joined by the crack of police and military sniper fire clearing the roof of the enemy. He later heard two of them died up there: they were presumably preparing the way for an airborne assault despite the shooting down.

George was beside him, breathing un-p.c. obscenities which if reported to HR would have had him disciplined. All the progress, the arrests, the progress and now this here, and even worse in Manchester by the sound of it, none of it had been enough.

These people were bigger, more pervasive than anything seen before; they seemed to have eyes and ears everywhere. The ground commander who deployed them had told him that a few BBC employees had got out, reporting over a dozen terrorists, well-armed…

They had shot down a helicopter for God's sake, scores of casualties, blown doorways and lifts, fires spreading inside. It sounded like a scene from Dante's inferno in there.

In the office reception where he was crouching Sky News was on screening a shaky video, taken by a smartphone, of four gunmen entering the opposite side of the building. A young hooded man with a silenced pistol appeared, shooting two, pausing and then entering the building as if in pursuit of the others. White hands, face shaded, expert shooting at range with a handgun, looked very fit. His mind was racing, too much of a coincidence; they would need the bullets from those corpses to run ballistics tests to be sure, but the same thing had clearly occurred to George who raised an eyebrow to him. "Pity he only got two... Wonder what he's doing there?"

"Must have been tailing them on his own, the only explanation." Then, as an afterthought. "Of course, impossible to ID from that clip."

"Can't say I'm unhappy about that, I hope he makes it"

Al-Benazzi still had phone reception, couldn't quite believe the authorities hadn't shut down the local transmitters yet, but it wouldn't be long. He called the leader on the ground in Salford; if he and the others were going to die here they wanted to know whether the other part of the operation was proceeding with equal success. It was. Entry had been gained to all three buildings, although many employed there had managed to escape from the multiplicity of exits, too many for even fifty brothers to seal off. Nevertheless, there was no shortage of targets, the studio and subsidiary office building had been set alight, the teams employed there still scouring the buildings and then attacking neighbouring offices. Keep moving was the plan, don't let the security forces pin you down, while the other team secures and holds the main building. Hostages were plentiful: it would be protracted. Security forces were arriving now, armed police, but at present they were heavily out-gunned and had pulled back to await reinforcements, allowing his comrades to expand the area under control. His brother there was confident they could outlast his team, said he could await him in paradise.

His own team were starting to take some casualties, not least the two on the roof; it was too dangerous to stay up there now, out in the open. Another had been shot by a sniper through a window, but no sign of an imminent assault. Good, his men would be more prepared and would have completed seizing the building in another thirty minutes, but disappointing because a rushed and chaotic intervention would generate greater losses for the enemy's armed forces, would be more spectacular. He checked the radio detonator for the van bomb parked half in reception, not that the security forces would come in that way, too obvious, exposed; he just hoped they couldn't jam all radio signal frequencies here; perhaps he should blow it now. Indecision was biting him, wait a bit, that might help to restore the initiative to us, it will drift away with time otherwise.

The Cabinet Office emergency centre was buzzing and crowded: the PM, senior ministers, Met Commissioner and Ted Armstrong, the heads of MI5 and MI6, Director of GCHQ on the phone, senior military officers, the Chief of the General Staff was on a plane over the Atlantic, his deputy was on the phone in a car on the way in, an indeterminate number of supporting staff, coming and going with messages, news channels on muted screens on the wall relaying camera footage. Ted Armstrong had made sure he sat next to Gerald, the Director of MI5. He could see the Home Secretary had noticed it too; she wasn't stupid, she was trying to read the eddies, the currents' flow, she even smiled at him. Hmm, she's worried; her ambitions are in danger of extirpation… The live screening of mass murder at the offices of the nation's premier broadcaster in two major cities. She needs all the friends she can get, especially those who've been breaking up an apparently huge terrorist network cell by cell.

And yet… and yet…

The sub-text of the discussion was, 'how can this be happening after all the arrests, arms seizures, the great work of the security forces?' Was anyone brave enough to tell them, shatter their carefully constructed illusions? They wouldn't be thanked for it, they never were.

The known facts, all too few, were run through once more: the clip of the terrorist's statement watched again. While it was on, one of the news channels repeated the video footage of the shooting of two terrorists in the street outside Broadcasting House, prompting a change in direction of the discussion. The PM looked around the room, "Which of your agencies is responsible for the attempt to stop this group, must have been following them? Why was that man alone?"

Everyone denied that of course, no knowledge, a foreign agency perhaps, or this new unknown force, must be them surely? If only the Chief of the General Staff were here, he was increasingly prepared to speak out, had handled the Chilterns decisively, no military casualties, only a few fellow traveller politicos and media types had questioned his ruthless application of force. He had gained kudos with the press, the vast majority of the population; these disoriented and frightened politicians would have looked to him to get them out of this nightmare. Where next they were thinking? When? Where? Tomorrow? The day after?

Gerald spoke up. Clearing his throat, he was hesitant, he saw the room as a panicky flock, apt to race away in the entirely wrong direction, even over the cliff.

"Whoever he is, he is a brave man, expert too, long range shot for a silenced pistol, must be slightly crazy to go in there after them. If we had a double zero section, I'd try to recruit him, if he survives."

His joke fell flat, poor timing.

"At least those in Broadcasting House are contained now, but it'll be some time before we can say the same about Salford: much bigger area, more terrorists, far fewer security people in the vicinity, our constant readiness military are so few now, years of cuts. They're all needed in Manchester and will take some more hours to be fully deployed. A break out there is still on the cards and even with more armed police on the way our people will be out-gunned for some time. It's up to my military colleagues to say when they will be ready to go, but I fear by then it will be too late for the poor devils still trapped inside and we will almost certainly need heavy weapons to dislodge the terrorists. They're not the type to surrender or negotiate; we must recognise that by now."

He paused, hoping someone else was going to take up the slack, but they just left him to it.

"Go on Gerald." It was the PM, ashen-faced, Churchillian pretensions absent today, at least for now.

The others breathed in gently, collectively, watching a man edge out on to the ice, unsure as to its thickness.

"These same factors don't apply at Broadcasting House. Special Forces are already arriving at the scene, there's a strong cordon of armed police, a confined space, single building, but too large for a smaller group, two dozen perhaps, to secure all access points. There're probably some of our people still alive in there, the sound of gunfire suggests it, but for how much longer if we delay? Besides, the longer we wait, the more they can booby-trap the building. So, we either starve them out, condemning any hostages they have taken, or others still hiding in there, to death, thereby looking weak and indecisive to the watching world, or intervene decisively, immediately and with overwhelming force. It's up to my military colleagues to say how and if they have sufficient resources to hand, but that's the choice, at least make it, either way."

All eyes turned to the Deputy Chief of Staff who had just arrived. New in post, this was a baptism of fire in so many ways.

"We have two troops of SAS on hand, with enough helicopters to lift them all on to the roof. Apache Gunships will be arriving shortly and a company of the Coldstream Guards is deploying as we speak, with another preparing to leave barracks, albeit a little under strength with leave and so on. We don't know how many terrorists are in there, or where they are, or even the state of the building. Casualties will be heavy, lack of tactical intelligence I'm afraid, no offence meant to my colleagues of course, but they would be going in blind. It could take hours, maybe days, to clear the building, and there might not be much of it left standing. If you sanctioned immediate unrestricted use of force, were prepared for dozens of casualties, then we could go shortly. I'm sorry, but it's not clear cut."

It never is, you numpties.

"I would like to go and patch another call through to the Chief if I may, in private, while you make a decision."

He left the room, you make the decision, after all you and your predecessors created this mess, if only by negligence.

The room was silent once more. No one wanted to be the first to advocate a course of action that could result in a bloodbath but stepping back was effectively conceding a similar outcome, while looking weak, played out. The PM was aware of their eyes drifting back to him like matter and light trapped in the gravity well of a black hole; the final decision was his, the blood would be on his hands, some pundits were saying it already was. It hadn't worked for Pilate, it wasn't going to work for him either; he was bespattered whatever happened now, to the grave and beyond.

"If the military say they can do it now or very soon, then I propose we order it."

He looked at those of his Cabinet in the room, encompassing them in collective responsibility; they nodded one by one, trapped in the glare of all the eyes on them. The deputy returned to the room, "The Chief concurs, go if we have a free hand, including the Apaches, but we'll need thirty minutes minimum to get ready."

The decision taken, many left the room, the security heads to the adjacent rooms that had been made available to them and their staffs, leaving the politicians and their advisers impotent and isolated around the table. The PM spoke, "Well, we better get working on some press releases for the different possible outcomes; agree the defined lines we must take in answering questions…"

Where had the other two terrorists got to? Sam looked up the staircase, no sign, they must have exited on one of the floors above, but which? Gunfire and explosions were spreading throughout the building like a virus, moving to commands he didn't understand around a body about which he knew nothing. The screaming was the worst, cries for help, of despair, shouts of jubilation in strange languages as well as English, mingling and mixing in a nightmarish cacophony.

Now what?

Rifle in one hand, pistol in the other, don't go too far up, you could be cut off; they had entered on the ground floor, but could be anywhere. Offices more likely to be above the ground floor, that's where most of the people working here would be. Up to the first-floor landing, the door's ajar, can hear shouts, running feet, some shooting a way down the corridor. Head ducks around the corner, pistol in hand, AK47 over back, a short corridor, offices either side, doors open, go right, it turns left into a larger open room, deserted, no, some bloodied corpses, one or two still living, just, nothing to be done for them now.

Retreat, what were you thinking? You're totally out of your depth here, you must be insane.

Reaching the first landing another burst of gunfire, screaming, comes down the corridor from the left. Head that way, quietly checking all the offices, cubicles, rooms on either side, more bodies.

Now the turn of the corridor rightwards, west that must be, peer around, a few yards further down it leads into an open plan office, large too. One man, armed, shooting at targets I can't see from here, sounds of another rifle, at least two then, screaming again, people running away, jamming the doorways, pleading, cut off, sounds of falling.

Advance down the short passage way, in and out of the small rooms either side, all clear, just a few yards to go now. Look into the large room again, only seems to be two of them; they've corralled lots of people into one of the corners, picking out the men, forcing them to their knees, shooting them one by one.

Sadism, pure and simple, the enjoyment of the power of life and death over complete strangers.

Crawl behind that row of work stations, twenty yards plus, you need to be accurate or otherwise your shots might hit those awaiting execution on the other side of the gunmen.

Closer now, behind the next row of work stations, rise up slowly, pistol braced, silencer mounted on the low partition between two desks, line up the further of the two gunmen who fires another shot, another falling body, and who beckons another victim to come forward.

Slow your breathing, don't want to kill one of the innocent, enough on your conscience already, steady your hands, good, two clicks, the man pitches forward. The other gunmen's shocked, turns half facing, he's quick, ducking, but not quick enough, two more clicks, he's down.

Over to the group, some are hysterical, not just the women, others in shock, but others seem more self-possessed, and listen to your questions and instructions. At least two other men have gone down the passageway, leaving just the two now on the ground, one's trying to move. Put a bullet in his head, no risks, then the final round in the magazine into the other, change-over.

Gather up their weapons, two of the lucid survivors claim to have some weapons experience.

"Here, take these, now, follow me."

There are sixteen plus me; eleven are women, on towards the first-floor landing stairs, the two armed ones following behind.

Right, the bend in the corridor, look around it, see no movement.

"On your way, quietly now."

A burst of automatic fire behind, then another, one of the armed survivors is down, shouting from the open plan office we've just left, two more down, one wounded, but the rest are safe around the corner. It's a sprint now to the stairwell, movement ahead, feet racing towards us, no one in sight yet, must be someone trying to cut us off, we're not going to make it, quick, into an office on the right, windowed, shoot it out, "Start jumping, you should be okay, I'll try to keep their heads down while you get away."

The last armed hands me his rifle, "I don't know what to say other than thank you. Who are you?"

"Just go, live, get them away."

Pulling out the little gold Celtic cross the monks gave me.

"I'm with them. Now jump, please."

Why did I do that?

The man's no coward, hesitates, part of him wants to fight, sees the young man turn away, crouching low, one rifle over his shoulder, the other grasped in both hands, feet race past the closed office door, they must think we made it to the stairs. He takes a step back to help, but the young man's gone, diving through the now open door, firing rapidly to his right and is then out of sight. He turns back, the last to drop to the ground, praying for the first time in years that they make it across before the bullets come for them in the open street, only the thinning dust giving them any cover. More shots from the building behind them, but inside, he's keeping them away from us; when I get out of this I'm going to make a programme about him, whoever he is.

Sam's diving shots took down the two who had run past from the left, but neither was killed, one making it into the stairwell, another into an open room. He could hear them shouting, someone else was racing back up the steps, must have already started descending.

Run! He turns left, races away; find another way out, this is survival now, nothing more. He heads through the open plan space into another, a right turn, new corridor, keep weaving, find some more stairs. In the distance he can hear voices behind, hunting him, the crackle of radios, how many more of them are there? Finally, a staircase, another fire exit, but there're voices down there too. Up then, second floor, quieter here, don't trip over the bodies, right, left, a drunken spider's path, they've lost him, but will be searching, for revenge if nothing else. Voices somewhere ahead, not English, don't stumble into them.

A room, looks like a radio studio, a body or two, broken equipment, a producer's cubicle. Not in there, that's the obvious place, out here, ninety-degree angle to it, behind that piece of equipment, whatever it is. From here, at the right angle, I can see a reflection of the doorway in the remains of the cubicle glass. Minutes go by, ten, twenty, thirty, have they given up? The sound of shooting and explosions is much more intermittent now; they must be running out of targets, their prey thinning out. No, there're voices somewhere out there, searching slowly, fearful of ambush, little idea whether he's even on this floor, they must be spread thin by now.

Another ten minutes or so passes, they're getting closer, two of them nearby by the sound of it, I'm like a rat in a cul-de-sac here, perhaps I should have kept moving. The door swings open slowly, no one's visible, but they must be there, one either side of the door probably, don't risk firing unless you're certain. Don't show yourself, wait, patience, let them expose themselves, become the hunter.

A blurred motion in the glass shards, one's in behind a recording station, the other's barrel sweeping the room from the doorway, the one inside crouching, moving left towards the cubicle, assuming I'm there, the other one covering him from the hallway outside. He's preparing a grenade, it's pitched into the cubicle, the remaining glass blown out, the man's springing forward to enter, he's sprawling... Too predictable sunshine. That used four rounds, plenty left still, fire a burst either side of the doorway, a yelp, winged the other, but he's firing back. Get ready for the grenade, another burst and dive for the cubicle, up and ready. But no follow up, the other one's withdrawn, can hear him talking to someone on the radio. Must be covering the exit from down the corridor, I'm trapped. What now? No way out other than though the floor or ceiling, wait, the authorities will surely be here soon, they can't allow this slaughter to continue.

Then what? Try to escape in the confusion?

Time passes, suddenly a huge earthquake followed by a crescendo of noise, dust falling, loose items shaken, lights going out, dark. Must be them, a tsunami of firing, rifles, machine guns, something heavier, further but mercifully smaller explosions.

Wait or move?

Safer to stay here but no chance of escape if I do, I'll be taken if I survive and the soldiers will be in a killing mood, so probably not then. Move then, darkness helps, find some stairs, the enemy are going to have their hands too full to worry about me anyway. Lord, forgive me; it's in Your Hands.

Edging to the doorway, still dark, the emergency lighting providing a bare minimum of eerie illumination.

Listening intently: is there someone there lying in wait for me?

Impossible to hear anything, given the rising noise of battle, seemingly closer now, building shaking, even some smoke filtering in. What do I do? Move or stay? I want to see Martha, Iltud, Narin, the others, my home again, not die here failing at the last. All those I couldn't save, dying in front of me, lost to the only ones who ever bothered, polluted by it all. Don't know what to do, so weary, nearly but not quite, not enough, falling short, just like me, always falling short.

Minutes pass, gunfire down the passage, an AK47 on automatic, but firing in another direction, no two of them, then something else, quieter, on semi-auto, more disciplined, much further away, it's prolonged, no one's going anywhere.

It's broken the paralysis of indecision, looking out, two dim figures firing back up the passage, in their excitement they've forgotten me. Too bad, empty the whole clip into them from behind, they're down, right down to Hell, feet racing forward, to run is suicide, detach the empty clip, hold out the rifle stock first, drop the other to the floor, the pistol's in the pouch pocket, too late to move for that now, they're here, all in black and masked, weapons and torches pointing at me, poising to fire.

"Don't shoot, I'm with you."

"Freeze, turn around, NOW, against the wall."

There are four of them at least, two race past to the right searching room by room, the rear one has checked the two he shot, joins the one covering him. Educated voice, posh almost.

"Who're you?"

"Undercover, intelligence, followed them inside, shot those two for you, at least four more."

"So you say."

This one's intelligent, examining me, finds the pistol, the cross around my neck, his eyes widen behind the facemask.

"Was it you, silenced pistol, outside?"

"Yes, two there, pursued the others in, lost them, lost myself, got some civilians out, but I've been trapped here, thanks."

"Ok, we'll have to hand you in. Here's the handgun if we run into any more of them, but do as you're told, ok?"

Sam nods.

"There's an emergency stairwell some way ahead, on the west side of the building, should be a police evac team there to take you in."

Following the others, he saw no chance to get away from these guys unless they're ambushed. One turn, then another, they must be near; the team leader's looking at a handheld map device. They stop, ceiling down, impassable, have to find another way, an internal staircase, another turn, then another, there it is, down they go, it's intact, just a body at the bottom, onto the first floor, more turns and corridors of darkness, nearly there, make a dash for it here, no, after the handover, outside in the confusion, the smoke. Gunfire behind them, one of them goes down swearing, then quietly fading, shock sweeping him away in its floodtide. The others return fire, spreading out.

"The exit's that way, they should be out there, go, now!"

One hurls a grenade down the passage, the others volleying fire in pursuit to cover his dash for the stairwell, around a corner, it's there. Where to now? Abscond via another way out? No, the cordon will be too tight now, if the soldiers were convinced, maybe the cops would be too, can always try to slip away when through the police ring. Who knows, there may be no one there to meet me anyway, ride your luck, someone upstairs has been looking out for me so far today. Wait here until the shooting dies away then go.

Some minutes later, Sam opens the door so very carefully, no one there, so step through.

Bowson heard through the radio that operational control was being passed to the military, they all knew what that meant. He was summoned back to the temporary situation base in the north-eastern corner of Cavendish Square, leaving his team in situ. He ran at full tilt, being joined by other similar officers with detachments on the other side of the BBC building, where they were met by a Major who briefed them outside the communications vehicle. Five minutes that's all, then race back to re-join the others. No, they had no choice. His job was to contain this side of the building, cover any civilians attempting to escape the building in the chaos, prevent a breakout, be ready to lead half his team into one of the side entrances on command to help with any evacuation. We aren't specialists in this, not properly trained for it, but resources are so stretched. He looked at the others, who to take in if required, some like George looked excited, some grim, others anxious: they picked themselves really.

People were checking weapons, making sure rounds were chambered, spare magazines fully loaded, divesting any unnecessary kit to speed movement, looking at the windows over the street for any sign of people, down the street for any hint of the direction the assault teams would take, anything to divert their minds from their rising heart rates, their anxiety.

Suddenly, the distant thump, thump, thump of rotor blades punching the air rumbled into earshot from the south, the vicinity of Oxford Circus. They couldn't see it from here, now more from the north, Regent's Park. There was a dramatic shaking of the buildings around them, a huge explosion to their right, must be in the courtyard between the two front wings of Broadcasting House, dust and debris fountaining up above the roofline of the building, then raining down onto the roof and some into the street in front of them. They were later told a laser guided missile dropped from a fighter jet had hit the van parked by the lobby, which had been presumed to be a giant bomb awaiting the assault teams, bringing down the lower floors at the front of the building, enveloping the streets around in a cloud of dust and smoke, deafening those not wearing ear protection.

A voice came on their radio frequency, the code word for the start of the assault. He motioned to his team to get ready, the entry squad sheltering by the door, the others training their weapons on Broadcasting House from the windows, only dimly visible through the plumes of smoke and dust, trying to spot any gaps of clear air through which to aim their firearms. Mouths dry, lips too, heart rates in the training zone: he'd once been told that the waiting was the worst. It was one of those hackneyed truisms beloved by the clichéd press. Well, they were about to find out if it were true; he rather suspected it wasn't.

Somewhere across the street, through the fog of war, men were abseiling down onto the roof, others gaining entry to the back of the building, still more preparing to attack the eastern wing while Apache gunships manoeuvred into position at front and back to give covering fire if required, point-blank range for them. As the aftershocks faded, the ringing of heavy debris falling ceased, the sound of other explosions, automatic and semi-automatic gunfire could be heard. It could be seconds, minutes, even hours, before they received the command to go... How the hell they could maintain this state of readiness for more than a few minutes he didn't know.

Abdul Al-Benazzi was thrown to the floor by the initial explosion. He had been in a corridor on the fourth floor not far from the front of the building when the van blew; taking away the suite of rooms between the corridor and the front, exposing his stunned form to the dust and darkness created by whatever angel of war had descended on them. He crawled away, trailing his Kalashnikov behind him on its strap; his wingman was dead, crushed by a fallen steel beam, his radio lost.

He found an inner staircase, got to his feet, stumbled up three floors to the seventh. Here, at the rear, they would make their final stand with over forty hostages in groups held around them. He looked at his phone, still in his trouser pocket, no signal, been shut down then. We need to start communicating with one another, identify the points of entry by the assault teams, begin triggering the bombs rigged at key exit and intersection points. More, smaller explosions from what sounded like the roof, so obvious, all the stairs to the roof were rigged, must have been triggered by those defending them; sounds of automatic weapon fire, grenades, even heavy cannon from outside, must be armoured vehicles or helicopters being used.

He was on a seventh-floor landing now, the air was poor here, not just dust, but smoke too, cordite and fire, parts of the floor upstairs must be burning. Good. Footsteps racing down the stairs from the floor above, he trained his weapon, it was two of his, no three; he motioned to them to come back into the seventh floor off the stairs just as there was a burst of automatic fire from above, and the lagging third brother was thrown forwards down the staircase. He and the other two, both fellow Moroccans, slammed the landing door shut behind them, retreated back up the corridor a little way towards the final refuge, built a barricade from office furniture while they told him what had happened. They must have used shaped charges to blow holes in the roof, ignoring the stairwells, just rolling grenades down them while others dropped through the newly made entry points after percussion grenades had been dropped in. He grabbed the radio off one of them, telling them to hold them here, retreat down the passage way if you must, fighting as you go.

He ran further back, trying to roll call what was left of his command. Fourteen it seemed to be, the rest dead or lost somewhere in the chaos. They needed to get a grip, wrest back the initiative, hadn't counted on the ruthless application of battlefield force in here of all places. It must've been a missile or bomb that hit the van in the lobby, now heavy weapons strafing parts of the building, must be Special Forces on the roof and floor above, no idea as to numbers. Others entering at the back of the building, probably larger numbers, a pincer movement, maybe other teams we don't know about yet. There're six of us on this floor here; the others can fight it out where they are, retreating here if able.

Get back the initiative, slow it down, think calmly. They are clearly not bothered about the building, ignorant of our hostages, are prepared to take military casualties; it's more like Syria. Let's show them we have hostages. He shouted an order; four were marched out of a room, all women of various ages. They were told to strip their tops off, unmistakeably women now, motioned to the corridor where the two Moroccans were awaiting the ingress of the enemy, wondering why there was a delay. The women were told to stand behind the door against the passage wall: human shields. He ran back to the rear where the other hostages were held, four more had been ordered to unclothe similarly. One of his men reported that the dust and smoke was clearing on the side of the building, visibility was returning, he had a view of the buildings opposite, several of the windows had been blown out too. He barked an order, the four women were led away, time to give them a gesture to make them pause, retract. Exploit their weakness.

One of Andy Bowson's team spotted movement through the settling dust high up in Broadcasting House and called out; Andy trained his carbine's telescopic sight on it to see four half naked women lined up on the edge of two blown out windows.

"Dear God," he heard himself mutter "Please Lord, not today."

He got on his radio to report, wasn't the first though. Someone else was behind the four, hard to see, suddenly the first woman was pushed out, still living, he didn't track her though his scope, didn't want to remember that for the rest of his life, kept looking at the others, they were shaking, looked like pleading, crying, that bastard must be just behind them, sheltering from our snipers. He got on the radio again, reporting the horror of it, was told there was nothing they could do, the assault teams were too deep in now, to suspend would be to fail. Get ready to go any minute. Can't you shoot that bastard? Not without hitting the women.

The next one tumbled out. He was in Hell now, wickedness he saw in his job frequently, evil too, but less commonly. Usually there was some psychological explanation or rationalisation that made it seem in part at least comprehensible, so that you could try deal with it objectively, go home at night sane even if angry or shocked. Today his modern, secular world view was being upended, its relativism shattered, confronted by primal, diabolical evil in the heart of his home ground. It was one of the things he and Sally had fallen out about, the existence of a personal force of evil; well today he could see it up there, in person, strutting about behind the two remaining women, forcing them into a place of utter horror, glorying in it, taunting them. God, if there's no Heaven, at least let there be a Hell for the likes of him

He felt eyes on him, they were George's.

"You alright Andy?"

He nodded in answer.

"You know, whoever they are, the ones behind Birmingham, the rest, they're right. I don't care if you report me for saying it."

"I see it, George. Let's hope they try to break out this way, I want to send them straight to Hell." George wasn't the only one who heard him, the rest were nodding too.

Al-Benazzi had just stepped behind the third woman when somewhere down the corridor behind him came two, no three, explosions, they must be coming through on to this floor now, more explosions, smaller, gunfire again. He pulled the two remaining women back, might need them to cover his retreat, he looked to his right down the corridor, smoke, dust everywhere, a fire fight was being played out that way, the odd round ricocheting past down the corridor. He forced the two women out at gunpoint, one was completely distraught, fell to the ground unable to function; he shot her.

Holding the other one in front of him, he retreated down the passage way, took a left into another, then another left towards their redoubt. Thirty-three hostages remained now, seven of his men here, a couple having made it up from the fourth floor, reporting troops everywhere, taking no prisoners, blowing every barricade and door with shoulder launched rockets and explosives, anyone close to the windows was liable

485

to be cannoned down by armed helicopters hovering nearby or shot by snipers perched in other buildings. He looked at his watch, almost three hours now. Is that all? It seems much longer?

He reorganised their defences, blew two corridors in to reduce the avenues of attack, put the hostages in one large meeting room with himself and one other armed man, split the others into three pairs to defend the routes to this part of the building, each fronted by four kneeling hostages across their corridors.

The firing down the passageway ceased, the Moroccans must have been overwhelmed. What had happened? Had they blown their way down through the ceilings again, ignoring or not knowing about his human shields? He tried the others who must still be fighting in different parts of the building, more distant explosions still shook it from time to time, gunshots, muted by their travel through walls and floors, more intermittent now, but smoke was becoming a greater problem. He could only contact two groups, four or five in total, one on the first floor, trapped, another on the third, trying to make their way up to his group.

They reckoned, oh, how many? Three hundred and eighty casualties at least, maybe four hundred; add the hostages still alive, pushing four fifty including security personnel. More importantly, much of the top management was gone, many of the news staff too, reporters, presenters, parts of the organisation would be crippled for months, years even, given what was also happening in Manchester. But here, he had wanted so much more, longer, dragged out for days, losing those two martyrs outside had been a shock when he had learnt of it, likewise the bombing of the van, the roof borne assault not following expectation. Perhaps they could delay the end for hours still.

Gunfire from the two open passageways to the right and left, the central one still quiet, several exchanges, both pairs there reporting signs of people gathering on the edge of sight, then two explosions, must be rockets, they're using rockets indoors again. Screaming, someone had survived badly injured, he looked out, partitions, ceilings down, passageways partly blocked.

The pair down the central corridor were firing at someone there, no return fire, he waved them back, they could be isolated, surrounded; they shot the hostages shielding them as they did so, plenty more to use still. They were near the north-western corner offices now, just back from the vulnerable windows. All bar four remaining hostages ringing their positions, the four youngest and prettiest being reserved for the last extremis. They were stripped, humiliated, placed in front of the windows. Hopefully television cameras were monitoring, broadcasting live from this side of the building. How long to wait? They weren't patient today, trying to sustain momentum even if it meant disregarding hostages, not their usual practice even if militarily prudent. No, they were now, had paused. He tried to contact the other brothers elsewhere in the building, no success; that must be it. No, there was still a little staccato gunfire a long way away, possibly near the street outside.

Andy Bowson received the command and sprinted across the street, followed by the others. Visibility was returning, only the smoke billowing out from parts of the building giving them any cover from unseen gunmen that might be lurking above, training weapons on them. They should have gone earlier, when a dust storm was still raging out there. They crouched by the shattered remains of a street level fire door, debris partly blocking the steps up, no sign of explosives. They entered, he and two others covering the stairs and ground floor doorway with their weapons while the others started to clear the debris, looking for booby traps, clearing a way out for escapees; secure it, that's all they had been told, don't go further in case you run into the assault teams who had been ordered to fire at will.

The gunfire had paused now, only the sounds of sirens and helicopter rotor blades, burning fires, settling debris, his own pounding heart, then a thump from behind like a heavy melon dropped on a kitchen floor. One of his team was violently sick; the broken body of a naked young woman had just missed him as he threw some wreckage out through the doorway. Satan was still at work up there he realised, George shook him.

"Andy, stuff orders, they must be right above us, several floors up. Let's get up there; these stairs should take us close."

Another crump of another falling body, he found himself saying, "Okay."

A large explosion, rattling this side of the building, dislodging more debris from the stairs, glass and masonry falling onto the ground, broken bodies, lying there. A smaller explosion from just above them at the top of the first-floor stairs, must be a booby trap set off by the larger explosion. It brought him to his senses: he put his hand on George to restrain him; his assistant was almost slavering in his hate, his rage, at those above. He called the command centre for permission to push on; it was denied, hardly surprising.

"Back to work, we're staying put."

Seven floors above he was just reaching to push another infidel woman to her fate when the office floor erupted behind him, lifting him off his feet, slamming him into the adjacent wall before hurling him back to hammer into the remains of the floor's metal beams and cables, leaving him suspended there. Broken, burnt, debris falling on him, his rifle dropping into the room below where a man appeared in view, black clad, masked, holding a submachine gun, silenced must be; the figure hesitated for a second, just slightly moving the muzzle of his weapon. Two tapping noises, two bullets, one in his stomach, one in his groin, fatal, but not fast; he hung there, bleeding onto the carpet below for a couple of minutes, couldn't be more, the pain was excruciating, sweeping aside the stunning of the shock.

Hands above dragged him up and out of the room by his broken ankles, his trailing head noting that much of the floor was gone: they had identified where they were, blown it from under them, not from above as before; filthy Israelis must have taught them that. One of the naked women was pointing at him, bleeding profusely, screaming hate, fear, blasphemies, from behind another black clad and masked man. There were several of them, carrying out dead and wounded women, several more of whom seemed unhurt, dragging him past the corpses of his last brothers, towards an office with a missing window.

Four strong hands lifted him and hurled him out feet first, not uttering a word as they did so.

The cease fire order came through, hold position; they pressed on with clearing the exit way. Five minutes passed, no more shots, another message. Building believed cleared, but searches continuing, recovering bodies and weapons, fire engines and ambulances approaching along with bomb disposal teams, building still believed booby trapped. He detailed the rest of the entry team to recover the bodies of the women on the ground outside, others of the team coming from across the street to assist while he and George stood their ground, watching the stairs and door opposite.

A sound from behind the door, the handle being turned so very slowly, so gently, so quietly, he motioned George outside to hide behind the door while he lay flat on the stairs, gun facing the exit porch. He heard the door swing open, a pause, his senses so keen, so sharp, he felt he could hear the stillness of someone there, listening, patient, so patient, sniffing the air, treading carefully forward towards the door. The smoke outside was thickening now, some blowing into where he was lying, the person standing, wondering if it were thick enough to mask their emergence outside.

It was a man, he covered him with his carbine, finger twitching, dying to pull the trigger, right between the shoulder blades. He was young, fit looking, hoody up, white hands though, seems familiar, can't be?

"That's far enough, hands up, turn around. Drop the gun, now!"

Yes, he was carrying a silenced handgun; it all just fitted, almost too pat. The man froze, turned his head slightly, saw the weapon on him, then that of George emerging in front, released the pistol onto the floor.

"Put the hood down, turn around, I want a good look at you."

He was standing directly behind him now; there was no escape, the man complied, white, twenties, steady eyes and hands, more than I would be in his place.

"George, make sure no one else comes in for a bit, block the door please?"

Now there's recognition in the man's face, he knows me. How?

"Did you shoot two armed men entering this building with that weapon? Is your name Matthew David Williams? Did you recently kill over thirty terrorists in the Chilterns, raid a house in Birmingham, another in Swindon or Reading as well, killing more of the same? You may as well tell me. Who do you work for? How do you know me, from Birmingham? Were you one of the ones who dragged us out into the back garden?"

"Where's this going Andy?"

It was George, looking over his shoulder from the doorway.

The man seemed to slump.

"If it was Chief Inspector Bowson, so what? Arrest me?"

"Answer my questions. Was it you who sent me those memory sticks?"

"So what if I did? They needed to get to the right people, like you."

"That young girl you took away?"

"She's free, safe with those who love her, happier now than for years. She was the slave of those monsters, kidnapped from Kurdistan, her family murdered… Are you trying to tell me we did wrong?"

"Who're you working for, the government?"

"In a way."

The man's confidence was rising now; he could see it, in proportion to his own uncertainty. George broke in again.

"Andy, he's on our side, fighting them. He's only helped us, let him go."

Dilemma, dilemmas, a career, nay, a life defining moment. George was staring at him; he sensed the force of his younger colleague's will pressing him to break his oath to the Service, to defy his sense of duty.

No, not duty, that wasn't so clear cut anymore. The images of those falling women replayed unprompted in front of his eyes, their naked broken forms strewn on the ground outside, the immense scale of what they were trying to combat, the vacillation of those at the very top of the chain of command, the descending greyness of relativism, politics, agendas, blurring the clarity of duty.

And finally, the words of 'Henry,' or was it 'John'... "For whom do we do it?"

"Andy, please, for me, for us all, those poor women."

What would Sally say? She'd had the clearest view on good and evil, much less grey than his own, almost medieval at times, he'd joked. Perhaps being a mother does that to you. What would the mothers, daughters, of those women on the ground outside say if they were here? How many more had this man saved, or tried to at least, on his own in that building, that circle of hell? How many more would those two he shot outside have slaughtered if he had just walked away?

"I suppose you've got no ID to confirm any of this?"

The man just smiled.

There it was done; the thought of her, those in there, outside on the ground, their imagined voices, entreaties, would ensure his conscience was clear.

"Pick the gun up, put it away. George, give him your baseball cap to identify him and get a couple of the others to guard this entrance and then catch us up. Follow me please Mr Williams, we need to get you out through the cordon and away."

A few minutes later he was standing in a side street with George and the Matt who he was now pretty sure no longer answered to his names on file.

"Where'll you go? Will you report this?"

"Somewhere safe. I can't tell you. You probably wouldn't believe me anyway."

Why had he said that, the flood of relief perhaps at this unexpected, nay miraculous, escape from his impetuous stupidity? The man's wife, a barely repressed desire to tell him she was safe?

"I'll report it, but not to anyone who will use it against you Mr Bowson, I promise. And thank you, for everything, and I'm glad neither of you were too hurt in Birmingham: we tried to avoid that. And can I have your number please, you never know?"

I owe you now and I will repay.

With that, he departed, hurrying away up the street, turning a corner into the large city's mist of anonymity.

"What have I done?" asked Bowson as he and George walked back to the building.

"Earned yourself a couple of drinks on me for a start," came the reply.

He turned to her, "I've failed, those poor people…"

Helena knew him well enough now to see what might come next; she hated his predilection for self-recrimination when he had no ability to withdraw from the fight, would emerge stronger for the conflict from these bouts of introspection.

"You haven't failed them."

She injected real venom, passion, into the words, causing him to register shock.

"Without you, what you have created from nothing, how many more would have died? Look at Birmingham, the others of them stopped before they could strike. The guilt is with those doing these things, those supporting them, the families and friends who don't report them, have educated them to think this way, those who've allowed them and their sick ideas to take root here, those who haven't spoken out, those who have condemned those who have tried. That's where the guilt lies. Not you, Sam, the others who have tried at huge risk and cost to themselves. Sometimes you make me so angry."

He looked at her, silent, stunned by her vehemence.

"I'm sorry…"

"God, don't start apologising again, I can't stand it."

She was almost shouting now, he flinched back, crestfallen. What to do? I've gone too far, but sometimes he needs to be shaken. She leant forward, put one hand on either side of his head, drew him forward, he didn't resist. She touched his lips with hers, gently, he didn't respond, then his nose and eyes, his forehead, then his lips again and drew back a little, far enough to see straight into his eyes.

"Don't you see, when you hurt yourself, you hurt me? Don't you know there's nothing I'd withhold from you? Sure, all the usual reasons, some I know you can't reciprocate, but most of all for your utter selflessness. I've seen so little of that in my life, so I understand its value better than you, you see? So, focus on what we need to do next, not pointless regrets. Please, for me, the victims?"

Lord, that hurt, took every ounce of self-control, I can't cope with much more of this.

He nodded, sighing deeply,

"Ok, ok, I understand the point, you're right as ever. Have you heard from Sam this afternoon?"

"No, he said he'd be back about six, after the nurse had gone. He was going to scout out some of the places associated with some of those names we recovered, try to identify them in the flesh."

"What d'you mean?"

She turned the TV off, shut down her laptop. The nurse was long departed; they had just sat there in silence watching the rolling news reports alternating between London and Manchester, confused, repetitive, speculative, maddening, but curiously addictive, almost sullying them with complicity. She sat down in front of him, on her knees, looked him in the face, unable to engage his eyes though. "I was going to tell you anyway before Sheena arrived and Sam got back, but got distracted by all that."

"Go on."

His concentration was burning her now with its intensity, searching her face, trying to provoke eye contact.

"Why won't you look at me Helena?"

"Sheena… She found out who ordered your killing, the others too, told me. It was just after you were shot. We tracked him down, Sam and I, kidnapped him, took him to the country, you know my place there? No, you don't, do you?"

Hold it together, it all rides on these few minutes, how he reacts.

"We, I, persuaded him to talk, give us the other names, important people, in government, the media, press, academics, even business. They were working with the people behind the terrorists, wanted to weaken the security services, told them who you are, where you lived. That's why they were waiting for you when you got home."

The tears were running down her face now, that first image of him lying there unconscious, not knowing, in the hospital.

"We were furious, wanted to hit back at them, keep things going, identify and expose them… That's what she's been working for all this time, pretending to be someone she isn't, infiltrating them; you know that."

"Can I see the list? How do you know he wasn't lying?"

"We knew some already, didn't tell him, so we could check. And by then he was a broken man."

"What did Sam do to him? It was Sam, wasn't it?"

His eyes widened when she shook her head, her whole frame was trembling, suppressed fear boiling over, fighting her desire to dissolve, to beg forgiveness from him.

"No, I did it, forced him to tell, finished him, for what he did to you. It was me, my decision, not Sam. I don't regret, only the dreams. Sam cleaned it up, no evidence left at all, the cottage is being sold, the car too. No one saw anything, we were careful."

"Was he the missing Permanent Secretary?"

"Yes." The tears were returning. "A coward and a traitor, I hope he's burning right now."

His eyes broke away; she shrank, fearing rejection, disgust, horror. He looked at the blank TV screen, into space, back to her, shaking his head.

"I can't leave you alone for a minute, can I? Why did you do it, risk yourself like that?"

"Do you need to ask?"

He leaned forward, held his good arm out to her, pulled her to him. She was sobbing, with relief, her eyes streaming onto his shirt.

"I think I'm going to have to take you there, if only to keep you out of mischief, so you can't get back."

"Would you?"

"Do you mean that, really?"

"Yes, but when we can go together, to stay."

"That maybe some time, your list to follow up, the fallout from today, we've also got to track down Sam, get him home. That reminds me: has a letter been delivered for me today, by hand?"

"I don't know, I'll go down and look in my post box."

"Later. First promise me one thing, you will never, ever, do anything remotely like that again without first agreeing it with me."

She nodded, tearful relief consuming her expression. The door buzzer rang. She got up, wiping her eyes: it was Sam. She let him in, asked him to bring up any post, had the door open for him as he arrived, startled him with her embrace. She whispered to him.

"Sam, he's here, he knows, prepare yourself. He's fine though, don't worry, he's really just worried for us, you know what he's like. Come on through."

Sam went in. He looked troubled, fearful; he handed her an envelope which she opened, passing one enclosed letter onto Henry and another to Sam. Leave them to it, I need to get myself together anyway, make some tea; all's well, he's here, he's not angry, he's so nearly...

Don't think it; don't delude yourself, that's not the deal.

The emergency sub-committee were all back in the main room: the ceasefire at Broadcasting House was over two hours old now and disparate reports were starting to be assimilated, an incomplete but increasingly coherent picture was emerging: if only they could say the same thing of events at Salford Quays. Confusion still reined there, the police perimeter remained weak, a couple more buildings were under attack, fires were burning in several more, drone camera footage added to that of helicopters and observers on surrounding buildings confirmed dozens of corpses outside.

Troops were being ferried in by aircraft and helicopter, three companies of the 2nd Battalion of the Parachute Regiment, two troops of the SAS with others being readied, one company of the Coldstream Guards diverted from London travelling by train, more gunships, drones as well, even a scratch company of local Territorial Army volunteers who had reported for duty. It was urban warfare up there; local Muslims were in the streets celebrating their 'forthcoming liberation.' The police were fearing the onset of darkness, riots, possibly even sectarian violence on a scale not seen before.

Ted Armstrong looked about him, again seated next to Gerald. There had been no celebration of the retaking of Broadcasting House, too many bodies being recovered for that, too many had been shot down trying to dash away across the street outside, too much damage, physical and moral. The military would be handing back control of the scene following their provisional report to the PM at this meeting, but a comprehensive analysis could take days. There was no power, fires still raged in parts of the building, booby traps were widespread, no one was even sure if all the attackers had been killed; none seemed to have been apprehended.

The Deputy Chief of Staff sat down at the table; he had acquitted himself well, been decisive, balanced, thorough, had grown in confidence in this forum. But to Ted the PM, the Commissioner of the Met, even the Home Secretary, seemed diminished, tired and understandably stressed, but no, more than that, shell-shocked, rocked by the revelation of things they had chosen not to recognise previously. They weren't the only ones; we're all guilty of that to various extents, not least those targeted in that building, in some ways they'd been some of the worst. Well, they'd paid a terrible price for it, but so had hundreds of blameless others just doing humble jobs there, their families and friends too. What a waste. He looked about, ashen faces, red-rimmed eyes; all that you would expect and this was just the starter, the main course was still being served up in Manchester.

The military man spoke, "PM, Ministers, Ladies and Gentlemen, we believe we're in a position to hand back control of Broadcasting House to civilian authority and to withdraw all military personnel other than one SAS troop, in case any isolated holdouts haven't been identified yet. We have now searched all parts of the building other than those inaccessible through blast damage, fire or undetonated booby-traps. Efforts are continuing to deal with these issues, but some may require the assistance of daylight."

He looked down at some brief hand-written notes.

"As of now four hundred and thirty-three corpses have been recovered, twenty two of which are believed to be terrorists with others still likely to be found. Of the rest, three members of the army are confirmed dead, three wounded, none missing, seven police dead, including the helicopter crew, and four wounded, the rest are civilians, with another ninety-two confirmed injured. The total numbers will take some more hours to collate, maybe another twenty-four."

"Moving on to Manchester, details are much more sketchy, but so far sixteen police dead and eight wounded, seventy one civilians reported to hospital so far, two military dead and five wounded, no word on others or those of the enemy. Escapees say there are several dozen in there, killing at will, taking hostages, expanding the part of the development under their control, although with the forces now deploying, and the use of air and drone strikes where required, we are confident that we can soon start to drive them back. However, I should warn you that casualties are likely to far exceed those suffered here, exceptionally heavy as they are already. I'm sorry, but we simply didn't have the forces in the area to respond quickly enough to close them down. They had far too much time to work their evil, too many of them too."

There was a collective intake of breath, many wondering about the public's reaction, whether the government could survive, the bonfires of promising careers, the distraught relatives they would have to face. The PM knew it was his place to respond.

"Thank you, err…"

The Deputy Chief wasn't done. "Sorry Sir, may I continue? There's one more oddity I should mention. That man we saw in the video, killing those two terrorists in the street and entering the building following two more? Well, one of the assault team leaders in the building reported they met him in there. He'd shot two terrorists they were exchanging fire with, claimed to have killed a handful more. They were taking him to a fire exit to be handed to an evac team when they were attacked. In the confusion he disappeared. They believed him to be some sort of secret service operative. We need to ask those outside, on the cordon, but with the chaos, the reduced visibility, who knows? Furthermore, some of the escapees say he rescued them, they'd been taken, were being executed one by one. This same young man came from nowhere and shot the two terrorists and fought off more, so they could escape. One even says he showed him a Celtic cross he was wearing around his neck, said something about being with them, that's all. The witness was quite emotional about it, hardly surprising, said he saved all their lives, called him a hero."

The discussion drifted off; speculation, denials, questions, suspicion that someone was withholding something, but what could they add now, it was left to others to fight and die, to clear up the mess in Manchester? It petered out; no one had the heart for it. Ted got up and walked out with Gerald; it was going to be a long night as it was, a press conference was being organised to keep the politicians busy, he had injured colleagues to see, plans to make, then letters to write.

"Gerald, do you really mean it when you say you don't know who that young man is?"

He got a wistful smile in response.

"Sadly yes. There are bits of the security apparatus that are not fully understood even by me, not in the light as it were. Just as well really, given the lives they must have saved by exposing what they have so far. I'd rather repress the curiosity of a lifetime and not find out."

"My sentiments exactly."

They headed off, leaving it at that.

He could hardly believe what he had been hearing from Sam. No, it was all too true, but he was avoiding some things, the girl, some of his motivations, but at least it wasn't what he had feared. Sam wasn't a practised enough liar yet to get away with evasion; sometimes, it was what people skirted around that revealed the most, but he had shown himself to be even tougher, more single minded than he had suspected, but not pathological. He was clearly besotted, even if not aware of it himself, and not just with the girl.

And Helena, almost stretching credulity, near savagery cloaked in that fascinating, bewitching persona, clad in that elegant form. Even her cousin, revealing new facets, surprising him once more with the sharp steeliness of her soul, a moral toughness well beyond mine. And what does that make me? The broken down old fool who lit the spark that turned into an uncontrollable inferno? What have I done? Was she right, did I do it in her name, but for myself? Lord, forgive my foolish arrogance, thinking I could control it and keep the edges of our surgery clean and hygienic.

"If you're thinking what I think you are, you're wrong, utterly."

She was back in the room, royal blue again, she didn't miss anything, far far too much for me, putting down a tea tray on a table, face composed. Sam was sitting there mute, still, talked out, fearing retribution, exile, admonishment. He's more scared of me than of going into that building. What have I become?

She came over with a cup of tea, placing it in his hands, and kissed him full on the forehead, standing back, hands on her hips, a smile on her lips, killing him with that look.

"Sam, has he told you that you're the bravest man he ever met? You are to me, and I know at least two others of huge courage. I don't regret anything, and neither should either of you, and I won't permit it. You're in my home now; you obey my rules, understood? Now, what do your letters from there say?"

"Sam's welcome to return, they attach no blame to him, only themselves, those who sent him out. I concur, it's mine as well. I will write that letter for you Sam. I suggest you go home, to your family, the girl, and rest. We'll need you back soon enough the way things are going. Besides, you're going to have to drop out of sight for a while, something tells me your fifteen minutes of fame will last a bit longer; everyone'll want to know who you are. Try to change your appearance a bit. Can we get him there for tomorrow night?

She wasn't fooled.

"Yes. Now, what does the letter say about you?"

He shrugged.

"Big developments, they want me to go to meet with them, praying for my recuperation, that sort of thing."

"When, how long?"

"Not before I'm fully better, and only for a few days. And no, you can't come through the barrier unless you don't want to come back."

She pouted. Was she playing, not always easy to tell?

"Thanks Sir." Why does Sam always call me Sir? "There's one thing I forgot to mention. The policeman who helped me get away thought the cordon, out of the building; it was him, Miss Bowson's husband. The other officer thought the same too, wanted me to escape, and they knew what I'd done previously. I don't know why."

Well, well, well. Perhaps providence at work again, certainly seems to follow this young man around.

"Thanks, very interesting, I think that could be useful. Why not go and wash up, get packed, see what the mistress of the house has in store for our palates tonight?"

She laughed.

"Home delivery I'm afraid, Sheena's vegan, but I'm not going to inflict that on you. She, and it, should be here within the hour."

She headed back into the kitchen, laid the table, easier here, opened some wine, that bottle of Chambertin they'd missed enjoying on the day of his shooting, time to catch up, make up. Ten minutes later she took him a glass through; he was back watching the news summarising the press conference spliced with live updates from Salford and Oxford Street.

"It's too horrible to contemplate, all those poor people trapped. And as for you and Sheena… You know, I don't know which of you two is the more remarkable, but I'm glad that it's you I'm staying with, the thought of vegan food…"

"Is that the only reason?"

"What do you think?"

The Turk was almost ecstatic, after all the set-backs, the doubts, only nine-eleven put this in the shade, and this was somehow more personal, more intimate, a stab at the heart of a major western institution. Yes, London had ended more quickly than he'd hoped, but Manchester was still going strong, better than expected. His one regret was what they could have accomplished if they hadn't lost two thirds of their organisation in the weeks before. His backers' doubts would be eased; more volunteers would come forward, more money, on to the next stage, bigger and better next time. He turned off the sound on the news channel, time to phone his key backer, arrange to meet.

Her cousin was slightly early, anxious, almost femininely dressed for her. She went through the hall as quickly as she could without being rude, straight in to see him, embraced him, sat beside him, almost passionately concerned. Helena smiled to herself, secure now with him, well, at least as much as I can be, the effect he sometimes had on others, and yet he thought so little of himself, believed she herself, the others, were far more exceptional.

The door buzzer rang again, dinner's here; you're getting lazy, mollycoddled by wealth. While she waited for it to be brought up images were screening in her mind: a simple life with him, primitive cottage, working with her hands, cold water and rooms, dark nights, physical exertion from doing the everyday things she hardly ever had to do.

Is that what you really want, all of that, just for him?

I don't know, maybe there's more than just that, I'd need to see.

If you do, it's not what you think with him.

That's not true, shut up.

Dinner wasn't quite what she had expected. The food was fine, although she knew he would rather have had something simple, made by her. He kept glancing at her. Sam said little, slightly overawed, but his thoughts were turning homeward she could see, the fear of exile dissolving in the aftermath of that letter in the Abbot's own hand, and his promise to write. Occasionally he would laugh, reveal something of himself in his relief, but his internality, the hard-learnt habits of his early life, would quickly reassert themselves. She knew that only Martha, whom she'd never met, had ever got really close to him, but maybe one other now could.

Sheena was conversationally dominant, sparkling, vibrant like she had never seen her before, something long buried by years of regret and subterfuge breaking through to bask in the sun for just a little while, speaking of her progress, those identified, the scale and nature of what they were uncovering, her horror at the killings, his injuries, her new greater resolve, her relief. What she didn't say, didn't need to, it was manifest, was her admiration, devotion, and a deep unsuspected faith.

He simply sat there, smiling that smile, talking when needed, disclosing very little, tut-tutting at their unauthorised activities, trying to extract a promise similar to that she had herself sworn, which Sheena adamantly refused to give, telling him straight that he wasn't invariably right, he needed to share the responsibility more. Yes, her cousin was on good form, even he retreated before her, promising to explain, consult more, bring others in.

He was looking harassed, looking to her in an appeal for assistance. No chance, she was enjoying the spectacle, smiling faintly at him, encouraging her cousin. His evasions got nowhere, Sheena was amusingly remorseless, pinning him down in a clinical way she could never manage herself; she could see he didn't know what to do. He started to concede, a little at first, throwing a bone to the cornering pack, but it wasn't satisfied, demanded the entire carcass, then more promises, to disclose more, consult more.

He was squirming now, Sheena triumphant, then suddenly something touched her leg lightly, must be his good foot. He was looking at her directly, beseeching; she ignored it. Then his foot was more insistent, stroking her, pleading for assistance, distracting, her pulse rate rising. Enjoy it; he's begging you now, pleading for mercy. His foot fell away, his final surrender, an exultant Sheena, the last demand conceded. That smile was back on his lips again, eyes skating over her, amused.

"Sam, remind me not to go unprepared to dinner with these two cousins again. I would rather have gone into that building with you than face them in this mood; they're utterly merciless to a poor wounded veteran."

Later Sheena left, taking Sam and all his gear to her flat in her car, promising to stow him there all day and then drive him to the West Country the following evening so he could walk the final few miles to the farm, before crossing the barrier when another party was ready, with his letter in his jacket pocket. He was bashful, embarrassed by the fuss she made of him; Helena musing to herself how her cousin would get on with him for the next twenty-four hours.

She had helped him get to bed. He had hated that, the loss of independence to her; had insisted she not help him get changed into his night things. It had taken him ages, so stubborn; she had left him to it, trying not to laugh. Later, after midnight, when the nightmare returned, stronger and larger than before, his form weaker, the other man not present, she had cried out, once, more times.

He couldn't sleep, the cramp from lack of movement, had hobbled out of his room using a frame to make a drink, had heard her cry, an incoherent low pleading. What to do? Nightmares were to be expected, normal after what she had seen and done, part of the encoded morality deep with the human persona, natural law the Scholastics had called it, hence the increasingly favourable modern reappraisal of their insights sparked by the developing understanding of the workings of the human genome. But she shouldn't have to face them alone, not like he and so many others; who else could she turn to other than him?

Another cry, more despairing, moaning sounds.

He hobbled to her door, knocked, no answer, what to do? Another cry, he turned the handle, it was unlocked, swung back the door silently, dark but for the odd shard of artificial light from outside slashing through gaps in the curtains; he never slept well in the city because of that. She turned over, restless, perhaps not, wait until the morning. He tried to back out, over-balanced, sliding remorselessly down the adjacent wall, gasping with the pain from his rib cage and leg, slumping prostrate and helpless. You idiot, now what? You can't move. Get your breath back.

She was standing over him, grey silk dressing gown, eyes grave.

"Are you alright? What're you doing here?"

"I heard you cry out, wanted to check you're ok." He laughed bitterly, "Some help I am, I can't even get myself up."

She got down on her knees, helped him sit upright against the wall. He tried not to look; she was distracting, consuming, glistening in that artificial quarter light reflecting off her dressing gown, hair and moist eyes, her skin almost unearthly radiant. She told him of her dreams, asked his help, advice. He looked at her.

"You're not alone you know."

Her tears were coming now.

"I am, even here, with you so nearby."

"What do you really want of me?"

"I promised never to ask. I know you can't."

She found herself pulled to him with surprising force, her head cradled against his shoulder.

"I'm sorry; I always seem to come up short for you. Are you really sure you want me here?"

"More than anything."

He closed his eyes, regain your self-control, it's like Zeno's Paradox, the distance between them kept closing, but would always enough remain to prevent them truly joining, no matter how fine the gap became?

"Then help me up to bed, stay and talk. It's much harder to beat these things alone."

She sat beside him in the bed, legs warm under the covers, just warm from his presence, his arm around her, talking about her dreams, their meaning.

"Who was the other man you mentioned, not just the broken down me?"

"I don't know, but something tells me I met him one Sunday."

That was all she could say; the realisation, her intuitive suspicion, held her back.

Surely not?

Later, as she fell asleep against him, content, breathing slowly, he lay awake, watchful. She had carried both his outer and inner defences now, only the citadel remained and its gate was reeling under her blows. How long? Hopefully long enough, so much more to do.

Wednesday, third week after Easter

He'd left the smuggling party behind on the way down to the valley, racing despite his heavy load, dawn was just arriving, a grey cloudy day, typical West Country Spring morning, promising mild showers: it was good to be back. A few early risers were about, country folk living with the available daylight, some waved to him as he jogged past, starting to blow hard. There it was, St Leonnorus' church, the station and warehouse, the small but growing cluster of houses and farms. Yes, there was Martha and Iltud's; they'd be up too, about somewhere. He went around the back, wet, dirty, tired, happy.

Martha jumped as he came in through the back door.

"Oh Sam, my love!" Enfolding him in her arms, "I prayed, I feared… What did we do wrong? Sit down, tea and breakfast are on; dump that kit, your boots".

She shouted out the back to the outbuildings of their smallholding.

"Iltud, Sam's back, safe!"

The farmer was there within seconds, wanting to hug him, but beaten to it by a young Kurdish woman who stood there with tears in her eyes, shaking. Martha looked at her; she was teetering between misery and ecstasy, so like me then.

"Come here Narin, it's alright; he's come back to us all."

Slowly, tentatively, with the gravest, most hesitant smile on lips moistened with running tears, she approached him. He stood there, not knowing what to do; she embraced him, trembling. Martha looked at Iltud, who was smiling, shaking his head, then at Sally who had come down to see what all the noise was about.

"That's enough now, plenty of time for that later. Breakfast, tea, talk, that's what we need."

Over her cup of tea Sally noticed that the boy and girl, as she still instinctively thought them, sat side by side, eating one handed, the others hidden beneath the table. It's a long hard road ahead of you both, probably several thousand miles, but at least you can see it; mine's still hidden.

After eating, Sam turned to her.

"Miss Sally? I have to tell you. I met your husband, spoke with him. He could have arrested me, knew some of what I had been doing, but he let me go, helped me get away. He's a good man, I'm in his debt. I'll tell you more later."

The head of the Counter Terrorism Command left the COBRA meeting accompanied by Gerald and the Director of GCHQ. These three had drawn closer, forging ties of renewed trust in the fires of horror and politics. Manchester was over just eight hours ago, it looked like a scene from the Apocalypse up there, burnt out and collapsed buildings, hundreds of corpses, hundreds more wounded, thousands more facing shattered lives, exhausted, harrowed security forces.

But, somehow worse, was the rippling effect across the nation and overseas. Faith in the country's institutions had been declining for years of course, but this marked a new low. Sectarian conflict was becoming endemic, arsons, assaults, even murders and kidnaps, rabble-rousing calls for jihads and crusades. In some areas the authorities had lost all control, hopefully only temporarily. Most people were confused, bewildered, stunned, but such things had a habit of evolving into either rage or passivity, who could tell which? For him though the worst was the refusal of the political and intellectual establishment to face facts; they were still wittering on about community cohesion and other modern shibboleths, in total defiance of reality.

Today he felt like resigning, admitting failure, but had been dissuaded by the other two accompanying him out. They said they needed to talk, openly, when the emergency was over, calibrate their approach, ignore their masters if required; he must stay on, there was no one else they trusted. What about the military, the Chief of the General Staff? A good man, we can work with him. Sounds like a coup in the making he had said. Not at all, more like a side-lining in particular operational matters. Surely, he realised that others were already at work with very different aims, who had grown strong?

Tell me more. Later. Intriguing enough to continue, at least for a while.

....

Chief Inspector Andy Bowson was shown into the flat by a well-dressed woman. This address, place, was far beyond him, but at least it wasn't flash like some of the foreign owned places he'd had to raid in his career. Restrained, elegant, reflecting its owner he thought. She showed him through to where 'John' was sitting, looking a hell of a lot better than when he'd seen him in hospital, leg still in plaster, arm in a sling which had been cast aside.

"Hello, good to see you Andy. I can call you Andy still, can't I?"

"How're you?"

"Doing fine, on the way back, more than well cared for, as you can see."

He smiled at the woman who returned it with real affection, triggering a pang of loss in himself.

"As you've probably guessed, I've been keeping busy, not surprising given everything that's been going on, but you must be frantic. I'm also looking further into the disappearance of your wife and son, unofficially you understand. All I can say is that you shouldn't lose hope. I can't say more, but we may be on to something. At some point I may need you to join me at short notice, come with me, in utmost confidence. Could you do that, do you trust me enough?"

He returned the man's look, shocked, not expecting anything like this. Can I trust him? What's he withholding, must be more to it? Do I trust anyone these days? Yes, George now certainly, some of the others, but less so, but a spook, even one who has always been decent to me?

"What aren't you telling me?"

"Some of it, until I have more of substance and no, before you ask, I haven't seen either of them, I don't think they've come to any harm or are in danger, and she certainly hadn't left you. I promised you I'd help you find her and I mean to, but you have to cut me a little slack, be patient a little longer, it could be months yet."

He shrugged.

"I suppose I've no choice, but I warn you, if you are misleading me, trying to use me…"

The woman interrupted.

"He isn't, he's trying to help you in his own way, like he does others. He doesn't lie about things like this."

"Okay, have it your way. I can be patient if I need to, but won't be strung along."

What other choice do I have?

"I understand. So, why're you here, other than a social call to a recovering spook?"

"To catch up, talk things through, as we agreed. Everything's upside down, but those at the top don't seem to care or want to recognise it, just going along like before. The chief isn't though and there are rumours that a few in the various security services are getting together, are frustrated beyond measure, are keeping things to themselves."

"I know. What do you think, how do you feel, about it? You can't be surprised?"

Do I trust him, really trust him? Who else is there? I must, to have approached him that time? He reddened.

'John' was watching the policeman carefully, sympathetically. He's trapped, but there's something that he's nerving himself to say, but

doesn't know how, if he can. Wait, no, save him the trouble.

"Is this about you and a colleague letting a young man go from Broadcasting House without reporting it? A man sought by the authorities, who was filmed shooting two terrorists dead and, it is claimed, killed several more in the building, someone all the various security agencies adamantly deny was one of theirs'?"

Bowson looked at the older man in astonishment.

"How did you know?"

"Part of my job to know, remember? The bits that fall between the cracks, the things no one else wants to look after, the future for those to come? Don't worry, I won't turn you in."

"He was English, definitely, sounded like a Bristolian, he more or less admitted being one of those behind the killings in Birmingham, Swindon and Reading. One of the hostages who met him apparently said he did the strangest thing: he showed him he was wearing a Celtic cross around his neck, said he was with them."

Then the realisation, the dawning light in his eyes.

"You, he's working for you; all of this, it's you!"

"Not quite, but close. So, what're you going to do, turn me in? How do you know this isn't official? There are parts of the secret state even the Cabinet doesn't know about, defending the nation from the more insidious threats, within and without."

Silence, the man was thrown by his unexpected revelation, hardly surprising, came here for a chat, some sympathy and suddenly I've dynamited his assumptions. Which way will he land? I'm pretty sure I know.

"Why've you told me this, now?"

"Because I think you've arrived at the same conclusions some of us have, and more are coming to, otherwise you wouldn't have disregarded your ostensible duty for something deeper by assisting the escape of that insanely brave young man. For that, I'm heavily indebted to you, and have redoubled my determination to reunite you with your family."

"What do you want of me?"

"To work with us, quietly, to defend our way of life, our civilisation, the things being forgotten or surrendered, the things that gave us everything. We think you're one of us, have proved yourself, you just need to prove it to yourself."

"How do you mean?"

"Join us, our little informal band of brothers and sisters, confronting things the normal authorities won't, searching out threats, going the extra mile to protect the things we love. Don't worry, we won't ask you to kill and, as you know, we are highly selective and our people are effective. How many do you think we've saved by our actions of the last few months, found things out that you couldn't? Thousands?"

He just looked at him, then the woman.

Henry could read the debate within, communicated by his facial expression.

What they were asking… but hadn't he already crossed the line? That's why they'd revealed themselves to him, reckoned he was already there. George was, he knew, would sign up in a flash, possibly some of the others.

"So, what's the end game, the objective, a coup?"

"Certainly not. No, to build an outer ring of informal defence, drive the threat from our shores, from others who share our civilisation, to protect the innocent, to watch the frontiers like the old Roman Limitani, to seek out those who would betray us. There's no pay, no status, no glory, just service, and risk of course."

"These rumours about people higher up getting together, is it related?"

"No, they're not there yet, but they're worried, near despair, but too high profile, too official. Maybe some in time, but this is about ground up people with the right mettle, one-by-one. We think you're ideal."

They talked for hours, over dinner; he tried to be objective, stand back, but couldn't. That young man, the lives that must have been saved, their attempts to spare the innocent caught up in their activities and, most of all, those women's bodies tumbling and lying broken on the ground, the cowardice and agendas that allowed it to happen… How many more to come?

"My wife, my family, do you promise on the Bible that you can help me find them?"

Why the Bible, given my lack of belief? What else was there though?

This man seemed focused on saving an entire civilisation, his culture, something based on that book above all others; if those things were so important to him, then it must be too…

"Yes."

The woman went out to find one, brought it back. 'John' swore an oath with his hand lightly, almost reverently, resting on its front cover as if in a court.

"You see, it's through this unofficial network of ours that we're tracing your family; official channels offer nothing."

"I know."

So that's it then, my only chance. Who else is there? And he's right, she is, George is. "Alright, I'll do it. What do you want me to do?"

"Nothing yet, just keep your eyes open as you have before and see if anyone else might, one day, be suitable to join our little group and, of course, be ready when we need you, have a coffee with your spook friend from time to time."

Not too much, early days, small steps.

"My assistant, George Edward, he was with me when we met the young man, look at him, he'd join up on the spot. I'd trust him with my life."

"We will. Thank you."

After he had left, Helena came and sat close beside him.

"You handled that well."

"It was providence really. He's a decent man, no fool; he's close enough to see the way things are going."

He called her cousin on a secure phone, met her the following day.

Seven weeks later, Chief Superintendent Dager disappeared while out jogging, never to be seen again; there were no clues at all.

His replacement was Andy Bowson.

The Abbot finished his prayer in the Duke's chamber. Everything was just as it should be, normal yet somehow, different. More equipment, goods, money, weapons, were arriving almost every month from their allies, the new training barracks was under construction in a side valley, one of the newer enclaves with little settlement as yet. But most of all what made him feel the difference was the new volunteers in training, with more arriving. Twenty from the Armenians, eight Greeks, even some strays, three Americans, one with a special forces background as a trainer, another Australian, even a Russian and a Serb. Their allies had been busy, things were moving too fast, but we are riding the wolf, or trying to. If only he, the Duke, were awake to give them the leadership they needed.

He smiled, not their greatest secret by any means, others lay hidden below the Abbey, the Basilica, the fort, elsewhere; after all, refuges protect more than just people. But one of them, his identity, Arturus, Dux Bellorum, Arthur, War Duke, Prince of Lethostow, asleep on the Isle of Apples, Avalon, awaking each year on the anniversary of Christ's rising from the grave for just one day, until needed. Well that need was coming closer, becoming more urgent. He, the others, felt more and more out of their depth. With His Blessing, hopefully their friend in Logres would be over his injuries soon, would come to confer, advise, share the burden.

To Terpsichore,

....

She who dances in the Sunlight to escape the shadows.

A mirror world; not quite, but sort of true,
Well, near enough, but still not quite you
Where evil can't enter, is purged at the door
For those who pass through, slain on the moor.
Where Helios shines always, his sky ever blue,
And night falls so gentle, ground cooling with dew.
Where love is the goal, and kindness the floor,
And pride is forbidden, but honour yet more.

So where go we today, and how shall we live?
Can Sins be erased, and can we forgive?
Shall we run together, to look at the view,
To smile and delight, and give the Creator his due?
Can souls be restored and faith be redemptive,
To find joy unconfined and lives held not captive?
So smile at me and climb, then let us construe
The challenge of the immortals: the wonder of you.

Real life is forever and divine love never tires,
So lift up your heart and hear the sound of the lyres.
There death has no dominion so let's resolve to pursue
All that is worthy and only love to accrue.
Now stand we at the gates, the moment of truth,
Discard we our burdens, regain the courage of youth,
Do we leap together, do what faith requires,
And land in the greater world, to the song of the choirs?

© JD de Pavilly

515